W9-CMM-311

6483

PS
3569
T337

Steadman, Mark,
1930-

A lion's share

DATE			

A
Lion's
Share

BY MARK STEADMAN

A Lion's Share
McAfee County

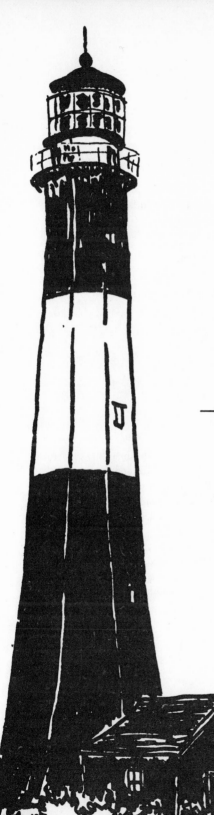

A Lion's Share

A NOVEL BY

Mark Steadman

Holt, Rinehart and Winston
NEW YORK

To Lois and Tom Wallace
Who Saw It for Me
with Patience and Cheerfulness
Always
and
To Charles Israel
Who Kept Me Going
and Whose Turn Is Yet to Come

Copyright © 1974, 1975 by Mark Steadman
All rights reserved, including the right to reproduce
this book or portions thereof in any form.
Published simultaneously in Canada by
Holt, Rinehart and Winston of Canada, Ltd.

"Kate" appeared in the November 1974 issue of
The South Carolina Review.

Library of Congress Cataloging in Publication Data
Steadman, Mark, 1930–
A lion's share.

I. Title.
PZ4.S798Li [PS3569.T337] 813'.5'4   75-5468
ISBN 0-03-015086-8

Designer: Madelaine Caldiero
PRINTED IN THE UNITED STATES OF AMERICA

10 9 8 7 6 5 4 3 2 1

"For a living dog is better than a dead lion.
For the living know that they shall die: but the
dead know not any thing, neither have they any
more a reward; for the memory of them is forgotten."

—ECCLESIASTES

BOOK I

Survivors:
April 12 and 13, 1956

Old Johnny and Rose

On Wednesday and Thursday, April 11 and 12, the sky closed in. It is something that often happens at that time of the year. Clouds the color of ashes hung over the town, capping it down under a pall of smoke from the fertilizer plants and paper mills along the river. Sea gulls were gliding in it. Flying with motionless wings, skimming in long, looping arcs through the grayness—sitting on pilings above the gray-brown stillness of the river, summing things up with their hard, bright eyes.

Sea gulls are stupid birds, but that's a slippery thing to keep in mind when one has its eye fixed on you. A sea gull's eye is a one-way proposition. It comes at *you;* there isn't any way for you to get at it. A very definite thing, that eye. It makes you forget that he sees things two ways at once—side to side. You never see the other eye. Everything focuses in the one that's on you. But the truth is there *is* that second eye, and whatever lies over the other way gets the same cold scrutiny that you are getting—a blank wall, a pile of old beer cans, or the whole wide world. Sea gulls are very nondiscriminatory. Which they have to be. They have little enough brain to start with, and if they had to divide that little into two, separating the right side from the left, they would spend all their time sitting around trying to make a choice, and would end up flying into pilings and buildings or down the smokestack of a steamship. The only thing that gets their undivided attention is something they can eat. They recognize that without even having to think about it.

Still, that hard eye is tough to cope with—even when you do remember the other one is there. Toughest of all on those cloudy April days, when lizards and snakes and black widow spiders seem to be the only animals left in the world, and they are all onto some stony secret with you at the center of it. People feel that coldness, and they go out to walk around in it as little as possible. Those still days in April slow them down, making them move about furtively with their shoulders hunched over, holding the screen doors back to keep them from slamming when they go in and out of the houses.

For two days the clouds were there—coiled, static, rising in a dome; the edges swung north and south to the marshes and salt creeks that ring the city; over the Atlantic Ocean to the east, the pines to the west.

Wednesday night the dirty streets and the corners of the squares were lit with a pale luminescence, the moon working in from outside the bell jar of clouds, filling the air of the town with a light that seemed to be snaking and streaming upward, out of the roots of trees and bushes. A light pale and luminous as water.

For two days the coiled clouds held the seal, capping the city down upon itself, still and quiet, with the measured whir of clockworks moving in the stillness. The twelfth, Thursday, at six in the afternoon, the dome of clouds unraveled, straightened into billowing ribbons that went sucking away over the eastern rim of the Atlantic. Suddenly. As if a wizard had called.

In the empty twilight sky the moon hung low and full and yellow, swung and fixed like a ball on the still eastern edge of the world. Hanging clear and yellow over the dark April ocean, with the black shadows of sea gulls gliding across it.

At one o'clock Friday morning, Old Johnny Curran stepped out of the Lighthouse Bar onto Bay Street. He tottered across the way into Emmett Park on the river side, catching a smaller, paler moon in the prismed cage of the Old Harbor Light—a gaslight beacon, dead now, gone to verdigris and rust at the eastern end of the park—the northeast salient of the old city, where Oglethorpe had first come ashore with his flags and debtors.

There was a woman behind him, walking with her arms folded. She was big, with a hard, taut face—impassive as a squaw's. Hair short and black, and long, spindly legs—a dark leathery woman. Walking very deliberately, making two-tap footfalls, heel and toe, as she came across the cobblestones of Bay Street and into the park.

Old Johnny hooked his bandaged hand onto the lamppost and went a merry-go-round around, sagging his weight against the one outstretched arm, the tingle of fire still in the skin of the hand.

"Moon's up, Rose," he said, hanging on the lamppost. "Moooooonnn's up. . . ." He shot it up into the dark, like a hound baying.

Old Johnny Curran was a big man—just short of being a freak—that big. And he was sloppy in a big man's way, dressed in a dirty black suit, with a dirty white shirt and a red tie. The narrow end of the tie turned back-to-front, and was hanging down below the big end. Three inches of dirty white shirt cuff hung out the end of his sleeve, and the pants flapped below his crotch, bunching over his shoes.

Rose stood watching him, looked up through the prism of the light, then at him again. Pierced earrings—gold, two inches in diameter—reflected flashes of light when she moved her head.

Old Johnny wore a gray fedora hat, the kind that men used to wear standing in breadlines during the Depression—tilted back on his head with the brim snapped down. His curly red hair, dark red, was bleeding out from under the brim of the hat across his forehead. He wouldn't wear his fireman's cap into the Lighthouse Bar. He was scrupulous about that—not absolutely by any means —but he didn't like to drink in uniform—even part of it.

"Mooooonnnmooooonnnmooooonnn . . ." he said, throwing his head back and hanging on the lamppost. It rattled in his throat and he coughed at the end. Then he went another merry-go-round around, lolling his head back, trying to catch the moon again in the prism of the light. The moon was gray-white now, hanging over the black hulk of the fuel storage tank below the corner of Bay and East Broad streets. It marked the very spot where the Trustees' Gardens had been in the beginning.

The woman watched him without speaking. She had black eyes that looked like holes burned in a drumhead, slanting upward slightly at the outside corners. Her eyebrows had all been pulled out and replaced by high-arching crescents painted onto her forehead.

Old Johnny's eyes were blue, tucked up under the deep ridge of his brow, under eyebrows that were bushy and peppered with gray hairs. Puffy eyes, with a squint. The flesh of the sockets was folded and velvety, like the eyes of a lizard.

"I had a dream," he said.

She looked over her shoulder into the window of the Lighthouse Bar across Bay Street. Billy Boy O'Day was putting out the lights, getting ready to close up for the night. The bar was small inside, long and narrow, with booths on one side and a yellow Formica counter on the other. At the back there was a Miller's beer clock, lit up pinkish yellow on the inside of the face.

She turned back to the moon, standing with her arms still folded, not looking at him. A small, curved sliver of light ran down the inside circumference of her earring when she turned her head.

"I had a dream last night, Rose," he said, speaking to her, but not looking at her. Hanging on the lamppost and looking up at the moon through the cage of the light. He coughed again. "Are you listening to me?"

She looked past him. "You've got the heart of a snake, Johnny," she said. "You're going to live forever? Is that what you think?" Her voice was low and throaty, lower than his.

He turned his head back toward her over his shoulder. "What?" he said.

"You think you're going to live forever? You outlived him, so you won't have to die yourself? God skipped you. Now you think you're going to get to live forever."

He hung on the lamppost with his ear turned toward her, not looking at her, looking back up at the moon.

She waited for him to speak to her. "How're you going to trust a man that never thinks he's going to die?"

She looked down Bay Street under the trees, the tunnel of live oaks with moss hanging down out of the branches. While she was looking, the stoplights changed, going yellow then green down the street to the west. Seven or eight blocks away, beyond the Cotton Exchange, were the headlights of a car. When the lights changed, they bobbed. The street was empty, and they could hear the engine winding up—a Ford. The driver pushed it hard before he shifted to second. At the third stoplight he had to brake for the red.

"You *know* better," she said. "I'm not talking about that. I mean the way you *feel*."

He looked at her, hanging on the post. "You know what a *blivit* is?" he said. He went on without giving her time to answer. "A blivit is four pounds of shit in a two-pound sack," he said. "That's what a blivit is."

"Are you *looking forward* to tomorrow?" she said. She shook her head. "You wouldn't be looking forward to it, would you?"

He swung on the lamppost, not answering her.

"You got no idea of being dead. That's what it means to you. No more idea than a snake."

"Finish your horseshit," he said.

She looked across the street into the bar. The stoplights changed and the Ford came up Bay Street two more blocks, the engine winding up too high. "Billy Boy's closing up," she said. "Let's get on home."

A big red tomcat poked his head over the top of the bluff at the end of the park. He watched them for a minute without moving. His head was wide and flat, with the ears pointing out to the sides. A piece of one of the ears was missing, and his right eye was marbled milky white.

"You don't ever want me to talk to you," he said. "When're you going to learn to *listen* to me, Rose?"

The tomcat came over the top of the bluff, melting along close to the ground, keeping his head turned with his good eye on them.

"You won't want to get up in the morning," she said. "You're going to be in fine shape for the funeral." She turned and started walking toward the street, her arms still folded, hugging her breasts. The car came whining up Bay Street, trying to make the light for the turn into East Broad. When Rose moved, the tomcat sprang away, running parallel to her toward the street. He and the Ford came together at the corner under the traffic light, his blind eye on the car side. He went under it between the wheels, and the back wheel on the right side caught him. The taillights of the car winked bright red as it braked around the corner, then the engine wound up again, and it was gone down East Broad. The cat flopped for a minute in the middle of the street, then it began dragging itself toward the curb with its front legs.

"Look," said Rose, pointing toward the cat.

"What?" said Johnny.

"It hit him," she said.

They watched him dragging toward the curb. He was leaving a slick on the cobblestones, a shiny trail reflecting the red from the traffic light.

"It hit him," she said again.

Johnny looked at the cat dragging toward the far side of the street. "He did it himself," he said.

Rose looked at him.

"He ran under the car," said Johnny.

She walked across the street to where the cat was lying in the gutter. Johnny walked across after her. The car had gone over him across his back legs, and they were twisted together, but there wasn't much blood. It was coming out somewhere between his legs, under the fur where it didn't show. He was over on his back— the top part of him was, the back legs were lying to the side. His front legs were spread and his claws were out, moving and feinting at them when they moved. They could see his chest pumping, and the red light glinting in his good eye.

Rose and Johnny stood over him, watching him move his claws like a boxer.

"He's game," said Johnny.

She didn't look up at him. "Put him out of his misery," she said, looking down at the cat. "I can't do it."

Johnny looked down at him. "He ain't going to just *let* me do it," he said. "I don't want him to claw me."

"Get something," she said. "I don't want to stand here and watch him."

Johnny tried to work a stone loose out of the street, but the edges were curved and he couldn't get a grip on it. "It won't come loose," he said.

"Get something else," she said.

He looked around. "I don't see nothing else," he said.

She looked up at him, but didn't say anything.

Finally he stepped up to the edge of the curb. He raised his foot up high, wavering as he tried to balance on one leg. Then he drove it down on the cat's head. It was a spongy blow, glancing to the side. The cat grabbed his leg with its claws and held on, so that Johnny had to shake it off, back into the gutter. It spread its front paws again, making a whining howl.

"He clawed me," said Johnny. He pulled up his pants leg to see the place. "I told you so."

"You got to do something," she said. "Listen to him. Do something to put him out of his misery."

"I can't get a rock loose," he said, rubbing his leg.

He pulled his pants leg down, then stood looking at the cat with his hands on his hips. "I don't want him to claw me again," he said.

He stepped down into the gutter and grabbed the cat's tail, lifting him up and holding him at arm's length. The cat growled and moved his paws around, but he couldn't get at Johnny. Then Johnny whirled him in a circle, holding him by the tail. He swung him around that way twice, and on the downstroke of the second circle he knelt and cracked the cat's head against the curb. After that the cat didn't move or make a sound, but he cracked its head that way two more times. Then he held him up to see. The front paws were hanging down limp, and he didn't move.

"What'll I do with him?" he said, holding him out at arm's length.

"Is he dead?" she said.

He didn't answer. Instead, he walked to the corner where the storm sewer was, dropped him on the grating, then shoved him into the opening with his foot. Afterward he came back where she was standing and sat down on the curb. He pulled up his pants leg. "Look where the son of a bitch scratched me," he said.

She looked down at him, then at his leg. "I don't understand me," she said. "Why would I want to hang around with a shitass like you?"

"I fixed him, goddamn it," he said. "I put him out of his misery, didn't I? There's worse things than killing a goddamn cat." He rubbed his leg. "He was going to die anyway."

She looked at the sidewalk, raised the toe of her shoe, twisting her foot, drilling the spike heel into the sidewalk. The long muscles along the side of her shin flexed.

"You're the one wanted me to do it," he said. He rubbed his leg. "I never did like cats."

She walked back to the glass window of the bar and leaned against it, her arms folded. LIGHTHOUSE was written across the glass in curving letters. The letters were white with a red outline. Under the curve of the letters was a picture of a lighthouse—black with white stripes on it. A long yellow spearpoint was pointing into the top of the lighthouse. It was supposed to be the beam from the lighthouse going out, but because of the way it was painted, it seemed to be going in.

"I'm sorry about the cat," he said, pulling his pants leg back down and looking into the street. "I mean, it's still just a cat, but I'm sorry about it for your sake. It was a favor to him. He was already dead." He paused. "Cats are stupid," he said.

"Let's get on home," she said. She was leaning against the window of the bar, and she didn't make a move to go.

"It looked bad," he said. "I couldn't think of another way to do it. He didn't feel anything."

She drilled her heel into the sidewalk again. "All right," she said. "I'm going to get on home."

He looked up for the moon. It was hanging just above the stoplight where the wires came together over the street. It seemed smaller than it was before.

"You think I *liked* doing it?" he said.

She looked down at him. "You can't trust a man who doesn't know he's going to die," she said.

"You get something up your ass and it sure does stick there, don't it?" he said.

She didn't say anything.

He sat for a while hugging his knees. "Did I ever tell you I killed a man once?" he said.

She waited for him to go on. "No," she said.

"It wasn't that I meant to do it," he said. "I hit him and his head got bashed in when he fell." He turned to look at her over his shoulder. "It was a fair fight," he said. "I hit him with my fist." He held up his bandaged fist for her to see.

She didn't answer for a minute. "How'd you feel about it?" she said.

"You mean did I feel good?" he said, not looking at her. "To tell the truth, he was kind of a friend of mine." He scraped his hand around in the gutter for a while without saying anything. "We used to drink together."

"I didn't mean that you'd feel good exactly," she said. "Just did you feel anything?"

He picked something up out of the gutter and held it up to the light to look at it, then he tossed it away. "It wasn't like when I was *trying* to kill the cat," he said. "I just hit him with my hand." He paused. "No," he said, "I didn't feel anything."

"You just can't get it into your head, can you?" she said.

"Goddamn it! I *wanted* to feel bad about it," he said. "We used to drink together. He didn't *look* dead, just like he was out cold. I didn't find out until later."

"What would you have to do, split his head open with an ax?"

"How're you going to feel it, if you *don't* feel it?"

"A snake's a snake, I guess." She sighed and looked up Bay Street, the lights going green down the tunnel toward the Cotton Exchange. "You ready to get on home?" she said. "Let's get on home. Billy Boy's closed up."

He was sitting on the curb with his elbows resting on his knees, his head on his arms. "Jack's dead . . ." he said softly and mournfully.

For a minute she didn't say anything. "You sure you can tell?"

He didn't answer.

"He's really dead, Johnny," she said. "It's not just words. He's really dead. How're you going to take that in?"

He was looking across the street toward the factors' warehouses along the river on the other side, behind Emmett Park. The park was between Bay Street and the warehouses, with benches and laid brick walks. Between the park and the warehouses ran a cobblestone street, ten feet below the park at the bottom of the bluff, with openings down the bluff to the river between the buildings. Along the fronts of the warehouses was a railed iron walk that was connected to the level of the park by iron bridges above the cobblestone street at the river level. The buildings were all deserted now, but this had been the center of the commercial life of the town at one time. The factors had bustled up and down the rattling iron walkway conducting their business. Ships went farther upriver now, passing the empty buildings to off-load and take on cargo at the new docks where the riverfront wasn't so crowded. But the old buildings with the railed iron promenade were still called Factor's Walk, though not two people in ten even knew what a factor was anymore. The cobblestones in the streets had been brought over from England as ballast by the sailing ships in the early days.

For a long time Johnny sat on the curb without saying anything —looking across the street at Factor's Walk. "Savannah River is full of turds," he said at last.

She looked at him sitting on the curb. "You've got a snaky soul, Johnny," she said. "A black, snaky soul."

"It's full of *turds*, Rose," he said, raising his voice.

She looked at him for a minute without speaking. "Okay," she said.

"I mean it," he said, not looking at her. "When're you going to learn to *listen* to me, Rose?"

She drilled her heel into the sidewalk, not looking at him. "Okay," she said again.

For a moment he didn't say anything. "You never did know how to handle me, Rose," he said.

"I'm going to get on home," she said. She didn't move to leave. "You can come on along when you get ready."

"When're you going to learn to *handle* me, Rose?" he said.

She looked away at the moon. It was moving up beyond the stoplight, getting smaller all the time. "Let's get on home, Johnny," she said. "Billy Boy's all closed up." The pinkish-yellow light from the clock stared out from the back of the bar. It was ten minutes to two.

He looked up at the moon. "Jack's dead . . ." he said.

"You can get a little sleep if we get on home now," she said. "You won't feel like going to the funeral tomorrow."

"He wasn't but twenty-six years old," he said. He turned and looked up at her over his shoulder. "Twenty-six," he said. He turned away again. "I'm fifty-four," he said.

"You're fifty-*five*," she said.

"He was just starting out," he said.

"No, he wasn't," she said. "He started out ten years ago."

"I'm fifty-*four*, Rose," he said.

She didn't say anything.

"Think of all the shitheads sixty years old," he said. "I bet there's a million shitheads sixty years old . . . seventy years old . . . *two* million . . ."

He stood up facing her.

"Couldn't you make it come out even?" she said.

"What?" he said.

"Where'd you learn to tie a tie? I wish you'd learn to make it come out even."

He threw something into the gutter. "I hate the goddamn black dirt," he said. "It smells worse than the river." He wiped his hands on his pants. "The water must get up underneath and make it smell that way. Just scratch it with a stick and it hits you in the face. It's worse than the river."

She didn't say anything.

"I hate to think about them putting him down in that stinking black dirt," he said. "Where they pile it up by the grave it'll smell like the goddamn river."

She looked up at the moon going over the trees. "Sometimes I almost think I know how to handle you," she said.

He looked at her.

"I just never did know him very well," she said.

[*13*]

"I know you never did," he said.

"You've got to go on living for something, haven't you?"

"Yes."

"He's really dead, isn't he?"

"Yes," he said. "He's dead."

"He was just a kid. I didn't mean it was over for him yet." She looked at him. "Twenty-six."

"I didn't know him that well either," he said after a while. "Kathleen wouldn't let me come around the house after she married Reilley. She couldn't stand me, even just to look at, after we broke up. The last time we were really together was when he was five," he said. "Jack and me."

He looked at the picture of the lighthouse with the yellow spear going into it on the window of the bar. "We went down to Tybee on the train. I took him down to Fort Screven, and the keeper let us in the lighthouse. It was daytime, so the light wasn't on. I could just reach across the lens with both my hands. It was that big." He spread his arms and the light behind him threw his shadow on the window of the bar.

"I don't remember," he said. "It must have been the summertime. We could see out over the ocean, all the way back to town the other way. There wasn't so much smoke in those days." He took his hat off and ran his hand through his hair.

"And Fort Pulaski . . . I didn't know it was that close to the ocean. You could see the places where the shells hit the walls— big pink spots in the bricks. I remember the ships coming in and one going out with the smoke laying out over the water in a streak. I told Jack it was going out to Ireland."

He stopped talking for a minute. "I didn't know where the shit it was going, but I told him it was going out to Ireland."

He stopped again, waiting. She nodded her head.

"It was a clear day. It must have been the summertime. The sky was blue, I remember. The river wasn't full of turds then, but it was brown going out into the ocean. You could see the long brown streak it made going out through Calibogue Sound."

He held his bandaged left hand up to the light, looking at it and rubbing the back of it with his bandaged right hand. "That's the last time we were really together," he said. "He was five years old. Kathleen broke it off afterward. But I remember that day we went up in the lighthouse."

He fumbled his hands in his coat pockets, then took them out, looking at the lighthouse on the window.

"The coast guard turned it out when the war came," he said. "They never lit it up again."

He looked down the tunnel of the street. "That was the last time we were really together. Kathleen couldn't stand to have me around after we broke up and she went in with Reilley."

For a moment he didn't say anything.

"He was a handsome child. He had his mother's face mostly, but he always looked so healthy. By the time he got around for you to see him he'd gone to hell."

"He wasn't a bad-looking boy," she said.

"He'd got puffy in the face," he said. "Allover bloated. I hated to look at what he was doing to himself."

"I could tell he'd been a good-looking boy."

"He was always so healthy-looking," he said.

She didn't say anything.

"It's just that he was my son," he said. "He wasn't but twenty-six years old. You know."

The moon was going higher, moving behind the oak trees and getting smaller as it moved.

"What about the dream?" she said.

"What?"

"You were talking about your dream," she said. "What was it about?"

"There wasn't much to it," he said. "I was flying."

"In a plane?"

"I was a bird," he said. "I was some kind of a bird, and I was flying." He hunched his shoulders. "I was a white bird."

"A swan?"

"No," he said. "A seabird. It was a gull. That must have been what it was."

"I see."

"I was gliding away without moving my wings. Just gliding."

[15]

"I see," she said. For a while neither of them said anything.

"I could see it down there underneath me," he said. "It was clear green. Like a bottle. The sun was out."

She looked down the street, then back at him. "What is it about Galway Bay?"

"I don't know," he said. "My grandfather was from there."

"You think about it that much?" she said.

"My people came from there," he said. "Galway Bay don't have turds in it."

"How do you know what it's got in it? You weren't ever there."

"I know Galway Bay hasn't got turds in it," he said. "That's one thing I by-God *do* know."

"How?"

He pointed his finger at her. "Keep your mouth shut," he said. "I'm going to say it, Rose, and I want you to keep your mouth shut." He held her with his outstretched arm. "There's . . . NO . . . turds . . . in . . . Gal . . . way . . . Bay. . . ." He said it slowly, spacing out the words.

She didn't say anything.

He dropped his arm. "Okay."

"Well," she said. "What about the rest of it?"

"What?"

"Your dream," she said. "What about the rest of it?"

"That's all there was to it," he said. "I went gliding away."

"That's all there was?"

"That's about it."

"There wasn't much to it after all, was there?"

"No," he said. "Just the gliding."

For a minute, neither of them spoke.

"Why'd you say I was fifty-five?" he said.

She looked up at him. "You *are* fifty-five," she said.

"I know," he said, "but why'd you *say* it? It really burns my ass for you to contradict me."

She didn't say anything.

"If I want to say I'm not but three years old, that's *my* god-damn business. You can keep your mouth shut."

"Pardon me."

"I don't want to hear it no more about Galway Bay either. That's another thing."

She didn't say anything.

He looked at her. "You're a nice piece of meat, Rose. But your soul's up your ass."

"That's just the only place you know to look for it."

He looked at her for a long minute. "You never did know how to handle me," he said.

"I know I didn't," she said.

They stood there for a minute looking at each other across the sidewalk without saying anything.

"Let's get on home," he said. "We'll have to be getting up early in the morning."

They went down the street together under the trees. It was a warm night, but he had his great, heavy arm across her shoulders. She was leaning in toward him, pushing her hands against the side of his chest.

"Don't step on the cracks," he said. "It's unlucky."

They widened their steps at the cracks, putting their feet over onto the blank spaces of the pavement. Their shadows stretched out along the sidewalk, bobbing ahead of them until they turned off at the corner of Lincoln Street.

2

Charlie Carne and Friend

"WELL, DEARIE, HOW ABOUT chicken tonight?" Charlie Carne held the two cans of dog food out to the small dog, leaning over slightly. He always expected her to make a choice, and, in fact, he always thought that she did. He was a tiny man, wiry, with a high waist. His dark pants were held up by thin black suspenders, and his dark tie was pinned to his shirt front by a plain silver bar. On his head was a coarse black wig. It didn't quite match his real hair, and the line where the two met was very obvious. He looked as if he were wearing a furry skullcap.

"Chicken will be good for you," he said. "I think chicken will be nice tonight." He put one of the cans on the kitchen counter and took the other to a hand-operated opener mounted on the wall.

The dog was small, white, with pink, batlike ears and a tail that curled over its back. She was smaller than a cat, bigger than a Chihuahua, her body elongated and sausagelike—without any neck, so that her head seemed to be embedded in her body. Her legs were short and bowed. When she walked, her nails clicked on the linoleum of the kitchen floor, and her outsized pudenda jiggled like a pink udder between her legs.

"Chicken isn't your very favorite," he said, taking the top of the can off the magnet of the opener and dropping it into a pedal-operated garbage can. "Chicken makes your bones strong. Dearie needs strong bones." The dog's ears were constantly pricked up. She watched him scooping the food out of the can and into a large ceramic bowl—yellow, with "Sub" written across it in green. The dog's name was Sub, but he always called her "dearie" when there were just the two of them.

"Tomorrow we'll have a little piece of steakie," he said. "Tomorrow will be nice." As he put the bowl down on the floor, she lowered her ears for a moment, then pricked them back up again. The mound of dog food was almost as big as she was. She sniffed it daintily—but she didn't eat any of it. Her nose was long and rat-like, with rat's whiskers and a very short lower jaw, from which the tip of her tongue often protruded. He rolled a ball of the dog food between his fingers and held it out to her. "Be a nice dearie," he said. "Eat your chicken." The dog licked at the ball of food between his fingers. Her tongue was darting and snakelike, and one of her upper incisors was missing. "Lovely chickie," he said.

When she finished, he rinsed his fingers at the kitchen sink, then went through the living room into the office to look at the map of the cemetery. After he had gone, the dog sniffed at the food in its bowl, then jiggled over to its basket and curled up.

The grounds keeper's cottage was a small building, stone on the outside, with leaded windows, so that it had a reverent appearance—like a small chapel. Inside the entrance, on the left, there was a tiny office off a hall. On the right was a small sitting room. Behind that was an even smaller kitchen and bedroom and bath. The walls were painted white, with dark oak woodwork. There were a number of crucifixes hanging on the walls of the hall and living room, and framed lithographs of Jesus on the cross. There were no pictures in the office, but there was a calendar with a photograph of the sun going down over the ocean.

On the wall of the office behind the desk was a framed map of the cemetery, done in brown ink on heavy yellowish paper. Stuck in the map were three pins with large green heads. While Charlie

Carne stood looking at the map, Sub clicked in from the kitchen.

"A rushing day tomorrow, dearie," he said. "Daddy will be tired out tomorrow." He held his chin in his hand. "Flynn at twelve. Murphy at one-thirty. Curran at three." The pins had flags with numbers on them. He ticked them off on his fingers. "Flynn . . . Murphy . . . Curran . . ." He shook his head. "Oh, dearie," he said. "Rushing, rushing, rushing. Daddy will be tired, tired tomorrow."

He stooped and picked up the dog, cradling her in his arm and adjusting the rhinestone collar. "No lunch for daddy tomorrow, dearie." He walked with her back to the kitchen, holding her in the crook of his arm and scratching the roll of fat behind her ears. "No lunch for your working daddy tomorrow." He sounded weary and resigned.

Back in the kitchen, he held her under the ceiling light fixture, pushing up the hairs on her back with his fingers, looking for fleas. "You're a clean little dearie," he said, putting her down on the floor again, and he rolled another ball of the dog food for her.

"Nice chicken, dearie," he said. "Eat your nice chicken." He went to the icebox and got out the ice tray, ran water on it at the sink to loosen it, then snapped out a cube and dropped it into her water bowl.

"Lovely steakie tomorrow, dearie," he said. "Lovely, lovely steakie for Sub and daddy tomorrow."

The dog stood in the middle of the floor watching him, the huge batlike ears cocked forward. Her look was so intense and intelligent that he was sure she could understand him.

He walked away into the living room, his slippers scuffing on the floor. "Flynn . . . and Murphy . . . and Curran . . ." he said, shaking his head. "Busy, busy, busy. A rushing day for daddy, dearie."

He picked up one of his shoes and a brush, walking backward and forward in the living room as he polished it. The dog was not looking at him. She was sniffing at the mound of dog food in the bowl. Finally her long tongue snaked out and she began to eat.

3

George

GEORGE BOGGER'S ROOM was nine by eleven. His family had given him the biggest bedroom in the house because of his epilepsy. His mother, in particular, held herself responsible for his condition, and spent her time thinking of ways to make it up to him. Actually, the seizures didn't take that much space. The bed itself would have been room enough.

He hadn't decorated it at all—his room—but he had accumulated a certain number of things into it which gave it a character. There was a bed—his mother's choice—limed oak, with a bookshelf-headboard; a dresser of the same wood; and a night table with a brown plastic radio on it. Over the bed was a framed picture in shades of yellow, brown, and black of a blond child fishing with a stick. He was sitting on a rock beside a small pool, and there was a puppy with him, looking up at his face. "A CHIP OF THE OLD BLOCK" was printed across the bottom of the picture.

In a corner of the room, George had put up a card table to work on his radio-electronics correspondence course and other projects.

On the dresser was a collection of druggist's vials with pills and capsules in them. It was a large collection. To the side of the vials were two slingshots. One was made of a sawed pine board, with red rubber strips cut from an inner tube for the sling. The other was a heavy affair, welded out of galvanized water pipe, with surgical rubber tubing, and a red bow tied around the handle. The lead slugs that he used for ammunition were scattered around the bases of the slingshots, which stood on their handles on top of the dresser, leaning against the wall. George made the mold for his slugs by pushing a rod into the ground. Then he would fill the hole with melted lead. When it cooled, he would pull out the lead rod and cut it into small pieces, about the size of a .38-caliber bullet. They were very effective on the frogs that he hunted with his slingshot. During the summer he made ten or fifteen dollars a month selling the legs to restaurants around town. He didn't normally hunt birds, though he was good enough with the slingshot to hit a Tipps bottle thrown into the air.

Across the single window at the side of the bed was nailed a sheet of unpainted plywood. The nails had been pounded in hard, and there were hammer marks around them.

George was sitting at the card table. The radio by the bed was on, and a mystery program was in progress. On the table were the plucked carcasses of three birds—two cardinals and a blue jay— and a birthday cake alphabet of blue sugar from the ten cent store, still in the cellophane package. The feathers from the birds were in separat> piles on the table, each graded according to color and size. The wings and part of the bodies were picked clean, but the heads still had their plumage. The birds were laid out in a row with the heads facing George, the blue jay between the two cardinals.

George bent over the table. He had made a cross of sticks, and was tying the feathers onto it with dental floss. It was meticulous work, since he chose each feather with care, one at a time— working the cardinal feathers in as the body of the cross, with the blue jay feathers to outline it. The only light in the room came from the ceiling fixture of translucent plastic. It was behind him, and he had to hold the cross out to the side to be able to see. The light was bad and the strain was making his eyes water.

Once in a while he would have to put down the cross and wipe his eyes, digging them with the heels of his hands. He started to whistle through his teeth, but he blew some of the feather piles away, mixing them up, and he had to sort them out again.

There was a knock at the door, soft and hesitant, three single raps spaced out like a secret sign. "George . . . George . . . are you all right, George?" He never heard his mother coming down the hall, though she dragged her feet. Always she was at the door before he knew it. He liked to concentrate on the things he did, so he was always being taken by surprise. She was whispering, but loud enough for him to hear her clearly through the door. He didn't answer. In the pauses, he could hear his father's voice from their bedroom down the hall, but he couldn't make out what he was saying.

"He may be having a fit," she said.

His father's voice was high, but there was a mellow quality in it. It didn't have much volume, for he was a small man.

"But what if he has a fit?" she said. "What if he swallows his tongue?" The thing that she worried about most was that George would swallow his tongue during one of his fits. She had vivid, terrifying dreams about it. Every time she went with George to see the doctor she brought it up.

His parents' bedroom was toward the front of the house, with the bathroom in between. The bulb in the toilet didn't rise enough to cut it off, so the water sang in it all the time.

"George . . ." she said. "Just tell me if you're all right, George."

He waited to answer her. "I'm all right, Mother."

The background music of the radio program came up, a prolonged high chord on an organ. It was the climax of the program, but he hadn't been listening.

He liked to have the radio on, but he didn't listen to it all the time. The commercials got more attention from him than the programs themselves. Sometimes he listened to the music.

He sat at the table with his hands resting on the edge of it, waiting for his mother to go away so he could get back to work on the cross. No one would have taken him for a sick man. There was a healthy look about him that came from the high color of his face—rosy cheeks over a deep tan—and even, white teeth, strong enough to crack walnuts. His eyes were dark brown, moist. In fact, he was a handsome man. His fingers resting on the table edge expressed it best, lifted and curled delicately, fresh-scrubbed and pink. There was no look of sickness or infirmity about him. Guessing his age, most people would say twenty-seven—maybe twenty-six. He was thirty-eight.

"Good night, George." His mother waited for an answer on the other side of the door.

He didn't speak right away, but sat looking at the feathers on the table, listening to the commercial on the radio. "Good night, Mother," he said.

She went away, her sliding footsteps dying down the hall under the sound of water running in the bathroom. George listened to her going away.

After she had gone, he began to work on the cross again. He finished tying the feathers on, then he opened the package of birthday cake letters and moved them around on the table, spelling them out. He picked them up one at a time and tied them onto the cross arms with blue thread. "GOOD LUCK" in blue sugar letters over the cardinal feathers. Afterward he tied the blue jay head at the center—between the GOOD and the LUCK.

The cross was small, delicate—a little over a foot high. He put it on the dresser, standing it up so that it leaned against the wall. Then he lay down on the bed and looked at it. The red and blue of the feathers gave it a rich texture, and he liked the way it looked.

The mystery program went off and a local news program came on. George got up and turned off the ceiling light. Then he got back on the bed, moving over near the orange light from the dial.

"Tomorrow at three o'clock . . ." the announcer was talking about the funeral. His voice sounded like Bill Stern and Walter Winchell, both at the same time—rapid and clipped with a lot of exclamation points in it. ". . . the most outstanding athlete ever to come out of Savannah . . ." He sounded as though he really meant it. Everything he said was in earnest. He went back over the events of Jack's life—the best of them—talking most about the one year, his senior year, that he played football for Boniface College—the Catholic boys' prep school. He called Jack a linebacker. Actually, he had been a center. In those days high school players had to go both ways. But it was as a linebacker that he had been best known. His number had been 55, and they had talked about retiring it after he graduated.

At the end of the program a commercial came on. "Mama—get—Cook—Kill . . . Mama—get—Cook—Kill. . . ." A chanting voice, with a tom-tom in the background. A high-pitched, idiotic child's voice. George lay on the bed, the side of his face lit by the orange light from the radio dial, chanting the words of the commercial along with the high-pitched voice on the radio.

He went to sleep that way, fully dressed, lying on the bed with his arms folded, the side of his face lit up orange from the dial light coming out of the radio. At one o'clock the local station signed off the air. For the rest of the night the radio wheezed static behind the orange glow of the dial. Stations far out in the night drifted in weakly from time to time—Kansas City, Missouri; Fort Wayne, Indiana. George didn't hear them. He lay stretched out on the bed rigid, with his arms folded across his chest.

4

Feeb

FEEB SIDDONEY HAD KNOWN JACK as long as anyone else in Savannah—from the time Jack and his mother had moved to the house on Waldburg Street in 1935. They had grown up together—along with Dendron and Mackey Brood—and both had been on the 1947 Boniface team, something that was very big to Feeb. The team had almost turned into a legend around Savannah.

Feeb owned two curb markets, and was personally running the one on White Bluff Road. He had to open up at seven o'clock in the morning, and hadn't had time to see the papers with the stories about Jack's death. A customer he was waiting on told him as he totaled the order.

"Jack Curran?" he said.

"Yes," said the customer. "Did you know him?"

"Jack Curran?"

"It's in the paper," said the customer. Then he cleared his throat. "The story made it sound like he was famous."

"Yes?"

"Well . . ." said the customer, ". . . what was he famous *for?*"

Feeb looked at him. "That'll be eleven dollars and fifty-five cents," he said.

There hadn't been anyone to go over it with at the curb market during the day. Only the customers. So he came in the front door talking about it that night—the whole day's stew and brooding coming out at once with a rush for his wife.

"He was the best of us all. The fucking best of us all."

She frowned when he used obscenity in the house, because of the children. But the times he was truly upset, it didn't have much effect on him. The habit was too old to break. And marriage had made her a passive woman.

"We were nothing," he said. He emphasized the words with a gesture of his hand. "Fucking zero." He made an O with his thumb and forefinger. "He made us a team. Ten and O. That's what it would have been. Worse than forty-six. Ten and O is what it would have been without him."

"O and ten," she said.

"What?" he said. "What?"

"You mean O and ten—you would have lost. That's what you mean."

"You know what I fucking mean," he said. "We wouldn't have done shit without him."

She looked at the boys, six and eight. Their eyes were big and round, and they were looking at their father. "Go to your room," she said. "Go to your room and get ready for bed."

"I've known him all my life," he said. "He was my fucking best friend. Since we were six years old." He held up the fingers of his left hand, and the index finger of his right. "Six fucking years old."

"Couldn't you just say 'six years old'?"

"Six *fucking* years," he said.

"It's sad for a young man to die," she said. "That's something that's always sad."

"Not just anyone. Not just fucking anyone." He stopped and looked at her. "Not just *anyone*," he said. "He could have been anything. He was the best thing to come out of this town. The best thing I ever knew . . ." he sputtered, looking for his word, ". . . *personally* . . ." he said.

[27]

"I didn't know him that well," she said.

"Like a piece of me was dead. That's what it is." He grabbed a handful of the roll of fat that hung over his belt. "A piece of *me*," he said, shaking it.

She didn't say anything.

"I'm sorry," he said. "With the boys . . ." He made a gesture. "I'm sorry for them to hear it."

"I know you're upset," she said.

For a while they sat without saying anything.

"We got any ice cream?" he said. "You got any ice cream in the refrigerator?" Eating in general, and chocolate fudge sundaes in particular—those were his great joys in life. He was never one for strong drink. Occasionally he would have a glass of Arak.

"Yes," she said. "There's no chocolate syrup."

"I brought some from the store."

He heated the syrup in a pan. There was a quart of vanilla ice cream in the refrigerator, and he put the whole quart into a soup dish, then poured the warm syrup over it.

"I wish I'd rather have a drink of liquor," he said, looking up at her before he started to eat it. "But this is what I want."

Eating it made him cry, because it made him remember the good old days of 1947, when they had been at Boniface playing football, and he and Jack would go to Theodore's Ice Cream Parlor, where he would eat chocolate fudge sundaes three at a time.

It was a silly kind of a key to have to unlock his memories with. And crying made him feel foolish anyway, though he was an emotional man and cried easily. But his wife sat down at the table with him, without any hint of ridicule for his weakness, watching him while he ate.

He scraped the dish, then licked the spoon. "I'd rather be a liquor head," he said. "I swear to God I would. You think I'm just always going to be a kid?" He dropped the spoon into the dish with a clatter. "Why couldn't I like *manly* things?"

She didn't answer his question. "He was your good friend," she said. "I knew you would be upset."

"He *was* that," he said. "Only he was something else. He was the best. You know. A-one. How many times in your life do you know what the best is? Even *know* what it is?"

"That was only the football."

"Don't contradict me," he said. "It wasn't only the football. He was the best there was."

"You didn't like the football," she said. "Not at the time you didn't."

"We all of us played for him. He was the one that made us able to do it. Without him—*beaucoup* zero." He made the O with his thumb and finger again. "And he *was* my good friend. That's what he was." He started to cry again. "I loved him. He was a good, sweet man."

His wife got up and came around behind his chair, putting her hands on his shoulders and patting him.

"Oh, the things he would have been able to do," he said. "Oh, the big, big things he would have been able to do."

She patted his shoulder.

"I was *counting* on him," he said.

5

Chicken Garfield

CHICK GARFIELD HAD BEEN the coach at Boniface College when Jack played there. In those days he had been "Chicken" Garfield— the boys at the school called him "Coach," of course—then when he stopped coaching and went to work at the Wheeler Insurance Agency, he eased it back to "Chick," which was a name he thought to be more in keeping with the idea of a businessman—friendly, but direct. He thought of it as a trustworthy name.

"Chicken" was a name that he had lived with for a good many more years than he had actually wanted to, and paring it down was something he had thought about doing for a long time. But his life connected with football was bound up in it, and he was afraid to tamper with it as long as his work was in the coaching line— though his record was such that it probably wouldn't have made much difference one way or the other. The only good years he had had were his first one and the one at Boniface that Jack played for him—which was 1947. That year the game with Oglethorpe of the city league—the big game for Boniface—had capped the best season the Irish had had since Horse Rooney played fullback in 1942. All the Boniface alumni went out of their minds with the excitement, including Mr. Wheeler, who offered him the job as he was walking off the field after the game. Chicken accepted at the 10-yard line, and shook Mr. Wheeler's hand under the green and white goalposts. Mr. Wheeler looked surprised when he took the offer right off that way, but he gave him the job as he had said he would.

His real name was Critchwood Laverne Garfield, which is a whole mouthful of a name and a very big conception—just fine for special occasions, but a little hard to live with on a day-to-day basis. Even his own family couldn't face up to all of Critchwood Laverne.

His father called him "Chick," which he liked—and his mother called him "Chicky." She could be thickheaded about some things, and talking to her didn't do any good because the name came natural for her. She called his father "Dicky" and his sister "Becky."

The children in the neighborhood stretched his mother's name for him and called him "Chicken." At the time, he regarded it as an improvement over what she had been calling him.

Through high school and on into college, he didn't think about it very much. But toward the end of his college career—he played guard at Millsaps College in Jackson, Mississippi—the notion began to come to him that a name like Chicken wasn't much of a name for a grown man to go by. Elaine was a big help in making it a matter of concern to him.

He started dating her at the end of his junior year, and she brought it up as a topic of conversation more or less all the time. She took the nickname seriously and thought it was undignified. (Her outlook on their relationship was high-minded and ambitious in a wearing kind of way; she was very refined and wanted the best of everything for the both of them, names included.) Going around with a man that other people called "Chicken" to his face was more than she felt she ought to have to put up with. So her first project for them was to get rid of the nickname. To begin with, she went to work on Chicken himself, sending him clippings

out of the newspapers with the nickname scratched out and
"Critch" written in in pencil, along with comments like, "A lovely
name," and "More *you* to me." Then she widened her scope and
started making complaining telephone calls to the *Clarion-Ledger,*
though the boys at the sports desk didn't pay a lot of attention to
her when she did it, and became pretty abusive and sexual about
it when she kept it up.

There were high expectations at Millsaps that he was going to
make the Little All-America team in 1941. None higher than
Elaine's, who was counting on that to go a long way toward
clearing up their problem with the name. She didn't think that
the people who picked the Little All-America team would put a
nickname like Chicken on their official list. But he didn't make the
team after all—losing out to a guard from Davidson College in
North Carolina. Elaine thought the name itself was responsible,
and used it to illustrate her point. But she didn't have time to
work on it much, because the attack on Pearl Harbor came in
December, wiping out her main topic of conversation for a while
—though World War II never did really get hold of her interest
the way the nickname did.

He didn't go into the army. A leg injury kept him out. And he
didn't go into the navy, the marines, or the coast guard either.
Four times he tried to enlist, but they always turned him down.
Just walking across a room, his knee joint sounded like a whole
troop of Spanish dancers. And his feet were flat as a bear's.

When the coast guard said no, he gave up on the war, and
married Elaine in the summer of 1942. That fall he took a job
coaching high school football in Eclectic, Alabama. On the team
that year there was a fullback named Lenny Pigot who was six
feet tall and weighed 210 pounds. There weren't many college
teams around in those days that could have put enough meat up
on the line to stop Lenny, and the other D division high schools
that Eclectic played against didn't even bother to try. Most of
them figured that just showing up for the game was pretty daring,
and about as much as could reasonably be expected of them.
Eclectic averaged 80 points a game, and the closest score of the
season was 53–12 against Fred High School of Arno, on a rainy
night when Lenny felt like he was catching a cold. The next week

there was a snide editorial in the county newspaper with the title, "Coasting."

After the season was over, Chicken and Elaine picked out the best offer, moving to the high school in Mobile, where he had a mediocre season in the fall of 1943. But by then the word about the 80-point games at Eclectic had drifted over as far as Georgia, and the offer came from Boniface. He went there in the fall of 1944 as head coach.

"I hope they don't ask me to make a speech," he said. Speaking in public turned him inside out. From a public relations standpoint it had been a bad failing for a football coach to have. Talking to the team was okay. It was a homogeneous group and he knew he could count on their interest. But standing up before a miscellaneous crowd tied him in knots. Even assembly programs at Boniface had done him that way, and the football banquet was pure torture. He didn't get many invitations to speak, because it was an ordeal watching him as well.

"*You* don't make speeches at a funeral," said Elaine. "The priest does it." She kept the house well. It was an old house, fronting on Abercorn Street between Thirty-fifth and Thirty-sixth Streets. The little things in the room were the nicest—small figurines and demitasse cups and other pieces of china.

"I don't mean a real speech," he said. "I don't even want to have to say a few words."

"I'm sure you won't have to say anything."

"I was his coach, Elaine," he said. "He played under me the best year he ever had. People remember things like that."

"I'm sure you won't have to say anything at the funeral," she said.

He wasn't listening to her, but sat with an abstracted look on his face. Elaine was gliding into middle age gracefully. She was a very attractive woman, and things around the house were relaxed and easy, now that people didn't call him "Chicken" anymore.

"What if I said, 'Jack was the backbone of the best team I ever coached'?" he said, looking up at her.

"I don't think you need to worry about it," she said. "They don't ask for testimonials at a funeral these days."

[33]

He looked away from her.

After a while she said, "You could just say he was the best player you ever coached."

He didn't look at her. "He was the best lineman," he said. "Lenny was the best back."

Lenny never played college football, though he was on the base team at Camp Lejeune in 1943. After five major landings in the Pacific, he died in a hospital when the war was over of an unidentified insect bite that gave him a wasting fever. Chicken didn't hear about it until 1946.

"You don't need to narrow it down that way," she said. Then she added, "Though I'm positive you won't have to say anything tomorrow anyway."

"I can't say he's the best player," he said. "Just like that." He stopped, thinking. "He was the best lineman for sure. No question about that."

For a while neither one of them said anything.

"Would you like some milk?" she said.

"What?"

"Would you like for me to get you a glass of milk?"

"Yes," he said.

She went into the kitchen and came back with a glass of milk on a saucer with some icebox cookies. He was looking at the ceiling. They were twelve-foot ceilings, not as high as the ones in the older houses closer to Broughton Street. Near the corner a spider was moving around on her web. The light from a lamp on the end table spread the shadow of the web into the corner of the room.

"Did you sell Dr. Baker the policy?" she asked.

"He didn't buy it today, but he's going to," he said. "I can't see him tomorrow because of the funeral."

He picked up the glass of milk and one of the cookies.

"Why don't we have supper out tomorrow night?" she said.

"Why don't we?" he said.

"We haven't had supper out in two months," she said.

"Yes," he said. He was looking at the ceiling again. "I hadn't even seen him for the last three or four years," he said. "I meant to go see him wrestle, but I never got around to it." He looked at different spots on the ceiling. "The last time I saw him he looked like hell," he said. "Bloated."

"Big men get that way," she said.

"He wasn't but twenty-six when he died," he said. "The last time I saw him he was twenty-one or twenty-two. Hell, he hadn't stopped growing yet."

"You know what I mean," she said.

"I mean I didn't *recognize* him, Elaine," he said. "Except for those gapped teeth and the tattoo he put on his arm for the Oglethorpe game that time."

She didn't say anything.

He was looking at the ceiling again. "Jack Curran was the backbone of the best team I ever coached," he said. He drank down the last of the milk. "Hand me the paper and a pencil," he said, motioning toward the desk.

She handed him a note pad and a pencil, and he began to write, propping the pad on his knee. From time to time he looked up at the ceiling and into the corner where the spider was walking her web.

"Jack was like a spider," he said, reading from the pad.

She looked at him. "Like a spider?" she said. She looked up into the corner of the room.

"He spun a web that bound the team together," he said. He looked up at her. "Spun . . . spun . . . spinned?" . . .

"Spun," she said.

"It sounds funny," he said. "Spun."

She cleared her throat. "You want some more cookies?"

He looked at the plate. "We owe him a lot, Elaine," he said. He picked up a cookie. "I feel like we owe him a lot."

The shadow of the spider's web wound into the corner of the room. Of the web itself, nothing could be seen. The spider seemed to be hanging suspended in the air.

6

Mary

"I DON'T THINK YOU OUGHT to go. I don't think you've got any *business* going. That's the way I feel about it," said the man. He wasn't speaking in a heated way. They had been talking about it all evening, and both of them were wearing out on it.

"Sometimes I do, and sometimes I don't. It comes and goes. Probably you're right. I'm trying to see just how I feel about it." Mary was small and delicate—more fragile than pretty, but pretty too.

"*You're* not Catholic," he said.

She looked at him. "You don't have to be Catholic to go to a Catholic funeral," she said. "A lot of the people there won't be Catholic."

"I know," he said. "It's just something else. I don't think you should go."

"The Catholic thing was part of the trouble," she said. "It wouldn't make any difference now." She looked at him. "It wasn't that important then really."

"He could have married again, couldn't he?" he said.

"I never did get straight about it," she said. "I don't think we *were* married from his point of view. I tried to get him to explain about his mother, but I never got straight about that either. He didn't like to talk about it at all. It was an old thing with him. I think we were living in sin."

He looked at her. "Well," he said. "It's your decision. You're going to have to make up your mind."

"It's yours too," she said. "I'm trying to think what Jack would say."

He got up and went to the window. "I think the moon's up," he said. "It's been so still. We should have had rain."

"It's not like being a widow," she said.

He looked at her. "No, it's not," he said. "It's not like being a widow at all."

"It is in a way," she said.

He looked at her without saying anything.

"I never believed in divorce any more than he did," she said. "Maybe he believed in it more, because of his mother. I never understood him that well."

He looked at his watch. "It's twenty to eleven," he said. "You'll have to think it out for yourself. *I'm* not going to the funeral tomorrow. *I've* got to go to work."

"I wouldn't want to do the wrong thing," she said.

"I'm going to bed," he said. "Will you put Fleetwood out?"

"Yes," she said.

"Where is he?"

"He's probably in the kitchen."

"I might have known," he said. "I'll put him out." He went into the kitchen and came back with a big gray tomcat draped over his arm. "All he does is eat and sleep," he said. Fleetwood yawned and stretched his leg. "Eat and sleep and make poopoo in the litter box." He went out the front door.

"The moon's up," he said when he came back. "The clouds are gone so I could see the moon."

"It doesn't feel as close," she said.

He looked at the chair by the fireplace. "He's tearing up the chair with his claws," he said.

[37]

She looked at the chair. "We need to make him a scratching post," she said.

"You need to give him a boot in the ass," he said. "I paid seventy-five dollars for that chair."

She looked at him. "I saw one in *American Home*," she said. "You make it with a piece of carpet."

"A boot in the ass would be cheaper than a piece of carpet," he said. "Two boots in the ass would be cheaper."

"You can't train a cat," she said.

"Who said anything about training?" he said. "I said give him a boot in the ass."

"Maybe I could spray something on it he wouldn't like," she said. "They have it for dogs."

"I vote for a boot in the ass," he said.

"What should I do, Pete?"

"I've told you about fifty times already. You want me to tell you again?"

"He was a good man in most ways. The religion thing was a big part of it. I didn't hate him. We just couldn't get along."

He looked at his watch again. "Let me put it this way," he said. "I've got to hit the sack, Mary. I have to go to work in the morning." He came over to the sofa and gave her a kiss on the cheek.

"I'm coming," she said. Standing up she looked more fragile than she did sitting down.

They went into the bedroom together. Then she took her nightgown and went into the bathroom to put it on. When she got back he was already in bed and the radio was on.

"It's about Jack," he said.

She went to her vanity and began putting up her hair, which was long and thin, light brown. Wearing it long wasn't the style, but she did it because Pete liked it that way.

They listened to the sports announcer talking about Jack and his football career. She watched Pete in the vanity mirror. He went to sleep while the announcer was still talking, before the sports program went off the air. Afterward there was a program of music, a special collection of Irish songs, but the disc jockey didn't say he was playing them for Jack. The first song was "Peg o' My Heart" by Perry Como. It had been popular in 1947. She liked Perry Como because the pictures of him looked so kind and calm. She also liked the song. Her favorite lines were:

Peg o' my heart, your glances,
With Irish art, entrance us.

She liked the two-word rhyme in the second line for the one word in the first.

When she finished with her hair, she turned out the light in the room and went to the window. The moon was bright enough to light up the side yard, and she could make out Fleetwood sleeping in one of the white wooden lawn chairs—a dark spot against the white of the chair.

The second song was "The Bells of St. Mary's" by Bing Crosby, which she remembered from the time before she met Jack. She liked that song, too. Her favorite lines from it were:

And so, my beloved,
When red leaves are falling,
The love bells will
Ring out
Ring out
For you and me.

It made her remember the leaves being red in the fall.

Pete started to snore, and she went to the bed and pushed him to make him turn over. There wasn't enough moonlight in the room for her to see his face, but she felt for his head on the pillow, then leaned down and kissed him on the cheek. Afterward she went back to the window and looked out into the moonlit side yard.

She thought about Jack's mother being at the funeral, and Susy. And all his Irish friends from the fire department.

"I wish I knew the right thing to do," she said, whispering it to herself. Then she started to cry, softly, so as not to wake Pete.

7

Mackey

MACKEY SCISSORED HER LEGS against the sheets, reaching for the warm spot that wasn't there anymore. Not upset about it, because she often woke up in an empty bed on the morning after—which was all right, provided the evening before had gone well. Most other people she needed only in a peripheral way.

She peeped an eye out from under the covers—a green eye flecked with brown. She could tell it was broad daylight outside, even with the overcast graying the sky. The room was filled with an ironlike gray-green light that had an eleven o'clock intensity to it.

She did not know about it yet—Jack's heroic death in the fire on Hull Street. No small voice inside her whispered what was lost and gone. The sounds of the fire engines going by her house, and of the fire itself two blocks away, none of that had come in to her where she was sleeping. She was accustomed to the city sounds at night, and unless they came into her own space—inside the walls of her apartment, and the bed itself—nothing distracted her attention from the important personal things that she lived by.

She lay in the bed, under the mound of covers—on her side, with her legs drawn up, her hands together under her cheek—like a statue of a supplicant praying, toppled onto its side.

At twelve o'clock she got up and took a hot bath, soaking and massaging herself slippery with white soap, thinking back to the triumph of the night before.

When she got out of the tub at one o'clock, she wound her hair in a towel and put on her robe, because the apartment was too cold to walk naked in. Then she went to the mirror on her closet door and opened the robe, holding it out batwinged, showing herself for her own satisfaction, her flesh pink from the tub against the pale blue of the robe, with coppery wisps of hair curled out from under the turban on her head.

It wasn't until seven o'clock Thursday night that she found out what had happened to Jack after he had gotten out of the bed. About the fire, and the heroic way he had died.

Her first inclination was to get a bottle and find someone to go home with her. But she settled for the bottle and herself alone.

Back in her apartment, she turned up the gas heaters as high as they would go, steaming the place back to something like Eden, or an island in the warm South seas. Then she took off her clothes and lay down on the bed naked, propped up with pillows, her legs spraddled wide, taking small sips from the bottle, which she held between her breasts like a crucifix.

When the bottle was empty, she dropped it on the floor beside the bed. Then she got up and did a tipsy pirouette in front of the mirror, holding her breasts in her hands, cupping them like melons that she was offering to the whole wide world—afterward sliding her arms together, holding and framing them, while she moved around the floor with short, whirling steps on her toes, almost doing a dance in the tropic heat of the room.

At twelve o'clock midnight, she turned off the heaters and got into the bed, pulling the covers over her head to seal herself in.

She pulled herself into a ball in the warm spot that she made in the bed.

And then she started to cry.

[41]

8

Dendron at the Firehouse

THE FIREHOUSE BARRACKS was a long, low-ceilinged room, with shaded lights dropped down over the corridor between the bunks. If he put his head at the foot of the bed, a man had enough light to read by. Turned the other way, his head was in the shadows and he could sleep.

Three men were in the barracks, sitting on the lighted ends of their bunks. Two on one side of the aisle, and one on the other, just across from them. The two men were talking. One had a very loud voice.

"It gives me the redass," said the man with the loud voice. "Words ought to goddamn mean what they say."

"Yes . . ." said the other man. He drew out the word. "Yeesssss. . . ."

There was a radio on but turned down low, its dial glowing at the dark end of the bunk of the loud-voiced man. Irish music was playing: "McNamarra's Band." When it was over, the next song was "It's a Great Day for the Irish." In between songs the announcer was telling Pat-and-Mike jokes.

The two talking men were smoking cigars, and the smoke hung in winding blue sheets along the corridor under the shaded lights. The man across the aisle from them was polishing a shoe.

"I never heard it," said the loud-voiced man.

"Yeesssss . . ." said the other man. He was looking at the shoe being polished across the aisle. "You're making too much of it." He took the cigar out of his mouth and flicked the ash with his little finger. Then he spit into a Sir Walter Raleigh tobacco can on the floor beside the bunk—a long drooling bomb of saliva that he dropped carefully into the can, holding his head still and looking down with his eyes. Afterward he wiped his mouth with the back of his hand. "You know what it means," he said.

An honor guard had been formed to carry the coffin and stand by at the cemetery—eight firemen all together—including the three in the barracks. It was something the department would do for those who were killed in the line of duty, or who died after retiring. The men were getting their things ready so they would make a good showing for the department at the funeral.

All three of the men had played football for Boniface. But Ducker Hoy, the loud-voiced man, had played on the same team as Jack. For two years Ducker had been the best tackle at Boniface. He was hard of hearing, and not always 100 percent accurate on his blocking assignments, but he had good size, and he wasn't afraid to hit.

The other two were Wilton Fosdick—"Horse" Fosdick—and Canty Greb. Horse had been a fullback on the 1952 team, and Canty had been the right end in 1949 and 1950. Horse got his nickname from a hope that he was going to be as good as Horse Rooney, the legendary fullback of the 1942 team. But giving him the name didn't work the charm. Deep down, he didn't really like to hurt people. Canty had gotten some scholarship offers from places like Southeast Georgia and the Citadel. But he hadn't been interested in going to college. He didn't want to leave Savannah.

"What's a *pall* anyway?" said Ducker. "They bury him in a goddamn casket. I never heard of a goddamn pall." Ducker held his cigar in the right corner of his mouth—way back, so it made his face bunch up on that side. He liked to chew the stub.

"You don't need to talk so fucking loud," said Horse. "I can hear you." Horse smoked his cigar like a man who had been given one as part of some kind of celebration—holding it with his teeth in the middle of his mouth, flaring out his lips so they wouldn't touch it. He smoked twenty a day just like that—a puff every ten seconds, six a minute. Steady. Like he wanted to get it over with and wouldn't be doing it again for a long time to come. Every ten puffs he'd try to blow a smoke ring, but he couldn't get his mouth right for it, and all that ever came out was just a wad of smoke. Horse never had much style at anything—least of all at smoking cigars. "I ain't deaf," he said, blowing out a wad of smoke. It wasn't even round. Usually the wads of smoke that he blew were long and tear-shaped. Once somebody said one of them looked like a whale, which perked Horse up. He tried to perfect his technique, thinking he would blow smoke whales if he couldn't do rings. But he couldn't get his mouth right for the whales either.

"What?" said Ducker. He had a high voice, and when he talked his red face began to shade off into purple. Even in high school Ducker had looked like a grown man, chunky and thick. His stringy white hair, greased up with Wildroot, made him look like a German butcher. After he quit playing football he would swell up another size or two every year. At twenty-six he looked middle-aged, with a face that seemed to be folding in on itself.

"It probably goes back a ways," said Horse. Horse had a raspy voice, creaky and weak, almost a whisper. Even when he was yelling he didn't make much noise. "A pall must be like a casket—what they used to call it." Horse was a big man, too, but with more bone showing. He wore his dark hair in a crew cut.

Canty looked more like an athlete than either of them. He was tall and thin, with curly blond hair—trim. And his muscles had a lot of definition. There was a quick tightness in the way he moved that came out even in the way he was polishing the shoes.

While Ducker and Horse talked about the funeral, Canty sat on his bunk across the way, working a spit shine onto his shoes. Dipping a rag into the top of the shoe polish can, which had water in it, then picking up the polish on the rag and swirling it on the leather until the drops of water went away.

"I don't like using a goddamn word that way," said Ducker. "I hadn't heard it."

"It probably goes back. You know, historic," said Horse. "Probably they *used* to call it a pall."

"What?" said Ducker. Since he really liked to chew it more than he liked to smoke it, Ducker had a hard time keeping his cigar going, and he was having to relight it all the time. He kept a big box of kitchen matches by his bunk.

"I said, they *used* to call it that," said Horse, raising his voice. "Goddamn, it ain't worth arguing about."

"I don't like it anyway," said Ducker. "I don't like to use a word that don't mean what it says."

"You know what a goddamn pall*bearer* is," said Horse. "You get your ass in a sling about the damnedest things."

"Bearer?" said Ducker. "Bearer? We're going to be *bearing* a goddamn *casket*." The cigar in the corner of his mouth jumped and shook with his talking. "That's what we're going to be goddamn *bearing*."

Horse took the cigar out of his mouth and blew a wad of smoke into the air. "Can't you think up nothing serious to argue about?" he said. He looked up at the wad of smoke he had blown. It was shaped a little like a whale.

"Look!" said Canty, holding up the shoe on his hand so they could see it.

"It looks good," said Horse. "But it takes too long for a spit shine. You been working on that all day."

Canty wrapped a towel around the shoe and put it under his bunk.

"Have *you* ever heard of a pall?" said Ducker, speaking to Canty.

"I heard of a pallbearer," said Canty. "We're going to be pallbearers tomorrow."

"Forget *bearer*," said Ducker. "You ever heard of just a plain, motherfucking *pall*?"

Canty wrapped the rag around his finger and began swirling polish onto the other shoe. "No," he said.

[45]

While they were talking, Jack's friend Dendron came in. Dendron Genneau. It was one of the town's ironies that Dendron never got a nickname. If anybody ever needed a nickname, it was Dendron. But no one even called him "Denny."

Dendron was small and fragile, light-boned, with a great big head, and glasses—very large, with thick lenses. His face was small in proportion to the rest of his head, which looked as though it had room for about three average-sized brains inside. The outsized head on that small body, with the glasses, made him look like one of those big-headed men of the future that were drawn to illustrate rocket ship stories in the science fiction magazines.

He was Jack's oldest and best friend—though they hadn't seen each other really to talk to for three or four years.

They had lived next door to each other since they were five. That was the secret of their friendship—not a matter of opposites attracting, or anything that would be so complicated to explain. Each was the one the other had known longer than anybody else. The truth was, they never did understand each other very well, and always had to listen very carefully when they were having their talks. Dendron didn't even particularly like football—though he went to the games to see Jack play the year he was at Boniface. As they grew older, they saw less and less of one another, but every once in a while they would still get together, and Jack would unload whatever was bothering him at the time. Dendron never solved any of Jack's problems for him—usually he didn't understand what the problem *was*. But Jack would keep on going to him with them just the same. The talking itself seemed to help.

It had been late Wednesday before Dendron heard about Jack's death.

"You ever heard of a pall, Dendron?" Ducker shifted the question to him. Because of his appearance, especially that watermelon head of his, Dendron had a reputation as a scholar. He wasn't especially smart, but he looked like he was. He was also interested in facts, though his memory for them was only fair. His chief trait—the way Jack saw him over the years they had been friends—was that he was loyal. And he was kind.

"What?" said Dendron. He pushed his glasses up the bridge of his nose with the middle finger of his right hand. The small face on that big head made it hard for him to get frames that fitted, and the glasses were always sliding down his nose.

"For Christ's sake, don't get started on Dendron," said Horse.

"Why do they call it a pall?" said Ducker. "Pallbearer. You ever heard of just a pall?"

"No," said Dendron. He looked around the barracks. "I guess they took everything to Mrs. Reilley," he said.

"What?" said Ducker.

"Nothing left in the locker," said Horse. "We had to make up a list."

"Jack's stuff?" said Ducker.

"That's what I thought," said Dendron. He looked around the barracks. "It's smoky in here." The blue smoke from the cigars hung in sheets along the barracks. At the end of the room, where the light came out of the head, the layers were very distinct.

"Sit down," said Horse.

Dendron didn't sit down. "I just thought that there might be something," he said, looking down at Canty polishing his shoes. "Something you wouldn't have thought about."

"We had to make up a package," said Horse. "Everything was in it." He stopped. "They're going to bury him in his uniform."

"Yes," said Dendron. "I hadn't seen him in three or four years." He sat down on the bunk with Horse. "We just didn't get together anymore. You never know."

Ducker was lighting his cigar, rolling the tip around in the flame and puffing on it in the center of his mouth. "We *worked* with him," he said, shaking out the match and dropping it on the floor. "I never see Dimmy Camack anymore." The others looked at him. He held up the stub of the cigar, examining the end. "It's been four years since I saw Dimmy Camack. Five, I guess." He thought a minute. "I don't know how long it's been." The others were looking at him, waiting. "You remember Dimmy," he said.

Dendron nodded.

"Dimmy and me would run around together," said Ducker. "We knew each other pretty good."

"You lose touch," said Horse.

"Dimmy used to be the best friend I had," said Ducker. "We knew each other all our life." Ducker put the cigar into his mouth, working it back up into the corner. He shook his head. "Dimmy was a crazy son of a bitch."

For a while they didn't say anything.

"Were you raised together?" Horse asked Dendron.

"On Waldburg Street," said Dendron. "We were about five or six when he moved there."

"Old Dimmy," said Ducker, shaking his head.

"Whose match gun is that?" said Dendron. He pointed to the gun, made from a clothespin, lying on a locker at the foot of the bunk across the way. The clothespin was taken apart and the spring arranged so it would light and throw a wooden kitchen match.

"Canty likes to play with it," said Horse.

"Does he play with it here?" said Dendron.

"It's a *fire*house, ain't it?" said Horse. Then he laughed.

"I haven't seen one of those since we lived on Waldburg Street," said Dendron.

"He likes to *make* them mostly," said Horse. "He don't really play with it much."

"I never knew how to make one," said Dendron.

"Canty would show you," said Horse.

Ducker's cigar went out, and he lit it again. They watched him while he rolled the end around in the flame of the match.

"He used to have crazy dreams," said Dendron.

"Jack?" said Horse.

"Yes," said Dendron. "He used to tell me about them."

"Curran had crazy dreams?" said Ducker.

"He just used to tell me about them," said Dendron. "We used to be pretty close."

"What kind of dreams?" said Horse.

Dendron looked around the barracks. "Just crazy dreams."

"Like a nightmare?" said Horse.

"Sometimes," said Dendron. "Sometimes just crazy."

"Like what?" said Horse. "What kind of dreams did he have?"

"All kinds," said Dendron. "The ones he told me about were the ones he had over and over."

"I see," said Horse.

"Were they like a nightmare?" said Ducker.

"No," said Dendron. "Sometimes they were. He dreamed all the time, but it was the ones he had over and over he worried about."

"I see," said Horse.

Dendron pushed the glasses up the bridge of his nose with the middle finger of his right hand. "I never have dreams," he said, wistfully.

"What kind of dreams were they?" said Ducker.

Dendron pushed the glasses up again. "Once he dreamed about some sharks."

"I see," said Ducker. "Sharks?"

"It was crazy," said Dendron. "They were double sharks. Like a P-38."

"A P-38?" said Ducker.

"That's what he said," said Dendron. "You know. Two sharks, but joined together by their fin. Like a P-38." He held his hands together with the thumbs touching, the fingers together and held out like wings.

"It was scary, eh?" said Horse.

"It didn't seem to bother him," said Dendron. "Just that he would have it over and over. He said it wasn't a scary dream."

For a while they sat and watched Canty polishing his shoe.

"I never had the patience to do a spit shine," said Dendron.

"Canty's got *beaucoup* patience," said Horse. "He's been working on it all day."

Canty held up the shoe on his hand, turning it so the light reflected on the toe. The shoe looked like it was made of patent leather.

"A spit shine lasts pretty good," said Ducker. His cigar had gone out again.

"That's really a good shine," said Dendron.

"Thank you," said Canty.

For several minutes they sat watching Canty swirl the rag on the leather. Ducker lit a match and got his cigar going again.

"I got something," said Horse. "I figured the family wouldn't have any use for them, so I didn't put them in the package." He reached under his pillow and pulled out a small brown paper parcel, holding it out to Dendron.

"What is it?" said Ducker, looking at the parcel.

[49]

"Was it something of Jack's?" said Dendron. Canty stopped polishing his shoe.

"Name tags," said Horse.

"Curran's?" said Ducker.

"I don't know what I wanted them for," said Horse. "I didn't think Mrs. Reilley would have any use for them."

Dendron took the parcel and opened it. There was a small bundle of cloth tags with a rubber band around them.

"He used to put them on everything," said Ducker. "He even sewed them on his socks."

There were a dozen or so of the small rectangles of cloth. Dendron laid them out on the bunk, ranking them side by side. Then he picked them up, making a stack of them again.

"You take them," said Horse. "I don't know why I kept them in the first place."

"We'll divide them," said Dendron, looking around at the three men.

"You take them," said Horse. "We had to send the other stuff to Mrs. Reilley."

Dendron looked at Ducker.

"I got no use for them," said Ducker. He picked up one of the name tags. "He used to put them on everything." He dropped the tag back onto the bunk.

Dendron put them back into the paper bag, which he folded around the tags. Then he put the parcel into his coat pocket.

"Thank you," he said.

For a while they sat in silence. Canty's rag made squeaking noises as he rubbed the polish into his shoe.

Finally Dendron stood up. "I'd better be getting along," he said.

"You can keep what you want and throw the others away," said Horse. "You were his best friend."

"Thank you," said Dendron. "I appreciate it. I don't have a picture of him."

For a minute he stood looking around the barracks. The smoke had thinned out a little. Two gray sheets of it wound down the passage between the bunks under the lights. He pushed the glasses up on his nose. "I'll see you at the funeral tomorrow," he said.

"Dendron . . ." said Ducker. Dendron looked at him. "We're going to put him away right. Everybody in the honor guard knew him."

"Yes," said Dendron. "I'm sure you will." He pushed the glasses up on his nose. "Thank you."

"Dendron?" Canty looked up at him, holding the shoe on his hand.

Dendron looked down at him. Canty moved the hand with the shoe on it. "I been polishing these shoes all day," he said.

"I never saw a better shine," said Dendron.

"Thank you," said Canty. He swirled the rag over the toe of the shoe. "You can have the match gun, if you want it," he said.

"Thank you," said Dendron. "I never learned how to make one."

Outside, Dendron opened the parcel and peeled off the top label and put it into the secret compartment of his wallet. The others he put back into the bag. Then he dropped the bag through the grating of a storm sewer.

9

Kate

KATE LEFT JOHNNY CURRAN—they left each other, against God's will—after eight years of marriage, when Jack was six years old. Johnny loved her to come home to. He really did. But the longer they were married, the more he drank like an Irishman. And the more he drank like an Irishman, the less he came home. There were some days—sometimes runs of three and four days—when she didn't see him at all, though the Lighthouse Bar was only four blocks away from the house on Warren Square. In October of 1935 he was away for a week. The sixth day went over Kate's limit, so she walked out on him.

Kate was phlegmatic in a fashion that could have been taken for patience, but the world had always appeared to her to be a certain way, and sitting around waiting six days for Johnny to come home didn't fit in with her sense of the proper disposition of things. That wasn't the kind of a marriage she had in mind, and she was never one to put up with a way of the world that wasn't to her liking.

So she moved out. Without nagging, and without discussing it with him—Kate was never much of a talker with those she had her deepest feelings for. Just—he came home and she wasn't there. Gone. With Jack and the few pieces of furniture she had brought into the house when they had gotten married. Pinned to the pillow of their bed was a note: "Enough is enough." The last words that ever passed between them.

It was a hard move that she had to make, because the Church was into her very deep, and she knew it was her immortal soul that was at stake. The family—except for her brother Donald—never forgave her for it. Nor did she ask them to. She took her husband's neglect for a long time without complaining about it. But finally, Johnny—the way he behaved—was more than she could bear, or thought she ought to, whether God expected it of her or not.

Her father died the year after she broke off her marriage, though they were never sure that was the cause of it. She went to the funeral, standing at the back with Jack, then leaving afterward without trying to speak to any of them. Kate was Mr. Lynch's favorite child, and his greatest disappointment. He never came to see her after she walked out on Johnny. The two or three times they met on the street he crossed to the other side without speaking. He didn't live to see her marry Gault Reilley. Which was just as well, or so the family thought. "It would have killed him for sure," said Jane, her ugly sister.

Kate wouldn't try to see any of them after the divorce, the more so since they had all opposed the marriage in the first place. Though she would dress Jack up and send him around to go to mass with them on Sundays.

She got a job with the Central of Georgia Railroad, in the payroll department, which is where she met Gault Reilley. They were married the year after the divorce from Johnny became final. After that, any kind of reconciliation with the family was out of the question. She never visited them, and they never visited her. They wouldn't have been able to talk about the divorce or the marriage, and there wasn't anything else to talk about. So she and Reilley went their own way, though the family was keeping up with them right along. When Susy was born, her sister Jane sent her a sympathy card with a black border on it.

Donald dropped around from time to time—usually for meals and a place to sleep when he was drying out. He brought her some of the news of her mother and Jane, but he didn't see much of her other brothers and sisters himself.

It was a willful family, and they all had a lot of what used to be called character, but Kate had the best backbone of the lot. Her marriage to Johnny was a kind of culmination of the whole tendency of her life up to that point, and the family's opposition to him was a great part of her interest in him to begin with—though after she got started she loved him mostly for herself. With a kind of blind tenacity that was beyond both explanation and understanding.

Her father wouldn't have him in the house at first, and Johnny was scared of the older man—who was also bigger. Later, when it got to be clear that his patriarchal will was going to be thwarted anyway, Mr. Lynch would go off into the bedroom upstairs the times Johnny came around, and Mrs. Lynch had to let him into the house to see Kate.

Mr. Lynch went to the wedding. The family argued him into that because of the way it would look if he didn't, though Kate wouldn't have anything to do with it—passing her plans for the wedding along to her sister Jane, who carried them back to the family. They got him to the church, but he tied his tie crooked deliberately, and wouldn't speak to say he was giving his daughter away when the time came. He just stepped back and sat down on the pew beside his wife.

The reception cost him a thousand dollars, and was held at the house. He didn't go to it himself, but after all the guests had arrived he came down from the second-floor bedroom in his shirt-sleeves and got a bottle of Jameson's from the sideboard in the dining room. He opened it with flourishes, standing there in the roomful of guests, and took a long pull straight out of the bottle. Then he took it back upstairs with him without speaking.

Kate had been raised in a house on Washington Square, with

fourteen-foot ceilings and windows that rose ten feet, starting at the floor. Her father was six feet five inches tall, two of her brothers were six feet four and a half, and Donald was six feet six. Her mother was five feet five, but the girls all got their growing genes from the father's side, though two of them looked like Mrs. Lynch in the face. Kate was the oldest and the biggest at five feet nine and a half inches and 155 pounds. Her dark hair was curly, different from the rest of the family, whose hair was dark and straight. Between her two front teeth was a gap, which she got from her father and passed on to her children. She wasn't a pretty woman, but she had a vitality about her that was appealing to certain kinds of men.

After they were married, Kate and Johnny lived in a house on Warren Square—two blocks away from the Lynches. They had the first-floor rooms and the use of the yard—another old house with fourteen-foot ceilings and windows up to the cornice at the ten-foot mark.

After she left Johnny, she moved into the ground floor of a slightly newer house near the Big Park, on Waldburg Street. It had twelve-foot ceilings, and bay windows on the back side, with panes of curved glass in them. She lived there for ten years, until after she sent Jack out of town to school. Then she and Reilley bought the house on Avalon Street in the Marshoaks project.

It was the first time she had ever had a whole house to herself, but most of the Marshoaks bungalow would have fitted into the living room of the place on Washington Square, and she had to make herself think about it to get used to the diminished proportions. The bedrooms were nine by eleven and eight by ten and a half. The living room was ten by seventeen, including the dining alcove at the end. The kitchen was so small that she had to back through the swinging door into the dining alcove to open the door of the refrigerator. And when she did baking and had to open the door of the oven, she banged her rear end on the cabinet under the sink.

Gault Reilley was a small, pink and gray marshmallow of a man, two inches shorter than Kate, and a total retreat from everything she had known before in the way of dimensions. The house was to a scale that suited him well enough, but it pinched and cramped her at first, and she had to go through a period of adjustment—pulling in on her gestures, and making sure she didn't make sudden movements—though she liked the coziness even from the first. Whenever she wasn't thinking about it, something got broken. Now and then she would begin to feel like the walls were closing in on her, and that if she tried to run away out the front door the whole house would stick to her like the carapace of a snail, and she would carry it off on her back.

They had to give up on floor lamps altogether. And Reilley, who was good at fixing things and handy around the house, got living room lamps with wooden bases, which he screwed down to the end tables so Kate wouldn't knock them off.

Eventually she settled into the coziness and really got to liking it. She and Reilley were happy together, and she learned to move with enough caution to keep the breakage down to a level that they could afford.

There had been a leak under the kitchen floor in front of the sink, and the flooring had rotted out. When Kate washed dishes at the sink, the spongy feeling of the floor made her nervous. Reilley didn't want to go under the house in the crawl space to repair the joists—the crawl space was only eighteen inches high, and very dark and spidery, with a soggy, damp smell to it, placenta-like, as if something fork-tongued and scaly had dropped into life down there. But he got a piece of plywood and covered it with linoleum that almost matched the kitchen floor, then nailed it over the rotten place so she wouldn't feel like she was going through when she stood there. He offered to take a turn at washing the dishes, but Kate wouldn't let him do it. Even though they were both working, she kept the woman things for herself. Reilley looked after the maintenance, which he was very good at and enjoyed.

Around the house Kate went barefoot, because she was a little sensitive about being so much taller than Reilley. But he never seemed to mind. When there were just the two of them, after Susy got married and moved out, he called her his "big hunk of woman." Which always made her shoot him with her gap-toothed smile. When she was standing on the plywood at the sink, she was nearly three inches taller than he was. He liked to watch her through the kitchen door, and would come into the kitchen and hug her when she was doing the dishes, tucking his gray-fringed bald head under her chin. "You big hunk of woman," he would say.

Jack's death came down on Kate very hard—harder than anything that had happened to her since her father died.

They weren't seeing much of him at the time, but he was her firstborn, and the boy. Reilley liked him, too—he got along with big people—but, of course, it didn't come over him the way it did Kate, because he only got to know Jack well the one year he had been in the house with them, 1947–1948 when he had been at Boniface. But it upset him the way Kate took it. It upset them both.

Kate was the kind to hold it in, but the night and the day after Jack died she was having to let it out. Her crying was like a man's —whole-framed and shuddery. It took her over so much that she couldn't stand up to do it. All day long she sat around the house that way, sobbing big pumping sobs that made the floors shake, and tilted the pictures on the walls. Reilley didn't know what to do for her, and he had to sit on the side and watch. Every now and then she would pull herself together long enough to move from the chair to the couch, or from the couch to the bed. But then it would come over her again, and she would collapse in a heap, and the sobbing would start up once more.

Susy came over as soon as she had gotten her husband off to work. But she was pregnant and having morning sickness very bad. Seeing her mother that way upset her and made her sicker than ever. She stayed for about an hour, trying to get Kate to eat something and pull herself together. But she couldn't get through to her mother any more than Reilley could, so she gave up and left— afraid that too much of it might do some kind of damage to the baby.

It might have gone on longer than it did. But late Thursday afternoon Kate saw the spider, and the spider stopped it.

She was afraid of spiders. In fact, there were a lot of things she was afraid of, but spiders were one of the things she was afraid of most. They went up near the head of a list which she had made and hung on the cabinet in the kitchen. Spiders sent her into a tizzy. So did frogs, lizards, snakes, rats, cats, birds, and big cockroaches. (Cockroaches are too common in Savannah to stay upset about as a regular thing if you live there. Everybody has to put up with them. Most of the city cockroaches are little bitty things, and know how to behave themselves. When you turn on the kitchen light, they will run away under the sink, or hide in the woodwork. But their country cousins that sometimes come in from the woods are another story. They are humdingers. Monsters up to three inches long, with wings. They can't fly very well, but that's just a liability and no comfort at all, since they might just as well buzz right up your nose trying to get away. It would be a lot better if they were ace fliers, and could go just where they wanted to go.)

Kate had uncomfortable feelings about some abstract things, too, like high places and going to sleep in the dark. But mostly she was afraid of things that were really there, animals that could move in and out of the spaces around her. Seeing them sent her into a tizzy, and she wasn't the tizzying sort, because of her size.

So she tried to get on top of it by making a list of all the things that scared her—from a list she found in a *Reader's Digest* article which gave the real medical names. The list in the article was a very long one, and it was comforting for her to see all of the other things that she *wasn't* afraid of.

She put up her list on the cabinet in the kitchen where she could see it every day, and maybe get used to the things she had written on it. It didn't really work, but it made her feel better about them in a theoretical way—when none of them were around where she could see them. Maybe it worked a little.

GOD MADE FEARFUL THINGS

Ophidiophobia—Snakes
Arachnephobia—Spiders
Batrachophobia—Frogs
Saurophobia—Lizards
Rodentiaphobia—Rats and Mice
Ailurophobia—Cats
Aviaphobia—Birds
Blattidaephobia—Cockroaches (big)
Acrophobia—High Places
Claustrophobia—Close Places
Achluophobia—Dark Places

After she hung it up, Reilley put stars beside Ophidiophobia, Arachnephobia, and Claustrophobia. Then he put a star at the bottom of the page, and beside it wrote, "Me Too!"

Seeing the spider—it had gotten into the bathtub and was trying to climb out—brought her back into herself in a strong familiar way, stopping the sobbing.

She came out of the bathroom and into the living room where Reilley sat slumped in a chair. "There's a spider in the tub," she said. It was the first everyday thing she'd said in over nineteen hours, and Reilley looked up at her from the chair. He was worn out over it himself, and the familiar sound of her voice was strange to him.

She stood in the doorway looking at him, biting her lower lip, clenching it in her teeth until it turned white, bulging out of the gap in the front.

For a minute he looked at her. "I'm sorry," he said. Since they had gotten the news, it was the first time he had been able to get at her to let her know how he felt about it.

She looked at him and nodded. Then she went into the kitchen and began fixing supper.

He went into the bathroom and ran hot water in the tub to kill the spider.

"It's the weather makes them come into the house," he said when he came into the kitchen. "Squeezes them the same as us."

They hadn't finished eating when Donald knocked, then slammed open the front door into the living room. Although it was basic to his personality, being a fireman also had something to do with the way he always came into the house—like he was coming to put out a fire. Shoving in the door so that it would bounce off the wall on the backswing, shaking the house and making the dust rise out of the rugs. Just being a Lynch had a lot to do with it. Donald was the biggest of Kate's brothers, bigger than the father had been.

Reilley knew Donald needed the whole doorway to be able to get into the house. What he couldn't figure out was the violence of it.

They had talked it over a number of times, he and Kate. "I wonder what he'd do if we ever locked it on him?" she said. "Get an ax and chop it down?"

Sometimes they would just sit and think about why he did it.

"Was he like that at home?"

"He moved strong. We all did. Of course, we had more room there. It was an old house, and they put them together pretty solid in those days. Donald was the biggest."

Donald's visits not only made Reilley nervous, they also cost him money. But since Donald was the only one of the family who came around at all, he didn't feel he ought to say anything. Still, just the way Donald opened the front door set them back five or ten dollars right to begin with. And what he did to Kate's lamps and china and knickknacks and things once he got inside made Reilley's breathing go smothery and turned him red in the face. Also, Kate tended to forget herself and move around too much when he was there. Though she would complain and carry on about it very big after Donald had gone, when Reilley added it all up for her.

When they both got excited and started moving together, Reilley didn't like to stay in the living room with them at all, but would go stand in the kitchen door where he would be out of the way.

He didn't like to be that way about it, but inevitably Donald's visits took shape as a column of figures inside Reilley's head. Joyful spending was one thing, and he was blithe enough about shedding his hard-earned cash when he could think of it as bringing back heart's ease and gladness. But his work in the payroll department of the Central disposed him to a very dollary view of waste and destruction, and, since Reilley literally paid for them, Donald's visits had to be figured out in terms of profit and loss. Always considering that he was the only one of Kate's blood relations who would have anything to do with her.

The most expensive visit they ever had from Donald came after the St. Patrick's Day parade in 1949, when he blew in very excited from the green Irish whiskey and the brass band music of the Irish-American Friendly Society. He turned over the dining room table chasing Kate around it, and broke four place settings of her Wedgwood china. Then, before they could get him anchored into Reilley's chair, he stepped on the Atwater-Kent radio, and crushed the right lens of Reilley's reading glasses. It came to $83.36.

This time the splintery sound of the door coming open, and the way the house shook on the backswing, lit up the double-entry sheets inside Reilley's head, and he knew like it was a vision that a new record was going to be set. Nothing broke, because by now everything was either screwed down or broken already. But it jumped the radio off the station it was on, and dropped the top seat of the toilet in the bathroom.

"Kate!" Donald had a high blurry voice, with a sound in the middle of it like air escaping from a tire. "Have you heard, Kate? . . ." he said. "Jack's dead."

They knew what he was going to say, but they didn't know what to answer him. Kate kept on eating, but Reilley put down his fork and watched her. .

"Yes," she said, not very loud.

"Jack's *dead*. . . . *Kate?*" he said. "Jack got killed last night. . . . Where's *Kate?*" He stumbled into the kitchen, flinging the swinging door open and catching it when it bounced off the refrigerator. He had to crouch to get through the doorway with his fireman's bill cap on.

"Jack's dead, Kate . . ." he said, trailing off, looking down at them sitting at the table. He leaned against the open door and took off his bill cap slowly, holding it over his left breast and bowing his head slightly. "It is my duty to inform you . . ." he said, looking down at the floor.

"I said . . ." she held on to it, ". . . yes. . . ." She looked at Reilley, then up at Donald.

He was still looking down at the floor. Up to now, he had been working along at getting out his message without paying any attention to them at all, the way they were taking it. The main thing was for him to lay down the burden he was carrying.

He was standing very erect, except for his head being bowed. For a long time he stood that way, then he rocked his head up slowly, pulling it back until he stood at attention, staring into the wall above their heads. "Jack's dead," he said, finishing it off, "Kate. . . ."

His face was a handsome face, but there was a gone-away look on it. Like the face of a half-wit—or of a man who is going to die soon, but not right away. His eyelids were droopy, folding down over eyes so black they seemed to be all pupil—or no pupil at all, just plain blank holes burned into his head. The skin had a painted-on white color—the color of an old woman's breast, with the same blue undertone from the veins just below the skin. Darker blue around the sockets of his eyes.

Across his left eyebrow and the bridge of his nose there was a scar, dead white against the blue-white of his face. The knife that had made it was in Donald's pocket—he kept it for a souvenir. The man it had belonged to was dead—which was something that still came up now and then around the firehouse barracks. Down there a real fair-fight killing was something that tended to have a very long conversational life.

"He was a good boy," Donald said, drawing himself up to attention to speak, and looking over their heads at the wall. "A . . . good . . . boy." The words came out one at a time, as if he had memorized them.

"Sit down and have some supper," said Reilley.

Donald looked at Kate, nodding his head downward. "How's she . . . taking it?" he said.

"I know about it already," she said. "I'm all right." She looked up at him standing by the refrigerator. "You want something to eat?"

"Sit down," said Reilley.

"You don't have something to drink?" he said, not sitting down.

Kate looked up at him. "We're not holding a wake," she said.

"Yes," he said. He ran his tongue over his lips slowly. "A little of the hair of the hound . . ." he said. "A *drop* of something . . ." His lips were pale, but clearly defined—thin. "It certainly would . . ." he said.

Kate got up and started to clear away the supper dishes. "I'll do the dishes," said Reilley. She didn't answer him, but took his plate, then started to run the water in the sink.

"You can have something to *eat,*" she said, speaking to Donald. "I'm not going to put any more whiskey in you."

Donald was sitting very erect in the straight-backed kitchen chair. He ran his tongue over his lips again. "A brew?" he said.

Kate turned to the sink and cut off the water. "I'll do the dishes," she said. "You two go in the living room."

Reilley looked up at her, then at Donald. Without getting up out of his chair, he reached over and opened the door of the refrigerator, taking out two cans of Miller's beer. "The church key's in the drawer," he said, pointing. "Give us a glass," he said to Kate.

She looked at Donald, then opened the cabinet. "One's all he gets," she said, putting the glasses on the table.

Donald tilted the can and the glass together, pouring the beer down the side to kill the head. He drank half the glass of beer, then he put it on the table in front of him and wiped his mouth with the back of his hand. Reilley was salting his, shaking the salt out into his left hand, then taking it up in pinches between his right index finger and thumb. The grains made diving trails of bubbles in the glass, foaming the beer on top.

"It ruins the taste," said Donald, looking across the table at him.

Reilley looked up, then back at the glass. "I like to watch it," he said, taking another pinch and dropping it into the glass, fluttering his finger against his thumb. "It doesn't make that much difference in the taste."

"It makes it flat out."

Reilley looked up at him. "I never noticed that it made any difference," he said.

They both watched the salt grains making strings of bubbles in the glass.

Donald was sitting at the table with one hand on his glass of beer, the other in his lap. "There wasn't a priest," he said after a while. "He was dead when we dug him out. There wasn't time for a priest."

Kate stopped moving her hands in the sink. For a minute she stood there without saying anything. "They told me that," she said.

Donald twirled the glass in his hand, rotating it between his thumb and index finger. "Mother says he won't go to heaven," he said. He unfolded his eyelids, glancing up at her. "Jane says he's going to hell." He paused. "Mother didn't say that," he said. "Jane was the one said he was going to hell."

Kate didn't say anything. Reilley looked up at her, then back across the table at Donald.

"They said you were hateful to God for what you did," he said.

[63]

"Leaving Johnny and going in with Reilley." He took a drink of the beer, emptying the glass. "Mother said that, too," he said.

Reilley looked across the table at him. Sitting down, they were more of a height. "Horseshit," he said. He said it as respectfully as he could, with the table between them. "They never even saw me."

"You know how they are," said Donald. "Just the two of them in that big house." He poured the rest of the beer into the glass. "When a priest says 'shit,' they both got to stoop and groan."

"It's nothing to do with you, Reilley," said Kate. "It's me."

"It's the priests," said Donald. "Mother's old and Jane's ugly. Just right for the bastards."

Reilley centered his glass on the place mat. "I wouldn't believe that Jack is going to hell," he said. He didn't look up at Kate. "I just wouldn't believe that."

"God does fearsome things . . ." she said. She had her back to them, looking out the window over the sink.

Donald drank down the rest of the beer. "They've got her by the short hairs, too," he said, talking to Reilley. "They know how to work the women all right. They kicked her soul out of the church, but they still got hold of her goddamn ass." He looked up at her, then back at the table. "God didn't put him in Hull Street Tuesday night," he said, holding the empty beer can upended over the glass. "He took himself in there." He put down the beer can and held the glass up to his mouth, holding it high to get the last drops out of the bottom. "It was too tight. When the wall came down, there wasn't any place to go." He held up the can between the thumb and index finger of his right hand, then he squeezed and the can folded in on itself with a snapping sound. He put the can on the table. "There wasn't any place to go," he said again. He looked at the can on the table. "Maybe *God* sent him in Hull Street," he said. "It wasn't no goddamn priest had anything to do with it."

Reilley shoved his can across to Donald, pulling the bent can over beside his glass.

"This weather's been getting me down," said Donald, pouring out of Reilley's can. "I feel like I've had my mouth full of a cat's tail, and my nose up his ass."

"It gets you down," said Reilley.

[64]

"We've been living in sin," she said. "I told you *I'm* the one. You weren't married before."

Donald looked at Reilley. "Makes you want to kick ass, don't it?" he said. He snapped the second can and dropped it on the table.

"Don't the love mean something to God?" said Reilley. "I would think he ought to notice something like that." He paused. "How is it *you* can be living in sin, and *I'm* okay?"

"I know it," she said. "It's just how I feel. I can't do anything about that." She looked down at him sitting at the table. "I'm not talking about *us*," she said. "I love you, too. I'm talking about God."

"You're talking about the goddamn priests," said Donald. "God wouldn't have nothing to do with it."

Kate didn't say anything.

Donald looked up at her. "Jack told Father Whelan to kiss his ass once," he said. "I heard him do it."

Kate turned back to the sink and began washing the dishes again.

"All they know how to do is sit around jacking off and scaring the shit out of the women," he said. "I hate the bastards."

Kate didn't turn around. "You two go in the living room," she said. "I'm not going to argue about it."

Reilley and Donald sat down in the living room, and Reilley tried to talk to him, going on with the talk in the kitchen. But Donald started closing up, folding his drooping eyelids up and down in big, slow blinks—licking and sucking his lips, with both arms stretched out along the arms of the chair.

The sound of Kate sloshing the water in the sink came in from the kitchen.

Later they got him into the bedroom and onto the bed. Reilley wrestled him out of his clothes as well as he could, having to do it without Kate's help. She would have undressed Donald by herself and thought nothing of it, but the two of them doing it— being there together—she wouldn't do that. So she went back into the living room to straighten things up before they went to bed.

Donald lay stretched out on top of the spread, filling up the bed. Under his clothes he wore an old-fashioned union suit that buttoned down the front, with sleeves. It looked strange on him, childish. Reilley looked back from the door before he turned out the light. While he was watching, Donald raised his arm and

[65]

crossed himself, making the moves with a quick, precise motion. He was moving his lips, but Reilley couldn't hear what he was saying.

After the lights were out and they had gotten into the bed together, Kate came over to Reilley and he put his arm around her. She was so solid that he had to prop up his pillow and almost squat on top of it to squeeze her in under his arm, but he liked holding her that way with the lights out in the room. Their bodies stretched out side by side under the covers, and he could feel her knee and the shank of her leg against his foot.

"Don't let go again," he said. "I couldn't stand it this morning."

"I'm all right now," she said.

He reached out to the table beside the bed and turned on the radio. "The Bells of St. Mary's" came up slowly as the tubes were getting warm.

She wasn't moving under his arm, and he couldn't see how she looked in the dark. "I thought a lot of Jack, too," he said.

"The Bells of St. Mary's" ended, and "An Irish Lullaby" came on.

"I was going to pieces."

"I know," he said. "I know you did. But I thought a lot of him, too."

For a while she didn't say anything. "There wasn't a priest," she said.

"It was too quick," he said. "It'll be all right."

"I can't help how I *feel* about it, Reilley," she said.

"I didn't know you still felt that way," he said. "I feel like we're good Catholics."

She didn't say anything. "I can't even open the casket," she said.

He moved away from her a little. "You're not going to open the casket, are you?" he said.

"I couldn't do it."

"You wouldn't want to do it," he said. "I'm sorry. You wouldn't *want* to do it. . . . It's not the Church that won't let you open it. . . ."

For a long time she didn't say anything.

"I can't even pray for him," she said.

"You can pray for him. What do you mean?"

[66]

"I can't *pray* for him."

For a while he didn't say anything.

"I'll pray for him for you," he said.

"An Irish Lullaby" ended, and there was a commercial for Pepsi-Cola. Then "Danny Boy" came on.

"Did you kill the spider?" she said.

"I ran some hot water in the tub," he said.

For a while they didn't say anything. "You'd better get some sleep," he said. "Tomorrow's going to be another bad day." He reached over and turned off the radio. In the dark they could hear Donald snoring in the other bedroom.

Suddenly Reilley sat up in bed. "He didn't break anything," he said.

"What . . . what? . . ." Kate didn't sound sleepy.

"He didn't break anything."

She lay back down. "Wait till tomorrow," she said.

After they had gotten quiet again, a big insect flew against the screen of the bedroom window. Until he went to sleep, Reilley could hear it beating its wings against the screen.

Kate was listening to it, too. It sounded as big as a bird.

J.J. O'Brien

"TWELVE THIRTY-FOUR?" J.J. O'Brien looked at his watch, then wound it, checking it against the brass ship's chronometer on his desk. Both the watch and the chronometer had cost a lot of money —more than they were worth.

"Twelve thirty-four is the time they wrote down on the report," said the man. "I wasn't there when it happened."

J.J.'s movements were strong, on the military side. To someone who had seen a lot of Errol Flynn movies, he would have looked like the commander of a Khyber Rifle regiment.

Deep down, J.J. wouldn't have favored the comparison. His preference was always 100 percent American, and the only other person he had ever wanted to look like was General Black Jack Pershing. He had served under General Pershing in the AEF, and that was his idea of a man to look like. The resemblance was there, and J.J. worked at it, but he missed by just a hair—on the coarse side.

Still, he was very dignified. From ten feet away his eyes looked clear and snappy and intelligent rather than shrewd.

"There wasn't no place for him to go when the wall came down. The whole goddamn wall. You can't dodge a whole block-long wall." The second man was ratlike and gray, with a bright tubercular glint in his eyes. When he talked too long, it brought on a coughing fit. The size-fourteen collar of his shirt hung very starchy on his neck, like a horseshoe on a peg.

"Ah . . . well . . ." said J.J. His suit was gray, too, but the fit was right. The drum-majory way he carried himself filled it out and made the tailoring worthwhile, though, as with the clock, he paid too much for what he got. The coat was double-breasted, with wide lapels, and the sleeves were shortened just enough for him to shoot the cuffs of his shirt and flash his shamrock cuff links, made of green Tara marble.

"A hero's death, Shube," said J.J. His eyes were a frosty gray-green, a lightened tone of the shamrock color of his cuff links. "The lad died a hero's death at the end."

"Stupid," said the ratlike man. "Stupid is what it was. They told him not to go in there."

J.J. looked up at him briefly, then brushed the wings of his great white cavalry moustache with his hand. "A hero's death," he said.

When the ratlike man opened his mouth to speak, J.J. raised his hand for silence.

"Hull Street's too narrow," said the man. "It was stupid."

J.J. picked up the telephone and dialed a number.

"J.J. O'Brien here. To whom am I speaking? . . . Are you the manager? . . . Let me speak to the manager. . . . J.J. O'Brien here. To whom am I speaking? . . . I'd like to order . . . a wreath . . . for the Curran funeral. Something suitable. . . . Something with green in it. Jack Curran was the lad who played for Boniface . . ." he snapped his fingers at the ratlike man. "In . . ." he snapped his fingers again.

"Forty-seven," said the ratlike man.

"Forty-seven. Nineteen forty-seven. . . . Something appropriate. With green in it, I think. A suitable memorial. . . . O'Brien. J.J. O'Brien. . . . Yes. Give me a price range."

The range was fifteen to seventy-five dollars. But the manager added that he could go as high as he wanted.

"Yes . . ." said J.J. He looked at the ratlike man. "Twenty-five," he said, stretching out the "twenty." He looked up at the ratlike man, then puckered his lips. "Thirty," he said. "Make it thirty."

He made a note on the desk pad. "That's right. Thirty. Thirty dollars. . . . Something appropriate for the occasion," he said. "He died a hero's death. . . . A true hero's death."

He hung up the phone and drummed his fingers on the edge of the desk. "We'll get in touch with Mrs. Reilley," he said. "If there's to be a wake, I'll furnish the beer."

"There won't be no wake," said the ratlike man. Something caught in his throat, and he had a coughing fit. J.J. drummed his fingers on the edge of the desk, waiting for him to get over it. It was a hard dry cough, coming in long whooping spasms that left him gasping for breath.

"*Jax* beer, of course," said J.J.

The ratlike man waved his hand at J.J., shaking his head. He held his breath to keep the fit from starting again. Finally he swallowed. "There ain't enough left of him for a wake," he said. He swallowed again and stuffed his handkerchief into his mouth.

"If there is, I want to supply the beer," said J.J.

"Stupid," said the man, working his handkerchief on his mouth the way a trumpet player would work a mute.

"But a hero," said J.J. "Nonetheless a hero. We have to remember our authentic heroes." He drummed his fingers on the desk, looking at the chronometer. "Even our stupid ones."

April 1 3

FRIDAY MORNING WAS BRIGHT but still. Under the live oaks, the shade in the cemetery was strong—full of dark grays, gray-greens, and mossy blacks. Where the sun came down through openings in the leaves, bright patches glowed on the ground—brassy green on the grass and leaves of bushes, silver on the sandy gray spots where no grass grew. The flowers dropping off the azalea bushes collected in thin windrows, purple-brown scatterings along the ground. A few last petals, still holding on the branches, made spots of dying purple-pink against the green of the leaves.

The cemetery was close to the marsh, with tombstones ranked and slanting up to the edge of the bluff under the trees. A procession led by a white marble angel on a pedestal, over the one word —STILES—the most eastward of the grave markers. She stood with her back to the marsh, facing the tombstones, her arms raised westward.

In the marsh, the tide was out, and the mudbanks made popping sounds drying in the sun. The water in the creeks was a brown and spermy broth, brewed down and thickened by the ebb. Along the edges there were swirls and eddies where the blue-shell crabs scuttled just below the surface, working their claws in the flotsam. The smell of the marsh came up the bluff in a sheet, spreading through the cemetery, passing below the marble angel and around the tombstones—moving heavy and slow along the ground under the trees.

George did not go to the mass at the cathedral. He was afraid to go into a Catholic church because of what he had heard about the Pope. At the cemetery, he was on time but not beforehand, and the casket was in place, with the funeral party already gathered under the awning of Fant's Mortuary. The priest was just beginning to speak—twanging the words out through his nose. ". . . *Deus, cujus miseratione animae fidelium requiscunt.* . . ." George was dressed in his good suit—which he had bought in 1947 at Levy's Department Store. The clerk who sold it to him had done it to win a bet with another clerk in the men's department. It must have been the last zoot suit sold on the east end of Broughton Street. They had never been too popular in Savannah at any time, but what lukewarm craze there had been was definitely over by 1947.

The color was a chocolate brown, and there was enough material in the pants alone to make up a pair of sleeping bags—or upholster a sofa. With the pleats, the legs must have been thirty-five inches around, pegged to nine at the cuff. Thirty-five inches all the way to the ground, like a pair of great, fallen knickers. And they came up above his waist as high as a pair of bib overalls. The shoulders of the coat were double-padded, and stuck out so much he looked like he was wearing a sandwich board, with lapels that speared out even wider than the shoulders. The clerk had told him that the way to tell if the coat was a good fit was to make sure that he could just reach the hem of it with his extended middle finger. George had a long arm, so the coat passed the test. It hit him slightly below the knee. "Better too long than too short," said the clerk. Which sounded pretty good to George, since it was just about the same thing his mother had always said when she had taken him shopping as a child.

After he sold him the suit, the clerk couldn't stop his momentum, and went on to sell him a tie and hat to go with it—which weren't part of the bet at all. The tie was yellow, with a hand-painted palm tree on it in green and brown. The hat was a Panama, with a twenty-inch brim and a feather sticking out of the band.

In the outfit, he made about the same general impression as Eagle McFleagle in the "Li'l Abner" comic strip—except that the color of his suit wasn't as gaudy as Eagle McFleagle's. Not that it made all that much difference, really. The cut was the suit's main feature—though the chocolate color did tend to fade into the background when George was out in the open—as long as he didn't move around too much.

The clerk had felt bad later about the hat and tie, but that was after George had already gone, when it was too late to do anything about it.

Anyway, George liked the suit. Wearing it made him feel good. It was looser than his work clothes, and he felt more stylish in it—especially when he would extend his middle finger and feel it just barely touching the hem of the coat.

As he came up behind the awning, he could see the high mound of flowers on the grave, the green imitation-grass carpet over the mound of dirt behind it, and wreaths on stands banked behind that. He hadn't counted on wreaths. They hadn't come into his mind's eye when he pictured the funeral and how it would be. Enormous wreaths—too many to count. There was one in particular, with dark red roses and—

BEST WISHES FROM J.J. O'BRIEN
&
BONIFACE CLASS OF 1948

—silver letters on a Kelly green ribbon. It stood out from the others—the dark velvet red of the roses against the green of the ferns in the wreath, and the bright shiny green of the silk in the ribbon at the center of it all.

The cross that he had made was in his hand, and he felt how small it was against the wreaths. The feathers were soft in his fingers as he stood looking at the mounds of flowers with the green

[73]

ribbon of the wreath centering them behind the mahogany coffin. He didn't look down at the cross, but turned it in his hand, gauging its size—a third that of the least of the wreaths. The colors—he had them in his head as they had looked standing on the dresser, backed by the pale apple green of the walls of his room. Here in the cemetery, looking at the wreaths, he couldn't make the colors of the feathers come into his head at all. The hard Kelly green of just the ribbon of the one wreath alone washed them away.

Even if it had been larger, with a streaked shine and glitter in its colors—he wouldn't have known how to take the feather cross up and put it on the grave. Everything was already in place—set and arranged. So he stepped aside and put it under an azalea bush out of the way, glancing down just once, quickly, to make sure it couldn't be seen.

Then he extended his middle finger to the hem of his coat—having to stoop a little to do it, because for nine years he had carried lead pellets and a slingshot in his pockets and the weight had stretched the coat. He bent his knees and held his arms straight at his sides, walking a little like Groucho Marx, coming up behind the awning to stand the last of the mourners.

All of the folding chairs were filled, and quite a few people were standing around outside the awning. But not as many as might have been expected. There was no breeze moving, and under the shade of the trees it was neither cool nor hot—though a few of the mourners were fluttering the bright mortuary fans. The honor guard from the fire department stood at attention to the sides of the coffin and behind the priest, four and four, facing the mourners. When the priest began to speak, Ducker Hoy took off his hat, then darted his eyes to the sides. When he saw that he was the only one, he turned red in the face from his chin up, slowly, like a thermometer rising, then he put the hat back on again.

On the first row of chairs sat Kate and Reilley, Susy sitting beside her mother. Old Johnny stood at the rear, his face red, with a clogged look, leaning on the back of the chair where Rose was sitting on the last row. Donald stood at the front, left corner of the awning, leaning against the pole. He was wearing his fireman's uniform, holding his bill cap over his left breast, but not bowing his head.

The priest spoke the words slowly, running them up through his nose for emphasis—afterward shaking the hyssop above the coffin with practiced negligence, sprinkling it with flourishes, incensing it with more careless flourishes of the thurible.

Kate was crying under the black veil of her hat, her shoulders heaving with the hard manlike sobbing, making the folding chair creak and groan. The creaking from the chair came in bursts as she let herself out, then pulled herself in—not giving in to it altogether as she had done the day before. Reilley sat on Kate's left-hand side, his right arm reaching up around her shoulders, the arm so short he looked like he was hanging on to her. Her crying made his arm flop up and down and shook him around in his chair.

He had on a bristly gray suit, the same shade of gray as the fringe of hair above his ears, so that the bald top of his head looked like some kind of growth coming out of the gray mound of his suit. There was a balled-up handkerchief in his fist, and he had it mashed into his face—though he wasn't crying. His face was very red—fiery. The wool suit was too heavy for the middle of April, even under the awning, and he was sweating in rivers and bucketfuls. Beads of perspiration stood out on the top of his head, breaking and running down his neck in quick zigzag trails.

"*. . . in sanctitate et justitia . . .*"

Under the droning voice, the crowd of mourners closed in upon itself like the petals of a flower. Only the priest felt the power of his function, making a glory of the moment.

Feeb cried. Mackey stared stony-faced with hard green eyes at the coffin before the green wreath. Chicken Garfield looked at his shoes and muttered under his breath with Elaine hanging on his arm. J.J. O'Brien scowled in regimental dignity, with the rat-faced man at his side holding a handkerchief to his face, his whole body shaking with the coughing like a man dangling on wires. Dendron stood with his hands folded, his eyes lost in the milky lenses of his thick glasses.

[75]

George was menaced by the gestures of the priest, but it was the first funeral he had ever attended, and he tried to take everything in.

When the man from Fant's Mortuary tripped the lever that sent the coffin down into the grave, only George and Mackey watched —and J.J. O'Brien. The priest was looking toward heaven.

Afterward, George waited behind the azaleas until everyone had left the cemetery. After they were gone, he went back to the grave.

Up close the flowers didn't impress him as they had when he had seen them from a distance. The wreath with the green ribbon looked better than most, but even it had too hard a shine.

He walked around the grave slowly, noticing the neatness of the shaped mound the Negroes had made with their shovels. At last he took off his Panama hat and put it on the wreath with the green ribbon. Then he crooked his finger to his mouth and made his hurt bird call. It was the trick Jack had liked for him to do.

When the birds came, fluttering and diving around his head, he held them there with the squeaking noise he made sucking on his finger.

"You were a good friend," he said at last, with great solemnity. Then he put his Panama hat on his head and walked away with his fingers extended to the hem of his coat.

On his way out, he stopped to get the cross he had made. But the ants were already into it, and were swarming on the blue jay head and the candy letters. So he put it back under the azalea bush.

Late in the afternoon, a single sea gull walked up from the bluff under the bushes, coming right up to the bank of flowers covering Jack's grave. He gave a long look at the wreath with the green ribbon, then pecked at it, dancing away and squawking when the wreath fell over. One by one he tried the other wreaths, pecking at the flowers and squawking, his eye growing brighter all the time, sometimes catching a red gleam out of the low afternoon sun.

[76]

He tried them all. Afterward, he stood for a minute in the middle of the shambles he had made, flowers coming in at both eyes from the fallen wreaths. Then he walked back stiff-legged to the bluff, the way he had come. Going out beneath the arms of the white marble angel.

BOOK II

Football:
1946-1947

The Fighting Irish

BONIFACE COLLEGE WAS THE Catholic boys' prep school, run by the Benedictine Fathers. The "Fighting Irish" is what they called themselves, and their colors were green and white. They liked to think of themselves as a little Notre Dame, though their actual record as a football team made that difficult, at least in the closing years of World War II and just after. They had had some very good football teams in the past, as the alumni liked to remind them—especially the Horse Rooney championship team of 1942. But, in the meantime, the lean years had come upon them. Four to be exact.

"Fighting Irish" had the right kind of ringing sound to it and associations that pleased everybody at Boniface, but it held up well only if it wasn't examined too closely—though it was certainly a pervasive state of mind.

A fourth of the student body was Jewish, sent there by their parents who were convinced that their sons would get a better education at a school that charged tuition than they would at the public high school, which did not. Most of the other three-fourths of the students were Catholic all right, but half of them were Mediterranean and Teutonic, with names like Debennedetto and Cortez and Schultz. The Irishmen were a sizable plurality, but not a majority by any means. Only the idea they represented set the tone.

It was an interesting melting pot of a student body, in which almost every ethnic group west of the Danube was represented (there was even one boy who was half-Chinese)—except that there weren't any white Anglo-Saxon Protestants, of course—or Negroes. Also, the student body was all male.

Boniface was a military school, and all the boys who went there were called "cadets," and had to wear a blue-gray uniform. Some of the boys from large families wore uniforms (or at least parts of uniforms) that had served five or six or even seven older brothers. The Fathers at Boniface were understanding, and didn't change the pattern of the uniform. Still, a pair of pants can only be let out and taken in so many times before it begins to give up the ghost. But the mothers didn't seem to understand that. They would give up on the coats, but not the pants. The pants they felt they were able to do something about. The brass never wore out, and sons took pride in wearing the collar insignia of their fathers, polished with Blitz cloths until nothing was left but the plain brass disk, gleaming in the sun. The brass didn't make up for the pants, but it helped.

The Benedictines were not only understanding, they were diplomatic—trying to place the hopelessly seedy-looking younger sons in the middle squads where they wouldn't be so conspicuous on parades. For the officers and noncoms, there were usually alumni, like J.J. O'Brien, who would chip in and help get them enough pieces of clothing so they wouldn't look too bad walking out in front where people could see them.

Jack Curran came back to Savannah in the summer of 1947, to play out his last year of high school football for Boniface. Kathleen Reilley had gone to work to send her son out of town to school, so he wouldn't have any more contact with Old Johnny than he just had to, and also because she was afraid that her second marriage to Gault Reilley would be embarrassing to him.

The first year she had sent him to a Catholic military school in Alabama. He was big for his age, and he played quarterback that year. But he was so unhappy at the school that she moved him to St. Francis, in New Orleans, Louisiana. He stayed in New Orleans for two years, where they moved him up onto the line—the first year to end, and the second year to center. In the three years he was away from home he almost outgrew his father. In New Orleans they said that when the barracks was quiet they could *hear* him growing.

When J.J. O'Brien heard about him, he made five long-distance telephone calls to New Orleans in two days, then went around to see the Reilleys.

"Six feet *three* inches, Madam?" J.J. O'Brien was inclined to be formal in the way he bespoke himself. "Two hundred and twenty-*five* pounds?" He ran his finger over his moustache, smoothing it down. "Madam, the Fighting Irish need—*need*—your son."

He offered to pay the tuition for Jack at Boniface, and to buy all his uniforms. He also promised to have him made a sergeant in the cadet corps—so he could play football there in Savannah, instead of wasting himself out in Louisiana. Kathleen couldn't turn down the offer, and Jack wanted to come home anyway, because of Mary Odell.

Boniface alumni fell into two categories. On the one hand there were the members of the small minority groups—the Jews and the Greeks were the largest of those—and on the other hand there were the Irishmen. The first group was generally more prosperous —most of the boys coming from families that had money and could send them on to college, where they would study for the law, or medicine, or dentistry, or business administration. A smaller percentage of the Irishmen went on to college, and a lot of them wound up running liquor stores or working for the fire department. Since Boniface was more or less the end of the line for them, the Irishmen were the ones who kept up their interest in the school, coming out to watch the football practice and following them to the out-of-town games. The other group was more inclined to sever its ties once it got away, going back into the smaller groups from which they had come in the first place.

J.J. O'Brien was one of the most prosperous Irish alumni of Boniface, if not the most respectable—though he *looked* respectable enough. He had graduated just before World War I, and had gone overseas with Black Jack Pershing's AEF, in the 118th Field Artillery, a Savannah outfit. Baseball had been the big game when he was coming along, and he had been catcher for the Boniface "Windmills," as they called themselves in those days. He was well known around town, since Boniface beat Oglethorpe High in 1916 —his last year there—and J.J. hit the home run that won the game.

He came back from France with a limp, for which he had received the Purple Heart—also a chestful of other decorations (including one that the French had given him). On the strength of the home run, the limp, and the medals, he borrowed enough money to become the Miller's beer distributor for Savannah— going down to the bank to negotiate the loan in his uniform, because that way he could legitimately wear his medals. He also carried a cane.

As the Miller's beer man, J.J. got acquainted with prosperity for the first time in his life. Chatham County never did pay any attention to the Volstead Act, selling beer and wine openly, and hard liquor only slightly under cover. The marsh creeks around town in the outlying districts, which had served as off-loading places for slaves a hundred years before, were ideal for rum running, and Savannah became a center for that activity—with J.J. always in the middle of it, skimming off his share, which grew larger every year. He piled up a very big stake, and after Prohibition was repealed, he expanded into the wholesale liquor business. He also gradually took over all the betting that went on in the white sections of town.

Like most of the Irish alumni, J.J. took a keen interest in the Boniface football team. But, unlike most of them, he was in a position to put money in to support it—giving presents of cash to the football players from time to time, or hiring them in part-time jobs after school, and helping the poorest ones with their tuition, so they could go there instead of Oglethorpe. As a present for the whole school, he bought a print of the Knute Rockne movie with Pat O'Brien, and gave it to them in the fall of 1945. Every year afterward it was shown to the whole student body at the first assembly of the year, and once a week to the football team throughout the season.

From 1942 on, J.J. hadn't been getting much of a return on his investment. In all that time, Boniface hadn't managed a winning season. In 1944—the year that Chicken Garfield had come to Boniface as head coach—they had lost seven games. That had been his best year. Since then, there had been a lot of talk about building, but it had been downhill all the way. The local competition wasn't very high class itself, but for the last three years, Boniface had lost to Oglethorpe—with the margin growing every year. That game was played on Thanksgiving Day in Grayson Stadium. For the team that won, it was a good season, since, finally, the local frame of reference was the important one.

The potential for a good team was there all right, and no one could fault Chicken on the players that he had chosen to fill the positions. He had all the right talents in the right places, but he was not an inspirational leader, and he could never get them to stop functioning as individuals and work as a team. Maybe Pat O'Brien was supposed to do that for them, through the movie. But it didn't work that way.

Still, man for man they had plenty to offer.

The quarterback was Aaron "Bomber" Stern. Sometimes they called him "Bomberstern," but generally they called him "Aaron." He wasn't the type for a nickname. Savannah has always been very big on nicknames, and only three of the football players at Boniface went by the names they were called at home by their parents. Mostly they were "Rat," or "Snake," or "Fish," or something even more colorful or descriptive. (There were three "Rat"s at Boniface, and twelve at Oglethorpe, which was the public high school and had a much bigger enrollment, being coed. Two of the "Rat"s at Oglethorpe were girls.)

But Aaron was "Aaron," most of the time.

He was a tall, rangy boy, with a calm, intelligent face and a great deal of style. Off the field he was a natty dresser—dark blue pegged pants and a maroon shirt were mostly his style when he was out of uniform. He was quiet and collected, and he inspired confidence, being president of the student body and commander of Company A. Everyone more or less looked up to him. On the football field he conducted himself with aplomb and presence of mind, and he undeniably understood what the game was about. He had an arm that seemed to have been made by the Winchester Company, and could stand on one goal line and throw a football over the other. He could do that all day long.

But with all that poise, and the great arm, too, Aaron had a monumental failing that canceled out all of his natural strong points. He would absolutely run out of the stadium and climb a light tower before he would let a tackler lay a finger on him. Routinely he would fade back thirty and forty yards to throw his passes, and although the fans loved it—and he certainly had enough arm for the distance—he tended to lose accuracy when he was going for a receiver more than fifty yards away. Half the time a fifty-yard pass wouldn't do much more than get the ball back to the line of scrimmage. And, besides, those fifty- and sixty-yard bombs spent a lot of time in the air. By the time the ball came down, there would be seven or eight people standing around waiting for it, arguing and shoving each other around.

Both of the ends were good—different, but good. Frog Finnechairo at left end and Flasher Lynch at right.

Flasher was the fastest man on the squad. Everybody in Savannah thought he was the fastest man in the world. He had a graceful, pointy-toed stride, and could do the hundred in 9.9. When the team ran sprints, Flasher would be down to the other end of the field and coming back before he met the first man of the rest of the squad somewhere around the 20-yard line. And not only could Flasher get down there in plenty of time, but he had such great style. A series of gazellelike leaps more than a run—floating him along above the field—his chest thrown out and his head thrown back, windmilling those long legs in slow motion, with every now and then the tip of a toe just brushing the ground.

He also had the reflexes of a bat. Before Aaron even turned around to throw the ball, Flasher would be off the line and twenty-five yards down field, which meant a forty-five-yard pass every time, since Aaron didn't feel really safe unless there were at least four yard stripes between him and the line of scrimmage.

Aaron tried to whisper the signals so Flasher couldn't tell when the ball was snapped, just to slow him down. But Ducker Hoy, the right tackle, was hard of hearing and also quick off the line, and they got so many off-side penalties doing that that he had to stop. Anyway, Flasher didn't need to hear. He had peripheral vision that gave him a 250-degree field, and he could have seen better only if his eyes had been set on movable stalks like a crab's.

But, of course, Flasher had weak points that washed out all the good ones—otherwise he would be up in Canton in the Football Hall of Fame by now.

The first failing was a bad habit. Flasher liked to show off. No matter what the play called for, he would break down the sidelines for twenty-five or thirty yards—it wasn't his fault in a way, it was just that he was out there that far before he could do anything about it—then he would cut and begin running from one side of the field to the other, to aggravate the secondary and show them how fast he was. Aaron would be back there yelling at him to turn around so he could see the ball coming, but Flasher would be putting it on, running circles around the defenders who were trying to keep up with him. Three or four times a game the ball would come in when he wasn't even looking, hitting him on the shoulder pads or the helmet and bouncing off. Those were the times that really got to Coach Garfield, though he didn't think too much of Flasher's habits in general. It was thrilling for the spectators, but Boniface never got many actual yards out of Flasher, in spite of all the mileage he put in scooting around in the secondary.

They said around Boniface that he could actually outrun the football, and had to slow down for Aaron's passes to catch up with him. But he liked to run so much that he forgot all about catching the ball. He remembered often enough that Coach Garfield had to let him play—though the times the ball bounced off Flasher really made him mad, and he would pull him out of the game, making him sit on the bench and wouldn't talk to him. But he always sent him back in.

The best field position for Flasher was when Boniface was around its own 20- to 25-yard line. That gave a lot of field ahead of him, and about the right amount for Aaron to fade back in without running out of the stadium. Aaron could boom the ball out there and let Flasher run under it somewhere around the 20-yard line going away. He needed a straight stretch to keep from being distracted. The closer they got to the middle of the field, the more he had time to start fooling around, running back and forth. From the 50-yard line in, he wasn't much use at all.

Flasher's hands weren't all that good either, to tell the truth, and he wasn't much on judging distances. He was all the time running back on the ball and having it sail off ten feet over his head, or sticking out his hands and having it bounce off his chest. Which was different from the times it bounced off when he wasn't looking. Coach Garfield didn't get so upset about those times, since Flasher was at least trying to get hold of the ball—though they certainly didn't thrill him to death either.

Frog Finnechairo was the one with the hands, and the one Aaron usually went to any time they got inside the midfield line.

Looking at Frog you would think—well, you would probably think all kinds of weird things, like you didn't know the circus was in town, and what was a freak doing going to Boniface College. The one thing you wouldn't ever think would be that here was somebody who played end on a football team. Frog was only five feet seven or eight inches tall, and his build was very peculiar. Two-thirds of his height was from his waist down, like one of those roly-poly toys with a weight in the bottom that you can't knock down. He was a kind of walking optical illusion, because even if you were taller than he was, you felt like you were looking up at him. He was all leg and butt and foot, with just a tiny little chest and a size-five head on his sloping shoulders. His arms were long, though, with hands that looked like feet on the ends of them.

Getting him suited up in a uniform turned out to be one hell of a problem.

Coach Garfield wrote six letters to the company that made the jerseys for the team, but he never was able to make it clear to them just what the problem was. So they got J.J. O'Brien to put in a long-distance telephone call to the president of the company.

J.J. finally got him to understand that what they needed was a size 12½/34 green football jersey. But then the president said he was sorry, they didn't have a knitting machine that was up to making a jersey that size. So J.J. asked him why not, and the president said he wouldn't even talk about a thing like that where one of his machines might hear him. Then J.J. got mad and said that was a hell of a way to run a company, and he might just buy them out and show them how it ought to be done. And the president said that would be fine, and if J.J. would mail him a check for fifty-eight million dollars, then he could take over and make all the fucked-up-sized football jerseys he wanted to.

"Did you say 'fucked up'?" said J.J.

The president said that's exactly what he'd said.

So J.J. got really mad and called the president of the company a son of a bitch, and the president called him one back, and the operator broke in and told them she'd have to cut them off if they didn't improve their language. Then J.J. told her to kiss his ass, too, and slammed down the receiver.

They solved the problem by ordering three jerseys with Frog's number in the biggest size the company could supply. Then they took them down with Frog's measurements to a tailor on West Broad Street to get one custom-made.

"Is this for a mascot or something?" the tailor asked after they showed him the measurements.

"No," said Quit Deloney. Quit was the manager of the team.

"The only thing that those measurements are going to fit is a baboon," said the man. "Are you sure you got them right?" He refused to take the order unless they brought Frog in so he could see what he looked like and measure him himself. So they brought him in. But it was dark in the shop, and the man took him out on the sidewalk so he could get a look at him where the light was good.

"I'm sorry," he said when he came back in. "It's just that I got stuck once before on a deal like this. It makes you careful," he said. "A guy came in here once—very well dressed. He had Italian shoes."

"Italian?" said Quit.

"Italians make very good shoes," said the tailor. "I asked him where he got the shoes, and he told me they came from Italy."

"I didn't know that about the Italians," said Quit.

"They make very good shoes," said the tailor.

"Did you know that, Frog?" said Quit. "Frog's Italian," he said, talking to the tailor.

Frog had a wad of bubble gum in his mouth, and they had to wait while he blew a bubble before he answered. "No," he said.

"Finnechairo," said Quit. "That's his name. I told you. He's Italian."

"Italians make the best shoes in the world," said the tailor, speaking to Frog.

Frog was blowing another bubble, so he didn't answer.

"Well," said the tailor, "this well-dressed guy came in here and ordered a size thirty-two long dinner jacket . . ."

"Thirty-two *long?*" said Quit.

". . . with three sleeves in it," said the tailor.

"Come *on.*"

"I know," said the tailor. "But he was so well dressed. After I saw the shoes I knew he could afford it."

"*Three* sleeves?"

"I should have known better."

"He had three arms?"

"No. I told you. He was very well dressed. He said it was a surprise for a friend."

"Did you see him?"

"I wanted to," said the tailor, "but I was too embarrassed. I didn't know how to *put* it. I thought it sounded funny." He paused for a minute. "The price was *very* good," he said.

"Where was the extra sleeve?"

"In the middle of the back," said the tailor. He didn't look at Quit when he spoke.

"I'd really like to see something like that," said Quit.

"It was a trick," said the tailor.

"It wasn't real?"

"He never came back."

"Just tricking you, eh?"

"A jacket with *one* sleeve, I could have put another sleeve on it."

"Yes," said Quit.

"How are you going to take off a sleeve in the middle of the back?"

Quit looked around the shop. "Look," he said, "we have a game Friday. I'll need to get these back by Thursday."

"I thought I could trust him, you know . . . because of the shoes."

"Well," said Quit. "Listen, we need to have these back by Thursday. We have a game Friday night."

"Wednesday," said the tailor. "You can have them Wednesday." He turned to Frog. "I hope I didn't hurt your feelings, young man," he said. "I just didn't want to get tricked again."

Frog stopped chewing on the wad of bubble gum and looked at him. "Huh?" he said.

Frog's size-five head gave him a brain-to-weight ratio that was about one leg up on a brontosaurus, and went a long way toward explaining a good many of his problems. But, even so, the helmet didn't cause too much trouble. After the hassle they'd had with the jersey, Chicken figured it wasn't worth arguing with the company. So he just ordered the smallest one they made, then pulled in all the strapping inside as tight as it would go, and put in some extra foam rubber for padding and to center it. The way it overhung Frog when he wore it made his head look like a toadstool and didn't help much with the general impression that he made, but it served the purpose. Frog was very happy with it.

The helmet and jerseys made Frog cost three times as much to fit out as anyone else, though the pants and shoes weren't a problem. He wore a thirty waist, with a thirty-five inseam, and size-fourteen shoes, which were standard sizes, and only looked peculiar when you saw them on Frog. But they didn't have to explain that to the suppliers, and so there wasn't any trouble about them.

What made the investment worthwhile were his hands and his jumping.

Frog was short, but he could outjump Nijinsky. In fact, his height gave him a psychological advantage. He could make a vertical leap of four feet from a standing start. And the really surprising thing was how effortlessly he could do it. One second he would be standing there with his feet flat on the ground, and the next second there would be a swooshing sound and he would be four feet up in the air, stiff as a board, with those number-fourteen shoes of his winged out like he was standing on a platform. With a running start, he could get up in the air five and a half feet.

He wasn't fast, so they used him on spot passes only, sending him out ten or fifteen yards where he would just turn around and stand there waiting for Aaron to get through dodging around and throw the ball to him. The defensive back would come over and stand there waiting with him, not able to figure out what was going on, because everything was so open and aboveboard. Then Aaron would turn and rifle one to him, putting it in about ten feet off the ground, and suddenly the defensive man would be looking at Frog's knees. There would be a splat up there in the air, or the sound of cartilage popping where the ball hit him, and Frog would come down with it wrapped up in that big hand of his.

Frog could usually get the passes with his hands before they got in close enough to do him any damage, but every now and then he would miss. The one time he took one of Aaron's bullets full in the chest all the color drained out of his arms and legs and head and settled in a big blue spot over his breastbone. He walked bent over for a week, coughing up black lumps and talking out of the top of his throat. But it sharpened up his reflexes, so he was always sure to catch the ball with his hands after that, or deflect it so it didn't catch him solid.

Toward the end of the game, there would usually be two or three men out there with Frog, waiting for Aaron to throw him the ball. But when they went up for it, it was always the same story. There would be Frog's pinhead and sloping shoulders up above everybody else, and that thirty-four-inch arm snaked out above that.

Frog's main trouble was that he didn't move too well after he caught the ball, and where he came down is where they nailed him usually. Also his sense of direction left a lot to be desired. He never did know where he was on the field. If Boniface needed twenty-five yards for a first down, Frog would go out and plant himself twenty-*four* yards down the field. He always seemed to be just a long stride short of the first down—though he almost always got the ball. Occasionally somebody would run into him and spin him around and he would go off in the wrong direction. In the game with Bibb High School in Macon, Flasher had to tackle him twice to keep him from running over his own goal line. It was a common enough occurrence that Coach Garfield had a "Stop Frog" drill that they used at practice every once in a while.

On running plays, Aaron's only thought was to get the ball off to the runner as fast as possible, then get the hell out of the way. There was no deception at all to his hand-offs because he *wanted* the charging linemen to see that he didn't have the ball. He would flash it around all over the place before he finally gave it to the back, then he would run off holding both his hands up in the air so nobody would make a mistake and tackle him. Whistler Whitfield and Cowboy McGrath, the left and right halfbacks, complained about it to Aaron and to Coach Garfield. They felt Aaron owed it to them to cover up for them just a little—because the way he waved that ball around on hand-offs, they weren't able to make it back to the line of scrimmage more than two or three times a game.

Their complaints never made any impression on Aaron. He was pretty one-track about some things, and he just went right on doing everything he could to make it clear who had the ball—short of calling in a Western Union boy to deliver it for him.

Coach Garfield couldn't do anything with him either, and he worried about Aaron ignoring him that way. But every time he would just about decide to pull him out for insubordination and let somebody else be the quarterback, he would go to tell him, and there would be Aaron lobbing those sixty- and seventy-yard passes down the field. So he just couldn't go through with it.

The most serious effort Coach Garfield ever made to turn Aaron around was when he got some game films of Frankie Albert running the Stanford "T" formation. He made Aaron watch them over and over.

"See, Aaron," he'd say. "Who's got the ball?"

"He's *hiding* it," said Aaron.

"That's right, Aaron," said Coach Garfield. "He's hiding the ball so nobody can tell who's got it."

"That's crazy," said Aaron. "Why would he want to *hide* the ball?"

"That's the 'T,' Aaron. That's what you're supposed to do when you're running the 'T.'"

"He played for Stanford."

"What?" said Coach Garfield.

"I never saw Lujack trying to hide the ball."

Coach Garfield tried to remember whether Lujack hid the ball or not.

"I guess that's the way they do things out at Stanford," said Aaron.

"That's the way I want you to do things around here," said Coach Garfield.

"This isn't Stanford, Coach. Lujack wouldn't pull a trick like that."

While Coach Garfield was trying to remember whether Lujack tried to hide the ball or not, Aaron got up and left. Whenever Garfield would get onto him about giving the play away, Aaron would look at him and say, "This isn't Stanford, Coach." By the time he got game films of Lujack, the season was over and it was too late to do any good.

As far as Dimmy Camack was concerned, it didn't matter one way or the other. Dimmy was the fullback, a Greek boy whose father had a shrimp boat out at Thunderbolt. He was five feet seven inches tall and weighed 195 pounds. No matter which way you turned him, he seemed to have the same dimensions—frontward, sideways, or upside down. He always ran looking down at the ground, so he couldn't see what Aaron was doing to him anyway. He would rumble by, and Aaron would sock the ball into his gut, dancing off to the side to get out of the way. Dimmy would hit into the line without looking up to see if the hole had opened or not, because, fundamentally, he didn't give a damn. "Hit dat line. . . . Hit dat line. . . ." That was about it as far as Dimmy was concerned. All of the net yards gained rushing came from Dimmy, since Whistler and Cowboy couldn't get out of the backfield, so he was the most valuable back on the team. But more than a few of his teammates thought how nice it would be if they could swap some of Dimmy's heart for just a little more head.

Since Dimmy never looked where he was going, he just had to run over whoever it might be that happened to be in the way.

From tackle to tackle, every Boniface lineman had scars on his back from Dimmy's cleats. The only reason the ends didn't have them too was that Dimmy was too slow to get that far in a lateral direction. He had a gyroscopic sense that told him where the goal was, and a kind of mental tunnel vision that sent him straight ahead until enough bodies built up to stop him. He felt that running toward the sideline was almost like cheating—or at least unmanly.

The way he ran, his center of gravity seemed to be down around his knees somewhere, but just the same he inevitably fell on his face on the fifth step, unless he ran into someone—in which case, he was good for two or three steps more. There were three yards in it for Boniface every time he carried the ball, but he punished his own team so much they hated to see Aaron give it to him. None of the opposing linemen ever figured him out. They kept trying to tackle him, and all they did was prop him up so he could keep going. If they had just stood aside and watched, they would have cut down on his yardage.

On the nights when Aaron's passing wasn't hitting, and he had to call on Dimmy to carry the load, there would be an argument every time they huddled to call a play. Aaron would have to work him back and forth from tackle to tackle to keep his interior linemen from just giving up and walking off the field. Dimmy never knew what they were complaining about. He would stand there in the huddle, flexing his knees and swinging his hands together, saying, "Gimme da ball. . . . Gimme da ball. . . ."

All of the linemen bitched about Dimmy, but none of them bitched more than Feeb Siddoney, the left tackle. The Boniface team was a kind of aggregation of Achilles heels, but Feeb was the one totally weak link in the chain. "Feeb" was for "feeble," and sometimes for "Phoebe," though everybody hated to call a football player "Phoebe," no matter how appropriate it was.

Feeb was a big Lebanese, with a nose like a banana, and long black hair that he wore in a ducktail. Not a tall boy, but big, with a strange, humpbacked profile, like a turtle walking on its hind legs. He had large soft eyes, brown like a calf's, and a round baby face. Feeb didn't want to play football in the first place. The only benefit that accrued to him, so far as he could see, was that it let him get into the knickers of a better class of girl than he would otherwise have been able to.

That's in a manner of speaking. Those were pretty innocent times, and the number of girls who were known to put out—actually certified to do it—was extremely small, and pretty much limited to dead-end bags. For them it was an avenue to social distinction—of a kind. They were courted on a more or less one-time basis by young men who wouldn't even look them in the eye or speak to them in a public place. The dates weren't much—usually a fast run out into the country where the car was parked under a live oak tree or in a slash pine thicket while the line formed at the trunk of the car.

Mackey Brood was the exception. She was certainly no bag. But then Mackey didn't go for gang bangs very often, and would only put out for boys who had real dates with her.

The great majority were what were known back then as "nice girls." Parking with them down at Fort Screven or on the road to Bonaventure cemetery could sometimes get pretty feverish and slippery, but was never much of a threat to the institution of virginity. After he let her out, the boy would go try to pull up a fireplug, or lift the back end of the car, and if that didn't work, the next night he would get a bunch of his friends together and take the run out to the live oak tree to unload his Fort Screven frustrations.

It could be a vicious innocence. But that was in an earlier time.

Still, Feeb wasn't all that much of a cocksman. His venality ran more to food than girls, and he didn't like the frustration of parking at Screven, though he bigmouthed about it as much as anybody else. What he really wanted to do was sit around Theodore's Ice Cream Parlor, eating chocolate fudge sundaes and talking dirty.

But he weighed 225 pounds—"an eighth of a ton of lard," as somebody put it—and anything that went to Boniface and weighed that much was going to have to play football, even if it had five legs and a hernia. His freshman and sophomore years he tried to sneak off into the band and the glee club, but his size made him too conspicuous. He couldn't get away with it. So his junior year, public opinion forced him to pack up his clarinet and go out for the team. There were plenty of 175-pound tackles in those days, and just having Feeb listed on the program gave Boniface a psychological advantage over most of their opponents.

The pressure from the school was fierce, but that was only the half of it. The other half was Feeb's old man, who ran a produce market on Montgomery Street. Somehow when Mr. Siddoney immigrated he had sloughed off his Levantine guile in exchange for a Celtic sense of honor—or maybe it was there, the guile, and only being worked out through Feeb. At any rate, *he* also insisted that Feeb play football. He put it that the family honor was involved, though who was going to notice was a good question, since there wasn't another Lebanese family within a hundred miles of Savannah. The Siddoneys had visitors from time to time—whole swarthy families that came in a truck with a lot of children in the back. Always they stayed for a week or more, with the children camped out on pallets around the living room and parlor at the Siddoneys', cooking things that smoked up the house and made Feeb's nose run.

"They wouldn't know a fucking football from a fucking eggplant" is the way Feeb put it.

Then he thought about it. "I take that back," he said. "They'd know you couldn't fucking eat the football."

Still, one way or the other Feeb got shoved into it, and the best he made of it was none too good.

He was useless on defense, except for the times he fell down and somebody tripped over him. On offense he would sometimes be able to get an angle on his man and push him off to the side, but on the plays when Dimmy was carrying the ball, he was more desperate to get out of the way himself than he was to take out his man. A good many times he would come out of the huddle still arguing with Aaron, trying to get him to change the play and send Dimmy off on the other side.

"One man calling signals," said Aaron. "One man calling signals."

So Feeb would line up with his head over his shoulder, arguing until the ball was snapped.

For the first two or three plays of a game, Feeb would sometimes bluster and bluff his way, trying to look ferocious and fake out the man he was playing against—saying things like, "It's your

ass, motherfucker," and "You ain't worth a motherfucking shit."
Feeb liked to say "motherfucker." Maybe it was being Lebanese,
since they go in very strong for genealogical cursing. But Feeb
had a high voice with a quaver in it, and three plays was about the
longest he could bring it off. By then the other players would
have seen how much of a coward he was, and would spend the rest
of the night getting even for it. When it was somebody he had
played against the year before, Feeb didn't bother cursing at all,
but would start dancing around and getting out of the way right
off.

As a matter of pure self-interest, Feeb devoted a certain amount
of attention to the game. He would study up on the opponents
they had to play, and would try to get his blocking assignments
changed so he could take out the smaller men. He made one disas-
trous mistake doing that in the season of 1946, when he got Coach
Garfield to give him a lot of cross blocking assignments on a little
145-pound guard at Richmond Academy in Augusta. It sounded
like a pushover, and Feeb was actually looking forward to the
game. But the little man turned out to be pure coiled steel and sharp
edges, and was so short Feeb couldn't get down low enough to
either block him or protect himself. By the end of the first quarter,
he was bleeding out of all eight of his body openings and was
backing off the line when the ball was snapped. It got so notice-
able that even the cheerleaders started commenting on it, and
Coach Garfield had to pull him out and keep him on the bench
for the rest of the game.

The only game that Feeb looked forward to all year was the
one with Glynn Academy in Brunswick, Georgia. That was because the left guard was a 135-pound bantam with weak eyes, and
the left tackle, a boy named Delmus Lamott, was even more faint
of heart than Feeb himself.

Feeb had nearly gone into cardiac arrest when he saw Lamott's
playing weight. "Two twenty-five! Sweet fucking Jesus!" He kept
saying "Sweet fucking Jesus" over and over, like it was the pass-
word to make a door open to a safe place, but he wasn't getting
the pronunciation right. "Sweet *fucking* Jesus . . . *Sweet* fucking
J*esus* . . ." and on and on. Finally, he broke down and cried.
Then, when that was over, he tried to think of ways he could

weasel out of the game. No way. His father would surely cut him off from his share of the produce business if he disgraced him by quitting the team, and life around Boniface wouldn't be worth living either if he did it.

He thought about shooting himself in the foot, or slamming a door on his finger and breaking it. But of course he was too much of a coward for that kind of thing, too. So in the end he just skipped practice on Monday and Tuesday, sitting in a back booth at Theodore's, shoveling in one chocolate fudge sundae after another and saying "motherfucker" after each spoonful.

He went back to practice on Wednesday, resolved to get himself hurt bad enough that he would have to miss the game. Not hurt enough to be really hurt, but just enough not to have to play.

It was the most furious week of practice he ever put in in his life. He did everything but run into a wall. The rest of the team couldn't believe it, and Coach Garfield called him off the field five times to talk to him and see what was wrong. He scared the B team so much that they all wound up keeping out of his way, so that not only did he not get hurt, but he broke the arm of a sophomore guard.

Everybody congratulated him on the way he was hitting, and he told them one and all to kiss his ass.

He went out onto the field at Brunswick, crossing himself and praying that he would get hurt early and not too badly, so he wouldn't have to stand up to the punishment for the whole four quarters.

When he lined up for the first play of the game, his knees were shaking, the tears starting in his eyes. And the sucking sound he made trying to breathe could be heard all the way up into the middle of the stands. He knew Lamott was crouched over there across the line from him, but he couldn't bring himself to look up to see.

And then.

Just what he had been praying for all week happened. A miracle. From across the line a dulcet voice, low and whispering and confidential, floated to him.

"It's only a *game*," said Lamott. The way he said it, it seemed to come out "gwame."

Feeb's heart nearly jumped out of his mouth at the sound. Just at the *sound*. He was too frightened to think about the words, and didn't hear them at first. Between Monday and Friday noon, when they had left for Brunswick, he'd burned thirty-five candles, but under the circumstances he hadn't really put much stock in that. The prayers had all been to get him out of the game. He figured that if they didn't do that for him, they wouldn't help much once it got started.

So he didn't get on to the words that Lamott was saying right away. He looked up into the face of the tackle, which was round and babylike. There was a ghostly pallor to it under the helmet, and big beads of perspiration stood out on his forehead and upper lip.

"What?" said Feeb.

"I hope you remember," said Lamott, his lips trembling, "It's only a game. *I'm* certainly not going to take it seriously."

Feeb looked at him, and he looked at Feeb. Then Lamott's lips twitched and he giggled.

The ball was snapped, and Feeb was so surprised that he forgot to back off the line. Lamott stood up and gave him a gentle shove. "I won't if you won't," he said.

Feeb looked at him, narrowing his eyes. "*Gwame?*" he said. He remembered the week of anguish he had just spent. He pointed his finger at Lamott. "It's your ass," he said. Then he added, "You motherfucker."

On the next play, Feeb was off the line before anybody else, catching Lamott off guard and driving him out of the hole. He danced back to the huddle. "Call it off tackle," he said. "Call the motherfucker off tackle." He slapped his hands together and did a little shuffle.

"What's the matter with you, Feeb?" said Aaron. Ducker Hoy took off his helmet and asked him to say it again.

Dimmy slapped his hands together. "Gimme da ball," he said. "Gimme da ball."

Feeb lined up, making growling noises, looking Lamott in the eye across the line.

"My father is *rich*," said Lamott. He darted his eyes right and left as he spoke.

"What?" said Feeb, "you motherfucker."

"I'll pay you five dollars," Lamott whispered, "not to hurt me."

Feeb looked at him levelly, then he darted his eyes right and left. "Fifteen," he said, also whispering.

They stood there dickering over the price while the ball was snapped, then Dimmy crashed into Feeb from the back, knocking him down along with Lamott. Lamott helped him up. "Ten?" he said, holding Feeb's hand.

Feeb got his breath back and nodded. "Eleven-fifty," he said.

"Shake on it?" said Lamott.

Feeb nodded again. "Yes," he said.

Lamott adjusted his helmet. "Football is a *terrible* game," he said.

Lamott's father was indeed rich. He had paid for the uniforms for the whole team, and had bought the scoreboard, which had an alligator on it that wagged its tail and lit up with red light bulbs for its eyes and made roaring noises when the Brunswick team scored a touchdown. Under the circumstances, the coach felt that he had to let Delmus play on the team. It didn't work out so badly.

In many respects, Delmus was a chip off the old block, reasoning that if his father could use his money to buy him on to the team, then he could use *his* money to buy himself safety on the field. It cost him about eighty-five dollars a week during the football season, which was a sizable amount, but not more than he could afford. Delmus stole most of it from his mother, and he figured it was money well spent. He paid all of the Brunswick players on the first and second teams two dollars a game—more or less so they would keep their mouths shut. He paid the fullback, James Farney, fifteen. James backed up the line on Delmus's side, and it was his job to rush in and take the punishment. Fifteen dollars was a good bit of money for one night's work back in those days, but even so James Farney gave good value, though he certainly had to shake a leg to do it, and wasn't much account at the paper mill where he worked on Saturdays. Delmus's father owned the paper mill, and Delmus was always dropping hints to James about how he was going to give him a nice soft job there when old man Lamott died and he took over. When Delmus told him that, it made James hustle more than ever, and Delmus would have to get down and roll around on the ground two or three times during the game just to get his uniform dirty.

The players on the other teams that Delmus had to go up against got anywhere from five to twenty dollars—depending on how big they were, and how good they were at dickering up the price. Delmus was shrewd, and it was hard to get the best of him in a bargain. Still, it was always safety first with him, though twenty dollars was his absolute limit.

In the two years of varsity football that he played for Brunswick, he bought every man that he ever had to play against but one—a guard at Jesup High School. But the guard only weighed 140 pounds, and was so stupid the center had to help him get into his stance before he could hike the ball.

After they shook hands on it, Feeb and Delmus made it look good, pushing and patting each other and shoving each other around. They might have gotten away with it for the whole game, only Delmus couldn't keep his mouth shut. He kept saying things like, "It's so *silly*," and "It's just a *dreadful* game." Until Bo Hoerner, the right guard, caught on to what was going on.

Bo was a phlegmatic German, who took the game seriously— just the way he took everything else. He was always the first one into the room on the nights they showed the Knute Rockne movie, and for ten straight weeks he cried when the Gipper died. At that point in the film, Bo would stand up in the darkened classroom, blocking out the screen, and say, "He was great, man, *great*." Sometimes in the huddle he would say, "Let's win this one for the Gipper." Usually Boniface would be about three touchdowns behind when he said it, and it never did any good. But he kept thinking that it might.

Bo finally got so irritated over the way that Feeb and Delmus were carrying on that he broke his stance before the ball was snapped to kick Feeb on the rear end and tell him to remember the Gipper.

"Watch out, young man," said Delmus, coming to Feeb's defense. "Keep your hands to yourself." Somehow he got a lisp into "yourself"—something like "yourswelf."

Boniface got a five-yard penalty for it, and Garfield called Bo over to the sidelines to find out why he had kicked Feeb in the behind. Hoerner told Garfield what was going on out there between Feeb and Delmus, and Garfield pulled Feeb out and sent in his substitute—Tally Dehoy—a 140-pound Spanish boy whose father worked in a fish market on the east end of Bay Street. Dehoy did a pretty good job of pushing Delmus around until they settled on $7.50 and a bottle of rosé wine. There were only three quarters left in the game, and Delmus wouldn't go as high as he had with Feeb.

In the third quarter, Dimmy stepped on Dehoy's hand and broke it, so Coach Garfield had to send Feeb back in again. Feeb and Delmus spent the fourth quarter haggling over how much Delmus ought to deduct for the two quarters Feeb had been out of the game, but they did it quietly, so Hoerner wouldn't hear and blow the whistle on them again.

They settled on $5.25.

Sorry as he was, Feeb was necessary to them in a way. He was the focus and excuse for the collective inadequacies of the team. With him, they had a reason for losing, so they didn't need to feel bad about it. Nor did they need to worry about winning. No one on the team was up to that—especially Coach Garfield. If they hadn't had a Feeb Siddoney, they would have been forced to invent one.

Well, one man on the team was up to winning, but he never got to play. That was Lulu Demarco, the first-string center.

Lulu was the first-string center, but he never got to play because he always got hurt in the first game of the season. He was the best man on the team for spirit—mean as a snake, and a boy who positively lived and breathed for the game of football. The trouble was, he was too little to be that mean and get away with it. He weighed only 140 pounds, when his general outlook called for a quarter of a ton at least.

The outlook came from the fact that Lulu had gotten his growth early, at just the time when he was beginning to decide where he fit into the scheme of things.

When he was thirteen years old, Lulu was five feet nine inches tall—which made him one of the biggest boys in the freshman class. Out of that one year's growth developed the way that he looked at the world. But then, that was the end of it. He never grew any more. Not an inch. By the time he became a senior, all of his classmates had grown on past him and made him a runt, but somehow he never noticed what had happened. So he carried his big man's perspective along with him, and none of the head-on collisions he had with reality because of it were ever able to knock it out of him.

Two years he started at center, and both years he got carried off the field in the first quarter with injuries that benched him for the rest of the season. In 1945, after eight and a half minutes of the first quarter, he threw a block on a guard that fractured six ribs and broke his collarbone. In 1946, a big tackle gave him an elbow on the third play, whiplashing his head back and cracking three vertebrae in his neck. Then, while he was lying on the ground, the big man stepped on him and snapped off the end of his coccyx. When the referee came over to see how badly he was hurt, Lulu called him a son of a bitch, and bit his hand so the blood came.

And then Jack Curran came, and everything changed. It was like having Lulu on the team all year, as big as he thought he was.

But it wasn't all silver and gold.

Not in the beginning it wasn't.

13

Teamwork

WORD ABOUT JACK HAD BEEN OUT in the town all summer, getting
stretched and improved on and amplified.

"New Orleans, man! New Orleans!"

They made it sound like Notre Dame.

"He played ball in New Aw-*leans!*"

In Savannah it was practically the next best thing to Notre Dame
itself, especially with the slant that J.J. O'Brien was putting on it.
Which was that the New Orleans high schools were like a regular
farm system, which Leahy himself spent a lot of time cultivating
and worrying about. That was J.J.'s story, the way he worked it up.

In fact, New Orleans did have some very strong Catholic high
school teams back in those days, so the idea didn't altogether drop
out of his pants leg.

The interest in football that blew up in Savannah was consider-
able, but it had to do mostly with high school teams, the reason
being that the nearest colleges were a full day's drive away by
automobile—the University of Georgia in Athens, and Georgia Tech

in Atlanta—both up in the northern end of the state, and, so to speak, a pretty abstract proposition as far as Chatham County was concerned. The Central of Georgia Railroad had a day train—the *Nancy Hanks*—that made a round trip to Atlanta, going up in the morning and coming back the same night, and some of the college crowd would ride it up to see the Tech-Georgia game, the years they played in Atlanta. But taking that excursion to see football games on a regular basis was limited mostly to doctors and real estate developers and wholesale liquor dealers. The man on the street didn't have the cash. So the average rabid football fan had to develop his conception of the possibilities of the sport out in Grayson Stadium on Friday nights, where the Fighting Irish and the Big Blue of Oglethorpe played their games.

Unfortunately, the local teams were terrible, on the average— though a good team would come along every now and then. Mostly they were nothing at all to get inspired about or build a myth on.

There were regular glimpses of what the game might be, which the fans got from the up-country teams that came down to stomp the locals into the ground. And once in a while there would be the good teams, or an isolated Savannah player who would pop up and fulfill their expectations on the legendary side—as Horse Rooney had done in the early forties, playing fullback for Boniface. But mostly they had to keep up their faith in football as a game of giants and heroes by sheer unsupported vision and willpower, anchored by believing in teams that were real—that is, teams that were from real places—but so far away nobody ever got to see them. Big Locker Rooms in the Sky, full of mean linemen and snaky backs, who finished their high school days getting scholarships to play football at places like Tennessee and Alabama and Georgia Tech. And even—the sweaty ultimate thought—at Notre Dame itself.

The Atlanta teams did show up in Grayson Stadium once in a while, because the Savannah schools would occasionally get on the schedule of Boys' High and Marist, though talking them into it was hard, because there wasn't much glory in it for anybody. Whenever they did come down, the Savannah team would get slaughtered, with scores that looked like odds against the sun coming up.

Especially when they were playing Boys' High. So there was a certain realistic dimension at the root of the Atlanta part of the myth.

Boys' High of Atlanta was good, but since it was a team that the fans actually did get to see now and then, it never did stir their imaginations in quite the same way as the New Orleans teams, or those of Knoxville and Nashville and Chattanooga. There was never any firsthand contact with those schools, and so reality didn't have to come in to cramp the vision.

There was also a certain kind of reverse mythology that said that the teams from Florida and California were made up of fairies and jelly beans, who spent all their time polishing their fingernails and slicking down their hair. The only things those states were noted for were just on the edges of the game—cheerleaders who put out, and hundred-member marching bands full of saxophone players with big fannies, and big-bosomed pom-pom girls. Nothing seemed to make a dent in that particular piece of folklore. Of course, nobody ever got to see a team from California, but it wouldn't have made any difference. Jacksonville High School came up to Savannah four years running in the forties and wiped up Grayson Stadium with the Big Blue of Oglethorpe. After they left, the field was gritty with teeth, and the trail of blood to the Big Blue locker room didn't fade out until the baseball crowd walked it away in the middle of the summer. But all the fans ever remembered were the bosoms on the cheerleaders and the fannies on the saxophone players.

"Two thirty, man! Two fucking thirty!"

They liked to talk about his size, but the truth is that the myth never did catch up with reality there.

Jack weighed 240, but even the biggest of the bigmouths were afraid to stretch the story that far. They didn't know how much he weighed really, but were building on his playing weight for the 1946 season, which they did know, because J.J. O'Brien had told them. It had been 215, which everybody assumed was a lie in the first place.

But it wasn't. And then Jack had had a growing spurt over the winter, going up an inch in height, to six feet four, and gaining twenty-five pounds. The standards of the time wouldn't let that be possible, and, besides, the ones who were making up the stories didn't have all that much imagination and had to hold closer to reality than is good for really artful lying. The only Savannah player then on the first team of a major college was Leon Hook, who was playing center for Georgia Tech at 175 pounds, and they felt like they had to keep that in mind. In those days a playing weight of over 200 pounds had to be sworn to on a Bible and signed by a notary public. Anything over 220 was regarded as an outright lie, just on the face of it. And even then, the really big men usually turned out to be lardasses, like Feeb, who were suited up mostly for the psychological advantage of having their weight listed in the program.

So nobody believed what was being said about Jack. Which should have been an encouragement to work it up bigger and better than ever, since that kind of lying is more a matter of entertainment than deception. But 230 was the sticking point, the place where their nerve gave out. Nobody would make the first move to lie it up from there.

Taken all together, J.J. and the alumni were pretty joyful about Jack and what he was going to do for Boniface football. J.J. even played a long shot and mailed a season ticket to the Pope. He never got an answer, of course, but he didn't want to overlook any possibility. Before every home game he checked the seats—just in case.

But the team—well, the team was another matter. Gloom was the word there. G-L-O-O-M. Black and brooding in capital letters. Jack's specter clouded their summer like a vulture's wing.

Most of the players knew him, and liked him well enough. But it wasn't Jack himself so much as the idea of him that was getting them down. He had always spent his summers in Savannah, and several of them had gone to school with him back in the elementary grades, before Kate sent him out of town to get him away from Old Johnny and the problem of her second marriage. But seeing him down at the beach, or at the CYPA, or in Theodore's Ice Cream Parlor was one thing. Dealing with the myth that J.J. and the alumni were cranking out was another. Eventually, the Jack that they knew and the one bagged up in the bigmouth idea of him came together in their minds, collecting in a resentful sediment at the top of their spinal columns. They didn't talk about it at all among themselves, because they couldn't. It wasn't the kind of thing that could be worked over out in the open. But it darkened their days, making them broody and distant.

All of them knew that having Jack on the team was going to make a very big difference to Boniface. But it was just that difference that hung them up. Every face on the first two teams sagged an inch and a half between June 1 and August 11, which was when practice was scheduled to start. Each of them was working it out on his own, but they were all coming to the same conclusion.

Jack had played three years for teams that didn't lose—or, at least, didn't lose as a matter of course the way they did. He had to be used to winning, and he would expect Boniface to win, too. So went the sad litany. Well, they wanted that, too—in a way. But the kind of speculation that Jack was stirring up was, after all, a reflection on them. And it caught them just there—between an abstract good, which they had to agree to, and a personal inclination, which they didn't want to admit. A moral dilemma is what it was, and they had to stew in it, each to himself alone, over the whole long summer. What they were locked up about wasn't Jack himself, but J.J.'s version of him, which, as it turned out, was an understatement at that.

So the locker-room crowd wasn't all that cheerful when practice started in the summer of 1947. All the regular members of the team were humpbacked and pouty, and sullen as a chain gang. They shuffled into the locker room, taking seats at the back and hunkering down in a constipated kind of way, without looking at each other or at Jack. Ducker rolled his eyes around at them once, then drilled his gaze into the floor at his feet and whispered the universal thought. "I feel like I got a turd wedged sideways."

"Fucking A," somebody said.

"Well . . ."
Coach Garfield always started his talks with "well." He did that to avoid starting them with "um," which he had read somewhere was the mark of a poor speaker. Books on public speaking had the kind of fascination for him that books on forensic medicine have

for certain morbid kinds of people—or illustrated books on cancer. He always had one checked out of the library to lay up on his bedside table and make himself miserable with.

Giving a talk at the first practice session wasn't what he wanted to do at all, and nobody said that he had to do it. But his sense of style wouldn't let him alone. It told him that giving a talk was something that he *ought* to do. When his sense of style didn't tell him that, his sense of obligation did. He felt that he couldn't just send the team out and let them start playing football. There would be something incomplete about it. Chicken's sense of style was all the time getting in the way of his inclinations and causing him trouble.

"Well," he said. He drew it out, "Weellllll . . . I feel pretty . . . good about the team. . . ."

"You do?" said Frog.

Being interrupted in the middle of a talk made him lose his place, and he would have to flounder around trying to find it again. When it happened right at the beginning, he just started over. Talking and answering questions were two things he couldn't do at the same time.

"Well . . ." he said.

Whenever he had to make a talk, he would write it out ahead of time and try to memorize it. But his memory wasn't all that good either, and the speech always got away from him when the time came. What happened was that he tended to just hit the high spots —those being the only parts he could remember. So nothing he said went together, and none of the players ever knew what he was talking about. But it never occurred to any of them to say anything about it. Football coaches were pretty much beyond criticism back in those days, except when they were losing. And at Boniface, even then.

The team was with him in spirit, and the words didn't matter that much. They knew him to be a kind and earnest man, and if he thought of anything that would help them improve the team, he would find a way to get it over to them.

"You boys . . . last year . . . I mean . . ." He sighed sadly. "It don't pay to *dwell* on that." He shook his head like a dog with a tick in his ear, then looked around the room, trying for eye contact.

"Man for man, you couldn't ask for better. . . ." He dropped his eyes to the floor and adjusted something in his crotch. "With the schedule we've got . . ." And on and on.

There were ninety-four boys in the locker room, about sixty of them just there for the first day. Boniface usually suited up thirty or so men for the squad, but because of the way they felt about football around the school there were always three times that many packed into the locker room at the beginning of practice in the fall and in the spring. Most of them would be gone the next day, because it was only a gesture in the first place. A few would stick it out for a day or two beyond that. But the first day—ninety-four.

It looked like a mob to Chicken. And the locker room was small anyway. Later, when only the playing squad was left, he would be more relaxed. He wouldn't make any more sense, but it wouldn't worry him so much. Words were never his strong point.

"Um . . ." he said.

The ones who were just out for the first day kept trying to follow him and make some kind of sense out of what he was saying, sitting on the edge of the benches and bobbing their heads up and down. After all, it was the only inside look at the game that most of them would ever get, and they wanted to work in as close to the core of the mystery as they could in the short painless time they were giving up to it.

The real team, the ones who were there for the season, were sitting off toward the back, slouching down. In other years a lot of them would bring funny books to read, and magazines like *Titter*. This year they sat brooding and empty-handed, silent mourners at dejection's black wall.

All except Frog Finnechairo, who had three pieces of Fleer's bubble gum in his mouth and was reading the comic-strip wrappers with a serious look on his face.

"So this year I know we're going to do it," said Chicken. He was skipping the last two paragraphs to get to the punch line, but nobody seemed to notice. Frog had a bubble going as big as his head, and most of the players were turned around watching him.

"Now I want you to meet a new man," said Chicken. "Jack Curran."

[*111*]

When he said that, everybody stopped watching Frog, just as the bubble broke and collapsed on his face.

"Curran's going to say a few words to you," said Chicken.

"Did you see it?" said Frog, his voice muffled behind the pink membrane of bubble gum that covered his head like a caul.

Jack stood up. He was sitting behind Coach Garfield during the talk, and when he stood up, at first he didn't look so big. But that was because he seemed to be standing right beside him—which he wasn't. He walked forward three steps, and when he did, it looked like his head was going to go through the ceiling of the locker room.

The trick about it was the way Jack was built. Until he got right up beside something that could act as a reference point, he looked like just an ordinary boy—well built. If you saw him half a block away, cut loose from things you might be able to gauge him by, you would guess he was about five feet eight or nine. Six feet four—that always came as a surprise. Something about him negated the rules of perspective. It was a difficult thing to adjust to.

"You all know me," he said. "Most of you do." He didn't like making speeches either, but Coach Garfield thought it would be a good idea. "Just a few words, Jack," he'd said. "Something to start us out." He had begun laying things off on Jack right away.

"We can have a good team." His way of talking was downright, but his voice was high for such a big man. Like Old Johnny's, but clearer. High, with just a touch of hoarseness in it.

"Louder, Curran." Ducker's voice was flat. He had stood up and was leaning against the wall at the back with his arms folded.

Jack looked at him, then went on. He had his knee up on the bench, and was leaning on it with his arms folded, hugging himself. "We can have a good team," he said. "But we've got to hustle."

"You got to talk *louder*, Curran," said Ducker.

"I think we'll have a good team," said Jack, without raising his voice. He pulled his nose with his thumb and first finger, then looked at Coach Garfield. "That's all I've got to say, Coach."

Chicken looked a little surprised. "That's all?"

"Yes," said Jack. "I think . . . you know. We can have a good team."

"Well . . ." said Chicken. "Okay . . ." He fiddled with his whistle, then put his stern look on. "Hit the field, men," he said.

For a minute Jack looked at Ducker, his head tilted a little to one side. Then he put on his helmet and went out of the locker room. The one-day boys followed. And then the team. All except Frog, who was blowing a bubble at the time. He pinched it closed with his lips and took it out of his mouth.

"Look," he said to the empty locker room.

"How can you eat *two* of those things?" said Jack.

He and Feeb had stopped by Theodore's after practice on Tuesday, and Feeb was finishing up his second hot fudge sundae. Jack was drinking a Coke.

"Wipe your mouth," he said, handing Feeb a napkin across the booth. Feeb took it and smeared the fudge around his mouth.

"Do it again," said Jack, handing him another napkin. "You go after that thing like it was a pussy," he said.

Of all the people on the team, Feeb was the one that Jack knew the best. The Siddoneys lived on Lincoln Street, just around the corner from the house on Waldburg. He and Jack had gone to grade school together.

Jack took the straw out of his cup and started eating the ice, tapping the bottom with his finger. "We got no hustle," he said.

Feeb was lifting a big spoonful of sundae to his mouth. He stopped and looked at Jack. While he was doing it, a long string of fudge sagged out of the spoon and into his lap. "Man," he said, "you got to be kidding." Then he shot the spoon into his mouth.

"No hustle. No drive," said Jack. "Everybody's dragass."

Feeb rammed another spoonful of ice cream and fudge into his mouth. "You think it's going to make a difference?"

"You don't hustle. You don't win," said Jack.

"Boniface don't win anyway," said Feeb. "Hustle or no hustle."

"That's the way we're acting," said Jack. "Everybody is acting that way."

"Ever . . ." He had a big spoonful of sundae in his mouth, and when he tried to talk, fudge ran out of the corners. He worked it around to the side. "Everybody knows the fucking score," he said.

"You've got to hustle," said Jack. "You've got to want to do it."

"This ain't New Orleans," he said. He reamed the sides of the sundae dish with his spoon, then licked it twice on each side. "It's hanging over from last year. The whole first team. We didn't lose a man."

Jack handed him another napkin. "I got beat twice in the last three years," he said.

Feeb looked at him over the napkin. "Twice?" he said. "Jesus. Get a grip on your ass."

"I hate to lose," said Jack.

"You get used to it," said Feeb.

"No, I wouldn't," said Jack. "I wouldn't get used to it worth a damn."

Feeb ran the spoon around the sundae dish again. "It ain't so bad, once you get used to it," he said.

"You beat Kose," said Jack. "I know how you did last year."

"So you know what I'm talking about."

"You beat Kose High School," said Jack.

Feeb looked at him. "Kose is a class C school," he said. "They got a hundred and sixty-eight students. Total."

"You came close to beating Glynn Academy."

"We wasn't hustling," said Feeb. "There was a flu epidemic in Brunswick. They had nine players in the hospital."

"Don't you give a shit?" said Jack.

Feeb looked at him, then scraped the spoon in the dish and licked it. "Not particularly," he said. "We hustled at the first of the year. We still got our ass beat." He jiggled the spoon. "Fuck it," he said.

"You're giving me the redass, Feeb," he said.

"Three games in four years, man," said Feeb. "Even with the Pope on our side. Go talk to my old man. He burned fifty candles last fall." He dropped the spoon in the dish. "You got to know where you stand, man."

"You've got something to do with where you stand," said Jack.

Feeb looked up at him, but he didn't say anything.

"Boniface had some good teams back during the war."

"All the heroes got killed," said Feeb.

"Horse Rooney is still around."

[114]

"Three motherfucking games, man," said Feeb. "You going to get beer out of horse piss sooner than you get a winner out of that bunch."

Jack crunched on his ice and Feeb ordered another sundae.

"What's Hoy's trouble?" said Jack.

"You know," said Feeb, digging into the sundae. "He's the bigshot tackle."

"You weigh more than he does," said Jack.

Feeb rolled his eyes. "Come *on*, man," he said. "You know what I fucking mean. He wants to beat your ass, only he's not sure how it'd come out."

"Hoy's a battler. He wouldn't be scared of me."

"He can't handle you on a football field," said Feeb. "You don't know the talk we been hearing all summer." He took another scoop of ice cream. "They made you sound like King Kong with a hard-on. It kind of makes *me* hate your guts even."

"Okay," said Jack. He stood up.

"Hey, man," said Feeb. "I didn't mean that."

"That's not it," said Jack.

"Where're you going?" said Feeb.

"I'm going to get me a brew," said Jack. "I want to think about it."

"Breaking fucking training," said Feeb. He scraped the sides of the sundae dish.

"Hoy's got the redass over me?" said Jack.

"He's the big man," said Feeb. "Not this year."

Jack started out the door.

"Wait a minute," said Feeb, squeezing out of the booth. "I'll go with you."

"You going to drink beer on top of that?"

"Sure," said Feeb, a surprised look on his face. "Something wrong with that?"

"Wipe your face," said Jack.

"I want you to put me one-on-one against Hoy." It was Monday of the second week, the first day of contact, and Jack had taken Coach Garfield aside to speak to him.

Chicken looked at Jack, surprised. "Let it go," he said. "Hoy's the best lineman I've got, next to you. I can't afford to have you busting each other up."

"Nobody's going to get busted up," said Jack. "Just put us one-on-one."

Chicken looked at him and fiddled with his whistle.

"You want to straighten out this team?" said Jack.

"I need the both of you," said Chicken.

"I know we do," said Jack. "Do what I'm telling you."

Jack was bigger than Ducker, but Ducker was meaner. And he was big, too. Even Jack didn't have enough size to just power him around any way he wanted to. But Ducker didn't understand the fine points of the game as well as Jack did. So Jack kept Ducker on his backside for half an hour, with Ducker's face getting redder all the time. When they thought Ducker wasn't looking, some of the B team players smiled at the way Jack was handling him. Ducker caught it, and tried harder than ever, but Jack was too quick for him to get a solid shot at.

"I want to see you a minute after you get dressed, Hoy," said Jack, when the drills were over. "Under the goalpost."

Ducker looked at him and spit on the ground. But he didn't say anything.

After he got dressed, Jack went out and stood under the goalpost, waiting for Ducker to come out.

"Stay right there, Hoy," said Jack, holding out his hand. Ducker was ten feet away from him. There was a dead look on his face, and his fists were clenched.

"You're the big All-American, ain't you, Curran?" said Ducker. His face was starting to get red again.

"You got a mind to beat my ass, Hoy?"

"What?" said Ducker. "I got a bad ear. Talk louder."

"I said, 'You want a piece of my ass, don't you, Hoy?'"

Ducker spit on the ground. "It crossed my mind."

"You're going to have to wait, Hoy. You can't take a crack at it till the season's over."

Ducker looked at him.

"That's what I wanted to talk to you about," said Jack. His hands were resting on his hips lightly. "Stash it away, Hoy. When we're through with the football, I'll give you a crack at it."

Ducker looked at him. "I never liked to put things off, Curran. Do it while the doing's good."

"You can't win, Hoy."

"What?" said Ducker. "What?"

"You'll have to cripple me to beat me. How's that for the team?"

Ducker looked at him frowning.

"I was just fucking around today," said Jack. "You ought to see what I can do when I put my *mind* to it."

Ducker was the best street battler in the school. That's what everyone said. A different proposition, not like football. He had never been known to lose a fight. And he wasn't particularly careful about who he picked them with.

"You got no choice, Hoy. Friday after Thanksgiving. I'll meet you down at Screven. Anyplace you want to." He stopped. "I'm not looking forward to it," he said. Then he paused. "I'll meet you anyplace you want to."

Ducker knew he was trapped. He couldn't cripple Jack and take him off the team, but he also couldn't handle him at practice.

"You ain't going to *enjoy* it, Hoy. It wouldn't be a walkaway fight. Either one of us. I'd have to try to rack you up altogether. You're too big to fuck around with."

The red was going out of Ducker's face. "You're a *big* asshole, Curran," he said. "I wouldn't walk through you. But you pushed me around too goddamn much today. Don't nobody get to do that."

"I pushed you around because I'm better than you are," said Jack. He paused a minute. "Coach Garfield needs the both of us. You're the only decent lineman we got."

Ducker spit on the ground. "All-American, Curran," he said. "You ain't forgetting that?"

"We can't bust each other up."

"Pushing me around . . ."

"You're big enough to handle me better than that."

"I ain't had the big-time advantages, Curran."

"Get on the team, Hoy. I'll meet you Friday after Thanksgiving. Fort Screven . . . anyplace you say."

"Pushing me around. Who the fuck you think you are, Curran?"

"You should be handling me better than you were."

Ducker looked at him, thinking. He spit on the ground.

"You like to lose, Hoy?"

"No," said Ducker. "I don't fucking like to lose." He thought a minute. "I don't fucking like to get pushed around either."

"Get on the team," said Jack.

"Curran . . ." said Ducker, pointing his finger at Jack. For a minute they stood looking at each other without saying anything.

"You want me to show you what you were doing wrong?" said Jack.

When the word got out in the school about Jack's deal with Ducker, the bookmaking began right away. They were tough odds to figure, and never were settled in a permanent way.

Jack was big in the bone, probably weighing forty or forty-five pounds more than Ducker did, but taller and trimmer. He carried his weight well, and most of his agility was in his legs. Ducker was on the flat-footed side. His speed was in his hands, which made him a good battler, but it wasn't of much use to him on the football field. His off-season sport was boxing, and he was very good at it. In the ring he didn't have to depend on anyone else, which he liked. Jack was a wrestler.

In a fistfight, Jack's weight wasn't all that much of an advantage. After all, Ducker weighed about as much as Jack Dempsey had. And Joe Louis had come near beating Primo Carnera to death. The Italian was even bigger than Jack was.

The odds were running about four and a half to five—in Ducker's favor, since Jack was the unknown quantity. But those were talking odds. There wasn't any money being bet.

Although the interests of the school didn't lie over that way, everybody would have liked to see the two big men go ahead and have their fight. It was more basic than football.

But in the meantime, Ducker got on the team.

As he said, he didn't like losing all that much either.

Having Jack and Ducker together went a long way toward getting the eleven men moving as a team, but that didn't mean that all the problems had been solved.

Since his play was going to be in the interior line, the line was Jack's first consideration. He wanted two good guards, and at least one good tackle. Feeb he more or less wrote off, having known him all his life. Everything Feeb did struck him as comical, and he couldn't take him seriously enough to work with him. He thought they could survive one weak link, if everybody else would hustle.

The first step was to get everybody's mind off himself, so he could see what was going on around him—after which they would be able to forget about it.

To do that, he suggested to Coach Garfield that for one day they swap around on the linemen's positions. So they did a round robin, every man taking a turn at each position from tackle to tackle, trying to get a feel for what the others were doing. Seeing how their part fit into the pattern. In the end, they began to trust each other, so they didn't have to cover a 360-degree field in their heads to feel safe.

The ends and backs were something else again. Whistler Whitfield and Cowboy McGrath were unknown quantities, since they had never had a line to block for them before, and weren't used to getting *through* their holes. Breaking out on the downfield side of the line did a lot for their morale just by itself.

Flasher, Aaron, and Dimmy were the real mountains to be moved. Frog—well, with Frog the dimension of the problem was different. There wasn't any real hope of doing anything with him except by working on him from the outside. To take care of Frog's sense of direction, the times he would get turned around, they kept up the "Stop Frog" drills. Jack solved the problem of Frog's being short on yardage by detailing two managers, one on each side of the field, to mark the down by blinking a flashlight with a green lens, so it would attract Frog's attention and show him where to go. He thought that the fans would take it for some kind of spirit thing, and didn't expect the officials to complain. Frog wanted the lights to be red, but they reminded him that the school colors were green and white, which would make the green light easier to explain to the officials if they ever had to.

"Red is my *favorite* color," said Frog.

Jack told Aaron to stop fading back so far. And when he kept on doing it, he had a talk with him about it.

"You don't need to go back there so far, Aaron. You're not getting the best out of your arm."

"I like to have room to move around," said Aaron.

"But you're not getting the best out of your arm."

Aaron didn't want to argue with him about it. "I like to move around back there, Curran," he said.

"You can get it out there pretty good, Aaron," said Jack, "but you're losing accuracy. Don't drop back more than ten yards. We're going to be blocking for you."

It was like talking down a posthole. Aaron went right on running for the goal line as soon as he had snatched the ball from Jack. Just like he always had.

"Stop fading back so far, Aaron," said Jack. "I'm telling you, you're using up your arm just getting it back to the line."

"One man calling signals, Curran," said Aaron. "One man calling signals."

"Goddamn it, Bomberstern, you don't need to run out of the stadium."

Aaron looked at him for a minute without saying anything. "Fuck you," he said.

He kept fading back his twenty and thirty yards, with Jack bitching at him after every play. Finally Jack turned around and chased him all the way into the end zone, where Aaron threw the ball away and climbed the goalpost. "One man calling signals, Curran," he said, looking down from the crossbar.

"You're going to stop doing it, Aaron," said Jack. "I promise you."

He called the guards and halfbacks aside and had a private talk with them about Aaron's habits. "We've got to harass him," he said. "If he fades back more than fifteen yards, whoever is back there blocking has got to nail him."

"You mean tackle him?" said Bo Hoerner.

"I wasn't thinking of anything that showy," said Jack.

"Our *own* man?" said Bo.

"He's too much out for himself," said Jack. "We've got to get him thinking for the team. He can't expect us to block for him if he's out for himself."

"I don't like it," said Bo.

"I like it fine," said Whistler Whitfield. "The son of a bitch ain't give me a good hand-off in the last two years."

"We'll work on that next," said Jack. "First we've got to stop him running out of the stadium."

Jack showed them how to do it. On the first pass play, he backed up with Aaron, and when he started to break and run for the goal line, Jack hit him. He did it well, so that it looked like an accident, but he drew blood on Aaron's leg.

"Look!" said Aaron. "Look at the blood! Goddamn watch where you're going, Curran."

"I was trying to keep up with you, Aaron," said Jack. "Stay up closer to the line."

"Look at my leg," said Aaron. "Look at me bleeding on my leg."

They had to hold up practice while he went into the locker room and put a bandage on it.

The next time, Whistler Whitfield got him. He didn't make it look as good as Jack did, but it didn't look clearly deliberate either.

"Goddamn, Whitfield," said Aaron.

"Sorry," said Whistler.

Aaron went into the locker room, and they had to wait for him again while he put on another bandage. The knocks they were giving him made him bitch and carry on, but little by little he began to unload the ball faster, just to avoid being hurt.

"It makes sense," said Jack. "By the time Aaron can make ten, Flasher can make thirty. Flasher won't have all that time to fuck around out there."

The next thing was to get Aaron using more deception in his hand-offs. Whistler and Cowboy had both been complaining to Jack about that right along, but he didn't want to push Aaron too much at once. "One thing at a time," he said.

But after he got the fading back under control, he took up the problem of Aaron's ball handling.

"Goddamn, Curran, don't I do nothing to please you?" said Aaron. "Lujack don't hide the ball."

"What the shit do you mean?" said Jack. "Lujack is an ace ball handler."

Aaron looked at him. "He is?" he said.

"You ever seen any game films of Lujack?"

"I've seen him in the newsreels."

"He has a nice touch," said Jack. "Nobody knows who's got the ball when Lujack is handling it."

"Well," said Aaron.

It didn't break him. He just began to look around for some other quarterback who handled the ball according to the way he thought it ought to be done.

"What're we going to do?" said Whistler. "By the time I get the ball, everybody in the fucking stadium knows where it's at, including the niggers in the washroom."

"He's out for himself again," said Jack. "Let's put him on his own. We've got to work with his self-interest just to get his attention."

"Okay," said Whistler. Then he thought a minute. "What the shit does that mean?"

"When you don't like the hand-off—don't take it."

"What?" said Whistler.

"I said, don't take it," said Jack. "Stick him with the motherfucker."

"Yes," said Whistler, and smiled. "Stick him with the motherfucker."

"Just go down in your blocking stance and let him eat it," said Jack. "Aaron won't keep up anything if he gets hurt doing it. We just have to make it in his own interest to hide the thing."

So Whistler and Cowboy stopped taking the ball.

"Take it! Take it!" Aaron had his arm stretched out behind him like he was trying to feed a snake, waiting for Whistler to take the ball and let him get out of the way.

"Hide it," said Whistler over his shoulder.

"What the fuck, Whitfield?" said Aaron. Then the two B-team guards nailed him.

"You try to give it to me on a stick, and you can eat it," said Whistler.

"What?" said Aaron, looking at the cut on his arm.

"We're going to have us a *team*, Bomberstern," said Whistler.

They didn't get rid of Aaron's bad habits altogether, but they cut them down to a point where they could live with them. At least they got him to paying attention and seeing their side of the problem.

Jack tried to reason with Flasher and Dimmy, but there wasn't any way to get through to either of them with just words. Especially Dimmy.

With Aaron getting the ball off faster, part of the problem with Flasher solved itself, since he didn't have that much time to fool around after he got downfield and had to pay attention to what he was doing.

But just for insurance, they began to work him over to slow him down—just a little. Jack would give him a heel on the instep coming out of the huddle. Then Ducker picked it up and started to sideswipe him coming off the line. They also got Whistler lining up behind him and telling him things like his fly was open, or his pants were ripped, to attract his attention just before the ball was snapped. They didn't want to interfere with him too much, because basically what he was doing was the right thing, though they wished his hands would improve. To help that, they gave him a rosin bag to hang on his pants, and made him carry a football around school during the day so he would get to recognize what it felt like. Even so, every third pass to him still bounced off.

Talking to Dimmy was not only a waste of time, it could also be harmful. Too many words coming at him at once seemed to clog him up and slow down his thinking—which wasn't much faster than a duckbill platypus's to start with. They didn't want to get him moody, or too attentive, but they did want him to look where he was going. So Jack and Ducker started pulling off the line and double-teaming him when he was going off guard. They hurt themselves about as much as they hurt Dimmy, but it surprised him, and got him to pull his head up just out of curiosity. Being able to see where he was going made him notice that some of his own men were out there in front of him, too, and stopped him from plowing into his own blockers from the back side and walking around on their vertebrae. Which improved their outlook considerably.

Two weeks into practice, the usual lethargy was gone. Everyone was attentive and alert. Well, relatively. Things weren't A-1, letter-perfect, but they were silver and gold to what they had been before.

A sense of how well everybody else was doing his job began to filter in under the helmets—even Dimmy's. The big thing was that they began to trust each other. Where they had all had a 360-degree field of apprehension before, the new attitude had cut it down to the 30 or 40 degrees that was the responsibility of each particular position. That alone meant an improvement of over 900 percent. Of course, some improvements were more important than others. Just getting Dimmy to run with his head up accounted for 300 percent of the improvement by itself.

They were coming up on the first real test, which came just before the season opened. The traditional varsity-alumni game.

Every year, on the Saturday afternoon before the season started, the Boniface varsity had to gird up what loins it had and take on the alumni in a real game, which was no pantywaist affair, but a knock-head session, where bright red blood was expected to flow. There were four twelve-minute quarters, with referees, and full equipment for the players. It never occurred to anybody who came to watch or play in the game that crippling the team might not be the best way to start them out for the season. Football, as they said, was a rough game.

Most of the alumni who turned up to play were out to get back a piece of the glory they had had two or three, some even eight or nine, years before. Taking it easy on the team was the farthest thing from their minds, and never came in as part of their view of the game. If the old guys had been able to go flat out for the full four quarters, nobody would have walked away from it whole. But half a game was about the most that ever came off. Partly that was because of the way J.J. O'Brien underwrote it—which may have been a calculated thing on his part. J.J. was a sport, but he was a smart one.

The bench on the alumni side of the field was a row of green canvas camp chairs, and there were little Negro boys to run up and down the line delivering pitchers of cold beer and cigars to the players, all supplied by J.J. himself. By the end of the first half, the beer and cigars would be coming down on the alumni pretty heavy, so the second half wasn't much more than a dance around the maypole, except for the varsity trying to get even for the punishment they had taken in the first half.

But the first twelve minutes were pure bloody murder.

The alumni weren't in that good shape; even without the beer and cigars they weren't. But their mad-dog outlook and their grown-man size made them a rough proposition for a high school team to take on. They outweighed the varsity twenty pounds to the man every year, and with that second moment of glory into them the way it was, they were like a herd of wild elephants until their wind gave out.

Usually the game was bad news for somebody in particular on the varsity squad. The whole idea of the game was crazy as hell anyway, but the height of all the craziness was that the alumni concentrated on the best players, trying to maim and disable them in particular. If one of them had a better reputation than the rest, that was the one they zeroed in on. Cutting him down to size gave a focus to the contest, making it more interesting for the alumni.

In 1947, it was Jack Curran. And the man to put the test on him was Horse Rooney, the All-State fullback from the 1942 championship team—the one that had beaten Boys' High of Atlanta.

Horse was as mean a snake as ever pulled a green jersey over his head, and as big a one as well. He had made the first team at Boniface in 1939 as a freshman at a playing weight of 185, attracting the coach's attention by breaking the collarbone of the first-string right guard during a practice scrimmage. His senior year he had weighed 215, and there weren't eleven men in the state who could stop him in less than five yards. For the four years since his graduation, Horse had had his natural snaky instincts honed up for him by the United States Marine Corps, which had put thirty more pounds of meat on him, and then had taught him eleven ways to kill a man with his bare hands. He wasn't in tip-top shape, but he figured to kill about four or five linemen before his wind gave out. Starting with Jack Curran.

Boniface had two defenses—a six-man line and a five-man line. Coach Garfield was going with the five-man line as a regular thing, since that would put Jack in the middle and let him operate from there. Anything between tackles would be his, with Dimmy on the left to help him, and Ducker on the right. And on Flasher's side of the field, because he could get out fast enough to turn his man in, the end sweeps would also be Jack's. His lateral movement was very good, and he was quick, if not fast. He could almost keep up with Flasher himself for the first ten yards.

The strategy of the alumni was simple and direct. Horse was setting the tone, and that was the way his mind worked. What he wanted was to get the ball on the first play from scrimmage, and go right up the middle with it, head-on at Curran.

"Just get them other cocksuckers out of the way," he said. "It's me and Curran, boys. Me and Curran." Then he slapped his hands together, and the skull session was over.

The alumni won the toss, and the varsity kicked off to them. It was a short kick, taken by the deep man on the 25. He bobbled it, and Bump Waddell, a twenty-eight-year-old guard from the 1937 team, fell on it at the 45-yard line. They didn't bother to huddle, but lined up right away, with Horse straight back behind the center. Before they got down into their stances, Horse raised his arm and pointed his finger at Jack.

"Off on three, Curran," he said. "Watch your ass."

All of the Boniface linemen turned around and looked at Jack. He had his hands on his knees and was looking down at the ground. Then the signals started and the center hiked the ball.

The charge of the alumni line wasn't all that hard. It was a big moment. Everybody knew what was going to happen anyway, and all of them wanted to see it so they would be able to tell about it afterward.

The alumni pushed off right and left, and the varsity backed off the line, checking. Then everybody stood up and turned around to watch Jack and Horse come together in the middle of the thirty-foot hole that had opened up in the center of the field.

Horse ran a good bit like Dimmy, only with his head up more and looking around, his knees pumping against his chest. He had a quick start, and was going flat out on the second step he took. But

Jack had the faster reflexes, and they came together on the alumni side of the line.

Talking about it afterward, everybody who was there to see it put it in terms of the way they'd felt seeing the newsreel pictures of the atom bomb going off in Alamogordo, New Mexico. Jack took him high, getting his right shoulder pad into Horse's face and wrapping his arms around him on the outside. Jack never broke stride. There was just a big cracking sound, like a fieldpiece going off, then the two of them were moving away toward the alumni goal line, Horse's head in Jack's shoulder and both legs sticking out under Jack's arms. The impact split the center seam on Horse's helmet, and flipped it off his head backward so it hung on his neck by the chin strap, like a Mexican bandit's sombrero. And his shoulder pads flapped up out of his jersey like the wings on a beetle.

Jack set him down gently on the 42-yard line and stood looking at him with his hands on his hips. Then he looked back at the other players. No one moved or said anything. They were staring at him, some with their mouths hanging open, jumping their eyes up and down from Jack to Horse and back again.

With everybody watching him, he walked back down the middle of the field to where the ball was, on the varsity 35-yard line, moving very slowly and deliberately the whole way. When he got to the ball, he put his foot on it. Then he reached down and tapped it with his hand.

"Our ball," he said.

As soon as he said it, the referee remembered and blew his whistle.

Right away the first-aid squad came onto the field and started to work on Horse, but it took a minute and a half of swatting him on the back to beat the first breath into him, and ten more of breaking ammonia ampules under his nose and pouring beer on his head, to get his eyes uncrossed and his mouth working right.

"How do you feel, Horse?" J.J. yelled it into his ear fifty or sixty times. In between, he would spread out his arms to push back the crowd, chewing on his cigar and yelling, "Give him air, boys! Goddamn it, give him air!"

When Horse's voice started to work back up into his throat again, all he could say was "*God*damn!" over and over.

J.J. stood over him, patting his shoulder and telling him he was going to be all right.

Finally Horse looked up at him in a way that showed he recognized who J.J. was. Then he blinked his eyes and crossed himself. "Goddamn, J.J.!" he said. He made a sucking motion with his lips, working his mouth, then spit out a big yellow tooth. He smiled up at J.J. through the gap. "Goddamn, J.J.," he said. "We going to have us a *team!*"

14

Dendron and Jack: Talking and Thinking

On Sunday afternoon following the alumni game, Jack talked to his friend Dendron about it.

"I remember going out to see Horse Rooney play when I was in the fifth grade," he said.

"Yes," said Dendron. "I wasn't much on football."

"He was the best football player I ever saw," said Jack. "I guess Blanchard was better."

They were on the ground floor of Dendron's house on Waldburg Street. The ground floor was down a step from the street, and was where the servants had lived when the house was first built. Dendron had the whole floor to himself, with his mother above him on the first floor up from the street. The two upper stories were empty.

Dendron needed the whole ground floor to himself because of the trains. They took up a lot of room. Trains weren't his only hobby, but they were the one he put the most value on. He also did chemical experiments, but those didn't amount to much. One Christmas he had gotten a Gilbert chemistry set, and he liked the part of it that had to do with magic. Occasionally he would make up a batch of disappearing ink, or a glass of green liquid that bubbled like the kind of thing Dr. Jekyll drank in the movies when he was going to turn into Mr. Hyde. He also liked to bend glass tubing with his alcohol torch.

But his serious hobby was trains.

He had an H.O. layout so elaborate that looking at it gave something like the sensation you would get riding the Goodyear Blimp over the Proviso switching yards in Chicago. He called it his "layout," but that's not what it was—not the way the H.O. people use the term. Dendron wasn't very strong on putting in stations and bridges and other kinds of scenery. Mostly what he did was put in track—nearly a mile of it, running it back and forth from one room to another, going under and around the furniture, and in and out of the closets. He didn't even pay much attention to the trains themselves (there were two: a 2–8–0 Richmond engine, with a Central of Georgia caboose; and an Atlantic Coastline diesel). It was the length and intricacy of the track system itself that he was interested in. He ran the trains slowly, and at a scale speed of forty miles an hour it took nearly two hours to get them around the circuit. But he did like dispatching, and he put up little numbered signs, and took an interest in making the trains hit the checkpoints on time.

The Atlantic Coastline diesel came out from under the bed where Jack was sitting, going between his legs. Then it went through the door of the room, and into the hall.

"Can't you shut that thing off, Dendron?" he said.

"It'll be in the other room for the next twenty minutes," said Dendron, looking at his Ingersoll.

They could hear the little train clicking off down the hall, then the sound faded away.

"I guess Blanchard was better than Horse," said Jack. He looked at Dendron. "Doc Blanchard. He played for Army. I'm talking about fullbacks."

"I see," said Dendron.

"Walker is great, too," said Jack. "Doak Walker. And Lujack."

"I know who Lujack is," said Dendron. "Father Dyer talks about Lujack in the English class."

"Anyway," said Jack, "Horse was the first one I *saw*. He was a good football player." He thought a minute. "You know, he weighed *more* than Blanchard. Blanchard only weighed two ten."

"Yes," said Dendron. "I've heard about how good he was."

"I wish he hadn't come at me like that," said Jack. "It's like he was everything there *was* to football to me. When I was in the ninth grade."

"I see," said Dendron.

"The eighth . . . the ninth . . . along there." He looked at Dendron. "It's the kind of thing you hang on to."

Dendron looked at him. "You're not sorry about it, are you?"

"I'm not *sorry* about it." He hesitated. "I didn't enjoy it."

"You can't avoid that kind of thing when you play football?" said Dendron, making a question of it.

"No," said Jack. "You can't avoid it. That's the way the game is."

"That's what I thought," said Dendron.

For a while neither of them said anything.

"Horse Rooney," said Jack. "I really think a lot of Horse, Dendron."

"I know he's a good player," said Dendron. "I hear he's kind of an asshole . . . you know—*off* the field."

Jack looked at him. "A lot of good football players are like that," he said. "You've got to take them for what they are *on* the field." He looked away. "Horse was the best player I ever saw. Except for Blanchard maybe. The best fullback."

Dendron nodded.

They sat without saying anything. Without looking at each other.

"I had a dream last night," said Jack. "I've been having it for about a week." Now and then Jack would have a dream that would come back more than once. The only person he ever talked to about them was Dendron.

"I was in the water," he said. "Under the water. It was deep, and I couldn't tell how far in I was. Everything was gray-green. Dark."

Dendron looked at him. "I hardly ever have a dream," he said. "Could you see it was green?"

"Gray-green," said Jack. "Yes. I can always remember the colors in my dreams. Sometimes it's more one color than another. Sometimes I'll have a red dream. Or orange. This was mostly gray-green."

"I hardly ever have a dream," said Dendron.

"I was in the water," he said. "Pretty far down, but I wasn't swimming. I was just floating down there in the water." He stopped. He was sitting with his elbows resting on his knees, his hands clasped together lightly. "All around me there was a bunch of sharks," he said. "They were swimming around me, but not like they were after me or anything."

"Like *Life* magazine?" said Dendron.

Jack looked at him.

"*Life* magazine always has pictures of sharks that scare you," said Dendron. "Sharks and fish. Like an octopus. Sometimes they're painted. Were they like the sharks in *Life* magazine?"

"No," said Jack. "These sharks weren't scary. They didn't seem to see me. They weren't just plain sharks, though," he said. "They were big. I couldn't tell how far away they were, but I could tell they were big. And there was something else," he said. Dendron looked at him. "They were two sharks apiece," he said.

"Two?" said Dendron. "What do you mean?"

"I mean there were two sharks, but they were joined together by their fin," he said. "Siamese twins. Two bodies side by side, with the fin joining them. Like a P-38."

"Well," said Dendron.

"They were doing loops and rolls, like they were fighter planes," he said. "It sounds strange to me now, but I remember I didn't think there was anything wrong with it at the time. I wasn't scared of them and I wasn't surprised."

"Like a P-38?" said Dendron.

"Yes," said Jack. He made wings of his hands, holding them with the palms down, thumbs touching, and moved them around in a sweeping motion. "Like a P-38. After a while they began swimming around me in a circle. There were a lot of them, but I don't remember how many. More than twenty, I think. Too many to tell.

"After a while one of them broke off and started to swim toward me. I couldn't tell how far away he was. He looked big, though. He kept coming toward me with his mouth open—he had two, I guess, but I only remember the one. He kept coming for a long time, and he kept getting bigger and bigger. He was farther away than I thought, because he kept coming a long time after I thought he would have got to me. And he kept getting bigger all the time. He got so big that I couldn't even see him anymore, just the big black place where his mouth was, with the white teeth in it. Then they got bigger, too, until finally they got so big I knew he wouldn't be able to bite a flea. Finally he was so big I couldn't even see the teeth anymore. I don't know where he was— all around me, I guess. I couldn't tell if he got to me or not. Just that he wasn't there anymore, and I didn't know whether I was inside him or outside."

Dendron looked at him.

"I guess I must have been inside," he said. "It didn't make any difference finally."

Dendron looked at him. "I hardly ever have any dreams," he said.

"Yes," said Jack. "I have one about every night."

For a while they didn't say anything, while Dendron thought about the dream.

"Horse Rooney," said Jack, shaking his head.

"Is that it?" said Dendron. "You had the dream after you tackled Horse Rooney?"

Jack looked at him. "No," he said. "I told you. I've been having that dream for a week now. It started before the alumni game."

"I see," said Dendron.

"Horse Rooney was a damn good football player," said Jack. "You know, he was bigger than Blanchard?"

"That's what I hear," said Dendron.

Dendron fidgeted around. He was sitting on a straight-backed chair that he used with his desk. On his head was a seersucker engineer's cap that he wore to run the trains.

"You weren't scared?" he said.

"Of Horse?" said Jack.

"Of the sharks?" said Dendron.

"No," said Jack. "It wasn't a scary dream."

Dendron looked at the ceiling. "This is a spooky old house," he said. "It's a good thing I don't dream."

Jack looked at him. "I like this house," he said. "The rooms are big."

"It's old," said Dendron. "The Marshoaks houses are nicer."

Jack didn't say anything.

"I like your house in Marshoaks," said Dendron.

"It's a little cramped."

"It's new. An old house gets you down."

Jack looked up at the ceiling. "I like a high ceiling," he said.

"There's something in the toilet," said Dendron. He said it quickly, looking at Jack, then he looked away. "The plumbing in an old house gets you down."

"It's better than the new stuff," said Jack. "You should see the faucets in our house. Plastic and crap like that. They couldn't get any metal fixtures during the war."

"Yes," said Dendron. "Did you hear me? I said there is something in the toilet."

"What do you mean?" said Jack. "The toilet doesn't work?"

"It works. There's something *in* it."

"In it?"

"I haven't told anybody, because it sounds crazy. There's something in it."

"Show me," said Jack. He got up and they picked their way across the tracks into the bathroom, which was between the front and back rooms.

"I don't see anything," said Jack. "You mean something got stuck in it?"

Dendron looked into the bowl cautiously. "It's something," he said. "I don't know. Some kind of animal."

Jack looked into the bowl. "An animal?" he said. "You mean something alive?"

"I never really see it," said Dendron. "You know, I don't get to look at it all over."

Jack looked into the water of the bowl.

"It's black," said Dendron. "I just see a piece of it at a time. Like a tail. Maybe a foot." He looked into the toilet bowl. "I don't know what I'm seeing. It's black."

Jack looked into the water. "Dendron," he said, "is this something inside your head?"

"What do you mean?"

"Is there really something in there? Because I never heard of a thing like that before."

Dendron looked at him for a minute. "It's real to me," he said.

"You mean it might be some kind of optical illusion?"

"Not an optical illusion," said Jack. "Something you built up inside your head."

Dendron thought about it a minute. "I couldn't answer that. I can *hear* something at night after the lights are out."

"Did you ever hear of anything coming out of a toilet?" said Jack.

"Yes," said Dendron. "The people next door had a rat in theirs."

"I never heard anything about that," said Jack.

Dendron looked at him. "If you found a rat in your toilet, would you spread it around?"

"I mean I never heard of anything like that happening anywhere," said Jack.

Dendron looked at him. "You mean I've got to furnish you a certificate that it really happened? I've got to *prove* it to you?"

Jack looked at him. "No," he said. "I didn't mean that."

Dendron started out of the bathroom. "Never mind," he said.

"Now wait a goddamn minute," said Jack.

"Listen," said Dendron. "I'm embarrassed about it already. I never thought about having to prove it to you. I just wanted to tell you about it."

"Come back, Dendron," said Jack. "You don't have to prove it to me."

Dendron came back. "I'm sorry I brought it up," he said. "It comes and goes. I didn't mean *you* were going to see it. I never told anybody else."

"No," said Jack. "That's all right. I'm glad you told me. It sounds funny, though."

Dendron looked at him in a hurt way.

"I mean it sounds strange," said Jack. He looked back into the toilet bowl. "Why don't you set a trap for it?"

Dendron looked at him. "I don't want to *catch* it," he said. "I just want it to go away."

"That would settle it."

"What if I didn't catch it?" said Dendron.

The diesel came in from the back room, circled the toilet, and went out the door into the front room.

Dendron looked at his watch. "Twenty-five seconds."

"What?" said Jack.

"It's twenty-five seconds ahead," said Dendron. He put the watch back into his pocket. "I just pee in it. I wouldn't *sit* on it for anything."

"I can see how you feel," said Jack. Then he chuckled.

Dendron looked at him with a hurt expression. "I didn't think your shark dream was funny," he said.

"I was thinking of a joke," said Jack. "It reminded me of the guy with the long dong, who got hiccups sitting on the john and pumped out all the water."

Dendron looked at him, but he didn't laugh. "What's the joke?" he said.

"It's like thinking about sliding down a razor blade."

"It is?" said Dendron. "What do you mean?"

"You have to think about it," said Jack. "It's in your head."

For a minute they both stood staring into the toilet bowl. Jack jiggled the handle. Then he flushed it.

"It could be a snake," said Dendron.

Jack didn't say anything.

"Which does it sound like?" said Dendron.

Jack looked at him.

"Does it sound like a rat, or a snake? Which does it sound like to you?"

Jack could see that the thing, whether it was there or not, had gotten very deep into his friend's head. What was outside didn't matter all that much.

"I wouldn't think a snake could get this far up the line," Jack said.

"I heard about an alligator getting in the sewers someplace. One of those Florida souvenirs. You know, some kid flushed it down the toilet, and it got into the sewer."

"It's probably a rat," said Jack.

"I wish it would go away," said Dendron.

"Probably it'll go away," said Jack. He had a bemused look on his face. "You remember the kittens?" he said.

"I'd forgot," said Dendron. "We must have been in the first grade."

"I'd forgot, too. It was Sookey's litter. I'd never seen a newborn kitten before."

"Three of them," said Dendron.

"Yes," said Jack. "It was a hell of a mean thing to do."

"How old were we?"

"We must have been about six," said Jack. "It was the first winter I lived on Waldburg Street. Sookey died that winter."

"I'd forgotten all about it," said Dendron. "You put them in, and I flushed the toilet."

"I think about it sometimes," said Jack. "It was a mean thing to do."

They looked into the toilet.

"You think it's a rat?"

"Maybe it's the ghost of one of the kittens."

Dendron frowned.

"It's probably a rat," said Jack. He decided to push for the rat, which was easier to contend with than the snake or the alligator.

"I guess a rat would be more likely," said Dendron.

Jack looked at him. "Yes," he said. "I don't think it could be a snake."

"I think about sitting down on it, and the rat would come out and bite me." Dendron looked at Jack. "I don't use this one," he said quickly. "Just to take a leak. I go upstairs for the other." He looked back at the toilet. "But I think about it," he said. "All the time. Even upstairs."

"A rat couldn't get up the drain line that far, Dendron," said Jack.

"Yes," said Dendron. "I've just got it in my mind. I can hardly sit down anywhere—thinking about it biting me."

"Well," said Jack. "Try not to worry about it."

"I guess they come up from the river," said Dendron. "The rats." They went back into the bedroom.

"I feel better," said Dendron. "It's probably my imagination. I needed to talk to somebody about it."

"You know," said Jack, "I didn't know you were afraid of rats."

"As a matter of fact, I'm not," said Dendron. "Not real ones."

For a while they watched the train. It went into the closet and started toward the bed.

"I could do without it, Dendron," said Jack. He raised his feet to let it pass under.

Dendron looked at his watch. "Thirty-five seconds fast," he said. Then he turned off the transformer. "I hate these old houses. You could always hear them in the walls."

"Yes," said Jack. He put his feet down on the floor again, looking up at the ceiling. He shook his head. "Horse Rooney," he said.

"Well," said Dendron. "I don't know much about football."

"It's not the game," said Jack. "I like the game." He looked at Dendron. "I like body contact. You know? I like to hit."

"Yes," said Dendron.

"But Horse Rooney." Jack shook his head. "I bet I made a thousand tackles. It's part of the game, Dendron."

"I know," said Dendron.

"But Horse was the first good football player I ever saw."

"That's what I hear," said Dendron.

"He set it up," said Jack. "And he hit me hard, Dendron. He hit me hard."

"Well," said Dendron. "It's just a game."

Jack looked at him. "No, it's not," he said. "It's more than that to me."

"I see," said Dendron.

For a minute neither of them said anything.

"You think it's a rat?" said Dendron.

"What?" said Jack.

"You think it's a rat?" Dendron pointed to the bathroom.

Jack nodded.

"I wish it was something I could talk about. It's not like a dream. I wouldn't want anybody to know about it. Mother would die if I told her."

"You can talk about it to me," said Jack. "A dream isn't all that easy to tell to somebody else either."

"Well," said Dendron. "A rat's better than a snake."

"Yes," said Jack.

"I wish it would go away."

"Probably it will," said Jack. "Try not to pay any attention to it."

Then he got up and started for the door, walking on tiptoes across the tracks.

"You got to go?"

"I've got a date with Mary."

"Jack," said Dendron. "Does it matter that much, whether it's inside my head or not? The rat?"

"No," said Jack. "It might matter to somebody that didn't know you."

Dendron didn't get up. "I'm not going to put out a trap," he said.

15

Where the Heart Lies

JACK THOUGHT THERE WAS only one woman in his life, but really there were two. Mary Odell and Mackey Brood. Mackey was the one he wasn't counting, though he had known her the longest, and still saw her now and then. Mary he had met at a house party in the spring of 1947, and over a single weekend at Tybee, she had transubstantiated for him into the living ideal of all womankind. By Sunday night he had worked her up into a niche from which he was never able to let her climb down.

It was still possible in those days—that kind of romantic worship of certain kinds of girls. In the movies, it happened regularly to women like Madeleine Carroll and Olivia De Havilland. And Mary was certainly the type to draw it out of a man. There was nothing especially healthy about it, that attitude. But it was fairly common. Only Jack took it too far, even from the beginning—into a dim wasteland, where nothing was solid or real. He would no more have laid a finger on Mary with carnal intent than he would have laid one on the Virgin Mother herself. Or on Kate, or Susy.

Everybody noticed the way Jack was feeling about Mary, but it bothered Feeb.

"Just think about her dropping her drawers, and taking a great big shit," said Feeb.

He was trying to swing Jack back into reality, the way he saw it, but the point didn't get home, and Jack hit him. It was one of the few times he ever took Feeb seriously.

"Shit, man," said Feeb. "Motherfucker." Rubbing the eye.

Afterward, Jack told him not to say it again, feeling sorry, but at the same time justified. Later he was the one who drove Feeb to the emergency room of the hospital.

It had been a bad weekend for Feeb all around. The girls were doing their own cooking, so the food was lousy. And all of the regular eating places were closed because the season didn't start until Memorial Day. There wasn't a hot fudge sundae to be had on the whole island, and the only decent hamburger was fifteen miles away back in town. But his date turned out to be the biggest problem of all.

Feeb was out with Corinne Feliciano, a small dark-haired girl with big brown eyes—and a peculiarity that was the subject of a whole lot of talk among the boys at Boniface. The thing about Corinne was that she never wore underwear when she went out with boys, and she liked to get her date to roll up his pants leg so she could straddle it, and ride it like a hobbyhorse. As a way to begin an evening, that would have been okay. But the trouble was the bareback riding never got any farther along than that. Nobody ever laid a finger on Corinne, and she was always surprised and indignant and loudmouthed about it whenever anybody tried. Corinne had a lot of first dates, because the whole thing sounded very interesting—before the boy got into it, with her up there humping on his leg, but screaming bloody murder when he made the first false move—but the repeat business was very slow, because there was just too much frustration involved. Though there was also a certain amount of challenge to taking her out.

Feeb knew all about it, but he had a secret plan to beat the game. He had gotten some inside information from Whistler Whitfield that he thought was going to make him the man to knock off Corinne Feliciano.

Whistler was acknowledged to be the biggest cocksman at Boniface, if not in the world, and whatever he had to say about pussy was carefully attended to. He didn't talk about it all that much, but Feeb had asked him a direct question.

"The surest way . . ." said Whistler, ". . . ain't no way *sure,* but the surest way I know, is to lay your joint in her hand."

Feeb looked at him. "What do you mean?" he said.

"I mean what I'm fucking saying, man," said Whistler. He held out his left hand, palm up, and hit it with his right. "Lay it in her goddamn hand."

Feeb looked at him, his head shaking from side to side.

"Listen," said Whistler, "women ain't much on looking, but put it in their *hand* . . ." he nodded his head, ". . . they'll cream in their jeans every time. *Feeling* is something else. Besides," he said, "It's bassackwards to what they're expecting. What they're expecting is that you'll be trying to get the old finger up the tube. Turning it around on them like that throws the shit out of them."

"I'll be goddamned," said Feeb. "You mean put it in her *hand?*"

"Feeb," said Whistler, "I'm telling you about the golden leg-spreader. The pussyville express. Get it out and lay her hand on it. You won't know what hit your ass."

"I be goddamned," said Feeb.

Whistler never did say specifically that Corinne Feliciano was going to respond like that, but the way Feeb figured it, gash was gash. And the part about women liking to feel more than look had a scientific ring to him.

So that's what he tried.

It took a long time to get Corinne's hand pried off, even with three of them working on her. Feeb wasn't moving at all, just sitting there on the backseat of Jack's DeSoto, with his eyes rolled back and his fingernails dug into the upholstery. But the moans he was letting out put everybody's nerves on edge and slowed down the work. Corinne never made a sound, just sat there staring straight ahead while they peeled her fingers loose one at a time.

"I thought we were going to have to wait for the sun to go down to get her to turn loose," said Jack, on the way to the hospital. "Or cut off her head like a snapping turtle."

"She sure had a grip on her," said Whistler. "For such a little girl."

The place where she had been hanging on was mashed and ropy-looking, but the other end was all swollen up like a balloon, and about the shade of purple of a damson plum. With Feeb holding it in his hand to protect it, it looked like a ball-ended watch fob.

"I hate to tell you, old buddy," said Whistler, with a sad note in his voice, "but packing that thing in a twat is going to be like trying to stuff a wet noodle up a cat's ass."

"You asshole," said Feeb. "You asshole." Over and over.

When they took him into the emergency room at Chatham General, the nurse took one look and fell down on the floor laughing. Then the doctor came in, and she pointed at it with her finger. "Look at his weewee," she said. When he saw it, he tried to look serious for a minute, then he fell down laughing, too.

Feeb stood there holding it in both hands like it was a baby bird, saying, "Motherfuckermotherfuckermotherfucker." Until finally Jack and Whistler couldn't take it anymore, and they fell down on the floor laughing, too.

"It's ruined," said Feeb, sadly.

When he was through laughing, the doctor wiped his eyes and got up off the floor to examine him. But there wasn't much he could do except reassure him that it would probably be all right.

"*Probably?*" said Feeb.

"Listen," said the doctor. "It may *look* a little funny. You never can tell. Maybe you'll be in demand. Women go for unusual things." He reached out to touch it.

"Keep your hands to yourself," said Feeb.

Afterward, Jack and Whistler took him to Our House, a drive-in at the corner of Skidaway and Victory Drive that specialized in elaborate desserts, and bought him a hot fudge sundae with a sparkler in it.

Jack didn't see Mary again until he came home for the summer, after school was out. But he wrote her every day, and thought about her all the time, elaborating his original vision of her and making it more and more refined. What he saw when he thought about her was just her face, framed in a glowing yellow light, with everything soft and hazy around the edges.

There was a chart in the biology class, which was in the form of a snaky tree, showing the divisions of the animal kingdom. At night, Jack would have a picture of the tree in his head, and it was like he would travel up it, starting at the base, where the little animals were that didn't have any shape to them. Then he would drift past the branches holding the seashells and the fish, and the reptiles and birds. On up, until he passed the branch with a man and a woman, holding their hands to cover themselves. Then he would drift on up past the highest branches, and there would be Mary. Very delicate and white, with a long dress on, and a light behind her. She floated up there as fragile and moony as the ornament that goes on top of the tree at Christmas.

Then he would go to sleep and dream about the sharks.

Mackey he didn't think about anymore at all. She would certainly have been down there in the branches if he had seen her in the tree. For him, she had never been an idea anyway—not something to come into his head and stick there for long hours after the lights were out at night. Mackey was too available for that. Though there had always been a good bit of tenderness in the way he'd felt about her—as there always was in his dealings with women. Jack didn't feel like he was writing her off. They had been partners and friends, but that was as far as it went.

If Mary represented woman on the spiritual side, then Mackey would have to represent woman in the body. And the way to her heart was straight up her leg.

Well, that's an oversimplification, and doesn't do her real justice. Mackey was smart, and truly kind to other people, and she had a lot of sensitivity for anyone who was hurting or sad or weak or dumb. There were a lot of ways to get into Mackey Brood's heart. But that physical yearning of hers was a big part of what she was, and the thing that people remembered about her—especially the boys that she went out with.

Maybe she got it from her mother—a trait that ran in the family, at least on the female side. What Mackey really wanted was a baby, not a man. Something growing inside her and filling her up. The motion of intercourse was just the reverse of what she really had in mind. But it was the next best thing, and the sensation was at least taking place in the right location. So she put in time doing it until the real thing would come along and swell her up with a new life.

Her preference was for Jack, for old time's sake as much as anything else, though she loved him, too, as well as she could love any man for himself and not for what he could put into her. But her real devotion was not to any one man, it was to something in herself, and when Jack wasn't available, she would take the next best thing—or the next. She wasn't one to pay much attention to details finally.

The Broods lived on Waldburg Street, in the 400 block, two blocks away from the Curran house. Mackey was the sixth child in a family of ten, the fifth girl. Mr. and Mrs. Brood both had to work to keep food on the table and a roof over their heads, except for the times when Mrs. Brood was coming to the end of a pregnancy and right after. Then, of course, she had to stay at home.

Mrs. Brood liked having children. At least that was the way she felt about the first eight. Toward the end she started to give out on the inside, and the ninth and tenth weren't so pleasant. Mr. Brood never was that thrilled about it, but his attitude was more statistical than hers was, and he didn't come in on the good side of it. Even from the first, they were more of an obligation than a joy to him. And as they accumulated and got more and more underfoot, they finally depressed him.

Maybe he just stopped dropping the seed into his wife, or lost the power to do it out of sheer dejection. At any rate, she went a year and two months without getting pregnant in 1934 and 1935, and the break in the rhythm seemed to do her in. The inside machinery began to break down, starting to sputter and miss. Then it went bad altogether, and had to come out in the summer of 1936. Whatever it was, she was never the same afterward. She even lost her interest in the children.

She never had kept up with them once the connection between their bodies had been broken. In the past that had been a matter of necessity. There was always another one coming along to take the place of the one that was falling away. But when she pulled the last one off her breast and set it down to go it alone with the other nine, there was nothing on the way to fill up the empty place. So she just lost herself in her work with the bundling machine out at the Union Bag, going off with her husband, and leaving the housekeeping to Arlene, who was the oldest. After her operation, little things gave her the jitters and made her weepy. The children got on her nerves even more than they did her husband, because she didn't know them anymore.

Mackey was half a year younger than Jack, and a year behind him in school. She was the girl in the gang through the last years of grade school, and the subject of Jack's first unclean thoughts. As he was of hers.

She made him his first proposition when they were nine. "I'll show you mine," she said, "if you'll show me yours." So they went out to the garage and she gave him the first clear shot of it he'd ever had. Then Feeb and Dendron got in on it, as members of the club. But only briefly. Dendron wasn't especially interested, and Feeb was so greasy about it that Jack got mad and wouldn't let him come back. Mackey was more interested than Jack, but they were both too young for anything to come of it. For the next four years there were just periodic sessions when they would go out to the garage and peep back and forth at each other. It wasn't until the summer of 1942 that they took the big step. Afterward, Mackey began to think what it would be like to have a baby growing inside her. Once it came up, she didn't think about much of anything else.

The Brood house was a wonderful place for that kind of thing, since Mr. and Mrs. Brood were away during the day, working at the Union Bag. And there was always so much confusion because of the mob of children that it was easy for Mackey and Jack to sneak off to the attic and explore each other's secret places in the dim orange light from the slatted ventilators in the peaks of the end walls, with the muffled sounds of the children below them drifting up the stairwell, and pigeons cooing under the eaves outside.

Jack tried to talk to her and tell her that he loved her, which he thought was an important point. But Mackey was absorbed with the way she was beginning to feel inside. It was the only thing she could talk about, and she never heard Jack at all.

"It makes me want to fill up. I wish you could crawl inside."

Jack didn't like that kind of talk. "It's like we were married," he said, trying to cut her off.

She looked at him, not even trying to understand. "I could take up the whole house. Everybody. They would come in and I could hold them all."

Jack didn't say anything.

"I love it," she said. "I love it. I love it." Hugging herself.

The sensations that she felt when they were together were only the shadow of something else. And the something else was what she wanted. When she was by herself, she felt so empty she could hardly stand it. Marriage had nothing to do with it, no more than storybook love.

Eventually it depressed Jack that she never understood what he was talking about and was so taken up with the things that were going on inside of her, which he couldn't participate in. When he tried to talk to her about love, which wasn't so private and could have included him, she didn't understand him at all.

Mary Odell was too ethereal to be sexy—at least most people wouldn't have thought of her that way. She was not only small, but frail, with the kind of face that would likely turn up on a bishop's Christmas card. She reminded Jack of the bride on a wedding cake, delicate as porcelain, and always fully clothed as her natural state —with only a dainty foot or hand showing at the most.

When the pressure in him built up to an unbearable point, Jack would drop around to see Mackey Brood. She was always glad to see him, and didn't fail to take him in. Nor did she take it unkindly that she was not much more than a pressure relief valve for him. To a large extent, that's what he was for her, too. Though she would have liked to have him all the time, if she'd had her choice in the matter.

Between Jack and Mary just about nothing physical ever took place—only some very chaste kisses.

The first time he saw her was on the beach at Tybee. There was a northeast wind coming off the ocean, and she was all bundled up in sweaters and a muffler and one of the long skirts the girls were wearing just after the war. But she had taken off her shoes to walk on the beach, and the sight of her small white foot, half-buried in the sand, stirred him more than the sight of Mackey's whole brown body had in the attic of the house on Waldburg Street.

From the beginning he found it hard to believe how fragile and delicate she was, and her shyness spoke to him in a sweet, whispering way.

"Are you from Savannah?" Her voice was low and faint, and he had to lean down to catch the words because of the wind.

"Yes," he said. "I go to school at St. Francis."

She looked at him.

"That's in New Orleans," he said. For him, her face had the beauty of holiness.

He saw her again that night, and they walked on the beach in the wind, his sweater draped over her shoulders and wrapping her around like a cape. Then they went up into a hollow in the dunes, out of the wind, to lie on their backs in the sand and look up at the stars. He spoke the word "love" to her, saying it time after time, to show what it meant to him. She didn't talk, lying there beside him on the side of the dune, but he knew that she was listening to him and understood the things that he said, the words that carried him over to her in the dark.

Walking back to the house on the beach, they saw the lights of a ship going out of the channel in Calibogue Sound. They hadn't touched up to then. But after they saw the ship, he took her hand and held it the rest of the way back to the house.

And that was the way it began.

Mary lived on Forty-first Street, between Price and East Broad, in a small house that was too new to have the style and character of the houses on Waldburg Street, but too old to be fashionable. Her mother was a small birdy woman with transparent skin, who was so self-effacing that Jack had to be careful when he was in the house to be sure that he didn't sit down on her. Mr. Odell had the look of an iron Indian—a tall, patrician man who wore gray suits and kept his tie on around the house. Mary was their only child and the apple of his eye.

"Curran's an Irish name, isn't it, young man?" Those were the first words he ever spoke to Jack, and there was a wariness in the way he spoke them that made it clear that he wasn't going to be happy, no matter what Jack answered.

"Yes, sir," said Jack. He wasn't afraid of Mr. Odell, but he wasn't comfortable around him either, because he wanted to please him.

"Are you Catholic?" said Mr. Odell.

"In a way," said Jack. He hadn't been to the cathedral in two years. Then he noticed the way Mr. Odell was looking at him. "Yes, sir," he said.

"We're Methodist," said Mr. Odell.

Mr. Odell wasn't particularly impressed when he found out that Jack played football, but he tried to talk to him about it.

"Baseball's my game," he said.

"Yes, sir," said Jack. "Baseball's a good game."

Jack knew he wasn't going to marry the family, but he wanted them to like him.

"You must come back again sometime," said Mr. Odell as Jack and Mary were leaving.

"Yes, sir," said Jack.

Then Mr. Odell took his watch out of his pocket and wound it. "Be in at eleven-thirty, Mary," he said.

When Jack went to see Mary after he left Dendron's, they drove out to the Triple-X drive-in on Victory Drive and sat in the car drinking Cokes. He told her about Horse Rooney, and the way he felt about him.

"I know," she said. "You hate to let go of something high up like that."

"Yes," said Jack. "I remember the way I felt about Horse. It's as clear as the day I saw him the first time."

"Sometimes you don't want to be the best man, I guess," she said.

"I wouldn't want to beat my father at anything," he said. "It would be the same way."

For a while they didn't say anything.

"Do you like football?" she said.

"I like the game. I like it when the team is working together."

"A girl doesn't have to compete the same way," she said. "We're supposed to get used to letting things happen. There's so much we can't do anything about."

"You have things to get over, too, I guess."

"I wish I could just knock heads like you do," she said. "In a way I do. It's so simple and direct."

Jack almost laughed at the idea of Mary knocking heads. "You're saying that because you don't have to do it," he said.

"Neither do you."

"I make myself do it?"

"In a way you do."

"That's what a man is, Mary."

"But you feel bad about it sometimes?"

"Yes," he said. There was a yellow neon sign behind her, framing her hair. "You do what you have to do. You don't like all of it."

She looked at him for a long time. "I love you, Jack Curran," she said.

"Because I do what I have to do?"

"Because I can trust you."

16

On, On, Big Green

THE TEAM CAME OUT of the alumni game in pretty good shape, without any broken bones or sprains, and with their spirit top-notch. Feeb was the only one to complain, first claiming he had a charley horse, then a pulled muscle in his neck. But even he didn't carry on the way he usually did when a game was coming up. All in all, they seemed to be going into the season in just about the right frame of mind.

"As long as we don't peak too early and slide off for the game," said Chicken, who was a born worrier.

The schedule wasn't too bad—with the hardest teams coming on at the middle of the season. The first game was with Richmond Academy of Augusta, but the game would be played in Savannah, and it wasn't the toughest school on the schedule by a long shot.

The Cavaliers had finished third in the league the year before, but had lost about half of their first team after graduation. Jimmy Dunn, the quarterback, and Danny Reese, the right half, were back from the 1946 team, along with Harper and Johnston the ends, and Stude, a tackle. In addition, they also had a left halfback named David Quill who would be starting for the first time. The sportswriters were all giving Quill the kind of thumb-in-the-dike treatment that they like to unload now and then, whenever a good little man comes along, to remind everybody about the character-building aspects of the game. They were calling him "Little David" and "the Giant Killer" and things like that, with plenty of quotations from the Bible and Grantland Rice sprinkled in. Quill weighed 140 pounds—which wasn't all that small for a high school halfback in 1947. Whistler Whitfield only weighed 150.

But it was the beginning of the season, and they were looking for things to write about.

From Coach Garfield's point of view, the bad thing about Richmond Academy was that they were a passing team. He had wanted Boniface to go up against a running offense the first time out, because of Jack.

"You can't have everything," he said.

Beginning on Wednesday, Jack started to point out the importance of good, hard knocking at the very beginning of the game.

"We've got to play the whole four quarters," he said. "And a good team won't fold up on you at the end anyway. But it won't hurt anything to set them on their cans right to start with." He looked at Feeb. "How much does the right tackle weigh?"

Feeb looked around at the rest of the players, then at Jack. "A hundred and ninety," he said.

"Program weight?"

"Yes," said Feeb. "That's what the newspapers said."

"That means a hundred and eighty. Maybe a hundred and seventy-five. You'll have fifty pounds on him."

Feeb seesawed his hand back and forth. "Forty," he said.

"You've got to set him on his can the first time off the line."

Feeb rubbed his leg.

"How's your leg?"

"A little stiff," said Feeb. He rubbed his neck. "It's my neck really hurts."

Jack looked at him. "I don't want you to fuck around, Feeb. I know you can't play the whole game. I'm asking you to hit the son of a bitch the first time across."

Feeb made a whiny face.

"What was the score last year?"

Nobody said anything. At last Bo Hoerner spoke up. "They had a great team, man," he said.

"They finished third," said Jack.

"They had the team to make it," said Bo. "They lost second place on a tie."

"I know they beat you," said Jack. "I just don't remember how bad. I don't remember what the score was."

"Twenty-eight to six." Ducker said it, speaking very low.

"Okay," said Jack. "We're going to turn that around."

There was silence. "Dunn's a good quarterback," said Ducker. "He was throwing to Harper and Johnston last year, too."

"Is he as good as Aaron?" said Jack.

Ducker looked at Aaron. "Shit no," he said.

"So we'll have to stop Dunn," said Jack.

Ducker thought a minute. "I fucking guess we will," he said.

"What'd he say?" said Frog.

"He said we'd have to stop Dunn," said Chicken. Then he turned to the players. "That goes double for me," he said.

Richmond Academy won the toss and elected to receive. Whistler got off a clean kick that Quill took inside his 5-yard line. He was fast all right, and he liked to jitterbug around a lot, but he didn't want anybody to get their hands on him, so he stepped out of bounds on purpose at the 25-yard line, just in front of Flasher and Chippy Depeau.

Jack called a defensive huddle.

"He's going to pass," he said.

"How can you tell?" said Dimmy.

"That's the way I feel," said Jack.

"Okay," said Ducker.

"Depeau," said Jack. Chippy Depeau played the middle of the line on the five-three defense. "You reach over and pull the center out as soon as he hikes the ball. Me and Hoy and Camack will shoot the hole. Feeb, you and Bo keep the guards from closing it up on us." He looked at Dimmy. "Are you listening, Camack?"

"What?" said Dimmy.

"We'll get Dunn," said Jack. "Just get through the hole and head for Dunn."

"Head for Dunn," said Dimmy.

They spread out on the line and the Richmond Academy center came up over the ball.

All three of them got through the hole, but Jack was the quickest, and he was the one that nailed him. Dunn was moving very gracefully and taking his time—like the whole thing was a foregone conclusion, or a drill of some kind. Jack caught up with him just as he turned around to deliver the ball, and he looked very surprised, then disappointed, when Jack drove in under his arm and cartwheeled him up in the air. He went straight up, did a slow turn end for end, with his arms and legs sticking out like the spokes of a wheel, then came down head first with a cracking sound on the 14-yard line. It was a hell of a jolt, but he managed to hang on to the ball. Jack reached down and gave him a hand to help him up.

"Fi-fi . . . fi-fi . . . fifty-five," he said, reading the number off Jack's jersey.

The Richmond team all looked at Jack sideways with their heads hanging down as they walked back to huddle on the 4-yard line. The longest look came from Quill, who was sucking his lips in and out and muttering under his breath.

"I don't think they took it serious," said Jack. "They're going to try it again." He looked at Chippy. "Pull him out of there again, Depeau," he said.

"How can you tell if it's a pass?" said Depeau.

"Start counting when they huddle," said Jack. "If you get to twenty, it's going to be a pass."

"What if it ain't?" said Ducker.

"Watch for Quill on a screen."

Dimmy squinted at the Richmond Academy huddle. "Quill," he said.

"Dunn," said Jack. "And, Hoy," he said, "you and Camack go in and take him. I'll stay back for the screen."

"Head for Dunn," said Dimmy, clapping his hands.

"And, Hoy?"

"Yes?"

"Try to give Quill a tap while you're in there. I don't think he really wants to play."

Camack caught Dunn by the jersey on the 6-yard line and slammed him down on the ground like a bad poker hand. Ducker veered off so he could get at Quill, who was down in his blocking stance with his elbows up, looking like a photograph out of a book on how to play football. Ducker went into him like a freight train going into a tunnel, and he almost came out on the other side.

Both Quill and Dunn got up slowly. But they got up.

Jack looked at the down marker. "I'd get it out of there if it was me," he said. "Did the kicker play last year?"

"Who's the kicker?" said Ducker.

"Watch the center's head for a quick kick. If he puts it down, pull him out of there."

Ducker, Dimmy, and Jack all got into the backfield, but it was Frog who blocked the kick, taking one of his Nijinsky leaps that put him eleven feet up in the air right in front of the ball. It hit him in the chest with a big splat that shook some of the stuffing out of his helmet. But it wasn't as hard as one of Aaron's bullets, and he caught it on the ricochet, coming down with it in the end zone.

"Is this the right end of the field?" he said, looking at Jack.

"Yes," said Jack.

"Then this is a touchdown?"

"That's what it is."

"I'll be goddamned," said Frog.

Whistler kicked the extra point, and Boniface led 7–0, with eleven minutes and nine seconds left to play in the quarter.

Nobody could believe it.

J.J. O'Brien was sitting on the Boniface bench, and when Frog scored the touchdown, he pulled out his checkbook and flashed off a check with the book braced on his knee.

"One hundred dollars to the man that brings me that ball," he said, waving the check over his head. "One hundred American dollars."

The whole Boniface team looked at him for a minute, then all of them got up and galloped down under the scoreboard behind the goal to wait for Whistler's kick to come down so they could catch it. But the referees didn't like the way it looked, and they hustled them out, threatening to hold up the game until they all went back to the bench and sat down.

"That's all right, boys," said J.J. "The offer stands till the end of the game." Then he lit a cigar and stuck the check in his lapel pocket, hanging it out where everybody could see it.

"What if we lose?" somebody asked him.

J.J. looked up and down the faces on the bench. "Who said that?" he said. Nobody spoke. "I'm a man of my word," he said. "Win, lose, or draw." Then he stuck the cigar back in his mouth and turned to watch the Boniface team coming down the field.

Boniface kicked off to Richmond again, then held for three downs, and Whistler took the kick on his own 35 and ran it back to the 50.

Somebody from Augusta must have thought that what was sauce for the goose would be sauce for the gander, because on the first play from scrimmage, their middle guard reached over and tried to pull Jack out of the line, the way Depeau had been doing to them. It was a bad move, because Jack took him on his shoulder and drove him into both linebackers, who were trying to get in through the hole he was supposed to be making. It jammed the whole defensive center of their line. While that was happening, Dimmy went by with the ball, pushing the guard ahead of him to the 41-yard line.

Aaron called Dimmy up the middle four more times to the 25. Then he gave Whistler the ball and sent him off the right side on a quick-opening play. There wasn't a Richmond Academy player standing at the line of scrimmage by the time Whistler got there, but he didn't get to see it, because he was running with his eyes closed, a habit he'd developed the year before. When he opened them, he was in the secondary, and Cowboy McGrath was putting his shoulder into Quill, just where the little man's jersey tucked into his pants. Quill's helmet was spinning up in the air like a big white poker chip, and the only thing between Whistler and the goal line was Dunn—who played safety.

Whistler took off, making big happy leaps. When he got to Dunn, he gave him his hip four times, and took it away five, then shot by him on the right-hand side. Dunn just fell down flat on the football field and rolled over on his back with his arms reaching up into the air. When Whistler went over the goal line he was practically walking. He stopped under the goalposts and jumped up and down a couple of times, then he touched the ball to the ground, very slow and dainty, with his leg pointing out behind him.

"Number two," he said.

By the end of the first quarter, Jack had collected a whole catalog of little moves and gestures that told him what Richmond Academy had in mind when they were on offense. He had his eye on Dunn to begin with, and right away he noticed that he would swing his head right and left when he was going to hand the ball off to one of his backs. On a pass, he would just get down behind the center and stare straight ahead. Quill was telegraphing, too, rocking his head back into his shoulder pads when the ball was going to him. And Stude, the right tackle, made a limbering-up flourish with his elbow, getting into his stance when the run was coming his way. Jack passed the information on to the rest of the team, and told them to keep their eyes out for other giveaway signs like that.

Boniface scored 14 points a quarter until the last quarter, when they scored 20. By then, four of Richmond Academy's first-string line were out of the game, as was Quill, and the coach was having to walk up and down the bench and hunt for the substitutes, who wouldn't answer when he called their names.

Whistler missed the last extra point.

"Sixty-two to nothing." Bo Hoerner kept saying it over and over. "Jesus H. Christ!"

"We took them by surprise," said Jack. "They thought they were playing us last year."

"We beat the shit out of them is what we did," said Ducker. "Sheee—it!"

"We didn't do bad for the first game," said Jack. "We got nine more to go."

"Bring on the motherfuckers," said Feeb.

"Who?" said Dimmy.

Jack was too pessimistic. The Richmond Academy game was a preview of the season.

The second game was with Waycross. They played the game out

of Savannah, and the score was 31–6. They should have beaten them more, only they were coming down off the high after beating Richmond Academy so bad. Also the word had gone out on them, and Waycross was up for the game.

Then they played Valdosta in Savannah, beating them 7–0 with their defense. Valdosta was about to begin twenty years of winning seasons under Coach Wright Bazemore, but they hadn't quite gotten their feet planted yet. Bazemore was taking a professional attitude toward the game, and had sent an assistant over to Waycross to scout them.

After Valdosta, there were three games on the road in the month of October—Decatur, which was just outside of Atlanta, on the tenth, Columbus on the seventeenth, and Bibb High of Macon on the twenty-fourth. They won all three of them—20–14, 38–6, and 14–13.

The scores made it look like Bibb had the best of the three teams, which they didn't. And Boniface ought to have beaten them worse than they did, only they were having to play against the officials that night. By the end of the game, Boniface had drawn over two hundred yards in penalties, with three touchdowns called back, and J.J. O'Brien was cooling his heels in the Bibb County jail for breaking the head lineman's sternum with his cane.

The team was still steamed up about it the next week when Kose High came up to play them in Savannah. Before the first quarter was over, the first team had run up three touchdowns, and Chicken was afraid they were going to hurt themselves, so he pulled them out to let them cool off. Then he cleared the bench for the rest of the game, giving everybody on the squad enough playing time to get a letter out of it for the season.

The way Boniface was rushing around made the Kose team nervous at first. Not because they were expecting to win, which they weren't, but because they couldn't keep up with it. The Kose players had a kind of built-in long view of the game, and were not inclined to get very personally involved, since their team had lost the last fifty-four games in a row. And as soon as the first team was taken out and the pace slowed down, they seemed to get about as big a kick out of the touchdowns Boniface was scoring as the

Boniface team itself did. Then the pace slowed down some more, and they began to get nervous again.

In the second half, the third-team quarterback came in and started throwing a lot of incomplete passes, so that there were whole series of downs when the clock didn't seem to be moving at all. The more the game dragged on, the more nervous the Kose players got. They were counting on it being over by ten o'clock.

The only reason Kose had been able to field a football team in the first place was that the coach had emphasized the broadening aspects of the travel involved, with trips to places like Pembroke, and Darien, and Willie-by-the-Run to look forward to. As far as the sport of it was concerned, the boys on the team would rather have gone down into the Dorchester Swamp to hunt alligators and water moccasins. But most of them had never been more than five miles from home, so taking the trips was something else again. Just getting a Savannah team on the schedule had doubled the size of the squad. Also the coach had sweetened the deal with a personal promise that after the game he would take all of them down to the Shalimar miniature golf course, then buy them a sundae with a sparkler in it at the Our House drive-in. The trip to Savannah was the high point of the season, and playing the game with Boniface was just the price they had to pay for it.

It was too high a price for the spectators who had come up with them to see the game. They all went out at the half and didn't come back. And the band sneaked off at the end of the third quarter.

It was tough on the players, because the Shalimar was just down Victory Drive from the stadium, and every now and then they could hear the bass drum beating and a trumpet run coming in over the back of the stands. The cheerleaders hung on until the middle of the fourth quarter. Then the Boniface quarterback threw four incomplete passes in a row, and they got up and left, too, after giving a locomotive for the Alligators.

It was eleven-fifteen when the whistle blew ending the game, and all of the Kose players who weren't actually on the field were halfway out of the stadium when it blew. The score was 85–0, but they couldn't have cared less. It was the hour they were worried about, not the score. All of them ran out of the stadium with their uniforms on, following the sound of the drum down Victory Drive, hoping they would get to the Shalimar before it closed.

For the Tattnall game, the team went up to Atlanta on the *Nancy Hanks*. During the ride, Jack could feel their spirits sinking, but he didn't know what was causing it, so he didn't know what to do about it. By the time the train pulled into the Central Station at one o'clock, the whole car was foggy with gloom.

Playing in Atlanta. That's what was doing it. The old Atlanta worm was into the apple, and the six-hour train ride gave them plenty of time to chew on it.

Jack tried to talk some backbone into them, but it didn't do any good, and Tattnall ran up a quick two-touchdown lead right away. They only put 12 points on the board, because their kicker got the holder's hand on the first try, making him gun-shy, so that he dropped the pass from center on the second one.

Having played in New Orleans, where there was no Atlanta myth, Jack could see what a sorry team Tattnall had. "They're shitty," he said. "I'm telling you—shitty."

But his teammates hadn't played in New Orleans, and they couldn't see it the way he did. Finally, the frustration took him out of himself, and with two minutes to go in the first quarter, he did something he had never done before. He took a swing at the Tattnall fullback when the fullback came up from the side and laid a block on him that carried him out of the play. The referee saw it, and threw him out of the game.

The whole Boniface team stood watching him walk off the field like he was the last messenger out of the fort, and the Indians were closing in. Feeb started to walk off with him, but Ducker grabbed him by the neck of his jersey and pulled him back. "We can do it without him," he said.

Everybody looked at him.

"Let's win it for Curran," said Bo Hoerner.

"Kiss my ass, Hoerner," said Feeb.

Lulu and Ducker talked it up as much as they could, and they hustled enough to keep Tattnall from scoring again, but they couldn't get up the punch to put one over themselves.

Then, just before the half ended, Aaron sent Whistler off tackle to the right on a lucky call that caught the defense moving to the left. Whistler found himself in the clear, and ran sixty-five yards for a touchdown just as the half ended. With the extra point, the score was 12–7.

Whistler came into the locker room at the half and threw his helmet against the wall. "They ain't worth a goddamn shit," he said.

"That's what I've been telling you," said Jack.

Whistler looked at him. "You're right," he said. "They ain't worth a goddamn shit." He looked around the locker room. "They ain't worth a goddamn *shit*," he said, raising his voice.

The second half they went out and scored 49 points, just to prove they could play with Curran out of the game. It was the best two quarters they had all year.

The Brunswick game was easy, though not for Delmus Lamott. All deals were off, and he had to move around a lot more than he was accustomed to doing. Under the circumstances, James Farney couldn't plug all the holes for him—not with the other team really playing he couldn't. Well, not *all* the other team. Feeb worked out his agreement right off, then he kept trying to negotiate with Jack in the huddles, coming in with a new offer after every play. But finally Jack told him flat out to keep his mouth shut, and Feeb had to go back to Delmus with the sad news.

Delmus took it hard, but it depressed Feeb, too. "He's only a goddamn rich pussy," he said to Jack. "You got to be a fucking hard rock."

It was an off night for Jack, but the team had found out they were able to go it without him, and they took up the slack, winning the game 28–0—though they should have won by twice the score.

At the end of the first nine games, Boniface had a record that made it look like J.J.'s letter to the Pope had gotten through. The cheerleaders painted a big poster and put it on the trophy case in the front hall. It was green on a white background, with shamrocks in the corners, and it was a very impressive sight.

    Sep. 19—Richmond Academy—62–0
    Sep. 26—Waycross—31–6
    Oct 3—Valdosta—7–0

Oct. 10—Decatur—20–14
Oct. 17—Columbus—38–6
Oct. 24—Bibb—14–13
Oct. 31—Kose—85–0
Nov. 7—Tattnall—56–12
Nov. 14—Glenn Academy—28–0
Nov. 27—COLD TURKEY FOR OGLETHORPE

The cheerleaders didn't put the statistics on the poster, but those were as impressive as the scores. Boniface had averaged 423 yards a game on offense—239 yards passing (which was a new school record), and 184 yards rushing (which wasn't quite as good as the Horse Rooney team). It was the highest total offense in the history of the school.

But the season wasn't over yet.

In fact, looked at from a certain point of view, even with 90 percent of their games already played, the real season was still ahead of them. The alumni and J.J. were delirious about the way the team had done up to then, all right, but the glory of the whole season would be wiped out if they lost to the Big Blue of Oglethorpe in the Thanksgiving Day game. That was the one that counted.

On Saturday afternoon before Thanksgiving, Jack and Feeb had agreed to meet downtown and go to a movie. They were only doing light work at practice, and the extra time between games made them edgy. Besides, there was a Betty Grable musical on at the Lucas, and Feeb liked Betty Grable almost as much as he liked hot fudge sundaes. Jack went in early to shoot a couple of games of pool in Wooten's pool hall on Duke Street, to get up some money for the tickets.

Striper Wooten did a lot of bookmaking on athletic events and horse races, and most of the football players from Boniface spent some time there off and on, especially during the season, when Striper was particularly friendly. He liked to have them around then, because he thought it was good for the betting, and he made them feel welcome, putting up autographed pictures of them behind the counter and letting them shoot a free game of pool now and then. Jack stroked a pretty good cue when he was feeling right, and that afternoon he took three in a row from Lulu

Demarco, who was not a bad player himself. He won enough to pay their way into the show and to buy them a couple of beers afterward.

Wooten's was just at the corner of Reynolds Square, and the Lucas Theater was down the street at the corner of Abercorn. It was a warm day, and the sun was out, so Jack went into the square to sit down on a bench and wait for Feeb. There was a little man in a gray suit, with a hat on, and Jack started up a park-bench conversation with him.

"Nice day," he said.

The man looked at him a minute, then wet his lips with his tongue. "Little dry," he said.

"The rain comes earlier in the fall," said Jack.

"I like about seventy-five percent," said the man. "Humidity," he added. "I'm talking about the humidity."

"I see," said Jack.

"Seventy or seventy-five," said the man. He wet his lips again as if he were tasting something. "About forty-five today," he said.

"You mean it makes you uncomfortable?" said Jack.

"No," said the man. "You can't get down for the low notes when you're too dried out."

Jack looked at him.

"Whistling," said the man. "I'm talking about whistling." He pursed his lips and gave a little trill.

"I see," said Jack. For a minute neither one of them said anything. "You live here?" said Jack.

"I'm staying at the Dobbs House," said the man. The Dobbs House was an old commercial hotel on the Bryan Street side of the square. "Just passing through."

"I see," said Jack. "You a salesman?"

"I'm retired," said the man. "Just moving around."

"Whistling around?" said Jack, and laughed.

"Yes," said the man. He didn't laugh. "I was down in Florida last month. Orlando . . . St. Pete . . . Jacksonville . . . *too much* humidity in Florida. St. Augustine wasn't bad. About sixty. Only it's right on the beach. The wind dries you out."

"You mean you whistle for a living?"

"No," said the man. "I told you. I'm retired."

"You mean you do it for a hobby?" said Jack. "Something like that?"

The man looked at him. "I never thought of it as a hobby," he said. "Maybe you could call it that."

"And you travel *around* doing it?"

"Yes," said the man.

"You mean you don't do anything else?"

"My wife died four years ago. We lived in Akron, Ohio, but I never did like it. Too hot in the summer and cold in the winter." He stopped and wet his lips. "We lived there thirty-eight years. I couldn't stand the goddamned place."

"What about the humidity?" said Jack.

"Rotten," said the man. "Just rotten."

While they were talking, Feeb came up, and Jack told him about the man.

"You mean you do it for a living?" he said.

"No," said the man, "I'm retired."

"It's a hobby," said Jack.

"And you travel *around* to do it?" said Feeb.

"Some places are better than others. We went to Phoenix, Arizona, once. That was when my wife was still alive. Phoenix is the worst place I was ever in for whistling. You wouldn't *believe* the humidity in Phoenix." He shook his head.

"Could we hear you?" said Jack.

"Sure," said the man. "What would you like to hear?"

"How about 'Heartaches'?" said Jack. Elmo Tanner's record had been popular the winter before. It was the only whistling music Jack could think of.

The man nodded. "Tanner don't have the range I've got," he said. "It's a good tune, though." He ran his tongue over his lips to wet them. "It's a little dry today," he said.

He whistled "Heartaches" for them, but without the background music it didn't sound as good as Elmo Tanner.

"That's pretty good," said Jack.

"You mean you just travel around looking for places to *whistle?*" said Feeb. "That's *all* you do?"

"I'm retired," said the man.

"I know that," said Feeb, "but goddamn."

"I like to whistle," said the man.

Feeb looked at Jack, then back at the man. "That's crazy," he said.

"It sounded good," said Jack.

"It's not a good day for it," said the man. "The air's a little too dry."

"Well," said Jack. Feeb looked exasperated.

"I'm going up to Wilmington, North Carolina, tomorrow," said the man. "I figure it ought to be just about right this time of the year."

"Savannah's too dry?" said Jack.

"I thought it would be about right, but it's a little too far from the ocean," said the man. "Wilmington's not quite so far. And the river is bigger." He wet his lips. "I might try San Francisco if Wilmington don't work out."

"Come on," said Feeb. "It's time for the movie."

"Thank you for letting us hear you whistle," said Jack.

"That's all right," said the man. He did a rapid version of "Good-night Ladies," with trills. It sounded as good as Elmo Tanner. "I like to try it out on people now and then."

"Come on," said Feeb.

On the way to the theater Feeb got more and more worked up about the man traveling around the country whistling.

"That's the craziest fucking thing I ever heard."

"He *likes* to do it," said Jack. "What difference does it make?"

"It's crazy, man. Crazy," said Feeb. "All he does is whistle. That's the craziest fucking thing I ever heard."

"I think it's pretty good, myself," said Jack. "He's doing what he likes to do."

17

The Shadow Twin

WHAT WITH THE STORIES and pictures in the newspapers, and the talk going around town, Jack got to be quite a celebrity in Savannah. The *Morning News* even went to the expense of getting an out-of-town artist to do a drawing of him, which they ran in a three-column box in the sports section on Sunday. It was a little like the ones that Willard Mullins used to do, only the style was pinched, with finer lines and less detail. The picture showed Jack head-on, down in his stance, about to center the ball. His helmet was off, so the artist could get the likeness of the face. In the background were smaller figures, showing number 55 tackling a runner and throwing a block. Three lines of eight-point type ran across the bottom of the box.

> Jack Curran: 6 ft. 4 in. and 240 lbs. of DYNAMITE! Number 55 is the keystone of the Boniface line, the nemesis of all opposing backs, and the despair of Coach Garfield's rivals.

Above the smaller figures in the background were balloons with "Not THIS Way!" and "HOLD It!" coming from Jack, and "OOF!" and "OW!" coming from the opposing players.

After every home game, droves of grade school boys would run onto the field to touch him. Even grown men would stop him on the street and ask to shake his hand. But the biggest fan he had was George Bogger. And Jack never knew about it, even though they were next-door neighbors.

George didn't know Jack at all personally. But he could see him out of his bedroom window, and he heard about him over the radio. Based on what he could see and hear, he started to walk with Jack in his mind's eye, not going side by side with him as a friend or equal, but tagging along as an unspoken observer of the great deeds being done. Jack wasn't the substance and George the shadow; they were never close enough even for that. All of it was insubstantial and a figment of George's imagination. But in that dark and quiet place, what light there was fell on Jack.

Jack had always been a golden boy. He was not a good student, but his openness and his uncluttered ways, and most of all the air of healthiness about him made his teachers like him, at the same time it made them leave him alone. George was always furtive and distracted; his epilepsy had made him a special case one way or the other. For one thing, it made him pay attention to what went on inside. For him, the simplest problem had intricate ramifications that would turn him into himself and keep him brooding and absorbed for hours.

Mrs. Bogger was embarrassed about him, and sympathetic over the problem that his case presented for his teachers. The teachers themselves seemed to respond in one of two ways. Some resented him and were nervous—like Mrs. Cole, the one he had in the third grade. Every day she would ask him, "Do you think you'll have a fit today, George?" When she led the prayer at the beginning of class, she would always end with, "And please, God, don't let George have a fit today." Maybe it was the way she said it—her voice was very nasal—but the plea didn't work well at all. He averaged about one fit a week for all of that year. When he had them, the rest of the class would crowd around to watch, while Mrs. Cole ran for the principal.

Others were like his sixth-grade teacher, Mrs. Brandt, who wanted to smother him with attention—making him sit in the front row, and not letting him play with the other children at recess. Mrs. Brandt had a large heart, and was truly moved by George's plight, but, sad to say, her attitude was the hardest for him to cope with, and was the reason he refused to go back to school for the seventh grade. Mrs. Bogger didn't insist, since she was worn out with it by then anyway.

Mr. Bogger was a small natty man, who had never taken any interest in his children, and very little in his wife, but George felt more comfortable about him than he did his mother, because he was almost the only one who didn't call attention to him.

John Spark, the head of the highway department survey party that George worked for, had once asked him what his happiest memory was. George had been moping around, and John told him that the best way to cheer up was to think of something nice that had happened.

"Something golden out of the past" was the way he put it.

"When I was little?" said George.

"Yes," said John. "Anytime."

"Grandmother took me down to Tybee on the train for my birthday once," he said.

John looked at him, waiting for him to go on. "She just took you *once?*"

"Yes," said George. "She died."

"Well," said John. He looked like he was about to start moping himself.

"She bought me a corn dog," said George. He thought for a minute. "Mama didn't want me to have a birthday party because of the attacks," he said. "But I always remembered the time grandmama took me to Tybee on the train."

John didn't say anything else. Up till then, he hadn't known about George's childhood.

"That was when I was little," said George. "Now I like to listen to the radio." Talking about it cheered him up for the rest of the day.

It was over the radio that George first heard about Jack and how important he was.

The bungalows in Marshoaks all had the same floor plan, but to give variety and a little class to the subdivision, the contractor had flip-flopped the plan going down the street as he laid the foundations. Then, after the houses were built, he painted them in different pastel colors. The Reilleys' yellow house flipped to the right, and the Boggers' pink house flopped to the left, which put the bedroom ends next to each other, with George's just across the side yard from the one shared by Jack and Susy.

After George found out about Jack he watched the comings and goings over at the Reilleys' house. Between what he saw through the window and what he heard under the orange dial of the radio, he began to send his thoughts after Jack—like a spider spinning filaments out of itself, invisible lines that went out of his bedroom window to the Reilley house and beyond. In George's mind, he and Jack came to be bound together, and he began to have a dark and secret share in the life of the famous young man. It was a light in the dungeon—something like a social life for him.

Whatever time George was at home—which meant nights, Saturday afternoons, and Sundays—he spent in his bedroom with the door shut, coming out only to eat his meals, to tend to the crickets that he sold for fish bait, to pour lead rods to make pellets for his slingshot, or to go off on frog-hunting expeditions along the canals that ran out into the country behind Marshoaks. Most of the time he would lie listening to the radio, his head down at the foot of the bed and propped up so he could see what was going on out the window.

When he was having a bad time with the epilepsy, George would curl up on his bed with his back to the window, the radio on to soothe him. His doctor would change the medicine periodically, as each newly recommended one appeared in the journals, and some of them fogged him up very badly. Whether he took the medicine or not, he seemed to average about one *grand mal* seizure a week. But when he didn't take the medicine the seizures were worse.

He spent a lot of time listening to the radio, memorizing the commercials that came on most regularly. He did that as a pastime, and because he liked to do it. But he also did it to some extent to prove that his memory was good, and to encourage John Spark to teach him to run the surveying instruments. His best one was the Colorback commercial, which was intricate and involved, and a long one compared to the Pepsi-Cola and Cook-Kill kind, which he could pick up after listening only six or seven times. He was especially proud of being able to recite the Colorback commercial, but he had to know a person well, the way he knew John Spark, before he would recite it in public.

George was a rodman with the highway department—that was his title and pay grade. His job was pulling the chain, setting stakes, and cutting brush so John Spark could run the line with the transit. John was a kind man and sympathetic, and he would try to teach George how to set up the instruments—getting them level, with the legs firmly set—because he knew George wanted to learn. But just about the time George would start catching on to it, a seizure would come along and wipe him out, and the whole thing had to be learned over again. It took two or three days for his head to clear up, which left only a couple of days to relearn what he had forgotten before another fit would come along and wipe him out again. He couldn't get ahead on it. But John let him keep trying, though he was afraid to let George carry the instruments, for fear he would have a seizure while he was doing it and would let them fall and get broken. The instruments were checked out to John, and he was the one responsible if anything happened to them. So he would carry them himself, and then let George work along learning to set them up, because he could see how he felt about it.

George didn't want to be a rodman for the rest of his life. More because of the job itself than the money. The thing that was especially hard on him was having to watch the college boys—high school boys sometimes—who would come on with the survey party in the summertime. George would be the one to help them get used to the details of the job, knowing that his $145 a month was just $10 or $15 more than they would be making. By the end of the summer, they would know some things about the work better than George did himself, though not many of them could ever get on to throwing the chain as well as he could, or handling a machete. And, of course, none of them could call birds or shoot a slingshot like he did. But if school hadn't started up in the fall, George knew they would have moved out beyond him, and would have been giving him orders by the time next summer rolled around.

In June, July, and August John would usually give up trying to teach George and would concentrate on the college boys, so they could take part of the work off him. Besides, George's seizures were worse in the hot part of the year. So John saved the lessons for the cold times, when there were just the two of them.

In the meantime, George spent a lot of the time when he was home lying on the bed in his room, listening to the commercials on the radio and trying to memorize them.

As it got on into the fall, and the weather got cooler, the outside activity at the Reilley house slowed up a good bit. George could see them coming and going, but they weren't out there hanging around in the yard very much. So mostly he had to try to keep up with them inside the house, through the windows. He made a point of watching for Jack to leave on the Fridays before the games. Then, after he was gone, George would fiddle with the radio, moving around on the dial, trying to pick up out-of-town stations, until it was time for the game to come on.

He would listen to the game, being able to picture what Jack looked like in his uniform from the photographs in the sports section of the Saturday paper—though he didn't ever get a very clear idea of what a whole football game would have been, since he had never seen one. He thought it must be a little bit like baseball, and he had seen a baseball game once—part of one. His father had taken him out to see Savannah play Jacksonville, but it was hot in the stands, and George got too excited, and he had a fit. His father had to bring him home before the game was over, and he never took him to another one.

George didn't go out to Grayson Stadium while Jack was playing, because he wasn't sure how to go about buying a ticket, and he didn't know how much it would cost. Besides, he knew how to handle the radio, and was used to taking things in that way. If he had a fit, he would be in his own bedroom.

After the game was over, he would sit up for them to come home. First, Mr. and Mrs. Reilley and Susy, and then, much later, Jack himself. George would always make a point of trying to wait up until Jack came in—though that was hard on him, since the survey party worked on Saturday mornings, and he would have to get up early.

After the Reilleys came in and the lights went on, George would lie in his room in the darkness with his head at the foot of the bed, the radio on, watching to see what he could of the activity of the house through the lighted windows. Most of the time all that he could see was Susy, since the room that she shared with Jack was right across the way, and she never bothered to pull down the shades. Jack didn't observe training very well, and especially on weekends he would be late getting in. But even during the week he was often out later than George could keep himself awake. So most of the time he would be watching Susy moving around in the orange frame of the bedroom window.

After a while he began to take an interest in her, since she was the only one that he saw on a regular basis.

Susy was a healthy-looking girl—big like her mother, but blond, her hair close-cropped and curly. There wasn't anything unhealthy in the way George watched her. She was only nine years old, and he was curious more than anything else—having got into the habit of watching the Reilley house because of his connections with Jack. George's sex drive was pretty tepid in general, and he wasn't taken with children at all. Anything that might have been going on in the house would have caught his eye. Once in a while it would pass through George's mind that she was, after all, a girl. But she was also only a child, and the activity in itself was what interested him —the *situation* in the Reilley house—something out the window.

Susy never did much of anything to stir up his interest in her especially. Just little girl things. She would disappear out of the room, and the bathroom light would go on two or three times during the evening. The rest of the time she would be reading comic books, or talking to the doll that she took to bed with her at night. Sometimes she would bounce on the bed. And, once in a while, when Jack was at home, they would have a pillow fight— mostly her beating Jack over the head with the pillow until he would grab it away from her and toss her around over his head a time or two, then stick her in the bed and kiss her good night.

Sometimes George would think about them. How unconcerned they were. He felt almost that they were putting on a show for him, but he knew they didn't know that he was watching. For a couple of nights he left the light on in his room while he watched them, but they never noticed. So he turned it back out because it bothered him. He liked the room dark, with just the light from the radio dial as a warm place by the head of the bed. One way or the other, they didn't know he was there. He thought about that some, too, and resented it. But after a while he stopped thinking about it.

One night while he was lying on the bed watching Susy, she got up and began to dance around the room. She wore a lime green nightgown made out of some heavy material like flannel, with long sleeves. She wasn't a very graceful dancer—being big for her age and gawky—and she moved without much rhythm, but slowly, holding her arms over her head in a circle, and doing a lot of spins. As George watched her moving around inside the window, he raised his hand and pointed his finger—sighting along it and following her movements. It was an idle kind of gesture, which he made without thinking about it.

For a long time that went on. Every night she would do her dance, and George would sight his finger at her, following her movements. While he was aiming at her, pinning her down with the outstretched finger, he would recite commercials that he knew. "Pepsi-Cola hits the spot. . . . A twelve-ounce bottle, that's a lot. . . . Twice as much for a nickel, too. . . . Pepsi-Cola is the drink for you. . . ." Short things that he could get off without thinking about them—one right after the other.

Then one night a kind of inspiration struck him, and he got his slingshot off the dresser and used that to sight at her. He was very good with the slingshot, and he knew how much to overshoot her so the pellet would drop in just where he wanted it to.

In the beginning, he would just aim at her indiscriminately—at the moving green figure in the orange rectangle of the window. But as he kept it up, he became more and more careful and particular. For a while he would zero in on the white bow of the ribbon at the neck of her gown. Then he moved the point up, holding on a place just above her eyes when she was facing him, just below her ear when she turned the other way. He began to look forward to his game at night. He even resented it when Jack was at home and in the room. On those nights he wouldn't aim at Susy.

After a while he came to the point where neither his finger nor the slingshot seemed to be the thing to use. So on payday at the end of the month, he went downtown to the Kress store, and bought a Colt .45 cap pistol that had real cartridges which could be put into the cylinders. It cost him four dollars, but it looked exactly like the kind of gun that Gene Autry carried in the movies he had gone to see on Saturday as a child. He smuggled it into the house, so his mother wouldn't see it and ask him about it. Then he tied a loop of string to it and put it on a coat hanger under his good suit in the closet, where she wouldn't find it when she came in to clean up his room while he was away at work during the day. At night he would take it out and point it at Susy dancing in her bedroom across the side yard. He kept the bullets for it in the pocket of his suit coat, and would take them out at night and load the gun. Before he put the gun away, he would take the cartridges out of the cylinder and put them into the pocket of the coat. He never put the gun away with the bullets in it.

Coming home from work in the evenings, he passed a pawnshop. Since he passed it every day, he didn't pay much attention to it. It had a display of knives stuck into a piece of log, a lot of musical instruments, military patches, and insignia—a great many small items radiating out from the display of knives, which was the main thing in the window. One day he broke the blade of his Barlow carving on a marking stake. He had caught the blade of his knife in a knot, then twisted it and broken it off. Going home he stopped to look at the display of knives stuck in the log. Then he noticed a display of pistols at the back of the window—three or four of them on a board with pegs in it. The pistols hung by their barrels on the pegs.

He went into the store and the owner came up to him, a small, fat, bald man in a sweater, with dark hair over his ears.

"I need a knife," said George.

"You bet," said the man. "Knives I've got plenty of."

The man went to a display case with a hinged glass front. He unlocked it and raised the front. "How about this one?" he said. He lifted out a wicked looking switchblade with a pearl handle, touched the button, and the blade leaped out too fast for George to see it. It had a long, daggery blade, with cutting edges on both sides. For a moment the man held it with the blade pointed at

George's stomach. Then he turned it and held it out to him handle first.

George looked at it without making any motion to take it. Then he looked up at the man. "You got a Barlow?" he said.

"What?" said the man. He jiggled the knife, holding the tip of the blade and rocking the handle up and down.

"I don't need no sticker," said George. "I got to *use* it. What I want is a Barlow."

"You want a carving knife?" said the man. "I mean a knife for carving with?"

"Yes," said George. "Carving. General cutting. You know."

"I see," said the man. He put his hand over the blade and levered it closed. Before he put it back into the display case, he whipped around at George and sprung it open again. "Too fast to see," he said. George looked at the tip of the switchblade pointing at his stomach. "Feel that spring," said the man, holding the knife out to George.

He looked at the knife, but he didn't take it. "Yes," he said.

After he put back the switchblade, the man brought out a knife with twenty-two blades in it. Then he started opening the blades, explaining the use of each to George as he did so. George watched, saying yes to every blade. All of the blades couldn't be opened at one time because there were too many and they got in the way of each other. When he finished, there were about thirteen of them open—forks, corkscrews—there were six knife blades in there somewhere, though it was hard to find them because of all the other things. There was even a pair of toenail clippers in it.

"Yes," said George, after the man had cut a notch out of his belt with the toenail clippers to show him how strong they were. "What I wanted was a Barlow."

The man looked at him in a disgusted way and began closing the blades of the knife.

"You got one in the log in the window," said George.

"Let me show you this one," said the man, reaching for another knife in the case. "This one has twelve blades."

"I don't want twelve blades, mister," said George.

The man looked at him, then he looked down at the tongue of

his belt where he had cut out the notch. "I thought you were going to buy it," he said. "I wouldn't have cut up my belt, except I thought you were going to buy it."

George looked down at the belt.

"I ruined my belt," said the man.

"I didn't ask you to do it," said George.

The man looked up at George. "That was a perfectly good belt," he said.

George looked around the store. "I got to get home, mister," he said. "What I wanted was the Barlow knife."

For a moment the man looked at George, standing there with his hand propping up the front of the knife case, holding the twelve-bladed knife in the other. Then he put the knife down and lowered the glass front and locked it. "Show me the one it is you want," he said.

George moved up to the door and looked into the window. He couldn't see the knives too well from the back side, since they were placed to make the best showing to people passing by on the sidewalk. So he had to lean into the window. As he did, he brushed against the display of pistols at the back, knocking one off its peg. George flinched and pulled back out of the doorway. The man stepped up quickly, poking his head through the door.

"What did you do?" he said quickly. He picked up the pistol, dangling it by the butt between his thumb and forefinger. Then he took his handkerchief out of his pocket and lifted it back onto the peg. George watched him handling the gun. "It rusts where you touch it with your hands," said the man. He ran the handkerchief over the gun to take off the fingerprints. Then he reached into the window and got a Barlow knife out of the log. "Here," he said. He handed the knife to George, then closed the door to the window and locked it.

"That's a good Barlow," he said.

George closed the blade of the knife and laid it on the glass-topped counter. For a minute he looked at it lying there. Under the glass of the counter was a display of military patches and brass collar ornaments. There was also a small cardboard box filled with loose medals, and a carton of Blitz cloths.

"How much is that gun?" he said.

The man looked at him. "The one you knocked off in the window?"

"Yes," said George. "Any of them."

The man opened the door to the window and took out the plank that the pistols were mounted on. There were four of them, hanging by their barrels from pegs in the piece of wood. The man put the display on the counter. All of the pistols were revolvers. Three had blued barrels and wooden grips. The fourth one—at the top of the display—was nickel-plated, with white plastic grips.

George looked at them. "How much is that one?" He pointed to the nickel-plated one at the top.

"Don't touch them with your fingers," said the man. "It makes rust spots. The perspiration in your hands makes rust spots." He took a pencil out of his shirt pocket and used it as a pointer. "That silver one is seventy-five dollars," he said, tapping it with the pencil. He looked up at George's face, which had folded in on itself at the price.

"Seventy-five, fifty, thirty-five, twenty," he said, stepping the pencil down the guns on the display case. The last one was an old, long-barreled Harrington & Richardson .22, with a drop-out cylinder. The bluing had worn away in spots, and there were light patches on it where the rust had been sanded out. The next to the last was a Smith & Wesson .38. It was in pretty good shape, though the bluing had worn a little on the cylinder and trigger guard.

George looked at the pistols. "What kind of bullets do they take?" he said. "The last two."

"Twenty-two . . . thirty-eight," said the man, tapping with his pencil.

"Twenty-two like a rifle?" said George.

"Yes," said the man. "Just the same."

"What does a thirty-eight look like?" said George.

The man went and got a box of cartridges and took one out and showed him.

"That's a real bullet," said George.

The man set the bullet on its butt end on the counter. "The army used to use thirty-eights," he said. "They went to the forty-fives when they couldn't stop the Morros."

"I see," said George.

"Did you see *The Real Glory?*" said the man.

"What?" said George.

"*The Real Glory,*" said the man. "The picture show."

"No," said George. He looked at the cartridge standing on the counter. "Can I touch it?" he said.

"Yes," said the man. "The bullets are brass. They don't rust."

George picked up the cartridge, rolling it around between his thumb and forefinger to look at it.

"Gary Cooper was in *The Real Glory,*" said the man.

"I don't go to the picture show much anymore."

"It's an old picture. I saw it a long time ago."

"No," said George, looking at the cartridge.

"It was about fighting in the Philippines. In one scene there was a Morro holy man that killed the commanding officer with a bolo."

"Is a bolo like a machete?" said George.

"Yes," said the man. "He ran all the way across the parade ground and got the commanding officer with his bolo. Gary Cooper was standing there shooting him all the time, but he couldn't stop him."

"I see," said George. He turned the bullet in his hand, weighing it and holding it up to the light so he could see it.

"The holy man dropped down dead after he killed the commanding officer, but they didn't stop him. Afterward, Gary Cooper counted the bullets. He hit him six times, but he killed the commanding officer anyway." He stopped, looking down at the box of bullets. He took one out and held it in his hand. "That's when they changed to forty-fives," he said. "They couldn't stop those Morros."

George looked at the bullet on the counter. "How much are the bullets?" he said.

"Two twenty-five the box."

"Twenty-twos are only half a dollar," said George.

"Two twenty-five for thirty-eights," said the man.

"That's high."

"It was just the Morros they wouldn't stop," said the man. "A thirty-eight is a lot of bullet. You could stop just about anything else you would want to with a thirty-eight."

"How much *each?*" said George.

The man looked at him. "I don't like to sell them that way. It's hard to get rid of a broken box."

"But how much would it be?"

"Mostly people want to buy a full box," said the man.

"I would expect I'd have to pay extra," said George.

"*Each*, they'd be a dime."

George figured it out in his head. "That's five dollars," he said. "That would be twice as much. *More* than twice as much."

"It's hard to get rid of a broken box," said the man.

"Well," said George. He didn't say anything else for a while. "Could I see the gun?"

"The thirty-eight?"

"Yes."

The man took out his handkerchief and wrapped it around the pistol. "Try not to touch it with your hand," he said. "It makes rust spots."

"Yes," said George, taking the pistol in the handkerchief.

He looked at it lying in his hand, trying to get the feel of it through the handkerchief. It was a bigger gun than he had thought, heavy.

"I couldn't pay for it until the first of the month," he said, handing it back to the man. "Would you keep it for me until then?"

"That's a week," said the man. "Could you put a little down on it?"

George took out a purse with a snap catch on it. He opened it and looked inside, then he turned his back to the man and took out his money. He counted it into his hand, then he closed his fist and turned back around, holding the money in his fist. "How much is the Barlow knife?" he said.

"The Barlow knife is a dollar and a quarter."

"A Barlow knife is generally a dollar even," said George.

"My Barlow knives are a dollar and a quarter."

"Well," said George.

"Look," said the man. He picked up the knife, opened it, and twisted the blade. "The blade don't have any play in it. It's a good knife." He closed it and put it back on the counter. "You get what you pay for, mister," he said.

George looked at the knife, thinking. "I could let you have two fifty," he said.

"That's not much," said the man.

"I'm not going to take the gun," said George. "It's only to hold it for me."

"It's still not much," said the man.

"That's the best I can do, mister," said George. "I don't make but a hundred and forty-five a month. I got to pay something for my board."

The man looked at him. "If you don't make but a hundred and forty-five, how're you going to buy anything?"

George looked down at the counter. "I live at home," he said.

"Well," said the man.

"I'll give you two fifty now," said George, "and the other thirty-two fifty next Saturday. If I don't, you can keep the two fifty."

"That's what it's for," said the man.

"I'll pay you the rest. Only you hold the gun for me." George slapped the money down on the counter—three dollar bills, two quarters, two dimes, and a nickel.

The man slid the money into his hand. "Okay," he said. "But not any longer than Saturday."

"Two o'clock Saturday," said George.

"Two o'clock," said the man. "And *all* the money. I don't do business on credit."

George took the Barlow knife and went out of the store. The next Saturday he came in with the rest of the money and got the pistol. He also bought six bullets for ten cents apiece.

He worried more about hiding the real pistol than he had about the cap pistol, of course, but he couldn't find a better place. He did get a cloth sample bag from the office and put the gun into that as a double disguise to hang it under his coat. And he couldn't think of anything better to do with the cap pistol, so he took it to work with him and buried it in the woods on his lunch hour.

Aiming the real gun at Susy was very exciting right from the first. He did it without putting bullets into it to begin with, but he didn't feel that he was really doing it then.

Before he aimed it live, he decided he'd better take it out and shoot it to see how he should handle it. So the Saturday after he bought it, he smuggled it out of the house and took it down to the Casey Canal, where he went hunting frogs.

The first shot kicked back on him so badly the pistol almost flew out of his hand, and the noise was much louder than he had expected. He wanted some frogs to try it on, but there weren't any to be found in November, so he set up a tin can and tried to shoot at that. He wasted four more shots, splatting mud out of the bank where the bullets dug holes going in, but he didn't even come close to the can. Down to his last bullet, he rested, with the muzzle almost touching the can, and pulled the trigger. There was a neat hole going in the front, but it blew away the whole back of the can coming out—a big starburst of peeled metal. Before he went home, he stopped by the pawnshop and bought six more bullets, since he didn't like to handle it unless it was dead full.

When he wasn't using it to aim at Susy, he would take out the bullets and keep them in the pocket of his suit coat, the way he had kept the toy bullets for the cap pistol. But before he would aim it at her, he would always put the bullets back in—all six of them.

For the first week he aimed the pistol with the hammer down, but that made him feel like something was missing.

First he cocked it but held his finger outside the trigger guard. Then he slipped his finger inside the guard but pushed forward with it, keeping it off the trigger. Finally, he aimed at Susy with the loaded gun, the hammer back and his finger on the trigger, the sights silhouetted black in the light from her bedroom window, her dancing figure pale green on the black bar of the front blade. At the end of the second week he began to squeeze off the trigger, holding the hammer back with his thumb and letting it slide down easily onto the cartridge in the chamber. He tried to keep count, and wouldn't do it more than six times without reloading, since there were only six bullets in the gun. But very often he forgot to count because he found it so exciting to aim the gun. Still, he was trying to make it as real as he could.

Sometimes he would almost go into a trance over it. The music coming out of the radio in the darkness of the room would set up a tempo for him, and he would keep time to it, cocking and squeezing with the beat of the song—twenty, thirty times in a row.

Sometimes the rhythm of Susy's dancing would set a pace for him. She would go leaping around the room in the wildest kind of whirling dance, and the tension and excitement would build in him along with the music and the dancing. At the end of the second week he worked himself up into a seizure, but he felt it coming on him, so he had time to ease the hammer off and drop the pistol on the bed before it hit him full. It worried him, though, so he put his finger back outside the guard again for the next few nights.

Then he moved it back onto the trigger.

During the day he would think about it. After a while he would hardly think of anything else. He remembered that he had missed the can with the four shots, and had finally had to put the muzzle of the gun practically up against it to hit it. So he told himself that he could hardly hit a moving target across the forty feet that separated the houses—not when he couldn't hit a tin can close enough that he could have reached out and touched it with his hand. But he worried about it just the same. It nagged along in the back of his head. Shooting the slingshot had given him a good eye, and handling the gun had given him the feel of it. He was afraid that if he ever did give in to the music coming out of the radio and Susy's whirling dance, everything might come together, and he would hit just what he was aiming at. And he remembered very clearly how the back side of the can had looked after he stepped up and put the bullet through it.

Finally he couldn't stand it any longer, so he took the gun out to the canal and set up a tin can on a stick—the same way he had done the first time. Then he walked off ten paces, took aim, and fired. The can went spinning up into the air, wheeling end over end. It didn't really look very much smaller than Susy whirling up there over the front blade. Before he even thought about it, he pulled the trigger a second time and hit it spinning in the air, sending it winging off into the high grass. It was easier than the slingshot.

He lowered the gun and looked at it. Then he stepped up to the bank of the canal and fired the four remaining shots into the water. Afterward, he flipped out the cylinder and ejected the shells into his hand. Then he threw them off into the grass as far as he could. He wanted to throw the gun away, too, but he couldn't afford a thirty-five-dollar gesture. In fact, he did throw it down on the ground, but he picked it back up and wiped the dirt off and put it into his pocket.

When he took it back, the man at the pawnshop would only give him fifteen dollars for it.

"You're cheating me, mister," he said.

"You think I sell one of those things every day?" said the man. "I can't do any better. It's taking up space."

George put the pistol back into the paper bag, and walked out of the pawnshop.

"It's a *business*, mister," said the man, calling after him.

He tried to sell it around to the men on the survey party.

"Where'd you get that thing?" said John.

"I paid thirty-five dollars for it," said George. "I ain't got no bullets for it, but I promise you it works."

"You supposed to be Gene Autry?" said John.

"I thought I would get to use it," said George.

"You can try to sell it to one of the guards on the gang," said John. "Put it back in the truck. I don't like to see you waving it around."

"I ain't got no bullets for it," said George.

"Put it back in the truck anyway."

The best offer he got from the guards was ten dollars cash, and a trusty to cook his lunch when the survey party was working in McAfee County.

So he took the gun back and threw it in the Casey Canal. For thirty-five dollars he couldn't afford it, but it was worth it for fifteen.

Afterward, he went to a lumberyard and bought a sheet of three-quarter-inch plywood for three dollars. For fifty cents extra they cut it to the dimensions that he gave them. Then he bought a can of black paint at the Kress store.

He tried to get into the house without his mother seeing him, but she was waiting. "What you got, George?" she said. "What are you going to do with that?"

He didn't answer her, but went straight through the house to his room and closed the door behind him, then moved the dresser in front of it. "Stop the banging, and I'll let you in after a while," he said to her, speaking through the door.

First he painted the panes of the window black. He did that to keep the piece of plywood from showing on the outside. After he finished with the painting, he put the piece of plywood over the window and nailed it down to the frame, beating the nails in hard so that he put hammer marks all around them. When he finished, he moved the dresser out of the way and opened the door, letting his mother into the room.

"What'd you do that for, George?" she said.

"It's *my* room, Mother," he said.

"I know it is," she said. "I know it is. But why'd you want to do *that?*"

He gave her what was left of the can of paint and the brush, then he got her out of the room and locked the door. With the window boarded up, the room was darker in the daytime than it had been at night before.

"It was wrong," he said, speaking to the walls of the room. It was all right to walk with Jack in his mind's eye, the way he had started out, with only the radio to go by. But it had gotten away from him.

He turned on the radio, then he put out the light and lay down on the bed, his head pulled over next to the night table—the orange light from the dial on the side of his face. He was lying on his back, stretched out, with his arms folded and his head propped up on a pillow. A Pepsi-Cola commercial came on, but he didn't follow along with it.

"It was wrong," he said again.

He went to sleep in that position, holding himself with both hands. Until he woke up in the morning he did not shift or change. Sleeping, there was more tenseness in him than there was when he was awake. An air of expectancy, as if he were waiting for someone to push a button and send him off to the moon.

18

Turkey Day

EVERYTHING THAT HAPPENS in the world is taken personally by the people in Savannah—the way a tidal wave used to be taken by the natives in those old Jon Hall movies about the South seas. Only, there is no volcano rumbling in the background, and no Maria Montez in a sarong to throw into it even if there were. Besides which, nobody, even in Savannah, is quite that pristine anymore. These days it's not something that hits you in the eye— nobody marches around with a severed head stuck on a pole, and virgins don't get thrown to the sharks. But, in spite of that, the circuits are still open between earthbound individuals and a cosmic infinity, and whatever happens, anywhere, is reduced to a local frame of reference in Savannah.

Whether or not that is a diminishment of the world, finally, is hard to say. It certainly tends to make life more important and interesting than it is when you start by admitting that nothing means anything, and whatever happens to you, personally, is of no special importance in the big scheme of things. Nobody in Savannah would admit to any such thing.

Father Dyer, the teacher of senior English at Boniface, tried once to get his class to agree with him that Macbeth's "sound and fury" speech at the end of the play was an accurate picture of the world in general.

" 'Life is a tale told by an idiot,' " he said, shaking his head sadly. He was baiting them, mainly to make them talk about it. But he was also a glum man, who went around with his lower lip in his teeth, tuned in to the world's sad song.

"What does it matter?" he said.

"Excuse me, Father Dyer," said Feeb. Feeb liked to talk in class. "That's like getting the word from a guy with a tack in his foot. Look at the situation. It ain't exactly an Abbott and Costello routine we're talking about." Feeb ticked off Macbeth's troubles on his fingers. "He's been sweating all those people he croaked. His wife just killed herself. A bunch of trees is attacking his castle. Macduff is going to kill the shit out of him. . . ." He didn't actually say "shit," even though there were only boys in the class. What he said was "sh—t," swallowing the "i." He looked around at the class, then back at Father Dyer. "What's he got to be happy about? That's Paul Muni stuff, man."

A good Savannah answer. Take everything personally, and don't try to push it out from there. The universe is something you don't fool around with. Even Feeb knew there were a good many people in the world who would go crazy if they had to sit in a booth at Theodore's eating hot fudge sundaes for the rest of their lives.

World War II was especially exciting for the people in Savannah, because they all assumed that when the Germans invaded the United States they would set up the first beachhead down at Tybee. And children went to sleep at night dreaming about Japanese planes coming down the river from South Carolina to drop bombs on the Dixie Crystals Sugar Refinery and the Union Bag Paper Mill.

But the things that were really local drew the most attention, and, next to the St. Patrick's Day parade on Broughton Street, the Thanksgiving Day game between Boniface and Oglethorpe was the biggest local event of all.

The Chamber of Commerce people thought so well of it that they listed it in the "Annual Events" section of the brochure they put out to attract tourists, along with such other things as the Miss Savannah beauty contest, the Chatham Artillery anniversary, and the annual interstate sailboat regatta at Wilmington Island. There were only eleven annual events listed altogether, one of which was the dog show, so by all local standards, even official ones, the game was very big indeed.

The two schools had been playing each other in intercollegiate sports for a long time, and the baseball series went back to 1894. But, in 1947, the football rivalry was only in its twenty-third year.

Up to 1925, the Boniface Fathers wouldn't let the boys field a team—though the Big Blue of Oglethorpe had been out there since 1919.

Knute Rockne had the George Gipp teams at Notre Dame in 1919 and 1920. Then Red Grange played at Illinois in 1923, and after that the whole country went football-crazy—which was an outside influence that did work its way into Savannah. The Fathers resisted that pressure until the end of the season of 1924. But that was the year of the Four Horsemen, and with the alumni practically beating down the doors, it got to be the next thing to a moral imperative that Boniface, being a Catholic school, should field a team. So the Fathers gave in in the summer of 1925.

It was so late in the year that getting Boniface a place on the Oglethorpe schedule wasn't an easy thing to do. But everybody could see that the game had to be played, so they finally settled on Thanksgiving Day—after Oglethorpe's regular season was over. It was a natural time for the game anyway, and once the series started, they never bothered to change it.

Boniface must have been picking up inspiration out of South Bend, because they won five of the six games they played that first season, then beat the Big Blue 30–10 in Grayson Stadium. J.J. O'Brien rushed out after the game and bought a turkey for every player on the squad.

The next year the signals weren't coming in too well, and Oglethorpe got even, wiping them up 43–6.

Over the whole series, Oglethorpe held the edge, having won fourteen of the twenty-two games, which was only natural, since they had ten times as many students as Boniface did—though half of them were girls.

But traditional rivalries are apt to turn up quirky games, and there was really no way to figure the odds on this one. You couldn't even predict the outcome on the basis of the season records in a given year. Some of the games that got the most hysterical advance notices turned out to be jaw-breaking bores once the teams got onto the field—shoving matches between the 30-yard lines, with baseball scores, like 3–2 or 6–3, that put even the cheerleaders to sleep. The only team in memory that came up to its pregame press was the Horse Rooney team of 1942. For the rest of them, one man's guess was as good as the next. So the sportswriters had a field day, knowing that nobody would hold them responsible for what they had said after it was over.

Every year there was a very strong urge—which tended to become irresistible—to call it the "battle of the century." Oglethorpe hadn't done too well in 1947—4–5–1, which, though it was the best year of the last three, was still not exactly grist for a legend mill. If they had called Boniface the "*team* of the century," that would have been accurate enough. But it was too close to an understatement to be considered.

"Have you seen him? Have you seen the motherfucker?" It was Monday morning, and Feeb was blocking the door to Father Dyer's homeroom, each hand on a jamb, and his head sawing from side to side.

"What're you talking about, Feeb?" said Jack. It never occurred to him that Feeb would be upset about anything connected with football.

"Ducker," said Feeb. "Have you seen Ducker?"

Jack looked at him. "No," he said.

"The motherfucker," said Feeb. "The fucking motherfucker."

"Well," said Jack. He waited. "What about Ducker?"

"He broke his leg," said Feeb.

Jack looked at him without saying anything, just pulling his eyebrows together a little.

"Him and Whitfield and Camack," said Feeb. "The motherfuckers went for the coffin."

"Hoy and Whitfield and Camack all broke their leg?"

"Ducker broke his leg," said Feeb. "All of them were going for the coffin."

In a traditional rivalry like the one between Boniface and Oglethorpe, one that keeps up year after year, a lot of little traditions tend to accumulate around the big one as time goes by. That way more people can get in on it and feel like they're taking part in the main tradition, even when they can't do it directly.

The big secondary tradition of the Boniface-Oglethorpe game was burning the coffin.

During the week before Thanksgiving week, a small select group of students at each school would go into hiding and build a big dummy coffin out of wood, which they would paint in the colors of the other school, with the name lettered on the side and crepe paper tassels and flowers all over it. On Monday of Thanksgiving week, each school would set up the coffin it had built on sawhorses in front of its main entrance, and post a guard to protect it. After the game, on Thursday night, the winner would take the loser's coffin out to Forsythe Park and make a bonfire and burn it for a victory celebration.

Part of the tradition was that once the coffin got set up under guard in front of the school, it had to be left alone. But during the week when it was being built, stealing it was the name of the game, if anybody could get onto where the hidden workshop was. A kind of guerrilla war developed, with hunting parties out every night cruising around town trying to find it.

The spirit of the search wasn't all that frivolous and innocent, and there was nothing in the tradition about the fights being barehanded. Nothing fatal ever happened, but whenever the scouts ran into each other, there were likely to be plenty of broken bones and blood on the ground afterward. That was a measure of how much was at stake. Bringing back the coffin was very big for status, being just a notch below playing in the game itself.

Losing your coffin was also very important. It could even affect the outcome of the game.

Because of the mayhem involved in the raids, both schools had strict rules that football players could not take part in the search, because they needed to be kept whole for the game itself. Ducker, Whistler, and Dimmy had broken the rule.

Whistler was the one who had found out where Oglethorpe was building the Boniface coffin. Which was no Sam Spade operation, since it was in Hoke Smith's garage, and Hoke lived right next door to him. Whistler watched them out the window until he couldn't stand it any longer, then he passed the word to Ducker. Dimmy got in on it because his father had a pickup truck and they could carry the coffin off in it.

The idea—it was Whistler's, and he had gotten it from watching Errol Flynn commando movies during the war—was that a small group of them could make a quick raid in the middle of the night, and get away before anybody knew what had happened.

"They'll never know," he said, "what fucking hit them."

The plan went just the way it was supposed to—up to a point. There were two Oglethorpe boys standing guard in the garage, but Ducker didn't even have to threaten them to back them off.

The trouble was Dimmy.

They had the coffin in the truck, with Dimmy at the wheel, and Whistler and Ducker in the back holding on to it, since it was too long to go in with the tailgate up. The truck was parked in the alley behind Hoke's house, a tight place to negotiate, and one that needed attention, which was the one thing Dimmy couldn't give it. He slammed into low gear, raced the engine, and let out the clutch, lurching the pickup in short, rocking hops that dumped Ducker into the alley on his head and shot the coffin out over the tailgate. When he banged into the garage across the way, Dimmy shoved the gear shift up into reverse and ricocheted backward over Ducker's leg. Whistler yelled at him through the window of the cab, but Dimmy was focusing his attention on the driving, and he didn't hear him. He put it back into first and went over Ducker again going forward.

Whistler finally got into the cab and jerked the key out of the ignition, but by the time he did, Dimmy was going over Ducker for the fourth time, the right rear wheel working down his leg with each pass, from just below his knee to his foot. The alley was sandy and loose, and Ducker's leg was such a piece of meat that the first three passes hurt the truck more than they did him. But the fourth pass was over his ankle, and that time something snapped.

After the doctors fixed him up, there was some serious doubt whether Ducker would ever walk right again. But that was a long-range problem and was Ducker's personal lookout. The immediate concern, which had more people involved in it, was that he wouldn't be able to play in the game.

"Why'd you do it, Hoy?" Jack looked down at the big white club of plaster of Paris, with Ducker's toes sticking out the hole at the end. Dimmy had already written his name on the cast. Once across the instep, and once, longways, up the side.

Ducker didn't want to talk about it. "Shit, Curran," he said.

"We *had* to do it, man," said Whistler. "They was right out my bedroom window. I was watching them all week."

"You could have told somebody else and let them do it. Why'd you have to go after it yourself?"

"It was right out the *window*, man," said Whistler. "There wasn't nothing to it."

Jack looked down at Ducker's cast, then back at Whistler. "I see there wasn't."

"We got the fucking coffin," said Whistler. "It was Dimmy backing up the truck broke Hoy's leg."

"I can still get around pretty good," said Ducker. He held the crutches in one hand, and hobbled back and forth on the cast to show them.

"No shit," said Jack.

"Fuck it," said Ducker. He put the crutches back under his arms, and went swinging away down the hall.

"We got the fucking coffin," said Whistler. Then he went away down the hall after Ducker.

"What're we going to do, Jack?" said Feeb. "What're we fucking going to do without Ducker?"

"You sound like we had a choice," said Jack. Then he added, "It's not the end of the world, Feeb. We've been lucky nobody got hurt up to now." He thought about it for a while, then he shook his head. "Maybe it's the end of the world," he said.

While they were talking, Dimmy came up. "Did you see the coffin?" he said. "Me and Whitfield and Hoy got Oglethorpe's coffin Saturday night."

"We heard," said Feeb.

"Hey," said Dimmy. "How about that?" He sounded pleased about getting the coffin. "It's kind of busted up, but we got it."

"Hard on Hoy," said Feeb.

"Yeah," said Dimmy. "He hurt his foot."

"I hear you were driving," said Feeb.

"My old man won't let nobody else touch his truck."

Jack turned and started away.

"It's got this clutch . . ." said Dimmy.

"Fuck off, Camack," said Feeb.

Dimmy stood in front of him, hunched over, his brows pulling down. His face clouded. "What'd you say?"

"I said you blew the fucking game," said Feeb.

"Oh," said Dimmy. He stood there, thinking about it, his eyes moving from side to side under the bony ledge of his brow, an expression on his face like a chimpanzee trying to decide between a coconut and a banana. For a minute and a half he didn't say anything.

"What game?" he said at last.

Coach Garfield didn't know what to do about it.

"I don't know what to do about it," he said, twirling the whistle on its chain, wrapping it around his finger. He had gotten Jack out of his English class to talk to him. "I swear to God," he said, "I don't know what to do about it."

"Demarco's got the best spirit," said Jack.

Chicken looked at him, then twirled the whistle the other way. "Demarco's too light to play tackle. What do you think?"

"Demarco can play center," said Jack. "I'll play tackle."

"Demarco can't play center," said Chicken.

"He played against Tattnall and Kose."

Chicken looked at him. "*Everybody* played against Kose."

"He played against Tattnall."

Chicken twirled the whistle again. "Demarco's too little."

Jack watched him unwind the whistle, then wind it up the other way. "If I wasn't here, who would be playing center?"

"It wouldn't be Demarco," said Chicken. "He would have something broke by now."

"Who would you have *started* at center?"

"That was in the *old* days," said Chicken. "I *got* a center. What I need is a tackle."

"We're lucky nobody's been hurt up to now," said Jack. "Lulu's the best man you've got for spirit."

"What about Sullivan?" said Chicken. "He's a hundred and eighty."

"Sullivan won't come on with the team the way Demarco will," said Jack. "Next year he'll be fine."

"You think Demarco can move them out?"

"He moved them out pretty good in the Tattnall game. He won't let them *in*. If we can get him to submarine, he might move them out."

"I wish he had forty more pounds on him."

"I wish he had a hundred more pounds on him. We got three days, Coach."

"I just don't know," said Chicken, twirling the whistle. "I just don't know."

So they moved Lulu in at center on offense, with Jack playing tackle. On defense, Jack went back to his old linebacker's position.

"I want your head in this game, Lulu," said Jack. "You pay attention. If you get something busted, we're really up the creek."

"I'll try," said Lulu.

"I know you'll try. I want you to be *careful.*"

There wasn't any point in trying to keep Ducker's leg a secret from the Oglethorpe team, not with Dimmy going around talking about it and lining up people to autograph the cast. The way Dimmy looked at it, Boniface hadn't gotten Oglethorpe's coffin since 1942, but they played the game every year.

Actually, the Oglethorpe team didn't need all the psychological advantage they were getting out of Ducker's leg.

They were a big team—ten pounds heavier than Boniface from end to end—though they didn't have any real stars to focus their game. The traveling squad had forty-nine men on it, and the first two teams had averaged just over two quarters' playing time per game, with a third-team average of eight quarters' playing time for the season. They couldn't get eleven men on the field all at once as good as the eleven men Boniface had, but there were thirty-five or so who were only a notch below that level, and they could run them in and out all day long. Depth was the thing that a team needed to play them. Which was the one thing Boniface didn't have.

"We'll have to get us twenty-one points in the first half to beat them," said Chicken. He and Jack had talked over the strategy for the game beforehand, but Chicken was the one who told the team about it.

"Their home game squad is nearabout twice the size of ours," he said. "And they've got the biggest third-team line in the state."

"Only they can't put but eleven of them out there at a time," said Jack.

Chicken looked at him. "Eleven at a time," he said.

It wasn't just the size of the squad that hurt. It was also the way they played the game. Oglethorpe was one of those teams that couldn't seem to score touchdowns, but they would beat you to death on the field trying. That was because Faro Wicker, their coach, knew all there was to know about conditioning, but didn't know the first thing about strategy. "Lacy-drawer stuff" is what he called it.

Faro had played end on a running team at the University of Georgia in the early thirties, which had given him a very physical conception of the game. He was in his fourteenth year as head coach at Oglethorpe, and in the fourteen years he had had one undefeated team—in 1938—and nine winning seasons. Considering the material he had, that wasn't a very impressive record. Oglethorpe had always had the biggest enrollment of any high school in the state, and Faro could have dressed out a hundred players a year, if he could have found somebody to put up money for the uniforms.

Faro was big and rawboned, and his years in the city had not rubbed the cracker off him. He still walked like he was hopping furrows, and he carried his elbows in tight to his sides, with his forearms winged out. Eighteen years after he left the ten-acre farm he was raised on in Woad, Georgia, you could have backed a plow up to him and the handles would have slipped right into his hands.

Faro's approach to football was strong on basics, but there wasn't any long view about it at all. Every year he would get a herd of big boys onto the team—"herd" was Faro's term, and it expressed just about the degree of sentiment he felt for them— then give them plenty of punishment during the practice sessions to harden them up and make them mean. The way he saw it, his job started on Monday afternoon, and ended after practice on Friday. Friday night was in God's hands. He was interested in the way it turned out, of course, but he didn't feel like there was anything he could do about it.

So Oglethorpe lost a lot. But they lost in a way that was extremely hard on the teams that beat them. The Oglethorpe players never seemed to get their minds more than five yards off the line of scrimmage. By the time they went away and left you alone, you would be hurting too much to notice how many points there were on the scoreboard anyway. It was shortsighted football, but it was pure bloody murder while the game lasted.

"We'll have to throw a lot of short passes and hit for quick ones into the line," said Jack. "We'll let you drop a bomb on them now and then, Aaron. But don't count on doing it all afternoon. The less time we have to spend pushing them around on the line, the better. We'd have to take too much punishment." He looked at Aaron. "Are you listening?"

"Quick stuff," said Aaron.

"Same thing for wide runs." He turned to Dimmy. "You're the one will have to carry us, Camack. You and Frog."

Frog ate his bubble. "What'd he say?" he said.

Losing Ducker didn't change the game plan, but it meant that all of them were going to have to take more punishment than they had planned on.

Thanksgiving Day was clear and cold—forty-two degrees, and no wind blowing. After an extra week of rest, the field was tight and hard.

When the teams came out for the pregame warmup, there were six rows of ten men each on the Oglethorpe end of the field, with three captains to call out numbers for the exercises. It was pretty much the same story year after year, so none of the Boniface fans was especially downhearted because of it.

J.J. O'Brien had broken out his World War I uniform for the occasion, ribbons and all. The last time he had done that was for the 1942 game, which Boniface had won, and he was out to work the charm again. Also he had pushed up the offer for the game ball to $150, though he didn't say anything about "win, lose, or draw." He had the money in silver dollars, and before the game he set it up on a card table in the locker room—fifteen stacks of ten—so they could all see what it looked like.

"No paper, boys," he said. "Silver." He held up one of the silver dollars between his thumb and forefinger. "Pure coin of the realm," he said.

After he was sure everybody had seen them, J.J. put the coins into the pockets of his cartridge belt, which he wore during the game.

When they went out for the toss of the coin, the whole Boniface first team walked to the center of the field. All of them were seniors, and they had decided that they would have eleven cocaptains for their last game at Boniface. Oglethorpe had three. It was the only time the Big Blue would be outnumbered that day.

Oglethorpe won the toss, and elected to receive. Bammer Kicklighter took Whistler's kickoff on the 5-yard line and ran it back to the 20, where Lulu and Flasher brought him down. Then Oglethorpe ran two end sweeps for seven yards, and sent their fullback up the middle for no gain. Whistler took the punt on his own 35, and ran it back to the 50.

Aaron threw two spot passes to Frog for a first down on the Oglethorpe 38, then gave it to Dimmy nine times in a row up the middle to the 2. The tenth time he faked to Dimmy, and gave the ball to Whistler, who went wide around end and walked into the end zone with the nearest Oglethorpe player fifteen yards away.

The kick was good, and Boniface led 7–0 with six minutes to go in the quarter.

"Nothing fucking to it," said Whistler, as they went back downfield.

The line play had been crisp on the drive, but the Boniface

team was holding up well, and even Feeb was taking out his man. "Bring on the motherfuckers," he said.

On their second series, Oglethorpe made two first downs, getting the ball out to the 50, then the quarterback fumbled and Lulu recovered for Boniface on the 45. Jack worried about Lulu being on the bottom of the pile, but they untangled and he walked back to the huddle all right.

"You okay?" he asked.

"We're going to fucking take them," said Lulu.

Aaron threw two short passes to Frog for a first down on the Oglethorpe 32, then the whistle blew ending the quarter, and the Oglethorpe second team came in. Their clean uniforms were crisp and sharp-looking.

Dimmy ran three times for nine yards, making it fourth and one on the 23. There were ten minutes and thirteen seconds left to play in the half.

"We shouldn't go for it outside the twenty," said Jack. "Whistler can lay it out inside the five."

"We got fourteen points to go," said Whistler.

Jack looked at him.

"Twenty-one points at the half. You said it, Curran."

"Can you hold them off for a long one?" said Aaron.

Jack looked at him. "I don't like to go for the chancy stuff when we're ahead," he said.

"We got two more to go," said Whistler.

"All the way, Flasher," said Aaron.

Jack didn't say anything, and Lulu broke the huddle. Digger Spode, who was playing middle guard over Lulu, got by him, and almost brought Aaron down. But Flasher was in under the goalposts before anybody missed him. The ball dropped into his hands, and he held on for another 6 points.

Whistler kicked the extra point, and Boniface led 14–0.

On the first play from scrimmage after the kickoff, Lulu got up limping from the pile.

"It ain't nothing," he said.

But Jack sent him to the sidelines, with instructions to have Sullivan come in as a replacement.

J.J. came up to Lulu and asked how he was feeling. "You're playing a fine game, lad," he said. "They need you out there."

Lulu tried to run sprints up and down the sidelines, but it was clear that his ankle was hurting him.

"Take him under the stands and fix him up," said J.J. Dr. Vespers looked at J.J., then he got his bag and took Lulu under the bleachers to look at him. He examined the ankle to be sure that it wasn't broken, then he gave him a shot of Novocain.

While Lulu was out, Oglethorpe ran seven plays to the 40. Then Whistler intercepted a pass, and Boniface had it first and ten at their own 45. On the exchange of the ball, the Oglethorpe third team came in, and their uniforms looked even cleaner and crisper than the second team's had.

"There's a million of the fuckers," said Whistler.

On the first down, Aaron threw a short pass to Frog. Frog caught it on the Oglethorpe 48, but the corner back came up fast and gave him a good sharp rap, which turned him around and started him off toward the Boniface goal line. The team was slow reacting, and he was down to the 5-yard line before Flasher caught up with him and brought him down.

"Kick it out, Whitfield," said Jack.

Oglethorpe's first team came in to attempt to block the punt, and Jack moved over to center the ball. The Oglethorpe left tackle grabbed Lulu by the jersey and yanked him out of the line, then got into the backfield and blocked Whistler's punt. The Oglethorpe end fell on it in the end zone, and they were onto the boards with their first 6 points. The kick was good, and with four minutes and twenty-three seconds left to play in the half, the score was 14–7.

After the kickoff, the Boniface drive stalled with fourth and four to go on the 38. Then Bammer Kicklighter got away from Flasher on the punt return, cut for the sidelines, and almost outran the team. Aaron bumped him out on the Boniface 43. Oglethorpe ran three plays for a first down on the 32, then Boniface held them for three yards on the next three.

With fourth and seven for Oglethorpe on the Boniface 29, and forty-five seconds left to play in the half, a substitute came out from the bench. There had been so many, nobody on the Boniface team paid any attention to him. Then, when they came out of the huddle, they lined up in place kicking formation.

Jack looked at the kicker—who was wearing number 99. "When did they get a kicker?" he said. Oglethorpe's kicking game had been awful for the last three seasons, but somewhere during the last two weeks Faro had found himself a leg. It was something Jack hadn't counted on.

"Get up there and block it, Frog," he said. "He won't get it in there from here."

Frog's reflexes were slowing down, and the ball sailed off just over his fingertips, coming down in the end zone bleachers. The referee threw up his hands, and with thirty-eight seconds left to play in the half, the score was 14–10.

"Where'd he come from?" said Jack. "Ninety-nine's not even on the program."

"How the shit would I know?" said Whistler. "They probably got eight more teams we never fucking heard of."

"I hadn't counted on a kicker," said Jack. "We're going to have to hold them outside the thirty."

Nobody said anything for a minute.

"Jesus God," said Whistler.

Going off the field at the half, Jack noticed the way Lulu was walking. "What'd they do to you, Lulu? You all right?"

"Yeah," said Lulu. "They fixed me up."

Jack looked down at the way he was walking. "Did Vespers give you a needle?"

Lulu looked at him. "He fixed me up," he said.

In the locker room, Jack complained to Dr. Vespers. "Getting hurt is the only thing that keeps him from getting killed," he said.

J.J. O'Brien heard him talking and came over and put his arm around Jack's shoulder. "Don't argue with the doctor," he said. "The lad's fine." He looked at Lulu. "How do you feel, young man?"

"I'm okay," said Lulu. "My leg's okay."

"Don't worry, Jack," said J.J. "The doctor always knows best."

Chicken came into the locker room twirling his whistle. "Where'd the kicker come from?" he said. "Oglethorpe don't have no kicker."

"They got one now," said Whistler. "Forty-five fucking yards."

"We're going to have to keep them outside the thirty," said Jack. "I hadn't counted on a kicker."

Nobody said anything.

"My ass is dragging, man," said Feeb.

"We got a better team," said Jack.

Feeb dropped his helmet on the floor and leaned back against the lockers. "Dragging, man," he said.

"Let's win this one for Ducker," said Bo Hoerner.

"That asshole?" said Feeb.

The truth was they were missing Ducker a lot. Lulu had the spirit, but he couldn't power into the backfield to jam up plays the way Ducker could do it. Just hearing his name made them sad and resentful, reminding them how tired they were.

"Feeling under the weather, boys?" J.J. had climbed up onto a bench where everybody could see him. "A little fatigued and dejected?" He held up a small bottle of tablets. "Here's just what the doctor ordered," he said. "Chase your blues away."

They looked up at the bottle. Chicken twirled his whistle, but he didn't say anything.

"What you got there, Mr. O'Brien?" said Whistler.

"Energy," said J.J. "En-ur-gee." He opened the bottle and took out one of the tablets, holding it up where they could see it. It was smaller than an aspirin, and pale yellow. "One of these little beauties, and you'll have your second wind in no time, boys." He sounded as if he was going to try to sell them.

"Hurry-up stuff," said Jack. Chicken looked at Jack, then down at the floor.

J.J. frowned. "Dr. Vespers wouldn't give you anything that would hurt you, young man. This is pure medicinal Dexedrine. I've got a signed prescription for every man on this team." He put the emphasis on "pure," saying it "pee-yore."

"You don't take that stuff in the middle of a game," said Jack. "Some people go crazy. You should have brought it around last week."

"You think Dr. Vespers would give you anything to hurt you?" said J.J. He began passing out the tablets.

Jack looked at Chicken.

"It's illegal," said Chicken, getting up. "You're not going to take any of that stuff."

J.J. looked at him. "Dexedrine is not illegal," he said. "We got a licensed physician to sign the prescriptions."

"*Taking* them is," said Chicken. "Thank you, Mr. O'Brien. I wouldn't want to get anybody in trouble."

J.J. looked at him, then he held out the bottle. "Put them back, boys," he said. "You've got to listen to your coach."

"Much obliged, Mr. O'Brien," said Chicken. He was looking down at the floor. "I wouldn't want anybody to get in trouble."

"Put them in your valise, Dr. Vespers," he said, handing them to the doctor. He didn't look at anyone, but walked out of the room looking straight ahead. "We'll be standing by," he said.

"My ass is dragging, man," said Whistler.

"Well, get it up," said Jack.

Chicken looked at Jack, not twirling his whistle. Jack didn't look at him. "Dr. Vespers gave Lulu a shot of Novocain." He looked at Lulu's leg. "He ought not be playing on that foot when he can't feel it."

Chicken looked at Lulu. "Come here, Demarco," he said.

"I'm okay, Coach," he said.

"Did Dr. Vespers put Novocain in your leg?"

"It feels okay, Coach," said Lulu. "I could tell if something was wrong."

"Come here," said Chicken.

Lulu got up, trying to walk naturally.

"You're out of the game, Demarco," said Chicken. "You could hurt yourself bad."

"I'm okay, Coach," he said. "I'm *okay*."

Chicken wasn't paying any attention to him. "You go back to center, Curran," he said. "Sullivan. You'll go in at tackle."

"Coach," said Lulu.

Chicken turned to him. "You stay here and get your leg taped up," he said. "You shouldn't even be walking on it."

"Get Dr. Vespers," said Lulu. "See what Dr. Vespers thinks about it."

Chicken looked at his watch. He seemed surprised. "Time to

go," he said. "You got to hang in there for twenty-four more minutes."

"Yeabo," said Bo Hoerner.

"Jesus Christ," said Feeb.

Boniface took the kickoff and got it back to the Oglethorpe 38, then ran out of gas and had to punt. Kicklighter took the ball on his own 10 and ran it out to the 25. They worked it up the field in short, steady bursts, three and four yards at a time, to the Boniface 26. Then Kicklighter fumbled the ball and recovered on the 25. It was fourth and three, so number 99 came in and kicked another field goal, making the score 14–13. The Boniface team was visibly sagging. They didn't seem to have any punch at all.

Whistler took the kickoff on his own 15, and four Oglethorpe players nailed him before he could take a step. Then Dimmy got four yards on three carries, and they had to punt the ball away.

In two series of downs, Oglethorpe was back down inside the Boniface 25. Somehow Jack got them to stiffen and hold for three downs, so it was fourth and six, and number 99 came in to kick the field goal that would put them in front. Jack called a time out to try to talk some backbone into them.

"Get up, Feeb," said Jack. Feeb was sitting down, which was strictly against the rules. They weren't even supposed to go down on a knee when they were on the field.

"Fuck it," said Feeb.

"Get up, or I'll kick you up," said Jack. Feeb looked at him, gave him a Boy Scout salute, then waved it into a finger. He got up, but he got up slowly.

"We're all fucking beat, Curran," said Whistler. "Look at that bench over there," he nodded his head to the Oglethorpe side.

"I played against four different men already," said Feeb. "How many more of the motherfuckers you think I got to go?"

Jack looked around at them. "This is the last game you're ever going to play for Boniface," he said.

"Is that a motherfucking promise?" said Feeb.

"You going to throw it away?"

"Man," said Whistler, "I'm fucking tired." He looked across to where the Oglethorpe team was huddling. "As soon as that little pissant puts it up there, we're going to be two points behind."

The referee blew the whistle, and they lined up for the play. Jack looked over the line at number 99, who was swinging his leg in little practice kicks, waiting for the ball to be snapped.

Number 99 was small and skinny, with two big yellow teeth poking out of his mouth, one lapping over the other, and no chin at all. He kept sucking on his teeth, sliding his upper lip down and back, so the teeth looked like they were popping in and out of his mouth. Nothing he had on fitted him. His jersey was too big, and his helmet was too small. It was a costume, not a uniform. He didn't look like a football player at all.

Jack was not inclined to hate a face, but he couldn't keep his eyes off number 99.

Before Digger Spode went down over the ball, he looked up at Jack and shot him a face full of teeth. "Watch your ass, Curran," he said. He held up three fingers. "Big three coming up."

When the ball was snapped, Jack was over Digger and into the backfield like a shot. The Oglethorpe quarterback heard the cracking sound, and the ball sailed by with him sitting there, his hands stretched out to catch it, but watching Jack instead. Number 99 froze, a terrified look on his face, his teeth sticking out bigger than ever. Jack put an elbow into them going by after the ball. He picked it up on the 41, then started for the goal without looking back.

Bammer caught up with him on the Oglethorpe 32, and rode his shoulders to the 22, where three other Oglethorpe players caught up with them and brought them down.

Bo Hoerner slapped him on the back. "Great, man. Great!" he said.

"Let's get it over," said Jack.

They huddled with more spirit than they'd had since the first quarter, and Dimmy in particular seemed to be feeling pepped up.

While Aaron was calling signals, Dimmy stepped back out of the huddle and ran around it twice on the outside in a funny, dancing kind of step, making a "rap-bap-bap," noise, like a child imitating a machine gun. Then he stepped back into his place and clapped his hands together. "Gimme da goddamn ball," he said.

They couldn't get his attention to run anything else, so Aaron called him up the middle. While Jack was taking out his man, Dimmy went by him like a freight train, picking up Digger on his shoulder and running off with him to the 9-yard line.

When they huddled again, Dimmy didn't come into the huddle at all. He spent the whole time running around on the outside in a prancing, high-kneed step, saying, "We got the *coff*-in. We got the *coff*-in." Over and over.

"What's got into Camack?" said Jack.

Whistler giggled, then reached across the huddle and tapped Jack on the helmet. "We took the fucking pree-scription, man," he said. Then he stood up and flexed his biceps like a picture in a Charles Atlas advertisement. "Feel that arm," he said. Then he stepped out of the huddle and high-stepped around with Dimmy a couple of times.

Aaron ran Dimmy up the middle again, there being nothing else he could do. Dimmy went into the end zone dragging three men behind him, and pushing two in front.

"Six points," he said, coming back to the huddle. "Six big points and the *coff*-in, *coff*-in. . . . rooty-tooty-tooty . . . bap-bap-bap . . ."

"We better run it over," said Jack. "I wouldn't trust Whistler's kicking."

So they gave it to Dimmy again, and he took it in for the twenty-first point.

"How many of you took the pill?" said Jack when they huddled for the kickoff. Nobody said anything, but Feeb giggled, and tried to give Jack a frog on the arm.

"Finnechairo?" said Jack. Frog was the one he was most worried about.

"Huh?" said Frog. He blew a bubble.

"Stick with your Fleer's, Frog," he said.

"What'd he say?" said Frog, trying to lift the flap of his helmet.

Dimmy was the hardest to control. Whistler calmed down pretty well after the first high passed off, and was no harder to deal with than he would have been with a couple of beers in him—though he was a lot more cheerful.

Feeb was happy and full of energy, and, for the first time in his football career, fearless. He began to do a real job on Conroy, which

Conroy couldn't believe, having played against Feeb the year before. It hurt Conroy's feelings, coming up so suddenly and in the
middle of the game. "Goddamn, Siddoney," he said. "What's got
into you?"

"Watch your ass, motherfucker," said Feeb. Then he giggled.

For three series of downs, Feeb pushed Conroy ten yards out of
the hole on every play. Faro finally noticed what was happening,
and he pulled Conroy out and put the first-string tackle back in.
Then Feeb did the same job on him. And, finally, with Boniface on
the Oglethorpe 26, Feeb threw the first rolling block of his life,
wrapping up the tackle's leg and breaking it.

"Goddamn," said Feeb. "We're going to beat the motherfuckers."

Aaron gave Dimmy the ball two out of three plays, and on the
ones when he wasn't carrying it, Aaron would fake it to him, so
he thought he was. The way he was hitting into the line, Oglethorpe had to pay attention to him. And with Dimmy sucking in
the whole secondary, Aaron flipped the ball to Whistler and sent
him around end. The second time he did that, Whistler went
twenty-six yards for the touchdown.

At the end of the third quarter, the score was 28–13. The energy
that Dimmy and Feeb and Whistler were generating spread out to
the rest of the team, and though Faro substituted players till it
looked like Oglethorpe was running a relay race from the bench,
there was no combination that seemed to work. The Big Blue
uniforms got dirtier and dirtier. But they couldn't stop Boniface.

In the fourth quarter, Whistler scored on runs of 35, 48, and 63
yards. Dimmy got 114 through the middle, even though they were
giving him the ball only two out of three plays.

After the fourth quarter started, Aaron kept begging them to
let him throw a long one. "Drop a bomb," he said. "Last game.
Drop a bomb." Jack kept putting him off, but after Whistler's third
touchdown, there wasn't much reason to try to keep the game in
their pocket any longer. The score was 49–13, and five of the Oglethorpe players were out of the game.

"Okay, Aaron," he said. "Drop a bomb."

Aaron faded back twenty-five yards—which was pure throwback
behavior, since not a single Oglethorpe player got across the line
of scrimmage to come after him—then he cocked his arm and

lobbed a sixty-yard floater out to Flasher on the five. Flasher waved to the Oglethorpe secondary, yelled "yoo-hoo" at them, then, when three of them came after him, he spent the next two and a half minutes running around and dodging them between the 15-yard line and the goal before he stepped into the end zone to make it 55–13.

With one minute to go in the game, Whistler went around end, got into the clear, and ran all the way to the goal line. But he didn't go across it. Instead, he stopped on the 1, put the ball on the ground, and stood with his foot on it waiting for the referee to come up.

"What're you doing?" said the referee.

"Blow your whistle," said Whistler. "That's where I want it."

The referee looked at him. "I don't think that's legal," he said. "Your knee ain't touched."

Whistler dropped down on his knee. "Blow your whistle."

"What the shit you doing, Whitfield?" said Jack. "That's crazy."

"I'm tired of scoring touchdowns," said Whistler. "I'm a bored fucker."

Jack looked at him.

"Call time out, Curran," said Whistler.

"You going to draw straws?" said Jack.

"Call time out."

"You go out, Sullivan," said Whistler. "Tell them to send Demarco in."

"Demarco's hurt," said Jack.

"It's the last touchdown," said Whistler. He looked across the line at the Oglethorpe team. Four of them were sitting down on the field. "Them cocksuckers're tired. Ain't nobody going to hurt him," he said. "Tell Coach we're going out the way we come in."

Sullivan started for the sidelines.

"You're going to play tackle, Dimmy," said Whistler. "Don't wait for nobody to give you the ball."

"Why would I be playing tackle?" said Dimmy.

"Because," said Whistler, "Curran's going to play fullback."

Jack looked at him.

"Like you been saying," he said, "we ain't never going to play football for Boniface no more. We're going to let you be a real hero for a change."

Lulu came up while he was talking. "What the fuck's going on?" he said.

So, with thirty-five seconds left in the game, Jack went over for the last touchdown, making the score 62–13. Then Whistler kicked for the sixty-third point.

Boniface got 563 yards from scrimmage—384 of them in the second half. It put their rushing average for the season up over the Horse Rooney team of 1942.

J.J. O'Brien took off his cartridge belt and swung it over his head, scattering silver dollars in a rain of shining cartwheels. "There's plenty more where that came from, boys," he said. "Plenty more where that came from."

Then he ran out onto the field and took off his Purple Heart ribbon and pinned it on Jack's jersey. "Young man," he said, "I want to shake your hand."

Just like the sportswriters said. It was the battle of the century.

19

In the Lighthouse

AFTER THE GAME, Jack went home for Thanksgiving dinner. The family was there before him, and Susy was watching for him out the window. When she saw him, she ran out of the door and jumped off the front stoop into his arms. "We won!" she said. "We won!"

Reilley shook his hand, nodding his head, but not saying anything. Then he stepped aside for Kate.

Kate wanted to be reassured that he wasn't hurt. "Are you sure?" she said, running her hands up and down his arms, checking for broken bones.

"Tired," he said. "But nothing's broken." He bear-hugged her, lifting her off her feet, and walked with her around the room to show her.

"Sit down and tell us about it," she said. Then she went out to the kitchen to get the dinner ready.

After dinner, Jack put on his Boniface uniform for the bonfire, and took the Reilley car—an old 1941 DeSoto that had seen them through the war—to go around to Mary's house.

"Doesn't he look nice?" said Kate. "I always loved a uniform."

Reilley shook his hand and slipped him a dollar bill as he was leaving. "Have a good time," he said.

Mr. Odell gave Jack his usual Indian's greeting. Very stiff and formal, but trying to be cordial for the holiday. He asked him about the game, and his part in it.

"I understand it was quite a good game," he said.

"Yes, sir," said Jack. "It was pretty good."

"Well," said Mr. Odell. He spoke carefully, as if he had been thinking over what he had to say. "Congratulations. Mary tells me you won."

"Yes, sir," said Jack. "Thank you."

Mr. Odell shook his hand again as they were leaving. "Be in at twelve, Mary," he said.

He took Mary out to Forsythe Park to watch the burning of the Oglethorpe coffin. There was a big bonfire going, lighting up the Confederate Memorial, with cadets from Boniface marching around it in their uniforms. The night was cold, and the heat from the fire felt good.

Everywhere he went, people came up to congratulate him. He saw Ducker on his crutches in the light from the fire and went over to him.

"We missed you, Hoy," he said.

Ducker looked at him, then back at the fire. "Not much you didn't," he said. "You beat the shit out of them." He looked at Mary. "Sorry," he said.

"We missed you anyway," said Jack. "It could have gone either way."

"Okay," said Ducker. "It was a good game."

They looked at each other, both thinking about the summer agreement to meet at Fort Screven after the game, but neither one saying anything, waiting for the other to bring it up.

"See you around," said Ducker, finally. Then he turned and swung away on his crutches.

After he took Mary home, Jack drove down to Bay Street. He hadn't seen Old Johnny since back in the summer, and he felt a need to look him up, it being a holiday and the end of the season.

He parked the car in Emmett Park, and walked across Bay to the Lighthouse Bar.

Jack saw Old Johnny once, twice—maybe three times a year. The fact that he saw him so seldom served to elevate the relationship, since, not knowing him, Jack could make of him anything he wanted to. Kate never talked about him, so most of the things he had heard came in bits and pieces from strangers and people whom he didn't know very well.

Jack liked Reilley, and he admired and loved him for the kind and patient man that he was. In every way that he could earn Jack's affection, he had it. But there was one simple, basic fact that Jack could not root out. Reilley was not his father. Not his flesh and not his bone. Because of the things he had heard, and those that he had worked out inside his own head, Old Johnny was the one he looked up to. It was something beyond fairness or choice.

The hands of the Miller's beer clock were pointing to twelve thirty-five when Jack came in the front door off Bay Street.

The Lighthouse was very small—more like a café than a bar, though they didn't serve anything but prepared foods, sandwiches wrapped in cellophane, and potato chips. It was about twenty-five feet long, and ten or twelve wide. With a yellow Formica-topped counter on the right-hand side and narrow, two-man, Formica-topped booths on the other. Behind the bar was a model of a lighthouse—some kind of advertising display originally, a trademark, but Billy Boy had painted over it—black-white-black, striping it after Tybee Light—covering up the name of the company when he did it. There was a red light in the lens of the revolving beacon. That and the pinkish-yellow Miller's beer clock at the back, and two porch lamps with dim yellow bulbs at each end of the mirror behind the bar were the only lights. They gave the place a cozy feeling at night, in spite of the Formica.

Old Johnny was there, sitting at the bar with a small man whom Jack did not recognize. Billy Boy O'Day was leaning on the counter polishing glasses with a rag. Old Johnny's back was to the door, and he didn't see Jack when he came in, but Billy Boy did. He put down the glass and reached over the counter, tapping Johnny.

"We got a visitor," he said.

Johnny turned around and squinted. "Is it Jack?" he said.

"Yes," said Jack. "Hello, Mr. O'Day." He nodded to the small man sitting beside his father.

"Well," said Johnny, "have a seat." He turned a bar stool out for him.

"Good game, Jack," said Billy Boy. "I heard it on the radio."

"Thank you," said Jack. He was speaking to Billy Boy, but he was looking at Johnny.

"I didn't hear it on the radio," said Johnny. "I heard it was a good game though." He paused. "You beat them, didn't you?"

"Sixty-three to thirteen," said Billy Boy. "Worst they ever beat the crackers."

"Ah," said Johnny. "I heard it was a good game."

For a minute, they didn't say anything. "This is L.D. Wyatt," he said, indicating the man on the stool next to him. "This is my boy Jack."

They shook hands. The small man looked several years older than Johnny. He was having trouble getting his eyes to focus.

"Pleased to meet you, Mr. Wyatt."

Mr. Wyatt seemed to be thinking it over.

"Wyatt works for the department," said Johnny.

"I thought you were running out of gas at the end of the half," said Billy Boy. "The announcer made it sound like you were going to get beat."

"We were tired," said Jack. "They've got a big team."

"You sure came back on them," said Billy Boy. "You must have got rested at the half. That Garfield is a great coach."

"Yes," said Jack.

"I meant to listen to it on the radio," said Johnny. "They ain't been talking about nothing else at the station for the last week."

"It was a pretty good game," said Jack.

Mr. Wyatt excused himself and left, walking with his left shoulder higher than his right.

"Baseball's the game I like to watch," said Johnny. "I never understood about football too good."

"There's more happening all at once," said Jack.

"To tell you the truth," said Johnny, "I ain't all that crazy about baseball. Not to *watch* it, you know." He turned up his glass and finished it off. "Boxing is what I really like," he said. "Boxing and wrestling. Just two of them out there—one man against one man. You can keep up with a thing like that."

"Wrestling's just a show," said Billy Boy. "You can see they ain't doing nothing to each other."

"Yes," said Johnny. "I mean the way it used to be. Back when Jim Londos was in it. Frank Gotch. Men like that. It's just a pile of shit these days."

"Amateur wrestling is still all right," said Jack. "At least it's honest."

"I'd even like to see Louis," said Johnny. He pushed his glass across the counter for Billy Boy to fill it up. "You want a beer?" He looked at Jack.

He nodded. He had never had a drink with Johnny before.

"Two Miller's," said Johnny.

"He looks like a good fighter," said Jack.

"You *seen* him?" said Johnny. He looked surprised.

"In the newsreels," said Jack.

"Oh," said Johnny. "The picture show." Billy Boy put the glasses on the bar and opened the bottles. "I heard him on the radio."

"He's a battler," said Jack. He poured his beer down the side of the glass, killing the head.

"Dempsey was the great one," said Johnny. He raised his glass to Jack, then put it to his mouth. "Looks like we ain't never going to see a white man take the heavyweight belt again." He wiped his mouth with the back of his hand.

"I saw the Mauriello fight last year," said Jack. "In the newsreels. There wasn't much to that."

"One round," said Billy Boy.

"I thought Conn might take him," said Johnny, "but he beat the shit out of him, too. There ain't any white challengers left. Who's this nigger he's fighting next week?" He looked at Billy Boy.

"Walcott," said Billy Boy. "He's an old man."

"Never heard of him," said Johnny. He took another drink from his glass. "There won't never be another Dempsey."

"They got a thick head," said Billy Boy, "niggers."

"Hardheaded as a brick," said Johnny.

[212]

"No," said Billy Boy, "I was reading about it somewheres. They really do. Scientific. Their skull is thicker than a white man. You can't hardly beat one to death with a stick."

"Yeah," said Johnny, "boxing ain't what it used to be."

For a while they drank without saying anything.

"How's your mother?" said Johnny.

"Fine," said Jack.

"She's a wonderful woman," said Johnny. "You don't give her no trouble, do you?"

"No, sir," said Jack.

"I think a lot of your mother," he said. He held up two fingers for two more beers.

"These are on the house," said Billy Boy. He looked at Jack. "To celebrate the game."

"Thank you," said Jack.

"Not many Currans left," said Johnny. "You and me are the last ones in Savannah."

"Two's enough," said Jack. He raised his glass to Johnny.

"What?" said Johnny. He raised his glass. "Goddamn right." They drank to the Currans.

"There must be plenty left in the old country," said Johnny. "My granddaddy used to tell me about it. We was numerous."

"I don't know much about the family," said Jack. Kate wouldn't talk about the Currans at all.

"We're from Galway," said Johnny. "Granddaddy used to know all about it. He was born over there."

"When did he come here?"

"Eighteen sixty-nine," said Johnny. "He was twenty-eight years old."

"He was from Galway?"

Johnny took a sip of beer. "He used to tell me about Galway Bay," he said. He looked at Jack. "He'd seen it himself. Clear and green as a mountain lake. Not full of turds like the river out there." He hooked his thumb toward the door.

"I'd like to go over sometime," said Jack. "We still got family there?"

"Must be," said Johnny. "Granddaddy said we was numerous. Anyway, why would they want to leave?"

[*213*]

"Granddaddy did."

"Yes, he did. And he cursed himself for it to the day he died. I wish we'd had the money to send him back to put him in the ground."

"You never went, did you?"

"No," said Johnny. "I'll never live to see the day. It costs money." He rubbed his thumb across the tips of his fingers.

"Maybe I'll take you and we can go together."

Johnny looked at him. "Two Currans going home?" He pushed his glass across the bar. "I'll drink to that."

"You never know," said Jack.

"I dream about it sometimes."

"You have dreams, too?"

Johnny looked at him, then back at the winking red lens on the lighthouse. "I'm gliding along in a boat like a swan," he said. "The water's clear and green." He paused. "Green like an emerald. And I'm sitting in a silver boat shaped like a swan." He poured his beer into the glass. "That's what Galway Bay would be like. Shamrock green." He took a swallow of the beer. "Maybe we'll go there someday. You and me, in a silver boat on Galway Bay."

Jack raised his glass, and they drank to Galway Bay.

"I have dreams, too—sometimes," he said.

"Listen," said Johnny, "do you remember the time I took you up in Tybee Light?"

Jack looked at him, then shook his head. "I don't think so. How old was I?"

Johnny squinted his eyes at him. "It was 'thirty-five or 'thirty-six. How old were you in 'thirty-six?"

"The summer?"

"Yes."

"Seven. Seven that summer."

"It was 'thirty-five. I remember. You and your mother moved to Waldburg Street in 'thirty-five." He took another sip of beer. "It was a clear day. We could see all the way back to Savannah. There was a boat going out for Ireland." He looked at Jack. "I told you it was going out to Ireland," he said. "I didn't know where it was going. Don't you remember?"

"Were there a lot of birds?"

"Yes. Sea gulls. They were landing on the walkway outside the light."

"I remember the sea gulls."

"We could see the storage tank," said Johnny. He hooked his thumb over his shoulder toward East Broad. The storage tank was just across the way.

"All I remember is the birds flying around."

Johnny took another sip of his beer. "That was the day. I think of it now and then." He looked at the lighthouse behind the bar. "It was a good day. Just the two of us up there in Tybee Light. The water wasn't dirty and full of turds then like it is now."

He looked at Jack. "How old are you?"

"Eighteen."

"You're getting some pretty good size on you. Stand up."

Jack stood up and Johnny slipped off his stool. He tried to measure his height by looking Jack in the eye. "How tall are you?"

"Six four . . . five."

"How much you weigh?"

"Two forty."

"You ain't outgrown me yet," he said. He sat down and put his elbow on the bar, his hand up. "Put it up there."

Jack sat down and put his arm up against Johnny's.

"Come around here," said Billy Boy. "You can't arm-wrestle with the both of you on the same side."

Jack went around behind the bar. "I better take this off," he said. He unhooked the collar of his cadet jacket, then unzipped it and took it off. Johnny took off his coat and rolled up his sleeve. His arm was as big as Jack's, but whiter, not so many freckles. The flesh inside his elbow was soft and puckered.

"Count to three, O'Day," said Johnny. He looked at Jack, but Jack was looking down at the counter where their elbows were braced together.

Billy Boy counted for them, tapping it out on the bar. On the "three" they pushed against each other, their fingernails going white from the grip, and their hands vibrating. Johnny had his lower lip in his teeth, and was holding his breath. For thirty seconds they were straight up and down, then Jack started to gain on him, and Johnny's arm began to sink toward the counter. He held for five more seconds before his arm started to go altogether. When it did, he reached up with his left hand and pushed back with both arms against Jack's one. Jack's hand went over and down onto the bar. As it dropped, Jack felt a catch in his shoulder, a sharp cutting pain.

"Best two out of three," he said, shaking his hand to loosen his arm.

"A boy shouldn't beat his father," said Billy Boy. "Let it go at that."

Jack looked at Johnny. Then he put his jacket back on and came around to the outside of the bar. He could still feel the catch in his shoulder, and he rubbed it with his left hand to work it out.

"Have another beer," said Johnny.

"Three's my limit," said Jack. He picked up his glass and finished it off. "I'll take you next time," he said, looking at Johnny in the mirror behind the bar.

"I know it," said Johnny. He rolled down his sleeve and put his coat back on. Then he slid his glass across the bar. "One Miller's," he said.

Jack watched him pouring the beer into his glass, then he swung the stool to the side and slid out. "I got to be going," he said.

Johnny took a sip of his beer. "Remember me to your mother," he said.

Jack didn't say anything. Kate wouldn't let him so much as mention Johnny's name in the house.

"Great game, Jack," said Billy Boy.

"Thank you," said Jack. He started for the door.

"Remember, we're going to take that trip," said Johnny. "Galway Bay. The two of us."

"The last of the Currans," said Jack.

"The last of the Currans," said Johnny. He looked at the mirror across the bar and raised his glass.

Jack wanted to go back and shake his hand—do something. But he already had his hand on the door. "See you around," he said. Then he went out into Bay Street.

The wind was coming up the bluff from the river with a cutting edge on it. A cold night. Jack rubbed his shoulder. He knew he had beaten Johnny, but he didn't know how he felt about it—taking on the burden of being the better man. He had been working his father up in his head for too long—something that went on up above him, and under which he could shelter. The new idea would be taking away his cover—snapping deep cords inside him and pulling the lines into a new pattern. He felt too much exposed and by himself.

The night was brittle and clear, with the stars out but no moon. "He could have beaten me in his prime," he said out loud to himself. A real phantom, that. No consolation in it. He felt like something was passing over to him that he didn't want to take on. But what had happened before—the things of the past that were over and done—those wouldn't give him shelter either. He felt exposed and feathery—cut loose from things. "Teamwork . . ." He said it in a new way, hugging himself, with his hands pushed up into his armpits to keep them warm.

The coat of the uniform wasn't thick enough for a November night. He was glad to get into the car and out of the wind from the river.

BOOK III

Love:
1947-1950

20

Tybee Light

FORTY-TWO SCHOOLS.

J.J. O'Brien was keeping up with it the way he would have done if he'd had honest-to-God money riding on the deal.

"Forty-two, gentlemen. Forty-two of the cream of our nation's schools." He had hoped it would get to fifty, fifty being a round number, but he had to admit that forty-two wasn't bad, considering the caliber of the schools. "The very cream, gentlemen." It was certainly a Boniface record. Better than Horse Rooney had done—though there had been a war going on in that case.

There was a blackboard in Wooten's Pool Hall, with all the names written on it—West Point, Annapolis, Oklahoma, Michigan, Notre Dame—each new one added as the offers came in, the very best places only. Every time a new name went up on the blackboard, there was a free round of beer—Jax—courtesy of J.J. O'Brien.

"To Jack Curran of Boniface, gentlemen. The *crème de la crème.*" He thought of it as the payoff on his years of investment.

The interest in Jack washed into town floodlike, and some of it spilled over onto other members of the team.

Dimmy Camack had firm offers from the University of Georgia and Clemson. He was having a hard time making up his mind—of course. "I don't know, man." He kept hitting his fist into his palm and shaking his head. Whistler hadn't gotten any offers himself, but was helping Dimmy.

Whistler nodded his head, taking it seriously. "I wonder which one would have the best . . . you know . . . pussy?"

Flasher got a combination football and track scholarship to the University of Florida. "Room, board, and tuition," said the recruiter, slapping him on the back, "and all the orange juice you can drink." He laughed with his teeth clamped together.

Frog got some cautious feelers, but one by one they caved in when the recruiters saw him up close, without his uniform on. Southwest Georgia was picking up the culls, and they were the ones that finally took him. But their man had to spend a whole afternoon watching Frog blow bubbles, and telling him how good they looked.

"That was a *good* one."

"I think the one before was better."

"Yes. They were both good. Those were two swell ones."

"You really think so?"

"The one before was bigger."

"Watch this. This is going to be a *good* one."

He finally got Frog to sign the papers, but by the time he did, his eyes were starting to cross, and there was a sound in his ear like a tire going flat. Afterward, he went to the Sapphire Room of the De Soto Hotel, and bought a whole bottle of Scotch over the bar.

"I got the fucker," he told the bartender, hitting his ear with the heel of his hand. "You know any Finnechairos?" He pronounced it "Finney-*chair*-ee-o."

"No," said the bartender.

He took a slug of Scotch. "Somebody else can find the goddamn organ grinder to go with him," he said.

"Don't you want a glass?" said the bartender.

Before he talked to Frog, the recruiter from Southwest Georgia had tried to talk to Feeb.

"Mister," said Feeb. "Fuck off." He thought that would put an end to it. Being disrespectful to grown people was very shocking back then.

When they sent him a letter, he tore it up in little pieces and flushed them down the toilet—hoping his father wouldn't find out that they were after him, because he was afraid that the family honor would come up again, and he would be in for four more years of damage to his soft, round body. Feeb had been as excited as anyone over the success of the season, but he didn't like playing any more than he ever had. When the recruiter tried to talk to him, all the pain and work and fear came back. As far as he was concerned, his football career was over. "A fragrant fucking flower in my garden of motherfucking memories" is the way he put it in public. What he wanted now was to get going in the produce business.

The University of Georgia had been courting Ducker in the early part of the season, getting more and more interested all the time. But after his leg got broken, that was the end of that. They never made any real effort to find out how bad it was. There were too many good players around to waste time on damaged goods.

It was a better than average year for the team as a whole, but Jack was the one they were really after.

He signed with Georgia Tech.

There were a number of reasons why he did it, and Tech was a major football power at the time anyway, but being able to get back and forth to Savannah was the overriding consideration, because of Mary. The trains made Atlanta very accessible.

J.J. O'Brien never understood at all, and was more than a little put out that Jack wouldn't even consider the Notre Dame offer.

"It's Notre *Dame*, son," he said. "Notre *Dame* . . . our very mother, my boy."

If Jack had gone up there, he would have been the first Savannah player ever to make it to South Bend—the furtive dream of every Boniface alumnus come true. But he wouldn't get to see

Mary at all if he did, and he never considered it seriously. Being honorable was very important to him at the time, so he settled it over the telephone with the recruiter, and didn't encourage him to come down to Savannah to talk about it.

"Something is *wrong* with that boy," said J.J. O'Brien, shaking his head. "Gentlemen, something is terribly *wrong*." At Wooten's, the free beer ceased to flow.

The University of Georgia people were fierce on Jack's back to the very end, and were harder to deal with, since they were in and out of town anyway, talking to other players. And the recruiter was very aggressive, if thickheaded. Two or three times a week he called Jack up, coming to the school and his house to argue with him about it.

"Anything, son. You name it." He elbowed Jack in the ribs. "Pussy every weekend," he said—adding, on a serious note, "off season, of course."

But Jack wasn't interested. He didn't like the recruiter's style in the first place, and in the second place, it took a train ride and three bus transfers to get there. Almost as bad as South Bend. He also didn't like the talk about pussy coming from an older man.

"He's so one-minded about it," said Jack, talking to Feeb.

"Maybe you ought to ask him for a sideways blue one with a wart on it—something he could really sweat over."

Jack didn't like the recruiter, but he also didn't like the *idea* of the University of Georgia. Coach Butts had had some very good teams—particularly in years when he had stars like Sinkwich and Trippi as a nucleus to build his team around. But what Jack heard about the attitude toward players made it sound more like a business than a game. And most of the glory seemed to go to backfield men.

At Tech the attitude was different—or was thought to be. Bobby Dodd had teams that played an interesting kind of football, with small, quick backs, and a lot of scoring from a long way out— though he was about as strong on basics as Butts was, having played at Tennessee under General Neyland. He liked to kick on third down in the early part of the game, and in 1947 Tech was second in the nation in defense. The thing was, the Tech game was more of a team effort, and the last four All-Americans to come from there had all been linemen.

Which is not to say that Jack was after glory for himself. To some extent he was, but it could have loomed much larger in his thinking than it did. Still, he thought that the styles of the two schools were indicative of something. Whether it was true or not, it boiled down to a matter of integrity for him. And the Georgia recruiter didn't help at all.

But the main reason he had chosen Tech was that Atlanta was easier to get into and out of than Athens.

On Friday after Thanksgiving, Jack went up to Atlanta on the Central of Georgia night train. He had tried to get out of it, telling the Tech recruiter over the telephone that he was definitely going to sign with them.

"We need to have you here," said the recruiter. "All of you will be sitting on the sidelines during the game. We want to introduce you during the half." He was very definite about it. "It's for the newspapers," he said.

Having him up for the big game with the University of Georgia was the final step in the campaign to woo him, and the way recruiting was handled in those days, nobody ever took a verbal commitment seriously. The final proof of intent was when the name went down on the dotted line.

So the recruiter wouldn't take no for an answer. "I'm sending you two stadium tickets for the game, and money for three train tickets," he said, speaking very slowly and distinctly. "Bring your parents."

Jack tried to talk him into letting him take the *Nancy Hanks*, going up in the morning and coming back the same night. But he wouldn't agree to that.

"It's a big weekend. We need you here the whole time. It wouldn't look right. Mostly it's for the newspapers, but it wouldn't look right to the others."

They wanted Kate and Reilley to make the trip with Jack, so they would be able to get the papers signed and wrap up everything while he was there. But Kate didn't want to take Susy—nor did she want to leave her behind. And Reilley claimed he had a chance to work overtime, because he didn't want to make the trip without her. Jack thought about asking Dendron to use one of the extra tickets and go up with him, but Dendron wasn't that interested in football. And riding on trains made him sick—in spite of his interest in the models.

Feeb would have enjoyed the trip, especially the eating places in Atlanta, but Jack didn't want to have to listen to him for eight hours going and coming.

So he cashed in the day-coach tickets for a Pullman.

Jack said good-bye to Mary, going over to her house just after supper. Then Kate, Reilley, and Susy took him down and saw him off at the station on West Broad Street.

The night run took ten hours—the train leaving Savannah at ten o'clock and getting into Atlanta at eight the next morning. It was one of those slow locals that seemed to spend half the time stopped in dark tank-town stations, and a lot of time backing up. A jerky, stop-and-go ride.

The Pullman berths were already made up when Jack got on the train, so he went up to the smoking car and had a couple of cigarettes. There was a good crowd in the car, well-dressed people going up for the game. One man recognized him right off.

"Jack Curran?" he said, and put out his hand.

Jack was polite, but after the second cigarette, he excused himself and went back to the sleeping car to turn in.

The first place the train stopped was Pooler, Georgia—which was ten miles outside of Savannah. The second place was Guyton, which was eighteen miles. And so it went for 316 miles. Every stop and start sent the couplings banging up and down between the cars. Lying in the berth, Jack would look out the window, hearing the sharp metallic sounds coming back from the engine, passing through his car and on to the end of the train. Back and forth along the line of cars, and through his berth.

Not every stop had a station, but most of them did. Dark sheds, with just a dim light here and there under the roof of the platform, and a sign on hooks creaking as it paddled in the wind. While the train was moving, he lost the feeling of things that were outside the car in the darkness. But when they were pulled up and resting in the stations, the remoteness would go away, and things would come up to the window where he could see them.

It was a black, upland night. Where quick, spidery shadows moved in the dim lights, he could tell the wind was up and blowing. By putting his hand on the glass of the window, he could feel the cold, and the high-pitched, singing vibrations coming down from the northeast.

He didn't sleep, but he dozed, waking now and then to look into the black square of the window, through which no motion could be seen while the train was moving. Only the black void of the night, with the reflection of himself, warm, on the inside plane of the window, lit up by the night light in the berth.

The angle of reflection on the glass of the window showed him his lower leg and foot. The leg was sturdy, plaited with cords of muscles and furred with reddish hair. But the foot was delicate, almost fragile. He bent his knee and pushed the foot under the blanket that was folded across the end of the berth. Beyond the winter-white shank of his leg, he could see the heavy folds of the green curtain next to the aisle. The folds moved gently with the motion of the train. They had the velvety plushness of an altar cloth.

His hand on the glass still brought the cold in to him, but the vibrations of the wind were damped by the motion of the train.

Now and then a pinpoint of light would move by in the dark, winking through the trees. A fixed point around which the train seemed to be swinging in an arc, giving no clue to the speed of the train, nor to the distance of the light. At longer intervals bright lights would suddenly appear, flashing by just outside the window —the headlights of a car at a grade crossing, or the window lights of a house hunkered up close to the tracks. For a moment, the outside world would leap up to the square of glass, rushing by and away toward the end of the train. Then, just as suddenly, the light would be gone, and he would be looking at the inside of the berth —at the heavy folds of the swaying curtain, and the bunched muscles of his lower leg.

Off and on, the lids of his eyes would come down, and he would doze, his ear picking up the still, muffled sounds out of the corridor on the other side of the curtain. A soft, sighing snore. The rustle of someone turning over in the crisp sheets of his berth. Now and then there would be the conspiratorial movement of the conductor and the porters passing in the aisle between the sleeping passengers. Once he heard two porters arguing about something, their voices muffled in harsh whispers.

In the dozing intervals, figures came into his head, shapes and forms that he sometimes recognized. He was trying to pull back the summer day in the lighthouse—the day that Old Johnny had remembered and talked to him about, getting it to materialize inside the berth of the Pullman car. He could see the gulls sailing in and out on stiff, motionless wings.

And in and out of his thoughts came the snaky tree that had wound its way upward inside his head in the dormitory at New Orleans, after he had met Mary in the spring—the branches of the animal kingdom, with Mary herself floating above the top like a Christmas angel.

But the image augmented and grew. First a single tree, then a whole snaky forest of them. With a path through the forest, and strange, moving things blooming like pale fruit on the branches. He walked the path between the trees. Then the trees opened out, and the path became an avenue. When he came to the end of it, he was standing under the lighthouse at Tybee, looking up at the black-white-black of the shaft of the tower. At the top, Mary stood on the walkway, leaning out to him over the railing, her face turned down. Then the top of the lighthouse faded, swimming like a water reflection, and it merged with Mary, until Mary became the top of the lighthouse, the shaft rising and melting into her, with her arms raised above him, and her face at the pinnacle, looking down on him and smiling. And then the gulls were there, flying around the shaft of the tower, with motionless wings, soaring and circling her head where the beacon sat like a crown.

When his eyes opened, the sun was up. Not first light, but full, clear day. Outside the window there were wiry brown cotton fields and dead trees.

Jack went into the washroom and splashed cold water on his face, then shaved. In the dining car, he ordered ham and eggs from a surly porter with a swollen, purple-gray face and eyes like wedges of tangerine. Afterward he sat on the morning side of the car, with the watery sunlight coming in the window, trying to pick up the movement of the trees from the moving train, to decide whether the wind had died down or not.

The man who had recognized him from the night before slipped behind the table on the other side. Jack nodded to him and lit a cigarette.

"Isn't it bad for your wind?" said the man.

"I don't smoke much during the season," said Jack. "You have to get up to a pack a day or more to notice it."

"Going to the game?" said the man.

"Yes."

"Have you signed with one of them?"

"Tech," said Jack. "I haven't signed yet, but I'm going to sign with Tech."

"Bobby Dodd is a good coach."

"Yes," said Jack. "Excuse me."

The surly porter came up to take the man's order. The rim of the quarter Jack had left for a tip showed at the edge of the plate. The porter noticed it and frowned.

"It was a good game," said the man. "Thanksgiving."

"Thank you," said Jack. He had to raise his voice over the rattle of the dishes as the porter cleared them away.

When he got back to the Pullman, the berths had been made up, so he sat and watched the train pulling into Atlanta. The sun was gone, pushed out by a front moving down from the mountains. It was going to be a gray day. The clearness of the night had passed off, and there was a low rack of clouds coming down over the tops of the houses they passed. The wind had died away, too, and the glass of the window didn't feel as cold to his touch.

The day in Atlanta was formal and organized, and it passed in ordered movement—a procession of numb, gray hours out of which he would later be able to retrieve only the discomfort of sitting on the sidelines in wooden folding chairs under a sky that threatened rain.

Tech won the game, 9–7, upsetting the odds—Johnny Rauch

was having a good year as quarterback for Georgia, but the Tech backs were very quick on defense. They intercepted four of his passes.

Ordinarily Jack liked a defensive game, but later, on the train, when the man from Savannah asked him what he had thought of it, he realized that he couldn't remember the score.

The recruiter wanted him to stay over and talk with a group of alumni. He knew that meant money was involved, but Jack told him that he had to get back to Savannah.

"I'm going to sign with you," he said.

"We've got to have your parents' signatures, too. When can I come down?"

"You can come down anytime you want to."

"Monday?"

"Yes," said Jack. "My parents work, so it'll have to be after five in the afternoon."

"I'll drive down Monday morning. What's the paper down there?"

"*News* and *Press*."

"Is something the matter with you, Curran?" said the recruiter.

"No," said Jack. He was surprised. "The train ride was bad."

"You look foggy."

"It's okay."

"I'll get a photographer out to take a picture of the signing," said the recruiter.

On the train, the lack of sleep on the Friday trip caught up with him, and he dozed fitfully going back down. It was a softer night, with the clouds out, and much warmer than it had been the night before. But the forest of snaky trees came into his head in the berth, and the lighthouse with the gulls sailing around it.

Reilley met the train alone, and they drove to Marshoaks in a drizzling rain. When he got home, he called Mary and talked to her, telling her what he could remember about the trip and the game.

"Tech won," he said.

"It was the first Saturday you were away. I'm sorry it wasn't a better trip."

"The game was all right. It was rainy."

"Will you come over tonight?"

"Yes." He was talking with his eyes closed, beginning to drowse and slip away. "I missed you."

"Get some sleep, Jack," she said.

After he talked to her, he fell into the bed and slept until three in the afternoon. When he got up, the rain had stopped, but the clouds were still hanging low. He borrowed the car and drove down to Tybee. The lighthouse was locked, and he stood at the base looking up at the walkway at the top—standing in close to it so that the white stripe was foreshortened, and the whole shaft of the tower seemed black. He couldn't see the light itself, only the walkway standing away from the tower at the top.

While he was standing there, a man came up and spoke to him. "Something I can do for you?" He was an old man, with a stubble of gray beard, and baggy pants that drooped at the crotch.

Jack looked at him. "It's not open anymore?"

"It's open," said the man.

"It is? Are they going to turn it on again?"

"It's on," said the man. "What do you mean?"

"I thought they cut it off during the war."

"They did," said the man. "The war's over."

"Could I go up and take a look?"

The man looked at him for a minute, and Jack could tell he was going to refuse him. "I'll get the key," he said.

Inside, Jack climbed to the top. The door onto the walkway was closed, but not locked, so he opened it and stepped out. When he came through the door, a pair of gulls rose flapping into the air, white spots against the grayness. The grating of the walkway rattled and shook under his weight, and he leaned in toward the glass panels of the dome as he moved around it.

Back toward town, a haze spread out, and he couldn't see the fuel storage tank. The sea was a leaden gray, with swells running past the jetties into Calibogue Sound, oily and slow. He tried to call up the image that Old Johnny had wanted to leave with him, but all he could remember was the gulls. Even Fort Screven, laid out below him, with the emplacements for the coastal defense guns facing the sea, all of it looked unfamiliar to him. He leaned on the railing, looking down at the pair of gulls circling the shaft of the lighthouse below him. They banked, came up on the opposite side, and lighted on the railing. Jack tried to look through the glass of the dome, but he couldn't see them. He inched around the rattling walkway, leaning in toward the shaft of the tower. The gulls gave him two hard, bright eyes, not taking off, but side-stepping down the cap of the rail, going away from him. He made a sudden, lunging movement, shaking the grid of the walkway, and they took off, flapping and circling the light.

He heard a voice calling him from below, and looked down through the metal grating at the man who had let him in. He didn't want to step out to the edge to look over the rail. "What?" he said.

"Get off the walkway," said the man, cupping his hands, and moaning out the words in long, hallooing sounds.

"All right."

"Be sure the door at the top is closed."

Jack nodded his head. The man waved, then went up the stairs of a house near the base of the light.

Jack put his back against the side of the tower, then slid down into a squat, leaning in away from the rail. On his right, the seaward side, there was a long streak of smoke. The ship was hull down, and only the black feather of the smoke, smeared on the grayness of the horizon, marked the spot. No other ships were in sight.

Inland, on his left, he could see Fort Pulaski, closer than he would have thought, with the light pink spots where the federal shells had gouged holes in the walls. He could see over the parapet and into the open center of the fort, where the top of the giant fig tree on the parade ground was clearly visible. But farther back toward the town, everything was lost in the haze. He couldn't see the fuel storage tank at all. But he thought he could make out a glint of light reflecting from some hard, metallic point where the town should have been.

Turning his head to the right again, he looked out over the heavy swells at the wisp of smoke from the ship. "I wonder which way Galway is," he said.

Saying it made him self-conscious. "I don't even know which

way Ireland is," he said. It would have been just the same to him if the ship had been going to China or Germany or Jacksonville, Florida. Galway. Nothing stirred or moved in him when he said the word for himself. Only if his father had spoken it.

He stood up and looked at the lens of the light inside the windows of the dome. The iron grillwork of the cage that enclosed it was white from the droppings of sea gulls. He stood up and began to climb to the top of the dome, working up the grid until his head was out in the clear above it. He stood with his feet braced in the iron web, his body bent forward and curving over the top, his chin resting on his arms. His head was higher than the topmost point of the light.

The smoke from the steamer had grown fainter, and the sky seemed to be closing in from the east. He shut his eyes for a moment, resting his forearms on the dome of the light, leaning his chin on his forearms, and hugging the curve of the roof with his body.

Looking down on everything around him—the sea, the two forts, the marsh stretching toward the town to the west—was a grand feeling. And then the thought of what a grand gesture it was made him feel silly. Climbing up to stand on the very top of the dome itself, taking command at the roof of the world. He thought of it as something out of a movie, and finally he found it amusing. There wasn't anything to it really. He was wedged firmly in the iron web of the grille.

When he climbed down off the dome, the iron walkway shook and rattled with every step that he took. He couldn't see the bolts that anchored it to the brickwork of the tower. He was glad that he didn't see the keeper when he left to go back to the car.

After he had gone, the sea gulls came back to roost on the grid of the dome—grave and humorless and deliberate, looking two ways at once with their bright, stupid eyes.

Jack and Mary:
Talking

MR. ODELL WAS LEANING out of the half-open front door, his left hand on the doorknob, and his right on the knot of his tie. "Be in at ten o'clock, Mary," he said.

Going out on Sunday night was something he didn't approve of, since she had to go to school the next day. But it was the end of the holiday, and she had insisted. When she was determined, he always gave in.

"Yes, Father," she said.

Jack drove aimlessly, while he thought over the things that the trip had left for him to say. They went out Victory Drive to Remmler's Corner, then south to Skidaway Road toward Isle of Hope, the lights of the DeSoto weaving the curves of the narrow road under the canopy of live oak branches and Spanish moss.

At Isle of Hope, he drove around the bluff and parked at Ballabee's Pavilion.

Isle of Hope was ten miles out of town, on the waterfront. The Isle of Hope River was not a river, really, but a tidal estuary. It made a long brown curve, sweeping against the crescent of a high bluff, going from north to south. Along the bluff a narrow road followed the sweep of the curve, open to the water and marsh on the river side, with a one-deep string of houses on the other. The front yards were long and wide, but in the back, second-growth pines crowded in close, with here and there an outbuilding, or a Negro shanty pushing up against the big main houses that fronted on the bluff.

They were slightly seedy houses, in a genteel way. Most of them had been built in the last part of the nineteenth century, and were occupied by the grandsons and granddaughters of the builders. They were not all alike—the houses—with individual patterns in the crenellations and towers. Some had widow's walks, and some did not. But they had all come out of the same basic conception of style—solid and fancy. They were all big, two-story, clapboard-sided, and mostly white—with wide, screened porches wrapping around them on the front and sides. From the high front steps, oystershell walks led down to the road, and across to docks and boathouses hanging on the bluff on the river side.

Midway between the horns of the crescent was Ballabee's Pavilion and Turtle Farm—the only commercial establishment on the island. There was not even a grocery store.

In the early 1900s, Ballabee's had been a thriving place, with dances every weekend, played for by Blue Steele and Tony Pastor and other well-known bands of the time. Excursion boats left on Sundays for trips to Beaufort and Tybee Island and Wassaw. A streetcar line ran out from Savannah, and townspeople would rattle out on it to spend Sundays and holidays in the summer, drinking beer and cooled lemonade in the afternoons under the roof of the pavilion, while the Chatham Artillery Band played the kind of heart-raising music that had been popular then—Strauss waltzes and marches by John Philip Sousa. Then, after the sun went down, there would be dancing in the light of Japanese lanterns to songs like "My Gal Sal" and "The Bowery" and "After the Ball."

For Isle of Hope and Ballabee's, the high point had come during the Grand Prix races in 1910 and 1911. Ballabee himself had worked for the Fiat team as a mechanic, and many of the drivers were put up at the houses along the bluff, taken in as guests by the families. Every night everyone would be down at the pavilion, the drivers bellied up to the bar, some wearing their helmets with the goggles pushed up on top, smoking black, hand-rolled cigars and talking about the trial heats in languages that rattled and hissed and grunted, or in halting, twisty-mouthed English. Barney Oldfield had been there, and Carlos Fellini, and Eric Steiner, who was driving for the Dusenbergs. The center of gravity of the whole town had shifted out to Ballabee's for the spring, with four extra cars running in tandem on the streetcar line, and a band every night, and crowds on the pier that swayed the pilings and made them groan, sinking them deeper into the mud under the bluff.

But in the years after World War II, Ballabee's had fallen into decline. Even the turtle farm had lost its momentum. In a way, James—the current Ballabee—was trying to keep up with the times.

There was a soda fountain and a gallery of pinball machines at the entrance, but the pavilion itself—the dance floor and the band-stand hanging over the river—that was graying out in the wind and weather. The profit margin on dances was too small and chancy, and James didn't think it justified the initial investment of fixing things up. All the paint had peeled off the railings and benches, and the wood had gone powdery and velvet to the touch.

James, who was the grandson of the Ballabee who had built the pavilion, seemed to lack the gay and festive spirit of his father and grandfather. No daring. Something they'd had came up petrified in him, compacted by two world wars and a depression. And, anyway, dance bands weren't his style. A jukebox was. With colored lights bubbling in the tubes, and a clear and certain profit of a nickel on every song that was played.

James's interests were businesslike and solid. There was a small boatyard, which gave him as much to do as he could handle by himself with the help of two Negroes. And he was also the Chris-Craft dealer for the Savannah area—selling about a boat and a half a year.

Except for the first ten feet in from the entrance, where a small amount of cash still came over the counter from the pinball machines and the soda fountain, he didn't pay any attention to the pavilion at all. Only the Wurlitzer.

The concessions were fenced off and locked at night behind metal grilles, to protect the pinball machines. But he left the main part of the pier, the dance floor, open since he didn't care about it anyway, and there wasn't anything that could happen to it, though he unplugged the jukebox and locked a metal grille around it, too.

Now and then one of the locals would wander down and drop a crab line off the floating dock, or set some baskets. Nobody came out from town anymore. The streetcar didn't run. At night the pier was deserted, even in the summertime, and Jack liked to go there and stand looking down into the water when he had things on his mind. It had just the right degree of loneliness—a deserted public place—with echoes of the other times in the loft over the dance floor to keep him company. Occasionally he would see a shark winding around the pilings down below.

Jack and Mary walked out to the end of the dance floor, then down the rampway to the floating dock. The tide was on the ebb, and the eddies around the pilings made sucking noises, like water going down a drain. Streetlights at each side of the entrance on the bluff lit up the sign-plastered clapboard, casting shadows of the railing onto the old dance floor and out over the river.

Jack stood looking down into the water, and Mary sat down on the end of the rampway.

He lit a cigarette, his face glowing orange from the match cupped in his hands. "It's cold," he said.

"It certainly is," said Mary.

There was always a wind on the waterfront, coming in across the marsh from the ocean. It was damp and still heavy from the cloudiness of the day.

Jack shook out the match and threw it into the water. Mary hugged her knees.

"It was a long trip," he said.

"You look tired."

"I feel okay now. It's hard to sleep on that night train."

"Did you talk with them about going to school next year?"

"Yes," he said. He made a gesture with his hand, and the

cigarette was gone from his mouth, the glowing end moving in an arc in the darkness. "He'll be here tomorrow for me to sign."

"My father thinks Tech is a good school."

"Yes. I guess it is. They have more of a team than Georgia." He paused. "A *team*," he said, coming down on the word. "Georgia's got Rauch and Porter Payne. That's all they've got."

Mary thought about it for a while. "They treat you better?"

"Yes," he said. "It's the way they think. A lineman's not raw meat up there."

"I see."

"Everybody's not out for himself. It's more of a *team*, you know."

Mary didn't say anything.

"It's big business anyway. Anyplace you go. College won't be like Boniface. They have to invest too much money."

"Are you looking forward to it?"

For a minute he didn't answer. "It'll be different. At least they have a *team* at Tech."

The lights in front of the pavilion swayed in the wind, throwing quick shadows out over the water. There were boats moored at the south end of the crescent, and their riding lights made a small, fallen constellation in the darkness, bobbing with the movement of the water.

"Look!" said Jack.

Mary didn't get up. "What?" she said.

"I think I saw a shark. It went under the dock."

Mary looked down. There were spaces between the planks, but it was too dark to see. For a minute neither of them said anything—listening to see if they could hear anything moving in the water. The only noise was the sucking of the eddies around the pilings, and the small waves slapping at the sixty-gallon drums that supported the floating dock. Mary pulled her feet up under her on the rampway.

"It was something big," he said. He got down on his knees and looked over the edge of the dock.

"Get away from the edge," she said.

"It was something big."

He stood up and lit another cigarette. Gusts of wind were coming across the river out of the marsh on the ocean side, making the

movement of the floating dock short and choppy. The waves breaking on the sides of the drums made pinging sounds that echoed
inside.

"You act like something's the matter," she said.

"Well."

"I don't mean the shark. I mean since you got back."

"It was a long trip. Atlanta's a crummy town."

"So is Savannah if you want to put it that way."

She waited for him.

"I saw my father Thursday night. After I took you home."

She didn't say anything. She had never met Johnny, though Jack
had talked to her about him now and then.

"I beat him arm-wrestling," he said. "He beat me, but he cheated
—I was going to beat him. I felt his arm going down, but he used
two hands. He wouldn't let me beat him."

He waited for her to say something. "He could have beaten me
in his prime. I didn't like it. He was always the biggest man I ever
knew." He paused. "You know. Big." He made a weak and un-
emphatic gesture with his hands.

"It was a bad time for it to happen. You were let down after
the game."

"It was a *good* game."

"You know what I mean."

"Horse," he said. "And my old man." He looked down at the deck
of the raft, listening to the slap of the waves echoing inside the
drums. "Mother says granddaddy was bigger. But he died before I
knew him."

"Maybe it's just the end of the season."

"Maybe it is. I feel like something is over."

"I'm sorry he cheated. That's the main thing that bothers you?"

"What would be like it? For a girl, I mean? If you were prettier
than your mother?"

She thought about it for a minute. "Just being younger, I guess.
It comes along slowly. I don't know what would be like it. It's
not the same thing with a girl."

"I guess so. We won't arm-wrestle again. He wouldn't bring it
up. It's like he lied to me. Cheated on me."

"Would you rather have won?"

He looked at her, then away. "I wish it hadn't happened."

"You sound like an old man, Jack. With the weight of the world on your shoulders. You're only eighteen years old. In a way, it's what you wanted, isn't it? Why did you want to arm-wrestle in the first place?"

"I guess so." What she said hurt his feelings. "Someday you have to start to lose." He folded his arms, putting his hands up into his armpits. "He bought me a beer. That's the first time he ever did that."

For a minute she didn't say anything. "I know you feel bad about it, but I think you're blowing it up too much." He didn't say anything. "I'm sorry it happened. I really am. I just don't know exactly how to get on your side of it. Mother's beaten already. I guess I'd have to outwhine her."

"You hate to let go of a thing."

"Do you think less of your father?"

He looked at her. "He cheated," he said.

"And you beat him."

"Yes. I would have."

For a while neither of them said anything. "Who do you look up to?" she said.

"I look up to you."

"I mean *admire*. What man would you want to be like? Right now. Tonight."

"I really look up to you, Mary."

She looked at his face for a minute. "I'm trying to get into your trouble. If you don't want me to try to help, just say so."

He thought about it a minute, beginning to feel sorry for himself in a totally new way. "Let me tell you a dream I've been having," he said. He forgot that she was involved in the dream, and it wasn't like telling Dendron, his friend who didn't have dreams. "I have these dreams sometimes. Over and over." He put his hands in his pockets, speaking without looking at her, his voice mournful in the dark. "I mean, I have a dream every night, but sometimes I'll have the same one over and over."

"All right," she said.

He told her about the trip, and the dream he'd had in the Pullman berth, with the forest of snaky trees and the lighthouse. "You're the top of the lighthouse," he said.

"What?" she said. "You make me sound like the Statue of Liberty."

"It's what I think about. Looking up to you." He felt more and more sorry for himself.

"It gives me a funny feeling. You're not saying you love me. You're saying you look up to me. It makes me sound like a monument."

"I love you," he said. "That's the *way* I love you."

For a minute she didn't say anything. "I'm not your father, Jack. I wouldn't want to arm-wrestle you whether you beat me or not. Don't look up to me that way."

"When I was in New Orleans . . ."

"What?" she said, interrupting.

"Last year," he said. "When I was in New Orleans last year, I used to think about you at night before I went to sleep. I saw this snaky tree that was on a chart in the biology class, and you were up there at the top. You looked like an angel on a Christmas tree."

With the streetlights behind her on the bluff, he couldn't see her face, the frown was in her voice. "My mother calls me her 'Angel.'"

For a minute he didn't say anything. Anger was beginning to come up under the hurt feeling, and he felt that it was very necessary to make his point clear to her. "Mary Mother of God," he said.

"What?" she said. She was really surprised.

"I don't go to mass. What would you say if I told you . . ." he stopped. "You're like Mary the Mother of God to me."

"That's awful," she said, standing up. "I'll be reminding you of a tombstone next thing."

"I'm telling you how I feel about you. I couldn't lie about it."

"Maybe you ought to lie about it."

"It's the way I feel."

"Feel some other way."

For a minute they didn't say anything. "Is this really the way you think about me?" she said.

"Are you going to get mad if I don't lie to you?"

"Is it really?"

"Sometimes," he said, lying a little.

"What are you going to do when you find out who I am?"

"I know who you are." He made the assertion the way he would have thrown a body block.

"I know you do. I know you do. You didn't hear the question. What are you going to do when you find out who I am?"

"I guess I'd better lie to you," he said, mournful again.

She stepped up to him and took his hand in both of hers. Then she put it up inside her sweater, holding it to her breast. It was a very small breast, warm, and he knew that his hand was cold from the air.

"Feel who I am," she said.

The small breast was exactly the kind he imagined that Mary would have—small and delicate, and hardly a breast at all.

"Your hand is like ice," she said.

It was the first time a man's hand had ever been put there, and Jack knew it was. There were secrets in those days between the sexes, and what she was giving him was a thing for him alone. It took away the need for him to make her see how he felt. He wasn't mournful, and he didn't feel like winning or losing. All he wanted to do was give himself up to her. He went down on his knees, taking both of her hands in his.

"Mary . . ." he said, "Mary . . ." He stopped, without saying it out all the way.

She pulled his hand out of the warmth of her sweater. "You're missing the point, Jack," she said. "You're missing the point. I'm Mary Cheney Odell of Savannah. And you've just had your cold, cold hand on the flesh of my body."

22

The Welding Widow

Jack wasn't so tired again as he had been after the Atlanta trip—
foggy tired and dreamlike. The way that he and Mary acted when
they were with each other afterward—on through the winter and
into the new year—there was a certain distance in their feeling.
After the one time, he kept his thoughts to himself, with an unspoken illusion that each of them knew who the other one was.
Mary's question about how he thought of her—that never did make
any sense to him. And it never had a chance to clear up, because
he wasn't able to think himself into it anyway. To do that, he
would have had to put aside the visions of her inside his head—the
snaky tree and the lighthouse.

So he told his dreams to Dendron, the way he had done in the
past.

He had the shape of her small breast in his memory—something
that went beyond words, and turned him into himself, and
buttoned him up into deep silence. He needed good things to
remember after the night with his father in the Lighthouse. Be-

sides which, he wasn't big for serious words anyway, and the way that she had taken him into herself—given him the intimacy—led him to distrust words altogether. His hand on her breast—that was the true thing that had happened, and the words he had used had only choked him, and mixed things up, turning him down a blind alley. They never came out with the meaning he had wanted them to have. Jack liked to talk well enough, but only when he didn't have to mean what he said.

At Christmas, he gave her a silver necklace, because silver was the metal that she brought to mind for him.

The jeweler who sold it to him kept calling it "this *number*," and congratulating him on his taste.

"Sterling silver, this number," he said. He held up the clasp, showing Jack the proofmark. It was too small to make it out, but Jack nodded because it seemed to mean a lot to the man.

"Yes," he said.

"Very nice number," said the man. "One of the best numbers I've got." The loupe of his glasses was turned up, and it magnified a mole on his forehead, bringing out the purple and brown colors, spongelike against the whiteness of his skin.

"How much?" said Jack.

"Listen," said the man. "You have very good taste." He gave Jack a wink and a nod over the counter.

Mary gave him a Swank key chain. One of the long ones that everybody was wearing then. It pleased him, because he wanted one, and because he knew that he had paid more for her necklace.

They had dates every weekend, and there was a house party at Tybee in March where it rained. Their intimacy did not grow, but they reached an accommodation with each other that made them think it did. The high point had been the time on the floating dock at Ballabee's after Thanksgiving. They never touched each other like that again. Not literally, nor in any other way. Jack could never bring himself to press in too close. And Mary never offered.

But he lived with the recollection of it just below the surface inside his head. And cupping his hand brought it back for him. He wished that she would do it once more—a long thought that wound in and out of his head and up and down his spinal column with a force of its own. But he couldn't try to push her. The best part of it had been that it was freely given. It created a feeling of respect and obligation in him.

Over the winter, George Bogger kept his ties with the outside world through the voices coming out of the radio. With the football season over, there wasn't much news about Jack. But there were the commercials, and the mystery programs, and the warm orange light from the dial. The epileptic attacks didn't come on as often in the cold weather. But he had them. Every time he came out of one, he had forgotten a little more. They erased most of the unpleasant side of the window business with Susy.

Forgetting let him keep on moving ahead, with the bad parts falling away behind him. While he had more sadness than most, because of the attacks the sadness worked itself off in a shorter time. Like a lot of afflictions, the epilepsy carried with it something of its own mitigation. Not that the attacks wiped away the past altogether, only that they softened it and blurred the edges, so that things didn't stick to him, hanging on and attracting his attention. He could have taken down the sheet of plywood that he had nailed over the window, but he had come to like it, that extra layer, the way it cut off the outside light and the noises that would have distracted him. So he left it up.

With the coming of spring, he began to get out into the yard a little. Even George had to break out of winter when the time came. There was too much daylight left when he got in from work, and there were things that he had to do—maintenance projects.

His first spring chore was repairing the hutch in which he raised the crickets that he sold for bait. It had a couple of rotten planks in it that needed to be replaced.

Toward the end of March he went out on a Saturday afternoon to take the measure of the boards, so he could begin to look around for sound ones to replace them.

"Steel's better. You can always rely on steel."

George didn't pull the voice out of the surrounding sounds just at first. His own backyard was not a place where he expected anybody to speak to him.

"You could spend your life building back a wooden thing like that. Steel's something you can *rely* on in this world." The voice was kazoolike, reedy; it sounded like it was coming up out of a coil of brass tubing. The second time George should have caught on that somebody was talking to him, but he was measuring the boards, and reading the numbers off the chain was tedious for him and required all of his attention, the way it did on the job.

"Hey, Pretty Boy," said the voice.

It looked like 4 feet, 3.2 inches. But it had been 4 feet, 3.5 the first two times he had measured it. He had trouble getting in close enough to read the marks on the chain, because he had to hold it in place with his arms spread wide apart.

A pebble bounced off his head, and he jerked his hands, letting the chain slip.

"You don't pay attention too good, Pretty Boy," said the voice. "Don't you never take notice?"

George looked back at the fence on the far side of the yard, shading his eyes with his hand. Just above the top boards of the fence, resting on it like a jack-o'-lantern, was a head that looked like a pink and white pineapple, with a red handkerchief knotted at the forehead, the ends pronging up in a V.

"You can rely on steel," she said.

George squinted his eyes to look at the head for a moment. It was round, like a moon, and chalky white, with bright red rouge spots on the cheeks, very distinct and blotchy. "You talking to me?" he said.

The head turned, looking left and right. "You the only Pretty Boy I see," she said. At the end, she tacked on a very distinct, echoey giggle, which seemed to shoot straight out the top of her head, coming on and going off like somebody was working a switch.

George looked around the yard, then back at the head.

"Steel's the thing," she said. "Steel don't rot out on you."

"I get the boards free for nothing," he said.

"It's a nuisance," she said. "You got to keep after it all the time."

George didn't say anything.

"You could scrounge up steel as good as those boards." Her elbows were winged out on top of the fence, her chin resting on her arms. Working her jaw when she talked made her head bounce up and down, wiggling the ends of the kerchief. "Wouldn't be but one time you'd have to do it with steel."

"I can *nail* the boards," he said.

"You can *weld* steel," she said.

George looked at her. "I can't weld," he said.

"*I* can," she said. She smiled, and he caught a flash out of a gold tooth in the front of her mouth.

"You a *welder?*"

"No," she said. "I'm a widow. I *used* to be a welder."

"How were you a welder?"

"During the war," she said. "Fred went off in the army, and I didn't have nothing else to do. I wasn't going to cheat on a man in the service."

"And you were a welder?"

"I figured I had to help with the war effort—getting Fred home, you know. You could look in his face and see he was going to need all the help he could get." She thought a minute. "It was like he was going off to the shooting with a bull's-eye painted on his chest." Then she added, "Fred was my husband."

"I see," said George.

"Born to lose," she said. "Fred." For a while she didn't say anything, and George thought she might be going to sing the song to him.

"I figured I might as well get *paid* for it, too," she said. "The working. You can't fight a war by going in the poorhouse."

"Yes," he said.

"So I learned to weld."

"That's right," he said.

"Welders get top pay," she said. "I worked at the shipyard."

"I see," said George. "You *used* to be a welder."

"I still got a rig," she said. "I like to keep it up, just in case." She looked at him. "I don't have to *work*. I got Fred's pension. From the army."

"Yes," said George.

"Fred was a corporal."

"I see."

"He got blown up at Anzio." She stopped a minute. "The government letter just said he got killed at Anzio, but they never sent any

[247]

of him home to bury. So I figured he must have got blown up. There wasn't even a dog tag. If there'd been any of him left, I figure they'd have sent it on."

"I'm sorry to hear it," said George.

"Thank you," she said. "I thought a lot of Fred. He wasn't much to look at in the face . . ."—she stopped—". . . like yourself," she said. "He had a good heart."

George blushed and didn't say anything.

"I'm about over it though. You can't drag out a thing like that too long."

"Live and let live," said George.

"What?"

"You can't drag it out too long."

"That's right," she said. "It gets morbid on you."

"I know what you mean," he said.

"Well," she said. "Get you some steel, and we'll fix it up right."

"Where do you get the steel?"

"Try a junkyard," she said. "It don't have to look pretty. That's the nice thing about steel."

"Just ask the man for steel?"

"Ask for one-inch angle," she said. She held up her first finger, marking it with her thumb to show him the size. "Inch, inch and a half."

George looked at her. "I didn't catch your name," he said.

"I didn't throw it," she said. She flashed her gold tooth at him, and gave him the frantic giggle with her neck stretched out and her chin tucked in. Very dry. Coming out of her like there was a blowhole in the top of her head. "Merle Verona Lee," she said, very serious. " 'Merle Verona' for short."

"Pleased to meet you, Mrs. Lee," he said. "My name's George Bogger."

"Yes," she said. " 'Pretty Boy' for short."

George blushed and started into the house.

"Bring it over here when you get it," she said, yelling after him. "I don't like to move my rig around."

"Yes'm," he said.

"Don't 'ma'am' me," she said. "I'm not that old."

George stopped. "How old are you?" he said.

For a minute, she just looked at him—a bare twinkle coming off the gold tooth, where her lips were parted. "That's a nigger question," she said at last. "Just you get the steel, Pretty Boy. Asking nigger questions don't become you." She took her head off the fence and went into the back door of her house, letting it slam.

"Who was that, George? Who were you talking to?" said Mrs. Bogger.

"She's our next-door neighbor."

"I know," said Mrs. Bogger. "What'd she want?"

"She's a welder," said George.

Mrs. Bogger looked at him. "A *welder?*" she said.

"No," said George. "She *used* to be a welder. She's going to fix the cricket hutch."

"What?" said Mrs. Bogger. "What? Who was that woman, George?"

George went into his room and shut the door on her. Then he lay down on the bed to listen to the radio and think about what he should do. But he couldn't pay any attention to the programs. So after a while, he got up and went out to look for a junkyard.

The Ideal Junkyard was down on East Broad Street, between Oglethorpe and Lincoln. A whole square block of undulating metal. Waves of it that pitched and rolled like a rusting Sahara. The office was a corrugated metal shack with a shed in front of it. Under the shed sat the proprietor. A small, heavyset, hairy man in a white T-shirt with two holes in it. Dark, curly hair stood out in the holes, and under the hair was the blue and red tracery of a tattoo. He was drinking a NuGrape soda, sucking on the neck of the bottle and popping it with his tongue.

"Howdy," he said when George walked up under the shed.

George looked at him. "I need some steel," he said.

The man looked at him, then swung his eyes around at the rolling hills of metal that surrounded the shed. "Buddy," he said, "you come to the right place." He turned the NuGrape up and sucked the last of the soda out of the bottle. Then he sucked his tongue into the neck of the bottle and took his hands away, letting it hang there like the clapper of a bell. He looked up at George as if he expected him to say something about it. When he didn't, the man pulled it off with a pop and threw it into a pile of broken bottles at the corner of the shack. "In general," he said. "Or you want something in particular?"

George held up his index finger, marking it with his thumb, the way Merle Verona had showed him. "Inch angle," he said.

The man rubbed his stomach, then belched loudly. "How long?" he said.

George looked at him. He held up his thumb and index finger again. "A inch," he said.

The man looked at George. "I know how long a *inch* is," he said. "I mean how long the piece. Twelve foot? ten?"

George thought a minute. "It's for a hutch," he said.

"A hutch?" said the man.

"For my crickets."

"You mean—" the man made a chirping sound with his mouth, "—crickets?"

"Yes," said George. "Like a cage."

"What kind of crickets you got, buddy?"

"I thought, you know, it's better than wood."

"They eat the wood?" said the man.

"Listen," said George. "You got any inch angle?" He held up his finger again, marking it with his thumb.

"How long?"

"Four foot, three and five-tenths inches," said George.

"Exactly?" said the man.

George looked at him. "Exactly," he said.

The man belched again. "Come on," he said.

He got George twelve five-foot pieces of angle iron.

"That's three dollars," he said.

George paid him.

"Where's your truck?" said the man.

George looked at him. "What truck?" he said.

"How you going to get it home?"

George looked at the pile of angle. "I ain't got a truck," he said. "I'm going to carry it."

"Carry it?" said the man.

"You got some wire to bale it up?" said George. "It ain't that heavy."

"It's heavy," said the man. "Mostly it's bulky. Where do you live?"

"Marshoaks," said George.

"Goddamn," said the man. "That's almost to DeRenne Avenue."

"Thirty-four blocks," said George.

"They ain't going to let you on the bus with it," said the man.

"I'm used to walking," said George.

"Listen," said the man. "Don't you have somebody would give you a lift? You could leave it here till you could come pick it up."

John Sparks would have come for him in the truck, but George didn't want to have to explain about the widow.

"I wouldn't want to do that," said George. "I'm kind of *into* it, you know. I don't like to wait around when I'm into a thing."

The man looked at the pile of angle iron. "For a dollar, I'd deliver it."

George thought about that. "No," he said. "I got too much money in it already. You bale it up for me and I won't have no trouble."

"I can't do it for *nothing*, mister," said the man. "It's more than a dollar's worth of gas to get out to Marshoaks."

"I understand that," said George. "It ain't your lookout."

The man looked at the pile of angle. "It's seventy-five pounds if it's a ounce."

"Just give me some wire and I'll bale it up," said George.

The man thought a minute. "I can't do it for *nothing*, mister. Just the mileage on my truck would be more than a dollar, not even counting my time."

"I don't mind," said George. "It's the kind of work I do. I can walk it home in an hour."

The man helped him bale up the pieces of angle iron. Then he found a piece of rope to rig a couple of straps so George could carry the weight from his shoulders. He was clearly remorseful about it, but he couldn't get down under a dollar for the use of his truck.

After they got the load up on him, George made a point of standing around for a few minutes talking to the man, so he could see that it wasn't bearing down on him too much. But when he started to walk out of the gate, he had to lean into the weight to be able to move.

Two hours. That's what it took him to walk it home. Half an hour of that was spent arguing with a policeman at the corner of East Broad and Henry Street. The policeman thought he ought to give George a ticket.

"What *for?*" George had his arms folded across his chest to keep the rope from sliding off. He would have put down the angle, but the circulation was cut off at his shoulders, and he was afraid he wouldn't be able to move his arms to get the load up again.

"It *looks* illegal." The policeman was tall and thin, with a nose that looked like a saltine stuck edgeways into the middle of his face. He fidgeted with his pad. "Blocking a public thoroughfare," he said.

"I can't walk in the street."

"You oughtn't to walk on the sidewalk. You shouldn't get by with a thing like that. What if somebody saw you?"

George looked at him. "*Everybody* saw me," he said. "What do you mean?"

"I'm *responsible* for this area," said the policeman. "What do you say to that?"

"Nobody else complained."

"It looks bad for you to get *away* with it."

"Get away with *what?*" said George. "You're the first one said anything about it."

"Can't nobody get by you. You take up the whole sidewalk."

"When I meet somebody," said George, "I turn sideways." He turned sideways so the policeman could see. There was plenty of space.

"Suppose you didn't *see* him?" The policeman nodded his head and winked his eye, as though he had made a telling point.

"Listen, mister. This thing's heavy. I got to get on home."

The policeman ended by giving him a warning. The ticket said, "Obstructing a Public Thoroughfare." Under the section on "Attitude" he checked "Fair." George's arms were too numb for him to take the ticket, so the policeman stuffed it into his shirt pocket. While they had been standing around talking, the numbness had crept over George's shoulders and was working its way down his back.

His arms weren't much use to him for the first hour after he got home, but as soon as the blood came back down into his hands, he got a hacksaw and cut the angle to exactly the same dimensions as those of the wooden hutch, taking the measure with the chain. From each five-foot piece, he cut off 8.5 inches.

When he finished, he went over and told Merle Verona that he had gotten the steel—though he knew it was too late for her to weld it up.

"We'll fix it tomorrow," she said. "Unless you don't hold with breaking the Sabbath."

"What?" he said.

"We'll weld it up tomorrow."

The next morning George turned out at six o'clock, the way he did every day. But when he knocked at Merle Verona's back door at seven, he nearly wore his knuckles out before he heard stirrings inside the house.

"Pretty Boy?" Her voice was a low, whispery croak, as if she had a fishbone pronged halfway down her throat. "What *time* is it?"

"Seven."

"Sweet Jesus." Her breath fluttered the curtain on the back-door window, but she didn't pull it aside where he could get a clear look at her. "Go back and do something. Come again at eight. I'm not letting you in before eight o'clock."

"What time you get up?"

"I'm up," she said.

"You didn't say what time."

"I just said it. Nobody gets a look at me before eight o'clock. Maximum. I wouldn't even take a chance with Fred before eight o'clock. And I had the papers on *him*."

"I get up at six," said George, pouty.

"I don't, buster. Not since V-J Day."

George started to leave.

"Don't you go off and sulk, Pretty Boy," she said. "You be *back* at eight o'clock. I wouldn't want to waste what I got to do to my face." She stopped, and through the door he could hear the joints popping in her jaw while she yawned.

When he came back at eight o'clock, she let him into the kitchen.

She was more civil, but her face didn't look all that good either.

"How old *are* you?" he said, coming up close.

"That's *two* nigger questions, Pretty Boy." She licked her finger and made a mark in the air. "You ask the third one and I'm going to fram you up side the head. *Think* about what you got to say." She pulled out a chair for him. "You had breakfast?"

"Yes'm," he said.

"I told you about 'ma'aming' me," she said.

"I wasn't thinking," he said, looking at her face.

"It's eight o'clock, Pretty Boy. I look better in the afternoon."

"Yes," he said. "I remember you do."

"You get up that early every day, or is Sunday special?"

"I meet John at the City Hall at seven-thirty," he said.

"Wait," she said. She got the coffeepot from the stove and poured two cups. "I don't want to hear about John until I've had my coffee."

George put four spoons of sugar into his, then poured evaporated milk into it until it ran over the top.

"I'm a night owl myself," she said.

George looked at her.

"You know. I like to sit up and listen to the radio."

"You like the radio?"

"Sometimes it's twelve before I get to sleep," she said "Twelve-thirty. Lots of times." Her mouth trembled and the corners turned down while she bit off a yawn. "A night owl," she said. She took a sip of her coffee. "You can't burn it at both ends."

"I like to listen to the radio," he said. He was sitting at the kitchen table, and he looked down at his hands resting on the oilcloth. "Pepsi-Cola-hits-the-spot-twelve-ounce-bottle-that's-a-lot-twice-as-much-for-a-nickel-too-Pepsi-Cola-is-the-drink-for-you." The way he said it, a key ought to have been winding down on his back. He didn't look up at her until he was finished. When he did, he caught her in another yawn.

Merle Verona had a Martha Raye mouth on her anyway, but when she opened it up all the way for one of her jawbreakers, her whole face faded off behind it, like she was beginning to turn herself inside out orally. For a dentist, her mouth was a dream come true—the kind of four-hand orifice God would provide to do molar root canals on if he ever got to heaven. But to an everyday nonprofessional, with a nondental point of view, it was a fearsome thing to see. Sitting across the table from it, in a small room, it was like looking head-on at a shark. George couldn't help calculating the size of the piece she would take out of him if she ever caught hold in a fleshy place.

"Excuse me," she said, when her face came back from behind her mouth.

"Are you all right?" he said.

"I'm not usually up this early," she said. "I was up till twelve-thirty last night."

He sat back down at the table. "I like to memorize the commercials," he said.

She looked at him for a minute. "Yes," she said.

"It's not too hard. You got to listen."

"I like the music shows," she said. " 'Hit Parade.' "

"Some people have trouble remembering them," he said.

"That's why they have it," she said. "So you can remember the songs."

"What?" he said.

She sang the "Hit Parade" theme song for him. "You like to dance?"

"Dance?" he said.

She whirled herself around a time or two, her housecoat swirling out around her legs, which were very nice. "Dance."

"I never knew how to dance."

"You look like you would be a good dancer."

"I never knew how."

"You've got a dancer's eyes," she said. "I can tell."

"I have?"

"A dancer's eyes have this look to them. You would have rhythm."

George drummed his fingers on the kitchen table. "Mother and Daddy will dance every now and then sometimes."

"You would just need somebody to teach you the steps. The natural talent is there."

George thought a minute. "I'd rather you teach me how to weld," he said.

Merle Verona changed into her shipyard working outfit—a pair of olive-drab coveralls, with a "Merlie V." breast patch and a white snood. "I always did love a snood," she said. "It's like the war all over again."

She set up her rig in the backyard, clipping the leads to the line side of the fuse box.

"Ain't that dangerous?" said George. Electricity was a scary thing to him. When he was a small child he had stuck his finger into a light socket, and his mother had talked it up to a point where he used to lie awake at night trying to hear the electricity surging and crackling in the walls.

"I keep my free hand in my pocket when I clip on," she said. "You got to be careful. The electrician I talked to wanted an arm and a leg to put in a two-twenty outlet. This works just as good."

She got everything set up and clamped, then she picked up two of the pieces of angle and banged them together. "Next time you see them . . . they will be *one!*" She thought a minute. "That's the thing I always liked about welding." She banged the pieces together again. "The *idea* of it."

"What?"

"They will be *one!*"

"I see," he said.

"You come back around ten."

George looked at her. "What?" he said.

"Come back around ten. It's just about sixteen inches of weld, but the setup takes time."

"How'm I going to see?"

"You ain't," she said. "That's why you better go home."

George looked at her.

"You can't have an *on*looker at a welding, Pretty Boy. It'll put your eyes out."

"How'm I going to see to weld when I can't look?"

"I don't have but the one mask. I got to be the one to see what I'm doing." She gave him a level and steady eye. "I mean it, Pretty

Boy. A couple of raisins on the half shell." She pronged two fingers at his eyes. "That'll be your baby browns."

"Well," he said.

"Blind as a bat." She closed her eyes, then opened them wide.

"I thought I was going to get a lesson," said George.

"It'll have to be a talking lesson till we get you a mask. You stand around here and you'll wind up looking at the arc. Can't help it. Go on home. I'll call you when I'm finished."

"How are you going to know what to do?"

"I was a *professional* welder, Pretty Boy. I know how to make a hutch. You got to get you another mask before I can teach you anything."

"*Buy* it?"

" 'Less they happen to be giving them away."

"This is commencing to run into *money*."

"It'll be worth it," she said. She banged the angle together again. "Next time you see them, they will be one."

George went back to his house, very morose and pouty. He could hear the buzzing and see the flicker of the arc through the boards of the fence. When she called him at ten o'clock, he waited for the third call before he came.

"It'll last forever," she said, showing him the hutch. "They are one."

"Where's the screen?" said George.

"You got to put in the screen," she said. "I can't weld screen wire on angle."

"How'm I going to get the screen to stay on if you can't weld it?" he said.

"It'll last forever," she said.

Then she began to use the investment she had made and capitalize on it.

"Let's go down to Tybee to celebrate," she said.

She had a 1941 Ford coupe, which she offered to let him drive.

"I can't drive," he said.

"You're a grown man, Pretty Boy. What you mean you can't drive?"

"I got epilepsy. They wouldn't give me a license."

[257]

"You got what?"

"Epilepsy," he said. "I have attacks."

Merle Verona looked at him for a minute. "You mean—" she stuck out her tongue and shook her head, "—'attacks'?" she said. "Like you swallow your tongue?"

"I *never* swallowed my tongue," he said. "I have epilepsy. So they wouldn't give me a license."

"I might have known," she said. "Fred had a face like a jewfish. Now you got the epilepsy fits."

"I never swallowed my tongue," said George.

"You know what I mean. I might have known."

"I'm sorry," he said.

"No," she said. "That's okay. I ain't no Betty Grable myself. Some people have all the luck." She looked at him. "You can *ride* in a car, can't you?"

"I ride to work every day."

"I'll drive," she said. "We'll go down after supper. What you like to eat, Pretty Boy?"

"I don't much care," he said. "I'm not big on eating."

"You like . . ." she thought, ". . . ham?"

"Ham's okay. We have it every Easter. I'm not much of an eater."

"You come over about six o'clock. I'll bake a ham for supper. Then we can go down to Tybee." She added, "With potato salad."

"Tybee's closed."

"The Rail's open. I like it better in the wintertime. We can listen to the jukebox. I'll teach you to dance."

"I got to go to work tomorrow."

"We'll be back by ten."

"I ain't no night owl."

"I did you a favor. Now you got to do me one."

He didn't say anything.

"I'm paying for it, Pretty Boy. You just come along for the ride."

"Well," he said.

"How *often* you have a fit?" she said.

"Attack," he said. "The doctor calls it an 'attack.'"

"How often?"

"Once a week."

[258]

"You had one this week?"

"Thursday."

"Come over at six. We'll have ham and potato salad."

"Don't put celery in the potato salad," he said.

They went down to the Brass Rail. George didn't drink hard liquor, so she bought him RC Colas over the bar. She drank Moscow Mules. She also gave him some quarters to play the racing game machine.

After a while she put some money in the jukebox and asked him to dance.

"I don't know about dancing," he said. The lights coming up from the machine blotched his face yellow and green and red, shifting as the wheel went around.

"I'll teach you."

"I'd rather not do it where people can see."

"You'll be a natural dancer. Don't worry about people seeing you."

"I nearly won," he said.

"What?"

"I nearly won the race game. I was betting on number three."

She didn't say anything.

"Number two won."

"You think you were close?"

"Two's next to three," he said. "I'd rather stay with it. Can you get somebody else to dance with you?"

The place was empty, except for two of the booths. In one of them four high school boys were draped around in a kind of Henry Aldrich angst, drinking beer and trying to turn Humphrey Bogart gestures into a way of life. In the other there was a couple. The man was bald with light eyes. The woman had shiny gold hair. Both of them had a deep tan. The man was talking, keeping his voice low, but making emphatic gestures with his hands. The woman was sitting sideways in the booth, smoking a cigarette, looking away from him and blowing clouds of blue smoke into the air without inhaling.

George played the race game and lost two more times.

"That's it," she said. "I don't have no more quarters."

"I nearly won," he said.

"You been *nearly* winning all night. That's the way they work it."

"I would win next time or two."

"I got no more quarters. You already put four seventy-five in that thing already."

"You're playing the music machine."

"It's *my* money, Pretty Boy."

"Well," he said.

"Let me give you a dance lesson."

"What time is it?"

"It's early, Pretty Boy. Listen. 'Sentimental Journey.' That's a real dancing tune." She did a step or two around the racing machine. "The night is young. Come on, let me give you a lesson."

"I got to work tomorrow. What time is it?"

"You got time for a dance."

"What time is it, mister?" he asked the bartender. The bartender hooked his thumb over his shoulder at the clock behind the bar.

"Is that ten-thirty?"

The bartender nodded without looking around.

"You said we'd be home early. I got to go to work tomorrow morning."

"You only live once, Pretty Boy," she said.

"What?"

"Let's dance."

"You got to take me home."

"You ain't going to let me give you a dancing lesson?"

"You said you wouldn't keep us out late."

"I done you a favor, Pretty Boy. Wasn't the ham good?"

"The potato salad had celery in it. I told you I didn't like celery in my potato salad."

"I paid forty-five cents a pound for that ham."

"I told you. Celery with my potato salad puts my teeth on edge." He started for the door. "We got to go."

"Well," she said. "I wouldn't want you to lose your beauty sleep on my account."

"I got a full day's work ahead of me tomorrow," he said. "I ain't no night owl on a pension, like yourself."

Merle Verona took a quarter out of her pocketbook. "Try the race game one more time." She put the quarter in the slot for him. He bet on number 3. It came in and he won twenty-seven dollars. "I'm your good luck, Pretty Boy," she said as the coins poured out on the floor. "Remember that."

Over the next three weeks, Merle Verona wheedled him into trips to the Brass Rail every weekend, luring him with rolls of quarters to play the racing machine in the hope that she would also get him to dance with her. But he was embarrassed about doing it in public, and only gave in enough to let her give him some lessons in her living room. He wasn't a bad dancer as long as people weren't looking at him.

Somehow Merle Verona found out about the slingshot, and she welded one up for him out of galvanized water pipe. "Aim for the Heart!" said the card that she tied on it with a red ribbon. With the pipe frame and some surgical rubber tubing for the straps, it must have weighed ten pounds. If George had had an eight-foot arm for the draw, he could have hunted elephants with it. Merle Verona had learned to weld putting ships together, and fine detail wasn't her strong point anyway. If he carried the slingshot in his hip pocket like he did his wooden one, it dragged at him too much to put up with day in and day out. But he liked the *idea* of it, so he thanked her, and put it on his dresser as a kind of trophy.

"You can *count* on steel," she said when she gave it to him.

On the night of April 26, she got George to take his first real drink. It was a Moscow Mule, which is very fizzy and smooth, without any liquory taste, because of the vodka. He sampled it, smacked his lips, then scoffed down four in a row. Merle Verona had trouble digging the money out of her purse fast enough to pay for them, but she didn't complain, because getting George drunk was part of her plan, and she figured it would about even out with the horse-racing machines as far as the expense went.

"That's a good drink," he said, after each one he tossed off. "I'll have another."

At least that's what he said after the first three. After the fourth

[261]

one he didn't say anything. He just sat there on the barstool with a froggy look on his face, his chin pulled down into his shirt collar, staring at a drip coming off the Pabst spigot behind the bar.

For five minutes nobody said anything. Merle Verona had had two Moscow Mules herself, so she wasn't paying much attention. But the bartender was looking at George like he might have had a fuse burning down in his ear.

"You better move, lady," he said.

"What?" said Merle Verona. When she looked at George, her first thought was that he was going to have a fit. "Get a towel!" she yelled. "He's going to swallow his tongue!"

George opened his mouth to tell her that he hadn't ever swallowed his tongue, but instead of words coming out, it was the five-course meal she had stuffed into him at her house two hours before.

"Swell, chief," said the bartender, moving away down the bar.

"Couldn't you see it was coming, mister?" said Merle Verona, talking to the bartender.

"You was the one buying them for him, lady. Four Moscow Mules of an evening is enough to turn anybody inside out."

"You could have brought that up about two drinks back."

"You pay for 'em, lady. I just mix 'em."

"You all right, Pretty Boy?" she said, speaking to George.

George looked at her and shook his head slowly from side to side. He didn't open his mouth to say anything.

Merle Verona moved away down the bar. "Just answer me, Pretty Boy," she said. "Point yourself the other way. I paid twenty-five dollars for this dress."

"I'm sorry," said George, staring over the bar.

"Let's get you some air." She helped him off the barstool and started toward the door. Then she noticed the look on the bartender's face. "Wait here," she said, leaning George against the door. She went back to where the bartender was standing behind the bar. "I never had anything but trouble out of life, mister," she said. She took a dollar bill out of her pocketbook and slid it onto the bar. The bartender looked at the bill, then rolled his eyes toward the mess George had made and raised one eyebrow.

Merle Verona dug out another dollar bill and laid it on the bar beside the first. The bartender didn't make a move to pick it up.

"You think this thing don't have no bottom to it?" she said, patting her pocketbook. "How much you make an hour?"

The bartender picked up the bills slowly with a sour look on his face.

"You joyful?" she said. "If I ain't buying happiness, I'm just wasting my money."

"Okay," he said.

"You sure now? I want thank-you-ma'am-come-again all over your face next time I walk through that door."

He put the money into his hip pocket, then leaned on the bar.

Merle Verona looked at his face closely for a minute, then she reached into her pocketbook and slapped another dollar bill onto the counter. "If that don't make you happy, you can go to hell," she said.

"Don't skimp with your pleasures," she said to George, as she helped him out the door.

Outside, she walked George up and down the seawall. The tide was out and there was a wide expanse of beach between them and the first lines of breakers rolling white in the dark.

"How you feeling?" she asked.

"Don't talk," he said.

She walked him the two hundred yards of seawall from the Brass Rail to the end of the parking lot. Down and back, then down and back again. After the second time she stopped at the steps leading down onto the beach.

"Let's go down on the beach," she said. "I love to walk on the beach at night."

He held on to the railing. "I'd rather not," he said.

"The air will be good for you," she said, pulling him toward the steps.

"I'd rather not," he said. From the seawall out to the water's edge was a hundred yards. In the daytime it wasn't so bad, though even then he would hold on behind the railing, putting that between himself and the openness of the beach and the water. At night it was worse. Far out he could see the lights of a ship, but they marked no point of reference for him. The horizon didn't end, but curved back on itself, going up and up and over his head behind.

"Let's go on back to the car," he said.

"You all right?" said Merle Verona. "You sure?"

"All right," he said. "I'll be better in the car."

Back at the car, he had an attack of the dry heaves. Merle Verona tried to rub the back of his neck to help him, but he waved her away.

Inside the car, he asked her to excuse him. "It ain't you," he said. "I feel awful."

She cranked up the car and started back to town, getting up to sixty on the long straight stretches lined with palm trees and oleander bushes on the shoulder, with the open marsh stretching away right and left behind. Coming onto the approach to Bull River Bridge at Wilmington Island she began to hear George's breathing.

"You okay?" she said, cutting her eyes over his way as much as she could, but without really seeing him in the darkness.

"I'm all right. I'm all right." He said it in a quick, gasping way, as if he were holding his breath.

She was on the bridge when he started to stiffen up, and she almost scraped the railing on the left-hand side.

"Pretty Boy?" she said. "Pretty Boy?"

When she came off the bridge on the Wilmington Island side, she pulled off on the shoulder and looked at him. His feet were jammed against the floor, and he had straightened out, arching over the back of the front seat, his face pushing into the roof of the car. Muffled bleating sounds were coming out from deep in his throat. His arms were winged out slightly, bent at the elbows, his fists clenched and shaking with the strain. She touched him, then drew her hand away. He was as rigid as a fiddle string, and his whole body seemed to be vibrating.

For thirty seconds, it might have been longer, she sat looking at him in the dim green light from the dash, hearing the choked whimpering sounds and not knowing what to do for him. It wasn't the way she had thought a fit would be, because nothing seemed to be happening. Then, while she watched, he began to relax, sliding back into the seat beside her as the tautness went out of him.

"George?" she said. "Are you all right, George?"

He didn't answer her, but opened the door and got out of the car and walked off toward a small group of live oak trees, looking down at the ground. She cut off the engine but left the lights on, sliding across the seat and out the door that he had left open. When she came up to him, he was leaning against one of the oak trees, his hands in his pockets, looking at the ground.

"Was that one?"

He nodded.

"You all right now?"

"I'm all right."

"You want to sit down?"

"Go on back to the car. I'll be there directly."

"You sure you're all right?"

He nodded again.

"It wouldn't happen twice?"

He looked at her. "No," he said.

"You're sure?"

"It wouldn't happen twice," he said.

She went back to the car, and in a few minutes he came up onto the shoulder of the road and got in beside her. She looked across at him, drumming her fingers on the steering wheel. "It wouldn't happen twice?"

He didn't answer.

She started the engine and pulled onto the road.

Back home, she herded him up the walk and into her house for a cup of coffee. "It'll clear your mind," she said, holding him by the elbow and steering him along. "Your pretty head."

In the kitchen, she put the pot on the stove, and didn't nag him about dancing with her. As she moved around the kitchen, she bumped into him with her soft places. For a long time he sat there without paying attention, sucking his tongue to get the taste of the Moscow Mules out of his mouth. But she had figured the odds on the attacks, so she kept on with it, ramming and butting with her hips and bosom, and as the tang of the ginger beer faded off into his sinuses, what she was doing crept up into the front part of his head, beginning to claim his attention.

"I'll be right back," she said. "I want to get into something more

[265]

comfortable." She spoke it like a Bette Davis line. The way it came out was too much on the leery side, but George had never seen Bette Davis anyway.

"What?" he said.

She came back in a housecoat that was the next thing to transparent. Tahiti purple with gold trim—very light and clinging. It also showed that she didn't have anything on underneath. But, it being Merle Verona, George didn't catch on to exactly what he was feeling right away.

"Where'd you get that?" he said.

"You like it?" she said, shooting him a flash off her gold tooth. "You ain't seen everything I got by a long shot." She jumped her eyebrows up and down and winked at him. The purple went strong with the red of her hair.

He frowned, looking at the smooth, silky cloth where it swelled over her stomach. "Damn near," he said.

She gave him two quick, high bars of her brass-plated giggle. "You want some cinnamon toast with your coffee?" she said. "*Pray tell?*"

George didn't know what it was. "I ain't hungry," he said, a whiff of the ginger beer coming up to him out of the back of his nose.

She fixed some anyway, so she could tend the oven, hiking her rear end up in his face where he could see under the skirt of her housecoat. While the toast was making, she crouched around the oven door, bending down this way, then that, for the sake of variety in the view he would be getting.

While she was doing it, the toast burned to a crisp.

"Golden brown," she said, and laughed. Then she threw the blackened pieces in the trash.

When she sat down with her coffee cup, she crossed her legs so the gown fell away right and left, all the way to her navel. Then she leaned forward so everything up top was bulging and hanging out in his face, and George sat there moving his eyes up and down while his coffee got cold.

Merle Verona was well built. And after four weeks, George had gotten used to her face so he didn't really see it anyway. She was chesty, but not a heavily built woman. And her legs were very nice.

"You're a good-looking man, George," she said. "How old are you?"

"Thirty," he said. "Thank you."

"I mean it," she said, "I bet you had all kinds of women in your life."

"What?" said George, looking up at her face. "What did you say?"

"A good-looking man like yourself. How come you never got married?"

He didn't answer.

"I never had but the one man," she said. "Fred wasn't much to look at." She thought a minute. "I seen better-looking faces on a frog," she said. "Let's be truthful."

"Yes," said George. He had seen the hand-tinted photograph of Fred in the stand-up gold frame that Merle Verona kept on the end table in the living room. Fred had a cast in one eye and looked like a pink-faced squirrel going into winter with his cheeks full of nuts. Even so, it was a flattering picture. The hand-tint artist had painted out the warts, and tried to line up both eyes in the same direction.

"But good-hearted," she said.

"It was too bad about Fred."

"Yes," she said. "He wasn't much to write home about in the bed neither."

"What?" said George.

"How many you reckon you got coming to you? I mean in a *lifetime?*"

"How many what?"

"I put Fred on the train at the Central of Georgia railroad station, March the fifth, nineteen forty-three." She held her left forearm with her right hand, spreading the fingers. "Ten o'clock at night," she said. "I watched the train going out of the station till I couldn't see nothing of it anymore." She looked up at George. "I cried my eyes out. I knew he wasn't coming back."

"Well," said George.

"That's over five years," she said.

"Yes?" said George, looking at her face again.

"*Five* years," she said.

George counted his fingers with his thumb. "Yes," he said. "Five years."

"I'm a normal, healthy woman, George."

"Yes, you are," said George.

"I been true to Fred. To the memory of him as he was when I put him on that train."

"I see," said George.

"But I'm a normal, healthy woman, George. And Fred ain't going to come back to me never."

"I reckon not," said George. "He got blowed up at Anzio."

"That's right," she said. "I won't never see Fred no more." She looked up at George. "I know you must feel like you need a woman sometimes," she said. "It's only natural."

George looked down at his coffee cup, frowning. For a minute he thought about what she had said. "I reckon not," he said at last. "Mother does for me pretty good."

"I don't mean feeding you and doing for you," she said. "I mean *needing*."

George looked at her, his brows knit in a frown. "What you mean?" he said.

"I mean the way a man *needs* a woman," she said.

"You mean? . . ." His eyebrows went up and his eyes opened.

"The way a woman *needs* a man."

George stood up. "Jesus God, Merle Verona. What kind of talk is that?"

"Do you know what I'm talking about, George?"

"You're a married woman, Merle Verona."

"I'm a widow," she said. "Fred ain't never coming back."

"I got to go," he said.

"I want you to go in the bedroom with me, George," she said. She stood up and opened her robe.

George looked at her, then he looked away. "Cover yourself," he said, whispering. "What if somebody looked in the window?"

She closed the robe. "I can't hardly remember what he looked like," she said. "I need you, George."

[268]

George looked away. "I ain't never had a woman that way. I wouldn't know what to do."

"Neither did Fred."

"He was your husband."

"I'd know what to do."

"It's a sin."

"It's a natural thing."

"We ain't married. I wouldn't know what to do."

"I can't *beg* you, George. I'm a normal, healthy woman. I'm asking you to do me a favor. Many's the man would jump at the chance I'm giving you."

"Who?"

"Come *on*, Pretty Boy."

"Merleverona . . ."

"You'd be a natural." She began leading him off toward the bedroom.

"Merleverona . . ." he said. "Merleverona . . ."

"I need you, George. I *need* you."

She had him almost to the bedroom before he pulled away from her and ran out of the house.

"Pretty Boy," she said.

He stayed up all night listening to the radio and thinking about what had happened. Finally he made up his mind about the right thing to do. At nine o'clock the next morning he went over to tell her about it.

She was all smiles when she opened the kitchen door for him. "This is more *like* it," she said.

"Will you marry me, Merle Verona?" he said. She had started for the bedroom, but his question pulled her up short.

"What?" she said.

"I need you, too, I reckon," he said.

"You're taking it serious, ain't you?"

"It don't *have* to be a sin."

"Come on, Pretty Boy. Let's just go on back in the bedroom."

"We'll get married," he said.

"Why would you have to take it so serious? Couldn't we just have a little fun?"

"It wouldn't be the thing to do."

She came back and sat down at the table. "I wouldn't want to be that serious about it," she said.

"You mean you wouldn't marry me?"

She looked up at him. "How much you make, George?"

"A hundred and fifty."

"A week?"

"A month."

She took a sip of her coffee, holding the cup in both hands. "I couldn't give up Fred's pension for a hundred and fifty a month."

"That's it?"

"What's it? I'm talking about a hundred and fifty dollars a month."

"We oughtn't to be getting in the bed and us not married."

She looked at her coffee cup. "I *been* married, Pretty Boy. What I wanted was a little fun."

"It's wrong, Merle Verona."

She looked at him. "You're not the marrying kind," she said. "It wouldn't work out."

"You said I was a natural."

"It ain't the first time I been wrong. I thought we could have a little fun." She finished her coffee and put the cup back on the saucer. Then she looked up at him. "I don't think you better come over here no more," she said.

"We could still go down to Tybee," he said. "We wouldn't have to go in the bedroom."

"Pretty Boy," she said. "You never did understand me."

"I'd pay *my* share," he said.

He brooded about Merle Verona, watching out the living room window as she went in and out of the house. In June he began to see her with a large red-faced man who wore seersucker suits and a Panama hat and smoked cigars in an amber holder. Several times he went over and tried to talk to her, but she wouldn't let him into the house.

In July a man came and hammered a "For Sale" sign into her yard. The Thursday after it appeared his mother met him at the door when he came home.

"She's gone, George," she said.

"What?" he said.

"That woman's gone," she said. "The moving van came today."

"I see," he said.

"I'm so relieved," she said. "I can't tell you how relieved I am."

"Yes, Mother," he said.

After supper he went over to Merle Verona's house and looked in the windows. Then he tried the back door and found it was open. Inside he wandered through the house, but with all the furniture gone, he couldn't recognize it the way it used to be. The only things he remembered were a smell of "Evening in Paris" cologne in the bathroom, and a pine-scented cleaner where she used to keep it under the sink in the kitchen.

He turned on the cold-water tap and let it run in the sink, thinking about the times with Merle Verona in the house. Then he turned off the water and went out through the back door.

"I can't tell you how relieved I am, George," his mother said when he came in the door to the kitchen. "That woman was out to get you."

On Saturday afternoon, he went downtown and had "Born to Lose" tattooed on a curling banner across a red broken heart. He had it put on his right arm—high up, where it wouldn't show when he rolled up his sleeves in the summertime.

Afterward he went back to spending his time the way he had before he met Merle Verona. Listening to the programs on the radio, and saying the commercials along with the announcers behind the orange dial.

Gradually Merle Verona and the things he had done with her settled into a dark place inside his head, alongside the trip to Tybee he had taken with his grandmother on his fifth birthday. He didn't forget about them and what they had done. He just didn't think about it anymore.

Finally he scrounged up some boards and repaired the cricket hutch.

23

Wedding Bells
and After

JACK'S FOOTBALL CAREER at Georgia Tech began on August 28, 1948, and it ended on March 18, 1949. Actually, it ended with the Thanksgiving Day game on November 25, but March 18 was when he came home from Tech to stay, so that was the time everybody found out about it. Even in Savannah, an ending that close to a beginning attracted a certain amount of attention. Seven months is a very short time. Though, at that, a good many people had started to forget about him. Most of those who did notice were unhappy about it. J.J. O'Brien felt betrayed.

"I'm disappointed in that young man," he said. "Bitterly—*bitterly* —disappointed."

Shube, the ratlike man, held a handkerchief to his face. "Boss . . ." he said, coughing.

"There was a wonderful career for the lad in the game of football," he said. "He threw it away. He simply—" he made a motion with his hand, "—*threw* it away."

"Yes, boss," said Shube from behind the handkerchief.

Jack did as well as anyone had thought he would do while he was playing. He made the first string at center on the freshman team and got written up in the Atlanta papers for his play in the Thanksgiving Day game against the freshman team of the University of Georgia. He made twenty-five unassisted tackles and won the award for the outstanding player in the game. "The best man at the line of scrimmage in Rambling Wreck history." That's what the sportswriters said. And Tech had had four All-American linemen in the preceding six years—including Paul Duke at center.

But when the grades came out in December, he had failed four subjects and gotten a D in the fifth. Jack wasn't stupid, but he also wasn't especially interested in periodic tables or differential equations. He couldn't get on to the theory courses, because he had never had to think that far ahead before.

And even the football wasn't what it had been in Savannah and New Orleans—though he couldn't *play* it badly.

There was no savor in it. *On* the field he was all right—at least during the games. The way he felt when he was away from it during the week—that was the important thing. He was not concerned about it—there was nothing sticking in his head, presenting him with interesting problems to be solved. He was thinking mostly for himself, and didn't believe in teamwork anymore. That had always been what the game meant to him.

"I want to win, but I don't think about it ahead of time. We're kind of out for ourselves up here." That's the way he explained it, talking to his roommate.

After the second quarter started in January, the school did what they could for him in the way of special tutors and help. But those wouldn't work, because he didn't want to help himself. When he got his grades in March, he had failed all of his courses.

He didn't *have* to leave school then. According to the regulations, the record wouldn't count against him until the end of the year in June. But by March he had made up his mind. And he didn't want to wait until they would tell him he couldn't come back. So he dropped out and went home to Savannah.

The way he worked it out for himself later, the schoolwork wasn't the most important thing. How he felt about football itself —that was the deeper motive. And Mary—she was the deepest

[273]

and most important motive of all. The one that had moved in behind the others.

The dreams came back, settling into spaces inside his head that should have been filling up with formulas and equations and the great dates of history—blocking the avenues of incoming messages.

He tried to talk to his roommate about his dreams of the snaky tree.

The roommate was a mechanical engineering major from Homer, Georgia, named Randolph Tarbutton. Randolph had to stay with the books ten hours a day just to pull his five C's, and lived with a constant, undistracted sense of impending doom. He didn't even care about the football, much less Jack's dreams about Mary. His academic problems were a buzz in his ear that drowned out everything else, and none of Jack's talk ever got through to his head. But he was about the same size as Dendron, and something in his manner encouraged Jack to talk to him.

All Randolph ever said was, "Man, I never have dreams."

At the end of the first quarter, when Jack was leaving for the holidays, he stopped at the door of the room and wished Randolph a merry Christmas. "Sometime I'd like you to meet Mary," he said.

"Mary who?" said Randolph.

Jack couldn't stand to be in Atlanta. It was hilly and windy and cold on the streets that had developed out of cow trails on the crests and ridgelines. September and October were dreary and wet, with a hard, antiseptic wetness, unlike the sea-wet falls in Savannah, where summer wasn't squeezed out of the ocean until it was almost time for the new year to come in.

Aaron Stern was at Tech, too—not on a football scholarship—and Aaron had a car. Every weekend that he could get away, Jack made the trip home to Savannah with Aaron so he could see Mary. He didn't even stay in town to see the varsity home games, though he had never especially cared to *watch* football anyway. During the winter quarter, when he didn't have to practice, he and Aaron made the trip nearly every weekend, leaving on Friday afternoon and coming back Sunday night.

When Aaron had to study and wouldn't leave Atlanta, there

were other Savannah cars heading south on U.S. 80. Jack was still a celebrity, and there was always a seat for him.

"What are you going to do?" Mary worried about it from a practical point of view. She had been counting on the college degree.

"It wasn't the same."

"You've got brains enough to pass your subjects."

"It wasn't a matter of that."

"That's why you're not going back."

"It wasn't the same. Were you counting on an All-American?"

"You always liked football," she said.

"So I don't anymore. Some things you get tired of."

"It doesn't make any difference to me."

"I didn't know what kind of a bargain you might have been counting on."

She didn't say anything.

"It's not fun. It's a business. Half the guys on the varsity are hurt some way."

"It lets people *know* about you. You wouldn't have to play football the rest of your life."

"I played because I *liked* to play it."

"You're the one I'm interested in. I just didn't know how satisfied you'd be."

"I'll be very satisfied. Knocking heads isn't the only thing I can do."

"It doesn't make any difference to *me*, Jack. As long as you're sure about yourself."

"It's just that wasn't *it* anymore. Atlanta is a crummy town. A cold, crummy town."

"That suits me fine."

"It just wasn't the same, you know?"

"I never cared one way or the other." She shrugged her shoulders. "Anyway, you're *out* now."

"I hope you didn't care."

Mr. Odell wasn't too thrilled about it either. Especially after they began to talk about getting married.

"What do you propose to *live* on, young man?"

"I'll be getting a job, Mr. Odell. I wouldn't ask Mary to marry a bum." Jack had been home for a month—collecting himself, thinking over what he would have to do. His plan was to go down and talk to J.J. O'Brien, counting on his influence to line something up. But he had been putting it off.

"What *kind* of a job?" Mr. Odell couldn't oppose a marriage outright, since Mary wanted it. All he could do was lay down stipulations that would push it off into the future as far as possible, where he wouldn't have to confront it. He insisted that Jack hold a full-time job for six months and have five hundred dollars in the bank.

"*Four* months," said Mary. "We've been going together for two years." She planned to go to work when she graduated from high school in June, and she thought that with the money she would be able to put into the account, they could get it up by August.

"Four months," said Mr. Odell.

J.J. wasn't very happy to see Jack, but he wanted to say his piece to him, too. He asked Shube to leave them alone because the coughing distracted him when he was trying to talk.

He began looking out the window, with his profile to Jack. "It was a disappointment to me, Jack. A bitter—" he shook his head, "—a *bitter* disappointment."

"I'm sorry, Mr. O'Brien. I'm sorry you feel I let you down."

"Not just me, Jack." He swiveled the chair to face him. "I'm thinking about you. It wasn't only me you disappointed. What about Boniface?" He adjusted the position of the chronometer on his desk. "You're letting down the whole school."

Jack didn't say anything.

"What about the young lads?" he said. "The young ones coming along? We need our heroes, Jack. Our great ones," he raised his hand, palm up, holding it above his head, "to look up to."

"Yes," said Jack. "Tech is a tough school."

J.J. looked at him. He drummed his fingers on the desk. "You're not dumb, Jack. Think of all those plays you had to memorize. Your mind is all right. You could have done the work."

Jack thought a minute. "Yes, sir. You're right. It wasn't just the schoolwork that was giving me trouble."

J.J. frowned at him across the desk. He shifted the chronometer. "It wasn't?" He sounded irritated. "My information was that you failed your subjects."

"Yes," said Jack. "It wasn't *that* hard."

"You mean you could have *passed?*"

"I'm not stupid, Mr. O'Brien. Football wasn't that much fun up there."

J.J.'s frown deepened. "Life is not always a game, Jack. You'll find that life is earnest, too. Work is a part of every man's life. Hard knocks." He rapped his knuckles on the edge of the desk. "Hard knocks."

"It wasn't the same."

"Doors open for a man in the public eye. Excellence has a price on it. It *pays,* Jack. It *pays.*" He held up his thumb and forefinger, pinching them together. "A jewel . . . a pearl." He dropped his hand. "Nobody likes a quitter. I thought you couldn't do the schoolwork."

Jack could see in J.J.'s cold green eyes that he was very dissatisfied. "I need a job, Mr. O'Brien."

For a minute J.J. didn't say anything. "I see," he said. "The world turns, doesn't it, Jack?"

"I'm going to get married."

J.J. swiveled his chair to look out the window again. "What kind of job did you have in mind?"

"You know a lot of people. I need something with a future to it. I'm getting married."

For a minute J.J. didn't say anything. "Well, Jack, people forget quickly. You won't be in the public eye anymore." He turned back from the window. "That's the choice you've made."

"People in Savannah know me."

"Yes. They *know* you." The way he said it, there was a calculation in his voice. "I have to figure these things in dollars and cents." He looked at him. "What do you think your cash value is?"

Jack didn't answer. "Can you help me get a job?"

J.J. looked down at his hands on the desk. "Yes," he said. "You know I can get you a job. I want you to set a value on yourself."

Jack thought a minute. "I'd do about anything. I don't want to work for the fire department."

J.J. frowned again. "Anything? That's a low price. You're going to sell yourself cheaply." He looked up at him. "The world will take you at your own value."

"You said I wasn't in a good position."

"That's right. If you don't think well of yourself, nobody else will. I didn't mean for you to give yourself away."

"Yes, sir," said Jack.

"Why don't you want to work for the fire department? That's an honorable calling."

Jack thought a minute. "It's a nothing job. I mean, to *me*. That's where all my family is. You can get to be a bum down there."

"That would be up to you."

"It's the way I feel about it."

J.J. looked at him for a minute. "So there's something you wouldn't do?"

"Not exactly *wouldn't*. I'd rather try something else."

J.J. shot his cuffs. "That's good," he said. "I like the way that sounds. Always draw the line somewhere. Keep your principles. . . . It raises the price."

"All my family just fell into it. They couldn't do anything else."

"Yes," said J.J. He thought a minute. "I could get you an insurance debit."

Jack looked at him. "Collecting?"

"It's legitimate. We pay off on our policies." He looked at Jack for a minute. "It's in niggertown."

Jack kneaded his hands together, not looking at him. "I don't want to be an insurance man in niggertown, Mr. O'Brien," he said. He was thinking of what Mr. Odell would say.

J.J. slapped the desk and laughed. "Splendid! I wouldn't want to work an insurance debit in niggertown either. You don't shake off a thing like that. You're restoring my faith in you, Jack." He looked at him across the desk and his face grew serious. "It would pay well," he said.

Jack thought a minute. "How much?" he said.

J.J. frowned. "Two fifty a month—minimum." He waited.

"No, Mr. O'Brien," he said. "I wouldn't want to work in niggertown for that. It's not enough."

J.J. slapped his hands on the desk and smiled. "Not enough," he said. "The very words. 'Not enough.' Keep your principles, but put a price on them." He picked up the telephone. "There's a place for you in this world, Jack. If you keep your principles." He dialed a number. "J.J. O'Brien here. Let me speak to Flynn. . . . J.J. O'Brien, Flynn. I'm sending a young man down. Put him on one of the trucks." He put his hand over the mouthpiece. "How old are you?"

"Nineteen."

"You'll have to get a chauffeur's license."

He took his hand off the mouthpiece. "Curran. Jack Curran. . . . Flynn, I said, put him on one of the trucks. I don't care what you think about it. . . . And, Flynn, the salary is two fifty." He winked at Jack. "That's right. Two hundred and fifty dollars. . . . Well, keep it to yourself. . . . Goddamn it, Flynn. I'm giving you an order." He hung up the phone.

"You see, Jack. You kept your principles, and it *paid.*"

"Yes, sir," said Jack. "What will I be doing?"

"To begin with, you'll be driving one of the delivery trucks. We'll see how that goes."

"Two fifty a month?"

"That's right."

"A beer truck?"

"Blatz."

Jack thought about what Mr. Odell would say to that. Mr. Odell was a teetotaler.

"It's a beginning, Jack. We'll see how it goes."

"Yes, sir," said Jack. He rose to leave.

"Don't disappoint me, Jack," said J.J. "Remember, you're looking out for yourself. I have to do the same."

"Yes, sir," said Jack.

"It's a matter of dollars and cents."

"A *beer* truck?" said Mr. Odell.

The $250 a month softened it, but not much. Mary headed him off, and wouldn't let him complain about it. "It's a *beginning,*" she said. "Mr. O'Brien is a very important man. Driving a truck is only a beginning."

What it came down to for Mr. and Mrs. Odell was—like it or

lump it. They could be part of the wedding or not. The choice was theirs. Mary was passing on, going away from them. All that was left for them was to get as many concessions as possible before the wedding took place.

Jack agreed to be married in the Methodist church—they didn't ask him to join it.

"Don't let him get you to make any promises about the children," Mr. Odell told her. "The priests will be coming around, but don't let him make any promises."

Mary put in a hundred dollars a month from her job at the bank, and they had the five hundred dollars in the account by the middle of July. She didn't insist on moving up the date of the wedding, but she did insist that they arrange to get the church, and that they start addressing invitations.

Kate supplied family names for the guest list, but the real preparations for the wedding were made by Mary. It wasn't Kate's church, and she and Mary had a hard time talking to each other. Mrs. Odell went with Mary for the fittings of the wedding gown, and to the jeweler's to pick out her china, crystal, and silver. "Very nice," Mrs. Odell said when Mary asked her what she thought of the dress and her patterns.

The wedding took place at the First Methodist Church on Friday, August 19, 1949, at four o'clock in the afternoon. J.J. was pleased with Jack, and had offered to let him off for three days, even though he'd only been working for four months. But Mary couldn't get time off from her job, so he turned down the offer. That pleased J.J. more than ever, and he gave them two place settings of their silver for a wedding present. "You're learning to get on in the world, Jack," he said.

For a honeymoon, they were going to spend the weekend at the SeaRoi Hotel on St. Simon Island, coming back to their apartment on Gaston Street on Sunday night. The Reilleys' wedding present to them was to pay for the two nights at the hotel, and to lend them the DeSoto to make the trip.

None of Jack's family thought of it as a big wedding, though there were 400 people in the church, and 250 at the reception afterward.

Dendron was the best man, since Jack felt that he had to choose someone not on the football team to stand up with him. Ducker, Feeb, Chippy, Lulu, Frog, Flasher, Whistler, and Dimmy Camack were ushers. All of them wore rented tuxedoes, except Frog, who had to buy his to get one that would fit.

There was a characterless lime punch with no alcohol in it at the reception that scandalized the Irishmen, sending them off by ones and twos to package stores and the glove compartments of their cars. After five o'clock, when the last trace of the lime Jell-O faded off into the alcohol, it wasn't a bad drink really, and no more lethal than the Chatham artillery punch they were used to drinking at Armistice Day celebrations and the Fourth of July.

Standing in the receiving line kept Jack away from the refreshment table until five-thirty.

"Not bad, man. Not bad," said Feeb, handing him a cup.

"Thanks," said Jack, and poured it into a potted palm.

He and Mary posed for the photographer, feeding each other pieces of wedding cake, then were out of the church and onto U.S. 17 by six o'clock. On the way to Brunswick, they stopped at a Stuckey's for some orange juice, and Jack bought a coconut carved like a head for a souvenir.

They didn't see anyone under forty-five in the lobby of the Sea-Roi when they went in to register at eight o'clock.

"Not exactly Honeymoon Hotel," said Jack, whispering. He felt silly carrying the scowling coconut head, and wished he had left it in the car. There were several people sitting in the lobby reading newspapers when they came in, and all of them lowered their papers and watched over their bifocals as Jack and Mary walked across to the desk.

When they got to the room, Jack tipped the bellhop a dollar. "Keep the change," he said. The bellhop was an old man who was shorter than Mary, and walked with a limp. He was wheezing too much from carrying the luggage to be able to say anything, but he touched his finger to his pillbox hat and thumped off down the hall.

Jack didn't notice at first that there were twin beds in the room. But Mary did.

"Well," he said. "We can push them together."

The room was just a little larger than the bedroom that he shared with Susy in the Marshoaks house, with flowered wallpaper, and a picture on the wall opposite the beds of a sailboat by moonlight. It wasn't on the ocean side of the hotel, but since they were on the third floor, they could see off toward the north along the beach—at least Jack could. He was tall enough to look over the airconditioner. Mary had to stand on the bed for the view.

"Do you want me to take a walk?" he said.

"What?"

"Do you want me to take a walk?"

"I can't hear you for the airconditioner."

He turned it off, then asked her again.

"Don't be silly," she said. "I'll just be a minute." She opened her suitcase and took out a pale blue nightgown, then went into the bathroom.

For the next hour, Jack lay on the bed, listening to the sound of running water and counting the slats in the venetian blind. The room got so hot that he had to turn the airconditioner back on.

When she came out, he smiled at her. "I was afraid you'd gone down the drain," he said. He got his pajamas out of his suitcase and went into the bathroom. The steam was so thick he could hardly breathe, but he took a quick shower and put on his pajamas.

Mary was standing on the bed, looking out the window when he came out of the bathroom. She didn't hear him come out, and he walked up and touched her on the shoulder. "Steamy, isn't it?" she said, getting under the covers and pulling them up to her chin.

He put his clothes in the closet, folding everything with elaborate care, so they wouldn't be wrinkled when the steam dried out of them. Then he came back and looked at her across the empty bed. He pushed it with his leg, and it slid over against hers. "Not exactly the honeymoon suite," he said. "I guess they didn't know we were coming."

"The way they looked at us in the lobby, I felt like Lady Godiva."

He put his knee on the empty bed and leaned across and kissed her. "Good evening, Mrs. Curran," he said. Then he turned off the bedside lamp and went around and opened the venetian blind. For a while he stood looking out the window at the whitecaps rolling up the beach. She stood behind him on the bed, her arms resting on his shoulders. They couldn't hear the surf because of the airconditioner.

"Tonight we begin our life together," he said.

"What?"

He cut off the airconditioner. "It sounds like a roller mill. I said, 'Tonight we begin our life together.'"

"It's the beginning of it," she said.

He began to feel her in the darkness of the room, putting his hand up under her nightgown and rubbing her smooth skin. She fell back on the bed—small and fragile under his hands. Lying on her back, her breasts disappeared, but her nipples were like blackberries as he rolled them between his fingers.

"Mary," he said.

Her body didn't arouse him in a sexual way, but the feeling that he had was intense and focused. With the lights out in the room, he could almost see her as he had seen her in his dream. Like a Christmas tree ornament. The soft child's body under his hands didn't connect with the image he had of her. But he understood what her expectations were, and he undertook to be her husband.

When he tried to make love to her, she grabbed him and turned rigid. He could hear her breathing in the dark.

"Did I hurt you?"

"A little."

He tried again, and this time she cried out.

"It hurts, Jack!"

He couldn't bring himself to hurt her. So he took his pleasure between her legs in a way that wouldn't cause her pain.

He tried to use his finger on her afterward, but the tenseness wouldn't go away, and she didn't enjoy it.

"It'll be better tomorrow," he said.

"Yes," she said.

Before they went to sleep she told him what Dr. Varnadoe had said when he examined her. "He said I was a perfect virgin."

"Yes," said Jack. "That's what you are."

The next day they walked on the beach, then drove into Brunswick and down U.S. 17 toward Jacksonville. It was after dark when they got back to the hotel. The people sitting in the lobby watched them over their newspapers as they walked to the elevator.

"It's just as bad without the coconut," said Jack.

What happened in the room was no more successful than the first night. Mary was too small, and he couldn't stand the idea of hurting her. So he did what he had done the night before, feeling ashamed afterward, as if he had masturbated in front of her.

"It'll be all right," he said. "It's not that important."

"It's important to me."

"It's important to me, too. I mean we don't have to rush things. I love you, Mary."

"I know you love me."

"It makes me hurt, too. You know the way I feel about you. It's not your body. That's not the main thing. You know how I feel about you."

"Don't start that holy business. It's not going to be that way."

"I mean, it doesn't matter to me. Really."

She sat up beside him. "Well, it *ought* to matter. I don't know what you have in mind."

"We'll work it out."

"Yes. We will."

"Shouldn't *I* be mad at *you*?"

"Well," she said, lying down beside him again. "Just don't start that holy business. It gives me the creeps. I don't want you to think of me that way."

He had a dream of Mary's head on Susy's body, in Susy's green nightgown. When he woke up the next morning, he was in the second twin bed. Mary was standing on hers, with her arms resting on the airconditioner, her chin resting on her arms.

"It's some honeymoon," she said, without turning to look at him.

"I'm not complaining."

"I know," she said.

She went into the bathroom to dress, closing the door. When she finished, she came out and he went in. They went down to the dining room and had breakfast, their first meal in the hotel. Everyone stared at them so hard that Mary couldn't eat. "Let's go," she said. Jack choked down the rest of his eggs and got up. As they were leaving the table, a little old lady with gray hair came up and laid her hand on Mary's arm. "I hope you will be very happy," she said. Mary looked at her, then burst into tears.

On the way back to Savannah, she sat pressed against the door, looking out the window and daubing her eyes with her handkerchief.

"It'll be all right," he said.

Back in Savannah, they set up housekeeping in an apartment on Gaston Street. They had the first floor, four rooms of an old three-story house.

Jack was affectionate to her in tender ways—kissing her when he came in from work—bringing flowers—putting his arm around her. But he couldn't bring himself to touch her again when they were in the bed. He was afraid he would hurt her.

"You don't love me," she said.

"I love you."

"Not in the right way."

It got to be a litany.

She thought about what was happening between them, and the part of it that was her fault. And finally she decided to do something about it. So she went to work on herself, to make herself ready to be a complete wife to him. She began with her index finger.

One night she came in and sat on his lap. "I think I'm ready," she said.

"What?"

"I've been getting myself ready. I think I'm ready to be a wife to you."

"You're a wife to me already."

"I mean a *real* wife."

He looked at her.

"Let's go in the bedroom," she said.

"Are you sure?"

"I'm ready."

"It's not dark yet."

She put on her nightgown, the blue one she had worn on their honeymoon at the SeaRoi, then she got into the bed ahead of him. When he came in from the bathroom he turned out the light, then sat down on the edge of the bed. For a long while he sat there as the room got dark.

"Jack," she said.

"I'm afraid I'll hurt you," he said.

"You won't hurt me."

"I'm thinking about the idea of it."

"You won't hurt me. I've been working on it."

He didn't say anything.

"Jack," she said. "It's dark now."

"I love you."

"And I love you," she said. "Come on. Come to me."

"I can't."

For a minute she didn't say anything. "What do you mean?"

"It's not *automatic*," he said. "I mean I *can't*."

"You mean you *can't?*"

"Don't ask me to show you. I mean I can't. I'm trying, but I can't."

"Now you won't be a husband to me."

"I love you, Mary."

"I don't want to hear that again."

"Well. It's the way I feel about it."

"I want you to *show* me," she said.

They sat for a while in silence, neither one moving in the dark. "All right," she said at last, her voice softer, almost a whisper. "All right." She reached out and touched his shoulder, then she took his hand. "You waited for me. If you *can't*." She gave him a light kiss on the cheek. "Don't take too long. I'm ready. I really am."

A week went by—two weeks. Then they were into the month of October. The longer it went on, the less Jack was able to think his way into it. He came to like the marriage the way it was, with Mary angelic and disembodied. There wasn't any frustration in it for him, because of the way he thought about her. If he had been a priest he would have been continent as a matter of course. "That is a way I might have chosen," he said to himself.

Mary's temper grew shorter and she become more cranky with the waiting. The way she felt about Jack started to poison everything that happened in the house.

[286]

"You're killing us, Jack," she said. "Us."

"I love you," he said. Calmly. Pronouncing it like a benediction.

On the sixth of November, she took things into her own hands. When he came home from work, she met him at the door naked.

He looked at her, then started for the back bedroom. "Put your clothes on," he said.

"No," she said. "I can't do that."

"I'm not thinking of you that way," he said.

"You're not thinking of me at all," she said. "I'm not Betty Grable. You knew that before."

"That's not it," he said. He came back to where she was standing in the front room. "You know that's not it. I love you, Mary." He dropped on his knees and put his arms around her legs.

She pushed at him to move him away. "Please," she said. "This is embarrassing enough."

He let go of her, and she stepped back away from him. "You don't call this a marriage, do you? This isn't a marriage."

He looked at her without saying anything.

"Go back in the bedroom and wait for me," she said. "I'm going to show you something."

"Mary."

"Go back to the bedroom," she said.

She came into the bedroom still naked. He was sitting on the edge of the bed with his clothes on. He looked at her, then he looked away.

"Look," she said. She was holding her hand out to him, showing him something.

"What's that?"

"That's a cucumber."

"A cucumber?"

"I had to peel it. It's got prickles on it."

It was a large cucumber. Maybe eight inches long, and an inch and a half in diameter.

"Watch," she said.

She squatted down facing him and slid the cucumber into herself. The whole time she was looking at him, and there was a hard, set expression on her face. She worked the cucumber in until just the last inch or so was protruding. Then she took her hands away, holding them up in the air.

He looked up at her face, then down at the tip of the cucumber, where it protruded. For a full minute he stared at the cucumber without saying anything.

"Say something," she said.

He looked at her face, then back at the cucumber. For a full minute he stared at it, his brows knit, a serious expression on his face as if he were considering some deep and perplexing riddle. Finally he looked back up at her. "Picklepuss," he said. He made a fishmouth and shook his head slowly from side to side.

"What?" she said. "What did you say?"

He cleared his throat. "Picklepuss," he said. He looked at her very seriously. "It popped into my head."

For a minute she didn't say anything. She had a slight frown on her face and seemed to be considering what he had said, weighing it very carefully, squatting there in front of him, her head cocked to one side. "It makes you think of *picklepuss?* . . ." Suddenly she sat down on the floor with a thump, squirting the cucumber out between her legs. She started to laugh, sitting on the floor with her legs stretched out, leaning on her arms. "Picklepuss!"

"Kosher dill!" he said. Then he fell back on the bed and started to laugh, too. "Oh Jesus, Mary!"

He rolled on the bed, burying his head in the pillows and wrapping the sheets around him. She rolled on the floor. The two of them filling the room with madhouse laughter.

Five minutes . . . ten minutes . . . The laughter almost died away, then they would look at each other and it would start all over again. Finally he got up from the bed, wiped the tears from his eyes, and lifted her in his hands, holding her the way he had held Susy when they had their pillow fights. "When do you start on the watermelon?" he said.

It started them laughing again. He staggered to the bed with her and dropped her on it. Then he picked up a pillow and swatted her over the head. She snatched the other pillow and hit him back. They traded blows until the pillowcases began to break open, filling the room with flying feathers. Finally he grabbed her arms and held them in his hands, bending over the bed and looking at her—looking into her tear-stained face.

"I love you, Mary," he said, brushing feathers out of her hair.

"Love me between my legs," she said. She sniffled and ran her hand across her nose. Then she spread her legs where she sat on the side of the bed.

He looked down at her.

She looked up at him, then she fell backward onto the bed. "Goddamn it, Jack, fuck me."

He looked down at her where she was lying on the bed.

She put her arm across her eyes. "Please," she said.

He went to the switch and turned out the light, then came back and sat on the edge of the bed. For a long time he sat there rubbing her leg without saying anything, stroking it with his hand.

"Don't do that," she said. Her voice was very small. "Don't do that, please."

"I'm trying," he said.

For a while neither of them said anything. Finally she got up and went into the bathroom. When she came out she had her gown on.

"What am I going to do, Mary?" he said.

"That's all right," she said. "I'm all right now." She started out of the door.

"Anyway," he said. "I love you."

"Yes," she said. "That's all right."

When he came home the next day, there was a note for him.

JACK,
I don't know how I feel. Ashamed. I've
gone home for a while. Don't love me so much.
MARY

In the kitchen he saw that she had made supper for him and left it in the oven. Propped up against the pillow on her side of the bed, like a severed head, was the scowling coconut he had bought on their honeymoon. When he saw it, he turned out the light and went into the living room to sleep on the couch.

24

Second Honeymoon

JACK DIDN'T WANT TO go around to the Odells' house where he would have to look at Mr. Odell's iron Indian face and hear the pulpit tone of reproach that would be in his voice. He wasn't up to that. But when he telephoned the house, Mary wouldn't answer the telephone.

If Mr. Odell answered, Jack would hang up without saying anything. By all the standards he knew, he was in the wrong, and the fact that he couldn't help it was no excuse, because not being able to help it was wrong as well. Being a man meant something specific to him, and he rode the grooves that had been cut and worn by those who had gone before him.

If Mrs. Odell answered, he tried to get her to coax Mary to come to the telephone. She always did what he asked of her, but she also did what Mary told her to do. Jack listened to Mary's words coming through her mother, but Mrs. Odell was a passive and neutral chamber, through which the words glided, distorting only to melancholy. He couldn't get any kind of feeling through her of the mood in the house. It was like trying to conjure up the whole Atlantic Ocean by listening to a conch shell in a shuttered room.

The only one he could think of to talk to about it, the one person with any insight into the problem, being a woman herself, was Mackey Brood. When Mary wouldn't come to the telephone, he went around to Mackey's place to see what she would have to say.

He didn't tell her everything—enough so that she could see what the problem was. He told her about his unmanliness.

"I love her, Mackey," he said. "I would agree that I'm in the wrong."

"I never did understand the way you talked about love," she said. "Don't let it get in the way. Get her into the bed."

"It sounds hokey, but I wouldn't care much for the world if I didn't believe in love, Mackey." He didn't look at her when he said it. "That sounds too hokey to tell just anybody. I don't care how much trouble it causes."

"I hate giving you advice," she said. "I really do. Why don't we stop talking and go back in the bedroom?"

"You were the only one I knew to talk to about it," he said. "I didn't want to put you on the spot."

"I think you'll wind up loving me someday," she said.

"I love you already, Mackey."

"You know what I mean."

"You wouldn't want to settle down to just one."

"If it ever comes the day, give me a try."

"If the day comes, I will."

"I don't know if I could take it, but give me a try."

Back at the house on Gaston Street, he tried to think of the best way to talk to Mary, since he couldn't call her on the telephone. He thought that it would be best to talk to her in person, but he kept seeing Mr. Odell's face behind the screen door of the house on Forty-first Street.

While he was thinking about it, she called him.

"I think it's gone on long enough," she said. "The whole thing is silly."

"I wouldn't say it's silly," he said. "I love you, Mary."

"That's what I mean," she said. "I love you, too. Stay there, I'm coming back."

"Pack a suitcase," he said.

"What?"

"Pack a suitcase. We're not going to stay here tonight. I'm getting a room at the De Soto."

"A new start?"

"Yes," he said. "A second honeymoon. Pack a suitcase."

"I love you, Jack Curran," she said.

"I love you, Mary."

When Mary arrived, Jack met her on the front stoop. He didn't want her inside the house at all. "After the honeymoon, we'll come back. I'll carry you across the threshold."

"I got to feeling silly about it. Telling mother what to say to you."

He kissed her—a gentle senior prom kiss. "We'll walk," he said, taking her suitcase. The De Soto was eight blocks away at the corner of Bull and Liberty streets. It was a cold night, foggy, with the threat of rain. They walked, leaning against each other, Jack carrying the suitcase and wanting to carry Mary as well.

At the hotel, the desk clerk recognized him. "Aren't you Jack Curran?" He looked at Mary, and there was an expression on his face as though he wanted to ask more questions. But he didn't say anything.

"We've got luggage," said Jack, holding up the suitcase. Then he signed the register.

"Does he know we're married?"

"I guess he's taking my word for it."

Mary looked around the lobby while they waited for the elevator. "I don't see a single pair of bifocals," she said.

"What?" said Jack.

"I was thinking about the SeaRoi. Our *first* honeymoon. No canes either . . . maybe it's an omen."

Up in the room, Jack talked to Mary about the love that he felt for her. Especially the love that he felt for her after she had left him.

"I didn't want to hurt you, because I love you."

"Don't worry about the hurt. It'll be all right. That's part of it, I guess." She didn't look at him. "Anyway, don't talk about it right now. I don't want to think about all of that. It was very embarrassing."

He turned out the light, then she undressed herself and they got into the bed together.

He was careful and as gentle as he could be—holding himself in, and moving delicately and with as much precision and care as he could. He could tell that he was hurting her a little, but he was as gentle as he could possibly be, and for the first time they made love successfully—carrying it through all the way.

When it was over, he kissed her gently on the mouth. "Did I hurt you?" he said.

"No," she said. She was pushing against his chest with her hands, trying to keep him from pressing down on her.

"Did you come?"

For a minute she didn't say anything. "Yes," she said.

"Was it good?"

She pushed against his chest. "You're heavy," she said.

He rolled off her. "For the first time, it wasn't bad, was it?"

"For the first time."

"I love you, Mary."

"I love you, Jack," she said. She kissed him. "I don't want to *talk* about it." She rolled away from him on the bed, curling up on her side with her arms clasped between her legs.

For a long time they didn't say anything. Finally he could hear her regular breathing, and he reached out to touch her on the shoulder. She didn't move.

"I love you," he whispered, very quietly.

Afterward he lay there in the bed, thinking about how fragile the lovemaking had been—the way that he had held in for it. There were gusts of wind blowing, and the fronds of a palm tree outside the window scraped across the screen. After a while he got up and put on his clothes, moving stealthily, so as not to wake her. Then he went down to the lobby. The desk clerk looked at him in a puzzled way as he walked out onto the gallery and down the steps to the swimming pool.

The chairs were all turned upside down for the winter, and the cushions had been taken inside. The pool had been drained, and the sunburst design on the tiles of the bottom showed clearly, black against the white. In the corners, there were small piles of leaves.

He turned up a chair and sat down beside the empty pool, looking back up at the lighted windows of the hotel.

He was thinking about his father, the last time he had seen him after the Thanksgiving game in the Lighthouse. Then his eyes caught the diving tower where it stood out above the roof of the hotel. He got up from the chair and went over to the tower. He looked up, standing at the base, then he started to climb the ladder, slowly and deliberately.

At the top, he held to the rail with one hand, and leaned out over the edge of the platform, looking down into the empty pool and the two diving boards below him. In the summer of 1948, Lulu Demarco had climbed the tower and jumped off on a bet, going out and over and coming down between the low board and the side of the pool. The space between the board and the edge of the pool was even smaller than he had thought it would be, a slot that didn't seem to be wide enough for a man—even a small one.

For a minute he looked down, pulling against the arm holding him to the rail. Then he stood up straight at the lip of the diving platform, looking out across the roof of the hotel. He collected himself, held his arms in a diving attitude, the hands together, thumbs locked, fingers of the right hand crossing the fingers of the left. When he was ready, he took a deep breath and looked down to the tiles of the pool. With the water out, it was nearly forty feet to the bottom. For a moment he stood there holding his breath and looking down at the edge of the platform, as if he were really going to dive. Then he breathed out heavily and stepped back away from the edge, taking hold of the railing with his hand— closing his fingers tight around it.

He couldn't tell what had been inside Lulu's head, because he was only going through the motions, and he knew how different that would be. He did know that he wouldn't have been able to do it. Even with the water out of the pool he could tell about that. It was a fair test, because he knew how to gauge himself. There was a kind of accuracy and conscious control involved that he wouldn't have been capable of.

"I couldn't do it," he said, speaking out loud to himself. He leaned against the railing of the platform, looking up and out, beyond the dark line of the hotel roof. It stood out sharply, running off at a slight angle, with the lights of the town brightening the low sky behind it. Below him he could hear the palm fronds rattling in Jasper Square behind the hotel. The air at the top of the tower was still, walled in on three sides by the roof of the hotel.

He thought of the day he had gone up into the lighthouse after the Atlanta trip. The way the platform had rattled when he walked on it, and the hard-eyed white birds stepping along the railing.

"I couldn't have done it," he said again.

As he started to climb down the ladder, he saw a man and a woman through a lighted window on the third floor of the hotel. The woman had dark hair. He couldn't make out her features distinctly, because he was too far away, but he thought of her as beautiful. She had on a pale blue nightgown, and her hair was tied with a blue ribbon. She was sitting at the dressing table in the room, doing something to her face with delicate, womanlike movements, while the man sat on the bed and watched her. Then the man got up from the bed and came up behind her, putting his hands on her shoulders very lightly. She looked at him in the mirror, not moving for a moment, then she raised her hands and put them on his—doing it freely and calmly, making a very natural gesture of it, one full of intimacy and affection. Then she leaned back, and he kissed her. It was an awkward position for her, but she made it natural and full of grace. The kiss was gently done, only their hands touching. Afterward, the man went to the window and pulled down the shade.

For a while Jack waited to see if he could detect any movement behind the blank orange rectangle of the window. When he couldn't, he climbed down the tower, moving very slowly and deliberately from rung to rung of the ladder.

At the base of the tower, he looked back to the platform where it was outlined sharply against the bright glow of the sky. The light in the window had gone off while he had been coming down.

Going up the steps and along the gallery, he thought of the way that Mary had pushed against his chest until he rolled off her. And how she had turned her back to him to go to sleep afterward— after the fragile, delicate lovemaking.

"It wasn't good for her," he said to himself. "She didn't enjoy it."

He went back into the hotel, going up the stairs to their room so he wouldn't have to pass by the desk clerk in the lobby again. Back in the bed in the room, he listened to Mary's breathing and tried to think of his dream of the snaky tree. But with her there beside him, the dream wouldn't come. All he could do was lie there in the dark, propped up by the pillow, hugging himself and trying to make it come into his head. Instead, he kept seeing the orange rectangle of the window, with the man and the beautiful woman behind it.

In the next room there was a radio playing late-night music. Perry Como singing "I Can't Begin to Tell You" and "Let It Snow." He moved his lips with the music, mouthing the words without sound. And under the words of the song was a descant—"Mary, I love you. . . . Mary, I love you. . . ." Also without sound.

At five o'clock he went to sleep that way, sitting up in the bed hugging himself, trying to make the snaky tree come into his head and seeing instead the lighted window, with sweet, delicate, lovely things going on behind it.

Mary moved back into the Gaston Street house with him, and they lived together, even slept together with no more fear of hurt for her. But something was wrong with the way they were living, the way they moved in the house—from Mary's point of view, too, but especially from Jack's. It wasn't like what would have been happening behind the shade of the lighted window. There was no delicacy in it. Mary suffered the lovemaking; she didn't enjoy it. It was uncomfortable for her—just awkward, not painful. His body was too big—ungainly. And when he made love to her, he was always aware of the size of his flesh and bones. He wore her out, and she was always anxious for him to come to the end of it and roll off her so she could breathe.

Afterward, she would be there beside him in the bed, and he would be thinking of how awkward and clumsy he was. Sometimes he would think of the delicate, natural gestures of the beautiful woman in the lighted window—gestures that were calm and freely made.

He began to turn on the radio at night after Mary had gone to sleep, playing it softly so as not to wake her, lying there listening to the music in the dark. The words of the songs were something that he took seriously, and he tried to think of them in relation to what was happening between them—himself and his wife—in the Gaston Street house. "I can't begin to tell you how much you mean to me. . . . The girl of my dreams is the sweetest girl of all the girls I know. . . ." That was the way it ought to be. It seemed to him that something was missing—something vital and irreplaceable and lovely. Something that he had a right to expect.

"What do you think marriage is?" she said, when he tried to talk to her about it.

"I'm talking about love," he said.

"Well, love, then."

"There's something more to it than this. You don't even like going to bed with me."

"You don't act thrilled to death yourself."

"That's what I mean. Something is missing. We have to think about it too much."

"I think you're asking for something that isn't there," she said. "You're asking too much of *me*."

"But I love you."

"Do you *like* me?"

"Yes," he said. "I like you. I like the way you look. But that's not love. That's not all there is to love."

"You're a grown man, Jack."

"Are you satisfied?"

She thought about it for a minute. "No," she said. "But I wouldn't blame it on love."

"I would," he said.

When the Christmas bills came in January, they had an argument about money. Jack had bought Mary a bracelet for Christmas that had cost over a hundred dollars.

[297]

"I'm going to take it back. We don't need to throw money away like that. A truck driver can't afford to pay a hundred dollars for a bracelet."

"It's engraved."

"I'll get part of what you paid for it. I thought we agreed we wouldn't go overboard."

"I thought you'd like it."

"I would have taken it back right away if you'd told me what it really cost."

"I'll take it back."

"You let me handle the money. We have to watch what we're doing."

They passed over the winter and into the spring, both of them waiting, thinking that something was going to happen that would make some kind of music and a sweet dance of life come into their Gaston Street house. But nothing happened at all.

Kate came to visit on Valentine's Day, and she and Mary had words, so she didn't come back. Kate reminded Mary of Jack, the way she looked and moved. And Mary had never especially liked the big woman anyway. When she had her in the house, Mary projected Jack's failings into his mother and then dug them out again in a way that she couldn't do with her husband. It made Jack mad, and he stayed out all night drinking.

He did that twice more in February, and four times in March.

Mary was tight-lipped about it the first few times it happened. After St. Patrick's Day she came out with her complaints, and Jack broke down and cried in front of her.

"Listen, Mary. . . ." His face was streaked with the crying. She didn't answer him.

"Listen," he said. "I've got to tell you something." He wiped his eyes, rubbing them with his fist like a small child. "I never told you about it. It's something you've got to know."

"What?" she said. Her face was stony, braced for the worst.

For a minute he didn't answer. He seemed to be thinking about what he was going to say. "We killed some kittens," he said.

"What?" she said.

"I did it with Dendron. When we lived on Waldburg Street."

He held up three fingers. "Three kittens. We flushed them down the toilet." He started to cry again, sobbing and wiping his eyes with his hand. "We killed them for *nothing*, Mary." He was sobbing so hard it was difficult to understand what he was saying. "Three little-bitty kittens. They didn't even have their eyes open."

"When you lived on *Waldburg* Street?"

He nodded, sobbing. "I never could tell you before."

She looked at him for a minute, then turned and walked out of the room.

"We *meant* to do it!" he said, yelling after her. "They didn't even have their *eyes* open!" He collapsed onto the couch, bawling over the kittens.

The marriage didn't work out. That's what everybody said, understanding everything in the neutral way of stating the fact. Eight months was a reasonable chance—at least Mary thought that it was, and Jack didn't argue. He harped on the love that was missing, the way his expectations weren't coming along the way they should have—but he didn't try to talk her out of leaving when she packed on April 9. She made a great gesture of it, perhaps hoping that he would stop her.

The marriage had died over the winter, but what made her leave was the warm spring weather. They argued over money when the bills came due in April, but the resolution had formed back in the cold rainy days of the months that had gone before. They couldn't carry it into spring, which heightened their expectations and made them less able to put up with what had developed between them.

For Mary, going home the second time was easier, because she already knew how her father and mother would take it.

"He wasn't the man for you, Mary," said Mr. Odell. "You wouldn't have listened to me. But I knew it couldn't work out."

Mary looked at her father, then ran into her room and cried for an hour. She wouldn't answer his knock when he came to apologize —for whatever it was he had said.

She wasn't happy about the breakup, and didn't feel justified by it. Her expectations weren't as high as Jack's, but she wasn't without them either.

After Mary left, Jack stayed on in the Gaston Street house by himself. In the bed alone he could almost have the dream of the snaky tree, with Mary fragile and delicate, the way he had thought her to be. The words of the night music coming out of the radio from the out-of-town stations stirred him in the right way again, without the self-consciousness. He didn't miss her as much as he had missed his dream of her when she was with him. Alone, propped up in the bed, with Perry Como crooning sweet words into his ears, he could close his eyes and speak the words into the room.

"I love you, Mary. I love you. Love you."

Sometimes he could see the orange shade of the window, and behind it Mary floated as light and dainty as a tinsel angel. And wonderful, calm things passed free and lovely.

25

In the Lighthouse

ON APRIL 13—the Thursday after Mary left him on Sunday—Jack went down to the Lighthouse Bar to see Old Johnny. He didn't go out to the Marshoaks house, because he wanted to talk about it and around it, without having to explain or argue, and he knew that his mother would tangle herself in his affairs with Mary, winding and draping them around herself and making a principle of the thing, while his father would keep it at a distance. And, finally, she wouldn't understand it from his side as well as Johnny would—though what he wanted wasn't precisely understanding so much as a passing of words.

It was a warm night, and he walked his long shadow around Emmett Park for a while first, breathing in the dark, rank smell of the river under the bluff. There were six or seven people in the bar, and he stood across Bay Street under the harbor light, watching them as they drank and talked, waiting for a chance to go in to his father when he would be alone.

At ten-thirty there were only three people left—Old Johnny,

Billy Boy O'Day, and a small man who seemed to be with his father. At ten-forty-five he followed his shadow across Bay Street, under the stoplight, and into the bar.

"Well, is it Jack?" said Billy Boy. Old Johnny and the small man turned to look at him as he came in the door. The small man was sitting on the far side of Johnny, and had to lean out to see around him.

Jack nodded to his father. "Haven't seen you for a while," he said.

"If it ain't the married man," said Johnny. "Sneaking out already."

Jack held up his finger. "One Pabst," he said.

"I thought you was working on J.J.'s Blatz truck," said Billy Boy. "Won't he take it unkindly?"

"I hope so," said Jack. "One Pabst."

Billy Boy put the can on the bar.

"You know Wyatt?" said Old Johnny, nodding his head to the small man sitting beside him.

"We met last time."

"L.D. Wyatt," said Johnny.

Mr. Wyatt knit his brows and looked to the side, thinking about whether or not he had met Jack before.

Jack put out his hand. "Mr. Wyatt?"

Wyatt shook hands with him. "He's outgrew you, Johnny."

"How tall you getting to be?"

Jack took a sip of his beer before he answered. "Six-seven."

"What you weigh?"

"Two sixty-five."

Johnny sucked his lip and rattled his can of beer, looking at himself in the mirror behind the bar. "Kids get more solid food these days. I had to fill out on pinto beans and cabbage."

"Vitamins," said Billy Boy. "Everybody's healthier than they used to be."

"That's a bunch of bullshit," said Johnny. "Pills is unhealthy. Solid food. That's what does it."

"He's bigger'n you, Johnny," said Wyatt.

"So was Kate's daddy. You ever see his mother?"

For a while they didn't say anything, drinking their beer and looking at each other in the mirror.

"How's it feel?" said Johnny, talking to him in the mirror. "Regular meals and such?"

Jack put his Pabst can down on the bar. "She's left me," he said.

Johnny looked at him in the mirror. "Hauled off on you?"

"Yes."

"Is it serious?"

"Second time. She went home in October, too."

Johnny took a sip of his beer. "Can't be too bad if she makes a habit of it."

"I think she means it this time."

For a while Johnny didn't say anything. Jack held up a finger to Billy Boy. "One Pabst," he said.

"I didn't ask how *you* feel about it," said Johnny.

Jack looked off at the lighthouse display with the red light revolving behind the bar. It made two revolutions before he answered, winking out of the mirror as it went around. "I love her," he said, speaking very low.

"Yes, shit," said Johnny. "Currans never was lucky in love. All we was good for was carrying the torch."

For a while they drank without saying anything.

"Wasn't but the one time your mother ran off on me. She wasn't the kind to fool around with a thing like that."

"Did you fight with her much?" Kate didn't talk about Johnny at all, and Jack had never found out exactly why she had left him.

"I never laid a hand on her," he said. "I loved your mother."

"I didn't mean that. I mean *words*. Did you have words?"

Johnny looked back at the mirror. "She didn't say word one to me. Just I came home and she and you was gone."

"We had words," said Jack.

"You can talk them out of the house. You'll play hell talking them back in."

"I wouldn't try."

"No use anyway."

"Last time she just came back on her own."

"Has to be that way. Your mother wouldn't let me see her to talk about it."

"That's mostly the way it was with Mary."

For a while they didn't say anything.

"I get along better with her gone," said Jack.

Johnny looked at him. "You mean that serious, don't you?"

"Yes."

"I know what you mean."

"You still love Mother, don't you?"

"I never thought about anybody since—not serious, I didn't. Don't a day go by and I not think about her once or twice."

"One out of four marriages breaks up," said Billy Boy.

They looked at him.

"I read it in the paper. Keep on and won't none of them be working out."

"It's the times," said Johnny. "Don't nobody give a shit anymore."

"That's not the way it was," said Jack.

"I didn't mean *your* case. It's just the way the times are going."

"Yes," said Jack. "It's a funny way I feel about it. I love her— you know—*really* love her. I like it better when she's out of the house. I can't do things to hurt her when she's not there."

Johnny tapped his head. "It's the idea of a woman drives you crazy." He looked down at the bar for a minute. "Fifteen years. Fifteen years Kate pulled out on me. I hadn't put it out of my mind a full day since. I keep on thinking how good it would be." He shook his head.

"I couldn't talk to her about it," said Jack.

"Talking ain't no use."

"She didn't seem to care whether we could talk about it or not. I don't know what it was she felt."

"You can't *work* at love. It just has to be right," said Johnny. "It wouldn't be worth it to just drag it on year in year out."

"Mary was like she was something holy to me," said Jack. "I wasn't much on the Church in a regular way."

Johnny looked at him. "I don't know about that," he said. "That don't sound too good to me."

"Just the way I thought about her."

"Kate got everything mixed up with the priests."

"I'm not talking about the priests. I mean I loved her like I would have felt about the Church if I'd been in it."

"You got that from Kate, I reckon. I never got into it much myself. Hocus-pocus is what I call it."

[304]

For a while they drank their beer in silence.

"I wouldn't want to live in a world where there wasn't any love," said Jack.

"I wouldn't either," said Johnny. "You get that from me. Most of the loving I seen got nothing to do with the Church."

"Yes," said Jack. "It's tied together some way. I feel like it's tied together some way."

Johnny held up three fingers. "Round again," he said.

Billy Boy opened three beers and put them on the bar.

"I'll get these," said Jack, digging in his pocket.

Johnny held up his hand. "I didn't send you nothing for your wedding," he said.

Jack let him pay for the beers.

"Whatever happened with the football?"

"Jack could have made it anywhere he wanted to go," said Billy Boy. "You should have seen the papers after the Thanksgiving game."

"I mean Georgia Tech," said Johnny.

"That's what I mean," said Billy Boy. "The Atlanta papers. He's the best natural player ever come out of this town."

"I wondered what happened."

"I had Mary on my mind."

"Atlanta is a crummy town," said Johnny. "I wouldn't want to live in Atlanta."

"Yes," said Jack. "I didn't like it up there." He took a sip of his beer. "Got to where I didn't like the football either."

"You always liked the football," said Johnny.

"I don't know what it was. Everybody was out for himself up there. It wasn't like Boniface—more of a business."

"That's the way it is," said Johnny. "To tell the truth, it always looked like a silly game to me. Where did it get you?"

"I didn't feel that way about it in high school. Everybody wasn't out for himself."

"I don't really care for baseball either, to tell the truth. That's a silly goddamn game." He looked at himself in the mirror. "Wrestling and boxing—you can tell where you're at in a boxing match."

"One against one," said Jack. "Not much point to that either if you stop to think about it. I like the idea of everybody working as a team. It's more of a long-range proposition."

"You can't do it, is all," said Johnny. "Everybody's out for himself."

"What about the fire department?" said Jack. "You got to work as a team putting out a fire."

"All you need is enough water."

"I wouldn't want to believe that," said Jack. "I just didn't like the way things were going up there. I missed Mary."

"Women can really screw you up," said Johnny, shaking his head. "They ought to be the ones have the peters on them."

"You screw yourself, I guess. They help you do it."

For a while they drank in silence.

"Wyatt never got tangled up with them, did you, Wyatt?"

The small man looked up at them in the mirror. He had been drinking his beer outside the conversation, wrapped up in his own thoughts. "What?" he said.

"Women," said Johnny. "You never got yourself tangled up with no women."

"Nothing but trouble," said Wyatt. "Love 'em and leave 'em."

"Easy said," said Johnny.

"Not if you ain't big and handsome," said Wyatt. "With me, they always liked it in and out—" he snapped his fingers, "—like that!"

Johnny looked at Jack. "Wyatt's the best man with a blade I ever see."

"Oh?" Jack looked at the little man.

"Show him, Wyatt."

Wyatt looked at them in the mirror. Jack never did see his hand move. He just heard the click and saw the red light from the lighthouse flashing off the blade.

"Where'd it come from?" said Jack.

"I think he keeps it in his shirt pocket. Some say he's got a special holder. Wyatt won't let out where it stays."

"It's an advantage," said Wyatt. "Someplace. I keep it someplace." He smiled without showing his teeth, just the lips pulled up in a thin line. With the knife in his hand, there was a new expression on his face—very confident and happy.

"Not your pants pocket?" said Johnny.

"You can't get it out when you're sitting down. I made some of my best passes sitting down. That's when they're not expecting it."

When he talked, his voice sounded firmer—with the knife in his hand.

"Come over here." Johnny motioned Jack around on the far side of Wyatt. "He's fast, but it's the control I never could figure out."

Jack came around until he was standing beside his father, next to Wyatt.

"Show him," said Johnny.

"It's harder when he's just standing there," said Wyatt. "Surprise is what I count on most." While he was talking he moved the knife, holding it the way a magician would hold a fan of cards to do tricks with them. The talking made Jack lose track of the blade. Before he got it in sight again, there was a light clicking sound on the floor. He lost the blade looking down, and there was the sound of clicking again.

"He'd take them all off if he wanted," said Johnny, putting his finger inside Jack's shirt and pulling it out to show where the buttons were missing.

"I'll put them back on, son," said Wyatt. "Your daddy wanted me to show you how I done it." His voice sounded apologetic, but strong. His smile was very firm.

Jack reached down and picked the buttons up off the floor. "That's all right," he said. He wanted to hit the tight grin on the face of the little man.

"I was watching him and I didn't see it," said Johnny. "You see it, Billy Boy?"

"No."

"He's the one opened up Donovan's face," said Johnny. He drew a line with his finger, through his mouth, going from ear to ear. "Donovan never knew what hit him till he tried to shut his mouth. His bottom jaw looked like a slice of tomater."

"I'm too little to worry about," said Wyatt, tightening his evil smile. Looking at him made the hairs stand up on the back of Jack's neck. He kept thinking of how it would be to smash the thin mouth with his fist.

He went around on the other side of his father and sat down on the stool again. When he looked in the mirror, the knife was gone from Wyatt's hand, and he looked like the air had been let out of him—folded over and subdued.

None of them had seen the place where he put the knife away.

"I never liked knives," said Jack. "Killing things."

"That's because you're a foot and a half taller than me," said Wyatt, leaning out and looking around Johnny at Jack. Without the knife, his voice sounded whiny. "That's a big man's point of view."

"Maybe so," said Jack. He was feeling sorry for the little man again. "I admire your skill, Mr. Wyatt. It's just the way I feel about knives."

"People pay attention to Wyatt," said Johnny. "Those that don't, wish they had."

"You ever tried to throw it?" said Billy Boy.

"I wouldn't let it out of my hand."

They settled down, drinking their beers again. Jack looked out the window on Bay Street. From the inside of the bar, the beam seemed to be coming out of the lighthouse painted on the window —not going into it, as it did from the outside.

"Did the guy paint the lighthouse from the inside?" he said, speaking to Billy Boy.

"Yes. He did everything backward—all the words. It came out all right."

"On the outside it looks like it's going in."

"What?"

"The beam," said Jack. "It looks like it's going in."

"I never noticed," said Billy Boy.

"How's the job?" said Johnny.

Jack looked at himself in the mirror. "I quit," he said.

"Quit J.J.?"

"It's a new start."

"J.J. could be good to you," said Billy Boy. "He likes football players. He's a sport himself."

"He reminds me of Daddy Warbucks."

"What's that supposed to mean?" said Johnny.

"I don't want to be his Punjab."

"He could do you a lot of good," said Billy Boy.

"He's got everything working for him," said Jack. "Everything and everybody."

Billy Boy tapped his temple with his finger. "Brains," he said.

"He knows how to get it out of the others," said Jack. He took a sip of his beer. "He's been good to me. I don't like driving his truck is all."

"He'll look out for you," said Billy Boy.

"I'll look out for myself."

"Don't talk him down, Jack. Lots of people know him," said Billy Boy.

"You ever see the way he treats the little guy works for him?"

"Shube?"

"Yes."

"Shube would be hustling niggers down on Indian Street if it wasn't for J.J. O'Brien," said Billy Boy. "I don't know why he puts up with him."

"I just don't like the way he treats him."

"You got something else in mind?" said Johnny. "A job?"

"No. I thought I'd take it easy for a while."

"Be your own man?" said Johnny. He raised the beer can and toasted him in the mirror.

For a while they drank in silence. L.D. Wyatt turned out his stool and stood up. "I got to be going," he said.

"Where you keep it?" said Johnny. "Ain't I your friend?"

L.D. didn't answer. He put out his hand to Jack. "Good luck," he said.

"Thank you, Mr. Wyatt," said Jack. For a moment he didn't know what he thought of the little man. Without the knife in his hand, he thought of him the way he thought about Shube.

After Wyatt left, Billy Boy moved off down the bar to polish glasses, leaving them alone.

"I went up in the lighthouse," said Jack.

"Tybee Light?"

"You talked about it last time."

"That was a good day. Did you remember the ship and how I told you it was going to Ireland?"

"All I remembered were the birds. They're still up there."

"I thought you'd remember the ship."

For a while neither of them said anything.

"I remember we talked about going to Ireland," said Jack. "The last time I saw you."

"Yes. I always did talk about going to Ireland."

"Let's do it," said Jack.

Johnny looked at him. "You mean right now?"

"We could go this summer. I don't much want to hang around town now. Nothing's here to hold me."

"Say," said Johnny, "wouldn't that be great?" He put his arm on Jack's shoulder. "You and me on Galway Bay."

"The last of the Currans," said Jack.

Johnny toasted him in the mirror. "The last of the Currans," he said.

"In a silver boat on Galway Bay," said Jack, raising his can to the mirror. "Shaped like a swan."

"Ah," said Johnny, "like a swan."

"I've got some money. A little bit. We could go there if we wanted to do it bad enough."

"Someday we will," said Johnny. "I promise you, someday we will."

"Let's do it."

"Two more, Billy Boy," said Johnny, calling to him down the bar. He raised his beer can. "Here's to Ireland," he said. "And the last of the Currans."

"We're going to do it?"

"Someday we will."

Jack emptied his beer, then crushed the can, folding it over between his thumb and forefinger, dropping it on the bar. "I guess I'd better be going," he said.

"Where you going? You're a free man now."

Jack thought about it a minute. He wanted to remind Johnny about the arm-wrestling. "That's right," he said. "No strings attached." He settled back to the bar.

Johnny slapped him on the back. "That's the ticket. We're the last of the Currans—after all."

"Tell me about Ireland," said Jack. "How did you feel when Mother walked out on you?"

Johnny ran his finger around the rim of the can, squinting his eyes and looking at himself in the mirror. He hunched his shoulders, leaning on the bar. Outside it was a warm April night, and the smell of the river was strong along the bluff.

"Ireland is a beautiful place . . ." he said.

BOOK IV

Love No More: 1950-1956

26

Gainful Employment

AFTER THE MARRIAGE broke up—through May and June—Jack floated around town, taking care of his needs in the least thoughtful ways—bunking in with friends and staying away from the Marshoaks house because he didn't want to have to talk to Kate about Mary—laying the blame on her. He picked up change hustling a little pool and arm-wrestling—though he couldn't get very good odds on the wrestling, of course, because of his size. He wouldn't play in Wooten's, since he didn't want to come face to face with J.J. O'Brien, not because he was afraid of him, but because of the debt he owed. But there were other pool halls, and not being so well known in them worked to his advantage in sorting out the easy marks and scrounging up games. He wasn't good enough to make a living at it, but he was steady enough to be able to eat on it.

When the Korean War broke out in June, he went to enlist—trying to hide the knee that had gone bad on him over the years of playing football, and that would have kept him out of the draft if he had wanted to use it that way, which he didn't. Like all young men in the early fifties, he felt that some time spent in uniform was part of the passage into manhood. Coming up through high school with the war going on—particularly at the military schools —there had been a lot of discussion of the merits of the different branches of the service—talks that floated off a base of the war stories told by returned old grads, John Wayne movies, and the assembly programs that were held occasionally to honor the school's own war heroes. There they would be brought together and addressed earnestly by members of the classes of the late thirties and early forties, in blue and green and olive-drab uniforms, sometimes with an empty coat sleeve or a trouser leg turned back and pinned. It was impressive. And the issues were clear-cut and undiluted. The last war where God was going to be on anybody's side.

With the war over, Jack hadn't thought much about the fact that football had made him unfit for serving his country. But now, with real shooting going on again, he considered it a very good alternative to the purposeless life he was leading, lounging around town and brooding about Mary. Even getting killed wasn't such a bad idea, as long as he was moving in some definite direction when it happened—though, to tell the truth, he didn't think of it in those terms, really. Only that it was something with a purpose for him to believe in without thinking about it.

The first place he tried was the marine corps recruiting office in the city hall. As usual, the marines had collected more than their share of attention through the movies and in the newspapers, and also Jack remembered that Horse Rooney had been in the marines.

The recruiting sergeant was a thick, gnomelike man, dark and Italian-looking, with just a small, leathery touch of Choctaw Indian in his face—a cross between a glandular John Garfield and Edward G. Robinson, buttoned up in tailor-mades, with stiff starch creases, and five rows of ribbons over his left shirt pocket.

"You're a hell of a horse, son. I wish we could use you," he said. He sat with his elbows on the desk, his hands lightly clasped as if he were holding a butterfly in them. There was a long white scar on his right cheek, and when he talked nothing moved but his eyes.

"You haven't looked at me yet. What do you mean?" Jack didn't have a limp, and he thought they would never put him under an X ray as part of a routine physical examination. The idea that he might be too big for the marines was something that had never occurred to him.

The sergeant held his hand over his head like an umbrella. "Too tall, son," he said. "Six-six. That's the regulations."

"You mean I'm too *big* to get in the marines?"

"I could send you up to Parris Island for a physical, but it'd just be a waste of time. They'd put the tape on you."

"I never heard you could be too big for the marines."

"You can be too big for anything," said the sergeant.

"Look," said Jack. He picked up the desk, lifting it away from where the sergeant was sitting. Then he carried it around the room, holding it like a serving tray, being careful not to let any of the papers and pens fall off. He took one full circuit of the office, then came back and set it down in front of the sergeant.

The sergeant clapped his hands without changing the expression on his face. "You're a hoss, son, but you're barking up the wrong tree. Six-six. It ain't up to me anyway. We can't waste money these days. It ain't like the big war."

"All right," said Jack. "We'll see what the navy has to say."

"Listen," said the sergeant, "don't take it personal." He scraped his finger across his brow like a windshield wiper. "Being big is just a liability when the shooting starts. I wouldn't want to be within twenty-five yards of you in a skirmish line. You think you just walk in there and scare them to death?"

"That's all right," said Jack. "Maybe the navy won't be so careful." He wanted to ask if they had any regulations about how short you could be, but he had respect for the uniform and the ribbons the sergeant was wearing.

"They'll be careful," said the sergeant. "Six-six. They know what they're doing." He took out his handkerchief and mopped his forehead. "The ideal size for a fighting man is under six feet," he said. He thought a minute. "Five-ten. If you're solid and quick." He adjusted the position of the calendar on his desk. "Plenty of times I wished I was about half what size I am."

Jack started out of the office.

"Don't take it personal, son," said the sergeant. "If the navy does let you in, ask for submarines."

Jack looked at him.

"They eat better," said the sergeant.

But the navy didn't want him. Neither did the army nor the air force nor the coast guard. So he went back to hustling pool and brooding about Mary.

He didn't think of trying the marine reserve unit. At least he didn't think of it soon enough. By the time he did, they were already gone. They left Savannah on August 8, and on September 15 went ashore with the second wave at Inchon. Most of them wound up with Barber's Fox Company at Toktong Pass during the fighting around Chosin Reservoir. The unit got a citation and the personal thanks of President Truman, but not everybody got to wear the ribbon. It wouldn't have mattered to Cowboy McGrath, because Cowboy was very phlegmatic about things in general and wouldn't have cared much one way or the other. But Bo Hoerner would have put great stock in it, as he had done the idea of the Gipper in the Boniface days. Bo was killed outright during the Chinese attack on the morning of November 28. And Cowboy bled to death on the night of the twenty-ninth because the corpsmen couldn't thaw the plasma containers to give him a transfusion.

It was the first foretaste of disillusionment with war to come to Savannah, especially sad after the palmy days of the great one, with its memories of raising the flag on Iwo Jima, and Bastogne, and Commander Cunningham radioing to send him more Japs just before Wake Island fell. Some of the old momentum still carried, and the papers wrote it up the way they had done the stories of the other war. But it was hard to get around the fact that thirty-eight days was a very short seasoning for the move they had to make going in at Inchon. And most of that was spent on the ships that took them there.

The father of one of the boys felt so strongly about it that he spent five thousand dollars—what it would have cost to send his son to college—to put up a big granite monument on some property he owned out in the woods near Bloomingdale—a little town fifteen miles up U.S. 80 from Savannah.

IN MEMORY OF 19 YEAR OLD
P.F.C. JOHN WESLEY BLANTON, JR., U.S.M.C.R.,
KILLED IN ACTION, NOVEMBER 31, 1950,
YUDAM-NI, CHOSIN RESERVOIR, KOREA
THE INCOMPETENT, GREEDY, VENAL, CONFUSED POLITICIANS
ELECTED IN 1948 WERE RESPONSIBLE FOR THIS BOY
BEING MURDERED IN KOREA.

Except for the landing at Inchon, it was a very bad beginning, even by inattentive Savannah standards. And wars had always been popular there.

At the end of September, Jack ran into Feeb, and when Feeb found out that he wasn't doing anything, he talked him into coming to work with him at the curb market. Feeb had gotten married, and his father had financed a kind of branch operation—one dealing in general groceries instead of produce only. Feeb was doing well and had it in mind to open a second branch. He thought that Jack could end up as a full partner, though he didn't say anything about that to begin with. What he wanted was someone he could trust and rely on.

"Listen," he said. "It's fucking good money. People got to eat."

At the beginning, it was nice for them to be together again, listening to Feeb talk dirty and going over old times. Every morning Feeb would come in with a play-by-play account of what he had done in bed with his wife the night before.

"Man . . ." he would say, in his loudmouthed confidential way, squinting his eyes and shaking his head. "Maaaaan . . . did my wife *cold* lay a fucking on me last night?"

"What?"

Then he would go into the intimate details, with Jack trying to cut him off. His wife had put him on a diet, and the compensation for taking away the food seemed to be that she was going to let him screw himself to death. The way Feeb looked at it was exactly the way he had looked at Theodore's chocolate fudge sundaes. It was just too good to keep to himself.

Jack didn't want to hear about Feeb's sex life, but he did want to know about the business, and he never could get word one out of Feeb about that. It wasn't that Feeb didn't trust Jack—that had been the reason he had asked him to come in—it was just the Levantine legacy he inherited from his father, along with his nose and his appetite. Business was business, and he took the cash home in a lockbox to total the receipts.

Finally, it didn't work out. Jack had thought of Feeb as a source of amusement for nearly twenty years. It was too late for him to start thinking of him as a boss. Feeb never insisted on it, but the situation itself generated its own rearrangement—at least it seemed so to Jack. Also, Jack couldn't fetch and carry for the customers gracefully. He wasn't surly, just that there was no side of him that could get pleasure out of ingratiating himself with strangers.

"I appreciate it, Feeb. It just wasn't much of an idea you had. I'm no businessman."

"I thought you'd come in as a partner. We wouldn't be small-time forever. It's a fucking good business. You could see that."

"I'm losing customers for you."

"It's not the fucking A&P. They want it, you get it. I ain't pushing snake oil."

"It's not my line, Feeb."

Feeb shrugged his shoulders. "I needed somebody I could trust. If you don't like it . . ." he shrugged his shoulders again.

"Thanks anyway."

"Let me know if you change your mind."

That was Halloween week of 1950. Afterward he went back to the poolroom, floating around, picking up small change but setting his own pace. Gradually, over the winter of 1950–1951, a blooming Curran thirst came snaking up his tongue. He tried to quench it first with Jax and Spearman's beer, but that ran into too much money because of the quantities he required. Then in the spring of 1951 he switched to a local sweet wine that was made of colored sugar water with grain alcohol in it. The syrupy sweetness was something he had to get used to, and the coloring they used in it dyed his tongue red, but it gave him the effect he wanted at a better return for the money he had to invest.

In July and August of 1951 Jack gradually lost his stroke, and had to give up hustling pool. From then until the summer of 1955, he worked off and on as rack boy in Dillon's Pool Hall on Jefferson

Street, sleeping in the backroom sometimes—sometimes finding a place to flop with someone who remembered him from the 1947 team, or a friend he had made over a bottle of Witch of Endor wine. His weight went up to 350 pounds, and his face swelled and sagged like a leper's.

At Susy's wedding in June of 1955, no one recognized him, and Reilley took him aside and told him he was killing himself. He went into the men's room and looked in the mirror, where he saw that Reilley was right. So he came home to the Marshoaks place for Kate to take care of him and dry him out.

During the summer of 1954, the group of college boys who came in to work on the survey party was a particularly scabby lot, loud-mouthed and cocky. Even John Sparks couldn't offset the effect they had, and for the first time they really depressed George and made him think in terms of widening his horizons by getting another job. However, it wasn't until later in the fall that the great bird of ambition flew down to perch on his shoulder. Maybe it wasn't ambition exactly, but a definite feeling of dissatisfaction—a delayed reaction that needed the rains and cold of winter to make it fester and bring it to a head. He began to cast around for some alternative to the highway department job.

There were a lot of things advertised in *Popular Mechanics* and magazines like that, which John Sparks passed on to George after he was finished reading them. Offers to learn meat-cutting and embalming in the privacy of your own home. But the one he zeroed in on finally was one that went:

$—RAISE GIANT FROGS—$
For Pleasure and Profit

There were other business opportunities involving animals—rabbits, hamsters, chickens, minks, and other things like that. There was one ad for giant earthworms that tempted him especially, since raising them for bait went with the crickets. But because of the hunting, George already had a kind of ongoing relationship with frogs, and his dealings with the restaurants gave him an inside track on the Savannah frog market. When it came to frogs, he felt as if he knew where he stood.

He sent away for their brochure, and in March wrote in his order, going for the full breeding pair to start him on the road to fame and fortune. He could have taken the low road and bought a hatch of tadpoles, which were cheaper, but he wanted to see what the animals themselves were going to look like so he could send them back if he wasn't satisfied. His expeditions along the canals and drainage ditches had brought him into contact with some pretty impressive frogs—four pounds being just a fair average for the ones he encountered. If the outfit he was dealing with didn't improve on that, there really wasn't much sense in paying for the things in the first place.

He got his money's worth, as it turned out, but he didn't get to go into the business after all, and was only left with consolation after the fact, because he wasn't there when the postman delivered the package, and his mother opened it for him.

The box had air holes, and the word "FROG" was printed on it twelve times in big green letters, but she missed it all, being so eager to get the top off and see what George was up to. So she opened it up and found herself eyeball to eyeball with eleven and a half pounds of inbred Louisiana frog. She didn't know exactly what it was she was looking at, because the dimensions of the animals were strictly prehistoric, and nothing in her experience gave her any frame of reference to apply to them. Sort of the King —and Queen—Kong of frogdom is what they were. And, anyway, the fact that there were two of them intertwined there on the bed of damp moss complicated the problem, throwing the whole thing further out of perspective, since she didn't know there *were* two of them. She conceived of them as one single beast—including the damp moss. All she could tell about it was that, whatever it was, it was slimy-ghastly, and—God help her—it seemed to be alive— something slick and shiny and green and hairy (the moss) that was looking at her with four yellow eyes. Not exactly the kind of thing you would expect the mailman to put into your trusting hands on a gray day in April.

"Barooomp!" said the frog—one of them.

"Sweet Jesus!" said Mrs. Bogger.

Then she did a quick Ann Miller high step and dropped the box on the floor in the living room, while she ran for her broom in the kitchen.

When she came back and saw that there were two of them—and that they were only frogs—she stopped being afraid, and started being mad because of the way they had scared her before. She chased them all over the house until she cornered them in the bathroom, where she swatted them out into a kind of double frog strudel on the black and white tiles of the floor.

George could tell from what was left of them when he got home that he had been onto the real article, for they were indeed monumental frogs. But the only thing they would have been good for after Mrs. Bogger got through with them would have been to drape a birdcage or paper a wall.

"What were you going to do with them, George? What on earth were you going to do with a thing like that?"

George didn't answer her, for fear of being disrespectful. He just took his lip in his teeth, then folded up the frogs and carried them out to the garbage can.

"You think I'd have a yard full of those things hopping around, George? Well, you've got another think coming. I wouldn't have a yard full of those things hopping around for all the tea in China."

George went back into his bedroom and checked the *Popular Mechanics* classified ads again, to root out a less chancy path to fame and fortune. He thought that it must be out there for him somewhere—free of loudmouthed college boys who thought they knew all the answers, when they didn't even know how to throw a chain.

The next thing he tried was a home-study course in radio repair, which guaranteed him vacations in Florida and total independence in exchange for a few pleasant hours of his spare time.

When the first lesson came, the first part of it was a long note of congratulations, full of exclamation marks and underlined words. The second part of the lesson was an explanation of electrical current, and the first sentence went as follows:

> When an electrical force, such as that provided by a battery, is connected across a conductor, the free electrons are guided in

an orderly fashion from the negative terminal of the battery, through the wire, to the positive terminal, or so it is conventionally assumed, although there is reason to believe that the current flow may be moving in the opposite direction, i.e., from positive to negative. Do not let this confuse you.

It confused him.

What that opening sentence meant to him was that he couldn't take any of the wiring diagrams at face value—not even the simplest. After such a tottering first step, even the plan for a bell circuit had depths and resonances that would set him musing and doodling on a scratch pad for hours, trying to clear up in his own mind just which way the current was *really* moving. He read the opening sentence thousands of times, and with each reading it grew murkier and more baffling.

"Why'd they have to bring it *up?*" he said, whiny.

Then he had an attack that wiped him out, so he had to start all over. Then he had another attack. He kept holding on and trying to get onto it for three weeks, until he finally decided that the pain it was causing him wasn't worth it—not even the vacations in Florida. So he gave up and canceled the rest of the lessons in the course.

What he really liked about the radio was the consolation of the orange light under the dial in his darkened room, and listening to the music from out-of-town stations. He didn't have to turn his head into a cauliflower for that.

As the summer wore on, the attacks wiped out the confusion of the electricity. And the new group of summer boys was nice enough, and respectful, and well-behaved, so that by the end of July his head was clean as a wind-washed bone—and he had just about forgotten the dissatisfaction he had felt for his job the summer before. The great bird of ambition had taken wing, and with the weight off his shoulders, he was peaceful and easy of mind and feeling as much satisfaction as he was accustomed to finding in his sad, gray, solitary life.

Television came to Savannah in the fall of 1954, and the wrestling programs and quiz shows were very big in those days. With nothing much to do but sit around the house while Kate put solid food into him, Jack spent a lot of time watching it. The star of the wrestling shows in those days was Gorgeous George, and he would regularly be on television several times a week. Seeing him made Jack angry at first. In fact, the whole medicine-show con game it was irritated him. But as he watched longer, the nursery-rhyme blatancy and artlessness of it began to amuse him and tickle his fancy. He thought he could tell that the wrestlers themselves— including Gorgeous George—were not deceived by what they were doing, no matter how much the audience might be taken in. And that started him thinking.

There was nothing that he was seeing on the programs that he didn't feel he could do himself, provided he could get back into some kind of shape. Most of the routines were such obvious frauds that it was hard to imagine anyone would pay good money to see them. But it was clear that people were doing just that, because the arenas were always full. Now that he was beginning to look respectable again, he would need a better job than racking balls in Frank Dillon's Pool Hall. So he began to think about not just losing a few pounds and getting the color back into his face, but of paring to the bone—hardening himself up again—the way he had been in the football-playing days—and becoming a professional wrestler. He figured that Gorgeous George had been forced to go to the gimmicks because he was actually a small man—for a wrestler— and wouldn't have attracted much attention without the hairpins and perfume. But Jack felt that his size, by itself, would be an attraction. And around Savannah he would probably be known well enough that he wouldn't have to make an absolute fool of himself to draw a crowd. He thought that he could manage it with a certain amount of style.

He started gently, doing a little roadwork to get back his wind. It was slow to begin with, because four years of Witch of Endor wine hadn't exactly set him up for the Olympic team. It had taken two full weeks just for the red coloring to fade out of his tongue. But he started out trotting once around the block, and pretty soon he was able to jog to Daffin Park, make a circuit of it, and get back to the house without breathing too hard—a distance of about three miles.

Once he got his lungs cleared out and was passing clear water when he urinated, he started doing exercises that would give him back his strength—especially in the muscles of his arms and neck and shoulder girdle—the muscles he would be using as a wrestler. Once a day he went down to the Y to use the weights. But twice a day he did calisthenics out in his own backyard.

The first period was around noon, because he felt that he needed to sweat the last trace of the poison out of his system. So from eleven to twelve he was out in the sun, doing his old football exercises. Just before supper, from six to seven, he would go out again in the cool of the afternoon.

That was the way he and George finally met. George saw him over the fence—heard him counting, really—and came up to watch him as he went through the routine. For three days George stood at the fence watching, his head balanced like a bowling ball on top of the boards. Only his eyes moving.

The first day Jack didn't notice him. The second day he ignored him, since it was hard to do the exercises and carry on a conversation at the same time. But the third day he couldn't let it go any longer.

"I ought to sell you a ticket," he said.

George looked around to see who he was talking to. "You talking to me?" he said.

"You're throwing me off."

"You used to be on the radio. I listened to you when you was playing the football."

"That was a long time ago."

"It was?"

"Don't you have something better to do?"

"It wasn't that long." George stopped and thought. "A couple of years."

"You going to just stand there?"

George looked at him a minute. "My name is George Bogger," he said, speaking very formally. He put his hand over the top of the fence. "Pleased to meet you, Mr. Curran."

Jack looked at the hand, then went over and shook it, also

moving formally and with stiffness, as the occasion seemed to require.

"I used to listen to you on the radio. You were pretty good. That's what they said."

"Thank you," said Jack. He thought a minute. "You going to just stand there and watch?"

"I'd be much obliged," he said.

"Well," said Jack.

"How big *are* you?"

"Too big," said Jack.

"What do you mean?"

"I been just sitting around the last few years. I need to work some of the lard off."

"You just doing that for *nothing?*"

Jack looked at him. "What do you mean? I need to get in shape."

"Couldn't you dig a garden? Chop some wood? You know—*do* something?"

"Work's not the same as exercise. You've got to isolate the muscles you want to get at."

"You do?"

"Listen," said Jack, "are you going to stand there all day and just watch?"

"What are you doing it *for?* You going to play football again?"

"I'm going to wrestle."

"You mean you're going to be on the *television?*" Television was more wonderful than the radio to George, though he didn't feel the same affection for it.

"Not hardly. Just around town."

"You could be on the television if you was good enough. Like the football."

"Excuse me," said Jack. He got down on his back to do the bridging exercises.

George watched him rocking up onto his neck. "One . . . two . . . threefour . . ." he said, calling out the numbers very hesitant and jerky.

Jack flopped down onto his back, looking up at the sky. "You're counting wrong."

"What's a *one?* I could count for you."

Jack rolled back up onto his neck. Then he did the exercise, counting out loud to give it to George.

"I got it. One . . . two . . . three . . . four." He nodded his head to the rhythm.

So Jack had a trainer, whether he wanted one or not. At least for the afternoon sessions. George was mostly discreet about it, and always stayed on his side of the fence. But he was out there as regular as regret. And that was how they came to know each other. First, with the board fence between them. Then, after Jack invited him, with George sitting cross-legged in one of the wooden lawn chairs in Jack's backyard, tapping out the numbers with his finger.

Some of the exercises were out of a Charles Atlas course Jack had taken when he was in the New Orleans high school.

"What's *that* good for?" Jack was doing an arm-opposed curl, holding hands with himself and pumping his arms up and down.

He drew his hand across his upper chest. "Shoulder girdle," he said. "And arms." He flexed his biceps.

"It looks silly to me. That one *really* looks silly. Wouldn't chopping wood do you more good?"

For a minute Jack looked at him without saying anything.

"I'm going to show you what it's good for," he said. He pulled up the table that went with the lawn chairs, then he sat down on the ground, putting his elbow on the table. "Put your hand up there," he said.

"What for?"

"I'm going to show you what it's good for. Put your hand up there."

"You're bigger'n me," said George, pouty.

"You keep asking what it's good for. I just thought I'd show you is all. You know, so maybe you could keep your mouth shut for a while."

George sat down and put his arm up on the table.

"When I count three," said Jack, "you try to put my arm down."

"I want to count."

"When *you* count three, then."

"You're bigger'n me."

[326]

"Count."

George counted, and on "three" they both stiffened their arms. That was when Jack got the surprise. George was deceptive. It was like arm-wrestling with a fireplug.

After three or four minutes, Jack looked up at him. "You aren't winning," he said.

"You ain't neither," said George. He was biting his lip, but he didn't seem to be straining particularly. Just, there stood his arm, like it was growing up out of the middle of the table, which was maybe anchored in concrete itself. Jack could feel from the way it was holding that he wasn't going to get it down.

"Ain't neither of us winning," said George. He spoke clearly and without panting. "It's a silly game, ain't it?"

Jack didn't answer. He leaned on the arm, putting his shoulder into it and as much of his weight as he could. His original idea had been to take George down gracefully, to make him be quiet. Now he just wanted to beat him. The force of his pushing lifted his rear end off the ground and turned his face red, but nothing would move for him.

"I guess it's a silly game," he said at last.

They relaxed little by little, until Jack let go of George's hand and took his arm off the table.

"I ain't been doing no exercises," said George, rubbing his arm.

"You've got a good arm," said Jack.

"That's my machete arm. I don't give it no exercises, but I *work* the shit out of it."

Jack leaned back on his hands and looked at George. It occurred to him that he didn't know what George did when he wasn't there in the backyard helping him with his exercises.

"George," he said. "What do you do—for a living I mean?"

And that was how they came to get acquainted. Over the next few weeks, other facts about George came out, a little at a time. But George only told him the things that he remembered. About the time his grandmother took him to Tybee. And about John Sparks, and the college boys who were working on the survey party—giving them a good report, because he liked the well-behaved group that was there this summer. Then he recited the

Colorback commercial for him, and told him about hunting frogs with his slingshot, and raising crickets, and about calling the birds.

"You mean you can call birds?"

"I use my hurt bird call," said George. "I can't call no *special* kinds of birds. I just make them come, you know, in general."

"You mean you could do it right now?"

George crooked the index finger of his right hand and put it into his mouth. Exactly what he did, Jack couldn't make out. It sounded like he was sucking on it—a high-pitched squeaking sound, like blowing on a blade of grass. As soon as he started to do it, the birds began to come, swooping in over the fence and the top of the house, circling around his head and giving him shrill answering calls. Soon there were maybe two dozen birds. When he stopped, there was a pause, then the birds beat their wings, the only sound the dry fluttering of their feathers. In less than a minute they were gone.

"Where did you learn to do that?"

"It just come natural. I don't remember how it was I got started on it."

"It's like St. Francis," said Jack.

"Who's that?"

Jack told him.

"It's just they come because it sounds like a hurt bird. I couldn't call up no rabbit—nor a deer."

"What is it you do?"

"I'll show you," said George, crooking his finger.

But even after he had showed him, Jack couldn't get the sound right so that the birds would come for him.

If Jack had stopped to think about it, he would have realized that it was a fresh start on friendship he was making, and he hadn't made a new friend since the time he was in Atlanta going to Georgia Tech—if the relationship he'd had with Randolph Tarbutton could have been called friendship. That's not counting the people he came together with over the Witch of Endor wine, but then he couldn't remember most of them anyway.

George never asked him any questions about himself, and the way they got along was like the undemanding friendship that had survived with Dendron—in a lot of ways it was. Like the direction-less friendships in high school days, when there weren't any ul-terior motives, and nobody was trying to make money out of it. It was almost like being back on Waldburg Street again, with someone right next door where he could walk out into the yard and get together with him thoughtlessly and without any effort. He couldn't do it with Dendron anymore, because Dendron was working, and he would have had to seek him out.

27

On the Mat

IN NOVEMBER, WHEN HE FELT that he was in about as good shape as he was going to be, Jack went down to the city auditorium and had a talk with Dewey Kalifa, who promoted the matches in the Savannah territory.

Dewey didn't exactly welcome him with open arms, though he did remember him from the Boniface football days, being a general sportsman. "I seen you play," he said. "You was a good one."

"Thank you," said Jack.

"Too bad nothing never come of it."

"Yes."

Kalifa had this thing about looking him directly in the eye when he talked to him. "It's not just being big makes you a wrestler," he said. "It's not as easy as it looks."

"Try me out," said Jack. "People will remember me from the old days."

Dewey put him onto the mat with Baliban Castanti, who was the local Masked Marvel—a large hairy man in his early thirties, who was half a head shorter than Jack, but more chunky, and very quick.

Baliban pretty much worked Jack the way he wanted to, and it turned out to be harder than it had looked on television.

After the match, Jack was very crestfallen.

"You didn't do bad, kid," said Dewey. "You've got a good build. Eye appeal is very important," he laid his finger alongside his nose, "for the lady fans."

"I wasn't handling him too good."

Dewey looked at him. "You don't handle him," he said, shaking his head. "You handle *yourself*. We don't have no shooting matches here."

"I thought I would move better." What had surprised him most was that no matter where he touched Baliban, he seemed to get a response out of him. There wasn't any place he could come at him without getting resistance—nowhere he could touch him and go on in. It was like trying to handle an octopus.

"Baliban's one of the best in the business," said Dewey. "He can't put on such a good *show* as some of them. If it was like the old time, he'd be doing all right for himself."

Jack didn't say anything.

"What did you think, Baliban?" said Dewey.

"He moves pretty good. I'd have to work with him some." He looked at Jack. There were red marks on the skin of Jack's chest and back where Baliban had manhandled him. "How big *are* you, kid?"

Jack told him.

"He's got a good build," said Dewey.

"Let's see how it goes," said Baliban.

"Give me a couple of days to think it over," said Dewey. "Come back Thursday."

When he came back on Thursday, Dewey had it all worked out. "What was your number? Your football number?"

"Fifty-five."

"Could you get a helmet?"

"Yes."

"We'll put you in the jersey and helmet. Probably a lot of people will remember you from the football. We'll work it that way. Like you're coming out of retirement."

"I've got my old sweater."

"Let's stick with the jersey. You'll have trouble enough getting out of that after you get in the ring. You can have too much crap to fool around with. Besides, I want them to see the number."

Dewey called him "Irish" Curran, the Green Knight, and set him to working with Baliban, getting up a routine. Ordinarily they wouldn't have spent so much time with a new man, but Dewey thought he might pull well with the local crowds. And the gate could use the extra attraction. In spite of the interest television was stirring up, the Savannah auditorium didn't come close to being full—even with Ladies' Night on Thursdays, and free dishes once a month.

Jack and Baliban decided on a combination body block and flying tackle for his specialty holds, but the emphasis was on getting him to respond more quickly in order that Baliban wouldn't have to carry him out in the open so much.

"We'll start out preliminary. Dewey tries to get bigger names down from Atlanta and Charlotte for the main events. If you go good, we'll get it up to forty-five minutes or an hour."

The pot for the night was divided up share and share alike, according to the length of the bouts. When a really big name came in, like Man Mountain Dean, they would have to guarantee a minimum. But that didn't happen often. In getting Jack ready to come on for a match with him, Baliban was looking out for himself.

After one of their practice sessions, Jack and Baliban got to talking.

"Does it ever worry you? It being such a put-up job?"

Baliban looked at him for a long minute before answering. "Don't start a shooting match, kid. I could take you. And Dewey wouldn't let you back within a mile of the place. This is a business."

"I understand that. I just asked if it ever worried you."

Baliban thought about it for a minute. "It's a job," he said. "I was working in a meat-packing house before I came on with Dewey. It beats hell out of that."

"I guess so," said Jack.

For a while they didn't say anything. "Listen," said Baliban. "In about six months, you may be able to take me. You got the size. If you get it on your mind, let me know. We'll come down here and see about it—on our *own* time. Just don't get funny with me in front of the paying customers."

Jack looked at him.

"You understand what I'm saying?"

"I understand."

"It's a business, kid. Let Dewey figure it his way. He likes to be the boss."

"That's all right."

"You can make suggestions—but wait a while. Don't never give him no surprises."

"I understand," said Jack.

Dewey decided that Baliban would win to begin with. Baliban was a born villain, and Jack was an unknown quantity. If the people liked him, the return match would be set up by the loss.

Jack had his first match on the night of December 2. He got a ticket for George, and they went to the auditorium together.

"Don't be disappointed if I lose tonight," he said. He hadn't been keeping George up with the refinements of the business. And the way George was talking, he knew he would be disappointed when he didn't beat Baliban. "I'm just starting out. The Masked Marvel is a tough one."

"You can take him," said George.

"Just don't be disappointed if I don't."

When he got into the ring, Jack noticed J.J. O'Brien sitting ringside. J.J. looked at him, but he didn't nod or make any signal. When he came back from getting the referee's instructions, he saw Dewey crouched down talking to J.J. Then the bell rang, and he and Baliban came together in the middle of the ring.

It was a good bout. At the twenty-five-minute mark, Baliban gave Jack the signal to lay on his body block and flying tackle. Jack put him down in the middle of the ring, and they held it for a count of two. Then Baliban gave him a squeeze in the crotch when the referee wasn't looking, and reversed him to take the fall and the match. They were only ten seconds over the thirty-minute mark when it ended. And Jack's tantrum and argument with the referee lasted for three minutes more.

Back in the dressing room Baliban congratulated him on the match.

"They went for it pretty good. I think we got something going."

Then Dewey came into the dressing room and told him he was pleased, too.

"Does J.J. O'Brien come to the matches often?"

"He likes to drop in once in a while," said Dewey. "Not every week. It depends on the program."

"Does he have anything to do with them? You know—on the money side?"

Dewey looked at him for a minute. "It's *his* territory, kid. I thought you knew that."

"You mean I'm working for J.J. O'Brien?"

"I mean we *all* are, kid."

"I see," said Jack.

"He spoke well of you," said Dewey.

Going back with George, he had to help calm him down.

"He squeezed your nuts! You had him till he squeezed your nuts."

"Baliban is a mean one."

"Couldn't you get the referee to say something to him?"

"He's got to see it with his own eyes. I wouldn't blame the referee."

"You going to fight him again?"

"We'll have another match. Maybe next week."

"Don't let him get away with it again."

"I'll be looking out for him next time."

"Next time you squeeze *his* balls," said George.

"You wouldn't want me to do that, would you?"

"Well," said George. "Don't let him get away with it again."

Jack thought about letting George in on it. He didn't like deceiving him. But he wasn't up to explaining how the whole business worked. And he thought he would be satisfied when he didn't lose the next fight. In a way, George was a bellwether of the manner in which the other fans were reacting.

[334]

While they were practicing on Monday, Jack talked to Baliban about J.J. O'Brien.

"I don't know him myself," said Baliban. "He runs an honest gate. You don't have to get up and count the house to get what's coming to you."

"It looks like I'm going to spend the rest of my life working for him," said Jack.

Baliban looked at him. "Don't fuck it up for me," he said. "Go ahead and quit, if that's the way you feel about it. But don't fuck it up for me."

Jack was sorry about quitting J.J. the way he had, because he didn't like quitting on any terms. But there was something about the green-eyed man. He kept thinking of the nursery rhyme.

> *I do not love thee, Dr. Fell*
> *The reason why I cannot tell*
> *But this I know, and know full well*
> *I do not love thee, Dr. Fell.*

Working for J.J. was so much a means to an end—so much a *job*. He could never feel like he was doing anything for himself—or just for the sake of doing it. J.J. was always there to get his share, making it serve his own purposes. What Jack wanted was to do something for the thing in itself, without any profit in it for anybody.

The second week, Jack and Balaban went to a tie. The third week they got a forty-five-minute match, and Jack won it. Their matches were getting good coverage in the Savannah papers, and the third week the auditorium was almost full.

Then Dewey sent them out of town, matching them in Pembroke, and Hinesville for the Camp Stewart crowd, and in Kose and Darien.

In January, Baliban's mother got sick, and he had to go down to Florida to see her. While he was gone, Dewey kept Jack in Savannah, putting him up against other opponents and letting him beat them—working on the press coverage.

It was February before Baliban came back, and Dewey held

Jack out for a week, letting Baliban wrestle instead. Then he had Baliban offer a challenge at the end of his match, and started publicity for a grudge match on Washington's Birthday.

The plan was for Baliban to win, on dirty tricks of course, and then start over the cycle they had run in December.

But Baliban's mother died on February 4, and he had to leave town again. So Dewey held Jack out of all matches, releasing a story to the papers that he wouldn't wrestle again until he could take on the Masked Marvel, who had left town because he was afraid to fight him.

The publicity worked, and advance ticket sales for the match sold out three-fourths of the auditorium. It was shaping up as an all-time record in cash receipts.

The program called for a full hour, with one fall for each of them, then a final two-count for Jack, with a reversal for Baliban, who would take the match.

For the first forty-five minutes, everything went as planned, with Baliban gouging Jack in the eyes and giving him squeezes in the groin when the referee wasn't looking, but with plenty of blatancy so the fans wouldn't miss it. By the time it came for Jack to take the three-count, the whole house wanted Baliban's head on a stick.

Jack took Baliban down, and they worked over to the edge of the ring, a technique that they had used quite a lot, as the fans seemed to enjoy it. Then, just as Baliban was starting his reversal, Jack looked out over the edge of the ring and saw J.J. O'Brien sitting in his ringside seat. J.J. was sitting very stiff-backed, with his hands resting on the head of his upright cane. He wasn't smiling, but there was a peculiar look on his face. As if he was waiting for something that he knew was going to happen. Something that would work to his benefit and make a profit for him.

For maybe fifteen seconds Jack looked straight at him, reading his eyes. When Baliban started the reversal, Jack balked him, but Baliban powered out of it, and they got to their feet, going head-to-head in the center of the ring.

"Let me win it," he said.

"What?" said Baliban.

"Let me win it."

"I can't do it. It's Dewey's program."

[336]

"I can't let you do it."

"It's good money, kid."

They walked each other around. "You'll have to do it on your own," said Jack.

"You ain't thought about this."

"I can't let you do it, Baliban."

For the next twenty minutes, the house watched Baliban, the Masked Marvel, bring Jack down for the three-count. For nineteen minutes they were both down on the mat, hardly moving at all, with Baliban driving to wear him out. What the fans were looking at was the real, old-time, genuine article. And it bored them to death. They thought it was a fake.

Jack hadn't come along quite far enough to be able to take Baliban. But he had the size and enough skill to make it very difficult for Baliban to take him. Baliban finally pinned him with a crotch and half nelson—one of the oldest and least spectacular holds in wrestling.

After the referee slapped the mat, Jack went limp.

Back in the dressing room, Baliban was hurt rather than mad. "If you felt that way, why didn't we talk it over with Dewey before the match? Why'd you have to fuck it up?"

Dewey came into the dressing room and counted out ten one-hundred-dollar bills, putting them on the training table next to where Jack was sitting.

"I won't badmouth you about it," he said. "But you're through in my territory."

"I couldn't do it, Dewey. I just couldn't do it."

"We got a good thing going, Dewey," said Baliban. "Give the kid a chance."

"If you felt that way, why didn't you come talk to me about it?"

"I didn't feel that way before I got in the ring."

"I told you when you first came in to see me. No shooting matches."

Jack looked down at the stack of bills. "I'm sorry," he said. "It just came over me. You know, while we were in there."

"It's the golden goose, Dewey," said Baliban.

"Not after tonight, it ain't. You heard them." He started out of the dressing room. "While he was getting his kicks they was bored to death. They thought it was a fake."

Jack was still looking at the stack of hundred-dollar bills. "What does J.J. say about it?" he said.

Dewey stopped at the door. "Listen, Curran," he said, his face getting red. "I work for O'Brien, but *I* run the territory. What I say goes." He pointed his finger at him. "And I say you're through." He walked out of the dressing room.

"He'll be okay in a month or two," said Baliban. "Give him some time to forget it."

Jack picked up the bills and counted them.

"Do you know J.J. O'Brien good? Really good?"

Jack put the bills down. "I know him."

"He owns the territory. Dewey would have to do what he says."

"I know it," said Jack.

"If you know him, go talk to him."

"Maybe I'll do that."

After they had gotten dressed, Baliban asked him if there were any hard feelings.

"I'm sorry I did it. For your sake."

"Listen," said Baliban. "You're pretty damn good. I didn't know if I was going to take you or not. Maybe we ought to come up here some afternoon and try it again, just so we both know where we're at."

"Maybe we'll do that sometime," he said.

"It didn't make a shit to me. You understand that. I couldn't afford to get Dewey pissed off at me. That funeral cost a shitpile."

"Yes," said Jack. He wanted to peel off a couple of the bills and give them to Baliban to help him with the funeral. But he couldn't afford to do it. Heroic gestures were behind him now—except when they didn't have to be paid for with money. "I guess it sets you back," he said.

On the way home, George complained about the dirty tricks Baliban had used to win.

"He beat me fair, George," said Jack. Then he told him how the wrestling business worked.

"You mean it ain't real?"

[338]

"We're good wrestlers. Baliban is one of the best there is."

"And he beat you fair tonight?"

"He beat me fair."

"I bet you could have beat him if you'd wanted to."

"No," said Jack. "No, I couldn't. I wanted to beat him tonight."

When he got home, he put his green jersey on a hanger in the closet. The helmet he would give to one of the kids in the neighborhood. Before he went to bed, he put eight of the hundred-dollar bills on the kitchen table, laying them out like a hand of cards. They would pay Kate and Reilley back for some of the food he had been eating.

For a few days he thought about going to talk to J.J. O'Brien and getting him to make Dewey take him on again. But he decided that Dewey had treated him decently, and he was the one at fault. He didn't want to get J.J. to force him down Dewey's throat, so they would have to admit who really ran the territory.

Besides, he wanted to be totally free of J.J. If he had to take a job, he wanted it to be one where he would at least be working for someone else—if there was such a thing in the city of Savannah —outside the fire department, which he knew was a job he could get for the asking.

What he wanted, deep in his heart, was for someone to offer to pay him for being a wonderful fellow, without any strings attached. Just to be himself and do things that were free and good.

For a time things were peaceful for Jack. The eight hundred dollars had bought him the feeling that he was paying his way in the house. Sleeping was what he did the most of—taking time to lie in bed in the mornings after he woke up, making his peace with the day slowly and working out his accommodations to it. After he did get up, he was content to sit around the place by himself, watching the programs on television—even the wrestling —seeing George now and then, and putting things off. It was a nice time for him—uncomplicated and mothery.

March was cold, with rain. But that was nice, too, because there wasn't any reason for him to go out of the house. He enjoyed the cold glow out of the television in the darkened living room of the quiet house—watching the pictures gliding on the screen, flaring and skimming, velvety, inside his head. With Kate and Reilley away at work during the day, he would wrap himself Indian fashion in a blanket and sit before the set in the best chair, a slight half-smile on his face, uncritical and at peace with the world, approving whatever happened to come on and move for him.

He thought some about the old days at Boniface, and now and then he would have a dream about Mary that was summery and nice—a concession to the past, much as the waking thoughts were—without any present urgency, or any sharp corners or angles. For the most part she wasn't in his thoughts except as a reminder of the really good times before she had come into the hard, every-day part of his life—when things had gone gritty between them and worn the marriage away. He didn't want to see any of the Boniface crew at all. They were only there to people his thoughts.

Now and then there was the lighted window, with the beautiful woman in the blue nightgown moving behind it in her secret way, doing delicate, gentle things for the sake of the man she loved.

But his friends from the football days, and his relationship to them—all that amounted to now was an unraveled hair ball of loose connections. Feeb had his curb markets and the beginning of his own swarthy brood of Siddoneys. And he never saw Dendron any-more. These days he felt closer to George than anyone else, but George was an outdoors friend—one for the backyard days of spring and summer, not the cold and rain of March. Getting to-gether would have to wait on the weather.

Then, just before St. Patrick's Day, Chippy Depeau had his car wreck on the Tybee Road, and hearing about that—and the opera-tion—pulled Jack back into the present. Afterward, going to the funeral brought him into contact with some of the old football crew again.

Burying Chippy was a hard thing to do. Not that it is ever easy, but some people just don't seem meant to die—which is one of the really dirty tricks in the veiled, black heart of the world—and Chippy was one of those seemingly immortal ones.

He had always had a brave, recruiting-poster vitality about him, dependable and rosy and pristine. The way Jack thought about him, he didn't have the spark to be a leader the way Aaron had.

And he didn't know as much about the game of football as Jack did—nor was he a star. But in the Boniface days, he had been the steady one—the one they could depend on. On the outside, Chippy looked like Tom Sawyer. That's not what he was like really, but it set the tone in his dealings with others. Whatever he said sounded right, coming out of that apple-cheeked face. He was very calm and even, and, of course, the way he looked did keep his head free of clutter and distractions, so he could see things whole and clear.

He had a good job with a shipping company down on River Street, and they were well pleased with him. His future was, as they used to say, assured.

Then, over the winter of 1955–1956, between Thanksgiving and Christmas, he began to feel a tightness just under his lowest ribs—a feeling of pressure that wouldn't go away. It didn't hurt, and could not really be called uncomfortable, but it made him aware of his breathing, and kept tugging at a corner of his mind.

He tried doing a little roadwork and lifting weights to see if he couldn't work it out. The job he had with the shipping company kept him at a desk six hours a day, and he laid to that the change he felt taking place inside him. On through Christmas and into the new year, he worked at toning himself up—not putting much emphasis on it, because his general health was very good, and he couldn't imagine that there would be anything really serious going on that wouldn't show up as an outward sign—in his face, or somewhere else. There wasn't anything like that. Just the slight pressure that wouldn't go away.

Finally, in February, he thought he saw something in his bathroom mirror—a small shift in the way that the corner of his eye turned down to join the line of his cheekbone. It suddenly occurred to him that it might be something serious and permanent—a peek over the dark hill of his own mortality—and he decided that he had better see a doctor about it.

"It's a tumor all right," said the doctor. He spoke in a matter-of-fact way—the way he might have spoken if there had been no one else in the room—studying the X-ray plate, standing there before it with his arms folded. The spot he had just tapped with the back of his ballpoint pen was very dark and clearly outlined, so that even Chippy could make it out—about half the size of a basketball, an irregular, oblong shape lying along the sweeping curve of his lowest rib.

"Cancer?" said Chippy.

The doctor looked at him. "At your age?" he said. "The shape you're in? Not hardly." He pulled back his upper lip and tapped the end of the ballpoint pen against his front teeth as he studied the X-ray plate. "I want to get it out where we can take a look at it and see what it is."

Chippy looked at the X ray with the spot on it. His face was calm, though he was frowning a little. The lines were rearranging themselves. "It's big as a cantaloupe," he said. "You don't think it's cancer?"

The doctor tapped his teeth with the end of the ballpoint pen. "I'd say it's a dermoid cyst. Is there a history of twins in your family?"

"Not that I know of."

"I want to have it out where we can take a look at it."

"Right away?"

"Yes."

Chippy looked at the X ray. "Whatever you say."

"Monday?" said the doctor, tapping the plastic shaft of the ballpoint against his teeth and looking at the X-ray plate. It was Friday afternoon.

Chippy nodded, not looking at him. "Monday will be okay," he said.

"I want to get it out where we can take a look at it."

"I want to take a look at it, too," said Chippy.

"I told you," said the doctor. He sounded delighted. Chippy was still woozy from the anesthetic and was having trouble getting the room into focus. "Dermoid cyst," said the doctor. Chippy couldn't see what it was; looking up through the bottom of the glass container distorted the contents.

The doctor put the container on the bedside stand, and Chippy rolled his head over to look at it. The curved sides of the glass distorted it a little even so, but he could make out the pasty white mass floating in the liquid.

"Negative biopsy," said the doctor. "What did I tell you?" His tone of voice was very self-congratulatory.

"What is it?" said Chippy.

"You said you wanted to see it. That's the first one I ever saw myself, to tell you the truth."

Chippy watched as he pointed out the features of the cyst as it revolved slowly inside the cylinder of the container. "Hair . . . that's a piece of bone . . . a tooth . . ." To Chippy it looked like a great, white lardy piece of meat, with small trashy things stuck in it—like a wad of dough after it had been dropped on a dirty floor.

"What is it?" he said.

"Dermoid cyst. What I said . . . a dermoid cyst."

"What's that?"

"I don't know *exactly*," said the doctor. "Twins, maybe." He tapped the container. "It never got any farther."

"That was going to be a person?"

"Not exactly. A little more and you might have had two heads." He looked thoughtful. "An extra pair of legs. Like you'd see in the circus."

"It started out to be a person."

"Probably."

Chippy looked at the glass container, trying to decide what his relationship might be to the thing he had been carrying inside him for twenty-six years. He was serious-minded, and thought in terms of his responsibility to the world.

"Could you tell what it was?" he said. "What it would have been?"

"I told you," said the doctor. "It wouldn't have been anything. Nothing itself. You might have had something hanging out somewhere."

"It would have started out something, wouldn't it? That's what you said."

"An egg isn't anything." He tapped the glass. "That was never what you would call an embryo."

"At the start it was."

"No. By the time it would have been something, it was nothing already." The doctor looked at him. "Do you understand me?"

[343]

"If it started as twins, would it have been a brother or a sister?"

"You're getting the wrong idea. I'm trying to tell you what it was."

"What would the odds be?"

The doctor looked at him a minute. "A brother. Three to one. You understand that doesn't mean anything?"

"It would have been my brother," said Chippy.

"It's a dermoid cyst," said the doctor. "You can't work up a relationship with a dermoid cyst." He started to pick up the container.

"Leave it there," said Chippy. "It's mine."

The doctor thought about it a minute. "Look at it long enough," he said. "You'll see what it is. I wouldn't have brought it in to show you, except I thought you were interested."

"It's mine," said Chippy.

"Three pounds of nothing." He made a gesture with his hand. "*Nothing* . . . a dermoid cyst. I'll leave it here now, but I don't want you getting attached to it."

He went out of the room and left Chippy looking at the glass container by the bed.

When he went home from the hospital, Chippy took it with him in a one-gallon mayonnaise jar. He kept it in his room, studying it through the curved glass of the jar, trying to put himself into some kind of relationship to it. Once he took it out of the alcohol, but the dead weight in his hands was only like a piece of meat, inert and small, and it was smooth and slippery to the touch—unpleasant. He put it back into the jar. Floating in the alcohol, it seemed to have an independent existence; he could think of it that way. When he swirled the liquid, it would turn and move on its own.

There was no human shape that he could give it, and the fact that he couldn't grieved him. Even medical books that he got at the library showed him pictures of things that looked like animals, with something in the way of real shapes, as if they might come and go on their own. What was in the jar was nothing. The change of direction away from life had been irrevocable. He had wrapped himself around it and carried it inside him for twenty-six years. That had been the determining factor—the way he had held it in.

He felt that his involvement in it was serious and not a thing that he could put out of his mind.

He thought about it for two weeks. Then he got into his car, putting the mayonnaise jar between his legs on the front seat, and for two hours he drove around the back roads out on the water-front, talking to it. Then he went out the Tybee Road, put the accelerator all the way to the floor and held it there, until he ran head-on into the abutment of the Bull River Bridge.

When they picked him out of the marsh, one of the ambulance attendants found the cyst and put it into the stretcher with the other pieces they had collected.

It would have been nice if somehow it could have been buried with him, but that's not the way it happened. It ended up in a porcelain basin under the embalming table in Fant's Mortuary, along with the other miscellaneous pieces that they couldn't fit in when they put him back together.

The funeral made Jack moody, and that night he drove out the Tybee Road to Wilmington Island, then around on the back roads under the trees. There was a drizzle of rain, and it was very dark. While he drove, he was thinking of Chippy, and he kept seeing the face of J.J. O'Brien, with the steady green eyes.

By the time he got home, he had decided that something was turning hard inside his head, and it was time for him to get up and go to work again. There was only one place left for him to go.

"I knew that was where the road would lead me to," he said. "Goddamn it, I knew that's what it would be."

28

April 11

On Monday, April 9, Jack went to work for the fire department. He had gone in on the seventh, which was Saturday, and, knowing that he was the son of Johnny, they welcomed him with congratulations—only the chief wasn't in, and they had to tell him to come back on Monday. He had thought about the fire department, turning it over inside his head and considering the possibilities until he lost track of them. Then he had given up and gone down to the station.

The way he looked at it, it was a dead end—one that had bagged his father, and his Uncle Donald, and Ducker, and any number of Boniface Irishmen. There was always room for one more mick at the fire department—the next thing to a retirement home. But, if it was a place to curl up and die, signing on was one way to get it out of his head and stop worrying about it. He couldn't help thinking how restful it would be—clubby and cheerful, and less like a job than the wrestling had been, more healthy than racking balls. J.J. probably worked a profit on it, too—so many firemen knew him and spoke well of him—but Jack thought that his hand would rest more lightly there. It was a shallow till.

Restful. That's the way he finally came to regard it. "Swimming upstream is all right for salmon," he said. "They don't have any choice in the matter."

While he was still thinking it over, the week before he joined, he stopped around at the station house on Oglethorpe Street, as if to look things over, without telling anybody that it was in his mind to come into the department.

"I'd recommend it," said Ducker. Jack had asked him his opinion of the work, speaking in abstract terms, so he thought.

"It's like you never left Boniface." Ducker spoke louder than ever because his deafness was getting worse, and he wouldn't wear a hearing aid—he thought of them as effeminate. "We're a team, Curran. A *team*."

Jack nodded, thinking how much he would have wanted to go back to *exactly* the way things had been at Boniface. At any rate, for him it was not going to be the same.

"Only *this* is important," said Ducker. He stabbed his finger down toward the floor.

"So was the football . . ." said Jack, ". . . at the time." They were sitting on bunks in the upstairs dormitory. Canty Greb and Horse Fosdick were there, too, but Ducker was doing the talking. They couldn't compete with him, since he never heard what they were saying.

Ducker rolled his cigar and flipped the ashes. "This is life or death," he said. "That's what I mean. This is no game."

"It depends on how you look at it," said Jack.

"No, it don't," said Ducker. "It don't matter how you look at it at all. Some things are important, Curran. Some ain't." He put the cigar back into his mouth. "Life or death, Curran. That's what it is. Life or death."

Jack got up from the bunk and started down the stairs. Ducker was beginning to give him a pain in the ear. "See you around," he said.

"*Lives*, Curran! We've saved lives. . . . Pulling them out of the *fire*. That ain't no high school bullshit."

Jack didn't answer. Ducker's remembrance of Boniface, the way things had been then, wasn't very clear. Jack had always respected experience, and lives were important, as he knew. But he didn't like being instructed by Ducker—not at the top of his voice. As a matter of fact, he didn't even like to look at Ducker, much less listen to him. His face had become puffy and swinish. It was a reminder of the way they were all going.

On Sunday the eighth, he went out with George, hunting frogs along the Casey Canal. It was the first time he had been with him to see how well George could shoot the slingshot. Jack talked about the way he felt as they went along—sounding himself out more than looking for answers from his friend. George was watching the bank, not seeming to pay much attention to him.

"I thought you could play football," he said. "That's what they used to say on the radio."

"I don't like to sit around too long. After a while I don't feel good." Jack could tell that his face was puffing up from his inactivity. He didn't have the constitution to do nothing and get away with it. The flesh gobbed up on him like tallow when he wasn't working his muscles.

"You *used* to play football." Wrestling was a dead issue with George, since he knew how they arranged it now.

"That was seven years ago. You can't just go get a job as a football player. I missed it when I didn't stay on in college. Besides, it never was a *job* to me. That's not the way I thought about it."

George watched the canal for a while. "You mean you missed your chance? I never considered that you had missed your chance. You used to be on the radio."

For a while they didn't say anything. Then George stopped and raised his hand. He aimed the slingshot, hunching his head over to one side and shrugging his shoulders. When he let it go, there was the slapping sound of the rubbers, and a dull plonking sound under the bank. George climbed down and came back with a bullfrog the size of a squirrel. He took out his Barlow knife and cut off the legs.

"Kill it, George," said Jack. He was looking at the frog, but he turned away after he spoke. George was holding the legless trunk in his hand and the mouth was pumping open and shut.

"What?" he said. He looked down at what was left of the frog in his hand, then he tossed it back into the water of the canal, spinning it like a chip.

Jack looked back in time to see the white underbelly, and the tiny front legs moving as it spiraled down out of sight in the water.

"You ought to kill it, George."

"I guess so. They don't never make no noise. If it was hollering and carrying on, I guess I'd kill it to shut it up."

George wrapped the legs in a piece of newspaper and put the packet into the hip pocket of his pants. "I'll kill the next one."

For a while they walked along the canal without saying anything. "I had a friend killed himself," said Jack. "Ran his car into a bridge."

George looked at him and thought about what he had said. "I seen a nigger killed once," he said.

"This was a good friend," said Jack. ". . . A pretty good friend. I hadn't seen him in a while."

"I didn't know the nigger," said George. "Grandmother just died. She wasn't killed."

"He was twenty-six. My age."

"Grandmother was eighty. I saw her in the casket, but they wouldn't let me go to the funeral. Mother was afraid I'd have an attack."

For a while they didn't say anything. "You ever think about killing yourself, George?"

George thought about that for a while before he answered. He didn't seem surprised by the question. "No," he said. "It never come into my mind. You?"

"No," said Jack. "I've thought about it once in a while. I guess everybody has."

"I never thought of it," said George. "Not personally." He turned the idea over in his head. "Why would anybody want to do a thing like that for? I have the attacks, but I ain't crazy."

"I wouldn't ever *do* it. Sometimes it crosses my mind."

"I never thought about it myself."

He shot another frog, and this time he stabbed it in the head before he cut the legs off. He had to stab it several times, twisting the blade of the knife in the bone. "They're hard to kill," he said. When he threw the carcass back into the canal, it didn't try to swim.

"Do you like your work?" said Jack.

"What?" said George, putting the newspaper back into his hip pocket. "The highway department?"

"Yes."

"The pay's not so good. I wouldn't want to work in no office."

"I guess you don't think about that either, do you?"

"Sure I do," said George. "It's not like I had a choice. This is the best job I ever had. I'd rather fly an airplane."

Jack didn't say anything.

"We have us some good times. You'd be surprised. John Sparks and me, we get along. I wouldn't work for no son of a bitch."

When they got back to Marshoaks, they had three pairs of frog's legs. "Don't think about it. What've you got to be unhappy about? You're too young to be morbid," said George.

"I'm all right."

"Well, listen. I wouldn't want you thinking about it. Maybe he knew something you don't know—your friend. You can't really tell about the other fella. Maybe he kept thinking about how he wouldn't never kill himself."

"I'm all right," said Jack, looking him in the eye. "I really am. Sometimes it gets you down a little, you know?"

"I know about that, old buddy," said George, "That's one thing I certainly do know about." He took the newspaper out of his pocket and held it out to Jack. "That's a dollar and a half worth of frog's legs—wholesale. You ever had any before?"

"No."

"Cook them up like fried chicken. Soak them in salt water first. That'll keep them from kicking in the pan."

"Thank you."

"Listen," said George. "You're a *young* man."

"Yes," said Jack. "I know it."

"You been on the radio."

"Yes."

"Good times going to come again for you. I always thought you was the luckiest man in this world."

"Yes."

"In this *world*," said George.

Only two calls came in to the station house on Monday, and both of them were minor. One was an ignition fire in an automobile on Price Street, which was out by the time they got there. The other was a grease fire in a kitchen on Jones. He went on both calls, but Chief Weeden cautioned him to just watch.

"Stay with the truck and keep your eyes open. You're just getting experience."

In between he sat around the station house while they showed him pieces of equipment and talked to him about the techniques of fighting different kinds of fires. It was very informal, though Ducker was talking loud enough for people out on the street to hear him.

"Mostly it's little stuff," said Chief Weeden. "You don't never know when the big one is going to come along."

"Yes," said Jack.

"Right now you're just learning. Ducker is going to take you under his wing."

"What?" said Ducker, recognizing his name.

"*Wing!*" said Chief Weeden, turning his face to Ducker, so he could see his lips moving. "Your daddy's a good man," he said, turning back to Jack. "I'm sure you'll get along."

"Thank you," said Jack.

"We're expecting big things of you," said Chief Weeden.

Tuesday and Wednesday there weren't any alarms at all. When he got off Wednesday afternoon, the stillness of the air and the overcast were squeezing his head, pushing against his eyeballs and eardrums. The heaviness was like the last thirty seconds before a thunderstorm breaks, but it had been hanging on all day.

Jack called Mackey Brood and told her he would be coming around to see her that night. Then he went out to the Marshoaks place and borrowed the car to drive down to Tybee. He had been thinking old thoughts all day—remembering the lighthouse, the time he had gone up in it after the Thanksgiving game with

Oglethorpe. He also remembered the time that his father always talked about, when the two of them had gone there before Kate and Johnny had separated—what a good time they had had, just the two of them. He wanted to go up and sit inside the glass dome at the top, looking out over the ocean. It seemed like the place to go for thinking—a bell jar under the bell jar of clouds, where he could trap old thoughts and be alone.

Since he had been there last, the coast guard had taken over the lighthouse. They had repainted the shaft, with a narrower white band in the middle and more black, making a darker tower than he remembered.

There were concrete walks with cut grass, and regular visiting hours posted on a sign by the door at the bottom. Jack didn't arrive until after the five o'clock closing time, but the radioman on duty let him in anyway.

"What happened to the keeper?"

The radioman was small and dark, and he talked through his nose. "I wouldn't know," he said. "Who're you talking about?"

"He was an old guy."

"Yeah?"

"How long have you been here?"

"Six months."

"I mean how long has the *coast guard* been here?"

"I wouldn't know," said the radioman. Jack's questions had driven his voice higher and higher into his nose. "You ain't even sup-posed to be here," he said.

"I thought you might have heard somebody say."

"No," said the radioman. He was looking at Jack in a nervous way. "How big *are* you, mister?"

"Six-seven. If you mean how tall."

"Don't bust nothing. And don't sign the register. You ain't supposed to be here."

"I'll be careful," said Jack.

He went through the inner door and started up the staircase. The way he remembered, it had been seedy and uncared-for, and he had liked the signs of neglect. They had made him feel that no one was looking, and he could have the tower to himself. Now the walls and stairs were freshly painted gray, and everything was worked over and spotless. It depressed him—too clean to be a dream tower now that somebody was investing money in it.

He pushed himself up the tightening spiral of the stairs without stopping, so that he was panting for breath when he got to the top. For a minute he stood on the landing under the dome of the light, leaning against the wall and looking up into the open bottom of the lens. That, too, was clean and shiny—even the railing had been polished, and the glass panels of the dome itself. He climbed the small ladder to the catwalk that circled the lens on the inside, with the heavy plate-glass panels of the dome on the outside, set in angle-iron frames.

The bulb of the arc light, with its filament like a piece of heavy spring, was suspended inside the curved bowl of the lens, brighter than it should have been, as if collecting the light from the over-cast. Outside it was darker, the sky gray, and the sea smooth and oily. There was no trace of a ship on the horizon, just the gray swell under the leaden gray sky.

There were two sea gulls on the lower catwalk outside the tower—the only things unchanged from the earlier times. Not the same two birds, surely—he didn't know what the life-span of a sea gull was. It didn't matter. They might as well have been—it was the principle that counted. Maybe their grandsons, or the sons of their grandsons. The eyes were as hard and red as he remembered them. And they seemed to be hungry still.

The heaviness of the air was having no effect on the birds. They were neither more nor less alert than he remembered they had been. Nothing intruded on their single-minded regard of the world. And everything that was important to them was going on outside and around them, where they could bring it into focus with their hard, bright eyes.

He rapped his knuckles on the inside of the glass, but they wouldn't pay any attention. There wasn't so much as a hard-eyed glance in it for him. Real threats would have been something else, and he thought about going onto the catwalk to drive them away. But that seemed to be more trouble than it was worth. Even if he could catch them by stealth and wring their necks, there would be two others just like them to give him the hard-eyed stare the next time he came—like ghosts of the dead and departed, and indistinguishable from any other two sea gulls in the world. He couldn't fight the principle that represented. Not when there was only the one of him. Besides, all he wanted to do was sit there inside the glass enclosure of the dome, looking out at the ocean, trying to bring back out of the past the two scenes from the lighthouse that were dogging him.

He wished that he would see a ship. And he tried to think of Ireland as a bright spot over the horizon, putting it in the light that he had gotten from Old Johnny. He was almost beginning to think of it the way his father did. In another year or two maybe it would be for him a green place of refuge, where the Currans were numerous and he would have blood ties that wound into the soil.

Galway Bay would be clean and free, and the wind off the open Atlantic would come cold and sharp, rolling over the far, sweet land.

He tried to hold his thoughts to that line, but the fresh paint and cleanness worked against him. What he finally decided was that he was only trying to talk himself into something. "It's not true for me yet," he said. "Or it's a bad day for pumping up sentiment." He spoke through the glass to the sea gulls. "Ah, well, it's a shitty world some days."

Then he went out onto the catwalk and waved his arms at the birds until they flapped into the air squawking, and spiraled down the shaft of the tower. The catwalk was painted a fresh shiny black, and it was firm under his feet. He leaned over the railing and cupped his hands, shouting after the spiraling birds. "Kiss my ass, sea gulls. . . . Sea gulls, kiss my ass."

Ireland was only his dream of a dream, and a foggy one at that. The lighthouse was a high, clean place that made him edgy and self-conscious. Finally, it was of no use to him. But he didn't want to leave it for the birds to have everything their own way either.

Mackey had to change her address a lot, because her landlords didn't like her life-style and the hours she kept. In the spring of 1956 she was renting the street floor of a house on Barnard, near Harris Street. Her "love nest" she called it, which was a pretty literal description, though the place wasn't anything special to look at—as was only to be expected, considering that it rented for fifty dollars a month, including the furniture and electricity. Mackey's frame of mind defined it, and that went a long way toward making up for the furniture.

"I was up in the Tybee lighthouse this afternoon," said Jack. He never had any trouble getting to see her, in spite of her crowded social calendar.

"You told me about it the other time." She wasn't especially interested in the way his mind worked, and nostalgia was never her strong point.

"It wasn't the same. The coast guard has it now. Everything's painted up." When he was with her, he liked to twang his heart-strings and say sappy things. He knew she would put up with it, and took advantage of her tolerance.

"That's bad?"

"I liked the old guy who was keeping it before."

"Nothing stays the same. The only thing you can count on is me."

"You can count on dead people. They stay the same."

She gave him a long look. "Are you changing the subject? Or was there something I missed?"

"I liked the old guy."

"Yes . . ." she drew it out.

He shrugged his shoulders. "Anyway, it wasn't the same."

"Maybe it's the weather."

"You never take me seriously," he said.

For a while they didn't say anything.

"Why don't we get married? You've got a steady job now."

"Three days," he said. "Steady."

"Steady enough."

"You'd be the best one for me, wouldn't you, Mackey?"

"We ought to have a baby, only I know how you feel about it. It doesn't make that much difference to me. You're the worrier."

"We ought to think about it. Nothing's going to get it off your mind."

"No. We ought to *do* it. Thinking about it's what we been doing. You always have to lay so much groundwork ahead of you. Like you put up walls for yourself to make it interesting."

"That's why you love me, isn't it, Mackey? I make it hard for myself wherever I go."

"I love you for your body, sport."

"And my fine, complicated mind."

"You're dependable. Mostly I'm tired of that vinegar douche—it's drying me up inside. When I move my legs—" she made a clicking noise with her tongue against the roof of her mouth, "I squeak."

"Come *on*," he said.

"Listen." She did a long-strided, Groucho Marx walk across the room, sucking her mouth to give him the sound. "Sounds like a calico cat licking his way out of a balloon. Squeeak! . . . Squeeak! . . ." She made the sucking noises with her mouth, going back to the couch. Then she sat down and crossed her legs. "I'm not crazy about having to hold everything up while you put on that Trojan of yours either."

"I never saw anybody so crazy to have a baby. Don't you know you've got to feed it?"

"That's a long time afterward. I'm not the one to make my trouble ahead of time."

He didn't say anything.

"We could make a beautiful baby, Big Boy."

He didn't say anything.

"Okay. We could make an ugly one—I just didn't know how you'd feel about it. Besides, what we're doing is a sin. Even if we were married it would be a sin."

"Priest talk."

"Well. What the hell. I've got to use the best arguments I can get my hands on."

"Try another."

"It's the way *you* think about it anyway. I don't really give a damn."

"Are you pregnant?" he said.

"If I was pregnant I wouldn't be talking about it."

"I know what a one-track mind you've got. Let's don't go into it again tonight. I was a married man once already. It's depressing to think about."

"Not hardly you weren't," she said. "Not what I'd call it." She stood up and took off her dress, pulling it over her head.

[356]

"Why don't you ever wear drawers? Isn't it unsanitary or something?"

"Don't be vulgar," she said. "Call them *panties*." She took off her brassiere and hugged her breasts, cradling them in her arms. "Don't you like to think that I don't wear them?" She cupped her breasts in her hands and looked down at them. "I do."

He watched her walking around the room, looking at herself. "I don't hear it."

"What?"

"Where's the squeaking?"

"Squeeak! . . . Squeeak! . . ." She began taking long steps, making the noise with her mouth.

"When was the first time, Mackey? The *very* first time?"

"I'm not the sentimental type, Big Boy," she said, looking down at him. "You ought to know as well as I do. June the fourth, nineteen forty-two. Three o'clock in the afternoon." She raised her right leg and sawed it back and forth on her thigh. "Squeeak! Squeeak! . . . You were there, you ought to know." She looked at him. "You cherry-popper."

"I remember the attic, with the pigeons outside."

"That was later. First time was in the garage." She put her finger in her mouth and popped it.

"It was?"

"All your love talk."

"You never did know what I was getting at."

"More than you thought, sport. More than you thought. I never was all that much on talking, that's all." She went toward the door to the bedroom. "Like now. As long as you're not going to propose, let's go on and get something started." She put her hands on the doorjamb, twitching her behind at him as she went through the door.

When he came into the room, she was sprawled on her back on the bed. "I got the Trojan," she said. "Come here. I'll fix you up."

He started to undress. "I'm not ready yet. Some things a man likes to do for himself."

"Waiting on you throws me off. You've got to work on your technique. Come here."

He got into the bed and she put the Trojan on him. The end was cut off, and the tip of his penis was sticking out of it. "Very funny," he said, looking down at himself.

Mackey started to laugh. "Don't it look sweet? You reckon that'd be all right with the Pope?"

He didn't say anything.

"I'd fix it for you, only I don't have my darning egg."

He started to get out of bed, but she pulled him back. "Why should it matter to you, if it doesn't matter to me? Take that broken rubber off, and let's *do* it."

"You're a shameless woman, Mackey."

"Big news," she said. "You're hurting my sensitive heart."

After they made love, Mackey went to sleep right away, as she always did, curling up with her feet pressed against Jack's legs. For an hour he lay there in the dark, listening to the whir of the electric clock by the bed, and thinking of Mary, and the lighthouse keeper who wasn't there anymore.

At twelve o'clock he heard a clock somewhere in the town striking, and he gave up trying to sleep. He slipped out of the bed carefully, so as not to wake Mackey, then he went into the living room to put on his clothes and let himself out of the house.

Walking up Barnard Street toward Orleans Park, he could hear his footsteps echo in the close, damp air. It was a hard, watery night, misty, with everything veiled in a fog that diffused the light from the streetlamps, making the air glow on the corners and casting indistinct shadows from the trees and shrubs. The beautification society hadn't gotten to Orleans Park yet. Maybe that was because it didn't have a monument. Except for a line of palm trees that ran around the perimeter, it was open dirt, hard-packed where the children of the neighborhood used it for softball games. Around the edges were a few benches, set out under the naked trees. Jack sat down on one stiffly, facing the municipal auditorium across the dark open space of the park.

For a long time he was lost in his thoughts, concentrating on the feeling inside, as of something slipping away—trying to work it up or down. When he looked up at the auditorium, he didn't see anything at first. By the time he noticed the flickering behind the doors of the entrance, he was beginning to smell the smoke. For another minute he watched the play of lights behind the glass of the doors.

And then it came to him.

There was an alarm box on the corner of Hull and Barnard, and he ran across the park toward it, feeling the pull of the muscles in his legs. Before he got there, the fire broke through the roof, sending a shower of sparks into the darkness before the flames themselves began to curl orange and yellow into the black air. Already he could feel the heat of the fire.

He was waiting in front of the auditorium when the first engine pulled up. Back to the south and east he could hear the wails of other engines as they moved toward him in the darkness.

Canty Greb and Old Johnny were on the ladder truck. He didn't know the other men on the night shift. Chief Weeden hadn't arrived yet.

After the truck pulled up, there was a certain amount of confusion. The pictures and lectures were only pictures and lectures, and the routine calls they got didn't really prepare them for the major fires and catastrophes that came along months and years apart. Jack helped as they unreeled the hose, laying it out along the curb. For a moment it was left unattended. He heard a noise and turned back to look at the building. As he turned, the roof collapsed inward, and flames leaped into the air all along the roofline. The reflection of the fire in the windows of the houses fronting on the square made them look as though they were on fire, too. For a heart-stopping moment, it looked as though the whole world was on fire and they were caught in the center.

In the pause after the roof collapsed, Jack picked up the nozzle end of the hose and ran into Hull Street with it, pulling it over his shoulder.

Looking back on what happened and trying to explain it later, the ones who had been there said that he probably intended to hose down the houses in Hull Street to keep the fire from spreading. The lectures he had been hearing had put a lot of emphasis on confinement and controlling collateral damage. But that kind of

talk was after the fact. What it meant to Jack was doing his duty—
not his job, since he didn't have to be there with the night shift.
Something he could give freely.

He was already into Hull Street before anyone noticed him—the
white ribbon of the hose snaking out behind him as he went. Canty
and two or three others yelled at him to stop, but the ladder truck
from the Henry Street station house was pulling up and the siren
drowned out their shouts. Old Johnny grabbed the hose and pulled
back on it to stop him, but Jack was moving with a goal-line determination, called back from his football days, and the old man
wasn't the one who could hold him up. Jack never broke stride, and
the surge pulled Johnny off his feet and dragged him along the
sidewalk until he let go.

There was a split second as the wall opened up, just before it
began to fall outward, when the fire lit up Hull Street, and they
could see Jack moving with the hose in his hands like a lance. In
the bright glare of the light from the flames, the polished brass
nozzle was gleaming like a jewel. He looked dwarfed in the glare
—only his shadow loomed large, gliding on the fronts of the
houses. Just for a second. Then the wall of bricks came down on
top of him with a long, angry boom, breaking like a wave and
rolling dust up onto the fronts of the Hull Street houses, and making the earth shake. Afterward, those who saw it happen would
only be able to gauge him by his house-tall shadow. They were the
ones who passed the word, making a parable of his death.

Some thought of him as an Irishman. And some also thought of
him as Savannah's very own. Nearly all of them thought of him as
something that had given them a moment of glory before the
flames behind the wall exploded his shadow into the dark air
above the roofs of the houses on Hull Street. They were convinced that he had broken out of the limits of a dwarfed and
twisted world. What everyone forgot afterward was that the flames,
which exploded his shadow upward into the dark sky, leaped
out from behind the wall that came down as bricks and mortar to
crush and bury his body. Chief Weeden came closer to seeing him
for what he was, but he arrived late, and missed the sight of the

shadow rising above the houses when the wall opened outward and started to fall.

Old Johnny was getting up, leaning on his hands when it happened, looking like a sprinter waiting for the starter's gun. He watched as the wall came down, then, as if that were the signal he had been waiting for, he began moving his legs, running along the white ribbon of the hose, following the line where it pointed, going into the rubble.

What happened next was something that only Old Johnny was to know and carry with him. It was too hot in there for anyone else to follow where he went. The ones standing by the trucks could see him clearly in the light of the flames, stumbling over the rubble of bricks, black in his knee-length slicker and boots, shining from the reflected light of the fire as if sheathed in fire himself. Then stooping and lifting great chunks of mortar and brick, holding his helmeted head down against the heat of the flames as he worked, with his shadow following the movement on the fronts of the Hull Street houses.

"Who is it?" Chief Weeden had just arrived.

"Curran. His boy's in there."

"Back! Back!" It was a nervous heroic gesture—his arms out, his face to the flames, as if to stem a tide. Nobody moved.

"The wall come down on his boy," somebody said.

"Get the hoses working."

He directed them to arch a stream of water onto Johnny, wetting him down to insulate him from the heat of the fire while he dug in the rubble.

They played the hose on him as he walked out, wetting the bricks to cool them, and making a path for him. He came slowly, placing his feet with care, looking down at the ground.

"He didn't get him," said a voice.

"Don't you never do nothing like that again!" Chief Weeden was relieved that Johnny had gotten out, but he was upset. It was the size of the fire, and the roaring it made in his ears. As his nervousness passed off, he began to get angry. "He couldn't have felt nothing anyway. It was a waste."

Johnny didn't look up at him. He went to the ladder truck and sat down on the running board, still numb from the soaking and the heat and smoke of the fire. He hadn't begun to feel the burn of the bricks in his hands.

"No . . ." he said. "No. . . ." Over and over.

"We'll call him a hero," said Chief Weeden. He was looking at the fire as it fed itself into the black night air. It was beyond stopping now, and he was beginning to relax. "We'll call him a hero . . . but it was a waste."

"We'll call him a hero," said Johnny. And then he began to cry.

29

Survivors:
April 13, 1956

KATE UNPINNED HER HAT and laid it on the table in the dining nook, stabbing the pin in through the top. "Jane would have been proud of herself," she said, raising her voice so Reilley could hear her in the back of the house. "You can't get away from God."

Reilley came in from the bathroom. He had taken off the coat of his gray wool suit and was mopping his face with a damp washcloth. His shirt was soaked and clinging to him with perspiration. "It's your family you can't get away from," he said. "Ugly sister Jane." He held the washcloth by the corners, fanning it out in the air to cool it. Then he refolded it into a pad. "That's what it'll do to you. Donald says she blames everything on God." His face was the color of a tomato. "She's got to take it out on something."

Kate pushed through the door into the kitchen without saying anything. Reilley followed her.

"I'm not going to cook anything for supper," she said. "I'll make you a sandwich if you want it."

Reilley squeezed out the cloth in the kitchen sink and ran cold water on it from the tap. "You figure to spend the rest of your life making up for it?"

"You know how I feel. Now's not the time to talk about it."

He sat down at the table, holding the cloth to his forehead. His fringe of hair was matted, darkened, and sticking to his head. "This is just all *your* decision, I guess—you and Jane?"

"I can't help the way I feel. It goes back a long time. My family always said *somebody* would have to pay it out."

He put the cloth down on the table and spread it, then began folding it carefully, creasing the folds with his finger. "God would punish you with the thing you loved most in the world," he said. "Isn't that the way it would be? The way you and sister Jane worked it out?"

She looked down at him. "I've had twenty years to think it over, Reilley."

"No," he said. "You've had twenty years to *dwell* on it."

She didn't say anything.

"You know. I thought a lot of Jack." He looked up at her. "I really did."

"I know how you felt about him," she said.

"I never was his father, but I thought a lot of him just the same."

"You're a good man, Reilley. I couldn't have asked for any more from you."

"Susy and I—we both thought a lot of Jack," he said, looking back down at the table. "Only . . . it ought to be over."

"Something's over," she said.

"No," he said. "No . . . it's like something was just starting up." He looked up at her. "I didn't mind sharing you. When he was alive. I really didn't."

"My son's dead, Reilley."

"Dead . . ." he nodded. "Dead . . ." He began to unfold the washcloth. "Just one of him, Kate. That's all there was." His voice was weak. "It's a hell of a thing. That's what it is." He shook his head. "Now's the time I ought to be keeping my mouth shut."

"Maybe so," she said.

"The thing is, it's not going to make any difference."

She watched him without saying anything.

He looked like he was going to cry. Slowly he put his head down on his arms. "I love you too, Kate," he said. "I love you too."

For a minute she stood looking down at him, his head bent over and resting on his arms. Then she came to the table and put her hand on his head, stroking the wet hairs and plastering them down with her fingers.

He reached up and took her hand. "I thought a lot of him, Kate," he said.

"I know," she said, patting his hand.

"Like he was my own son."

Then she started to cry. Not the manlike way she had cried on Thursday, but softer—more like a woman. "I know," she said. "I know. I know."

Reilley stood up and put his arms around her. She was standing at the sink, on the piece of plywood he had fixed for her. With her high heels on, his head barely came up to her shoulder. He tucked it under her chin, laying it on her bosom, and she put her arms around him, holding him and stroking his wet hair. For a while they stood like that, holding each other.

He said something, but his voice was muffled in the front of her dress and she couldn't make out what it was.

"What?" she said.

He pulled back his head so she could hear him. "My big hunk of woman," he said. Then he sniffled, burying his head in her bosom again and hugging her tight.

She hugged him back, looking up at a spot on the ceiling and stroking his wet hair with her fingers.

"I told you you wouldn't have to make a speech." Elaine had gone with Chicken to the funeral, because they always went together to social functions.

"Yes," he said. He hung his coat in the hall closet, then loosened his tie.

"Don't take it off," she said.

"What?"

"We're going out to eat. Remember?"

"Oh," he said. He sat down on the couch, a furrowed, thoughtful look on his face. "It was such a good luck team," he said. "Chippy just a month ago, and now Jack."

"Coincidences, Chick. It doesn't mean anything." She thought a minute. "They were both nice boys."

He turned it over for himself for a while without saying anything. "Jack was always so healthy-looking."

"I remember the Depeau boy was very clean-cut. A nice-looking boy."

"They both were—in the old days. Jack let himself go afterward. Jack is what you need if you're going to have a team."

"They were both nice boys."

"Do you think I did the right thing, Elaine? Getting out of coaching?"

She looked at him for a minute. "Are you serious? It was the smartest move you ever made in your life. You wouldn't worry about it after all these years?"

"I think about it sometimes. There were a lot of good things about it. The boys."

"It was driving you crazy, Chick. Can't you remember? It was driving *me* crazy, too."

For a minute he didn't say anything. "Nobody even knew I was there," he said. "At the funeral."

She looked at him. "You don't *like* to be the center of attention, Chick."

"I know," he said.

For a while neither of them said anything.

"The bad things fade out, I guess. I feel very strange about it. First Lenny, now Jack. Lenny and Jack could have played for anybody."

"Lenny died in the war."

"Both of them," he said. "I know. That's just the way it was. Strange coincidences." He looked up at her. "Funerals do that kind of thing to you," he said. "They were the two best men I ever had. With both of them gone, I don't know, it's like everything was wiped out. I feel like I ought to go back and do it again."

She looked at him without saying anything.

"I know," he said. "They were bad years except for the good times. It's just that this wipes *everything* out."

She came and sat down on the couch beside him, taking one of his hands in both of hers. "I'd say we have a good life, Chick. Selling insurance is important, too."

"I guess so," he said. "But, you know, there were good times. You'll have to admit that there were good times, too."

"And better times since," she said.

"Not better," he said. "Not as bad."

"Well," she said, standing up.

"I don't know whether I'm up to selling insurance for the next thirty years. Where are the *high* points?"

She looked at him for a minute without speaking, then walked out of the living room and into the kitchen.

He leaned back on the couch and looked up at the ceiling. The shadow of the spider was still there in the corner of the room— poised and motionless in the shadow of the web.

After a while he got up and went into the kitchen where he put his arms around her and apologized for the way he had been feeling.

"I'm glad we're going out tonight," he said.

"We have a good life, Chick," she said.

J.J. and the ratlike man went to Wooten's Pool Hall after the funeral, where J.J. stood the house to a round of Jax beer in honor of Jack.

"A sterling lad, gentlemen. A sterling lad." He raised his glass with a flourish.

Afterward they went to J.J.'s office.

"The consistency of it, Shube. Ah, the dreadful consistency of it."

Shube looked at him, but he didn't say anything.

"Disaster. Nothing but disaster. Right up to the lip of the grave."

"Yes, boss," said Shube.

J.J. lit a cigar, puffing it and rolling the end in the flame. "That boy was a disappointment to me, Shube. A great disappointment."

"The wreath was nice."

"A tasteful wreath, Shube. Thirty dollars' worth of good taste." He blew a cloud of smoke. "What would you think of this, Shube?"

He paused and looked at the cloud of smoke. "What would you think about a *permanent* memorial?"

Shube looked at him. "I think you done enough for the bum already."

"The Jack Curran Memorial Plaque." He made a C with his thumb and forefinger, lining it out in the air. "For the outstanding Boniface player of the year."

"Good money after bad, boss. Good money after bad." Talking brought on the coughing. Shube squeezed the words out, then clamped the handkerchief to his face.

"*He* didn't make anything of his life, Shube. Maybe *we* can."

Shube was coughing into his handkerchief and couldn't answer.

J.J. rolled the ashes off on the edge of the ashtray. "I invested a good bit in that young man. A good bit of money."

Shube was not coughing, but he was still holding the handkerchief to his face, waiting to see if it would be starting up again.

"A sizable investment, Shube." J.J. took out a pen and wrote a figure on his note pad. "How much would a plaque cost? Something—" he made a gesture with his fist, "—with dignity. It wouldn't have to be elaborate."

Shube waved the handkerchief at him, swallowing to hold off the coughing. "Let it go, boss. Let it go."

"It will be something for the lads to aspire to, Shube. Something to stretch them and make them grow."

Shube was coughing again, and couldn't answer.

"Jack Curran's memory is *worth* something, Shube. The example he set will be something to take note of. After all, he was a hero." He took a puff on the cigar. "An authentic and actual hero. Right up to the day he died."

Shube was coughing so hard he could barely get his breath. It collapsed his chest and bent him over on himself, reddening his face and making the veins stand out on his forehead.

J.J. looked at him. "You ought to do something about that cough, Shube. It's driving me crazy."

Mary sat watching Fleetwood digging his claws into the wing chair by the fireplace. She was tired of correcting him, and probably the cat knew it. Fleetwood was a house cat, and she didn't like putting him out in the yard. She was afraid that something might happen to him, and, besides, the fun of having him was in seeing him move around the house, resting on the furniture and taking his ease. The post with the carpet would solve the problem, but it had gotten to be a point of honor with Pete by now. She almost felt as if she were nagging him. Eventually she knew she would get the post.

"Stop it, Fleetwood," she said. Since she didn't make a move, the cat paid no attention to her, but went on pulling at the upholstery of the chair.

"Fleetwood!" she said. When she got up, the cat stopped. For a moment she thought of walking across the room and kicking him, the way Pete had suggested. And she smiled at the picture of surprise that doing it would have put on Fleetwood's dignified face. Fleetwood was arrogant, and thought he was a very classy number, but basically he was stupid—even for a cat. Mary ran an orderly household, but Fleetwood didn't understand about that. As far as he was concerned, he was the one that made things go.

Instead of kicking him, she picked him up and carried him out to the kitchen where she poured him a saucer of milk. Fleetwood lapped at the milk in a disinterested way, then walked to the kitchen window and leaped up onto the sill. The sun coming in the window lit up his fur, tipping it silver along the curve of his back. She admired the picture that he made sitting in the window, thinking what a beautiful cat he was.

At three o'clock she went to her bedroom and sat on the bed, thinking about Jack and their marriage. All of the sordid parts had dropped away from her memory. She really didn't have any recollection of them anymore. Pete would never have found out about it in any case, because she could never have brought herself to tell him. But now there was literally nothing for her to tell.

Most of her memories of Jack went back to the time before they had gotten married. She remembered the house party where they had met. And the time on the floating dock at Ballabee's Pavilion when it was cold and they had seen the shark. By now those memories had been shuffled over onto the other side of their wedding day, and her remembrances of Jack as a husband were rather fond ones. In any case, she had never hated him.

What she could remember of the incompatibility—which was the word that came into her head when she thought about them together—had all been the fault of the Church. His Church. She had a clear recollection of Jack talking to her about the Virgin Mary, and the way it had made her feel when he did.

Afterward she went into the bathroom and ran the water for her bath. It was nearly time for Pete to come home, and before she got into the tub, she put the lock on the door. She recognized something fragile in herself on this particular afternoon, and she didn't want Pete to blunder in and catch her, the way he sometimes did.

He slammed the living room door when he came in and called to her. She heard him, but didn't answer. There was a picture in the dark recess of her mind, behind a fluttering veil, and it was holding her attention, though she wasn't trying to remember what it was.

He tapped gently on the bathroom door. "I'm home, Mary." He spoke softly, putting his face close up to the door.

For a moment the veil twitched.

Pete knocked again.

"Yes," she said. "I'll be out in a little while."

"I'm home," he said.

She lowered herself in the water, resting her head against the back of the tub. On the counter by the sink were the containers of her lotions and creams—pink and pale blue and white against the white tiles of the bathroom. She thought of the pink and white wedding dress that she had worn when she married Pete—Mr. Odell had wanted her to wear white. And the bouquet of pink roses with white lace.

"I'll be out in a little while," she said again, softly, to herself. The bridesmaids had worn pink dresses, too. Thinking about it, she smiled her fragile, angelic smile. Then the veil twitched feebly, and was still.

George looked at himself in the bedroom mirror, turning this way and that to get the whole effect from different angles. He ran his hands around the brim of the Panama hat, following the snap of the brim in the front. Then he extended his middle fingers to feel the hem of the coat. While he did it, he gave himself a sly, Humphrey Bogart look. Then he smiled. He wouldn't want to dress up that way all the time, and the work clothes that he wore on the job were more easy and comfortable for him, but he did like to feel stylish now and then.

He took the hat off carefully, lifting it with both hands, and put it on the shelf in his closet, hanging the snap of the brim over the edge of the shelf. Then he took off the suit, folding the pants carefully so as not to double the creases, and put it on a coat hanger with a newspaper section on the crossbar. Over the coat hanger he put a laundry bag, which he pinned shut at the bottom with safety pins. His tie he put into the tie box in the top drawer of the dresser.

Something of the sadness of the funeral stirred inside his head as he put the clothes away. But he didn't have a wide experience with funerals—or with church things in general—and he decided that was the way you were supposed to feel, so he didn't worry about it. He wasn't struck yet with the fact that Jack was dead, and what it chiefly would mean to him—that they wouldn't be seeing each other anymore day by day. Just going to the funeral had been occupying his mind, being out of the ordinary and not a thing he was accustomed to. What it would lead to hadn't really come up as a problem for him yet.

He turned on the radio, then snapped off the room light and lay down on the bed. As the tubes were getting warm, music came up from behind the dial. Dean Martin singing "Volare." He could tell by the clearness of the music that it was a local station, but he waited until the song was over before he turned the dial knob. It was a kind of courtesy on his part. He hated to interrupt a song.

Finally, he fiddled up a voice with the fuzziness in it that told him it was coming from somewhere a long way off. It was the weather report from Fort Wayne, Indiana. George listened, thinking how different from the Savannah weather was the weather they were having in Fort Wayne. In Fort Wayne it was raining, and they were expecting a freeze that night with ice. In April. It was nice to hear about it when he was a long way off and the weather was warm outside. Even in the middle of winter it didn't freeze often in Savannah.

After the weather report, the music started. Slow and mellow pieces that George could recognize, with violins in the orchestra that he could hear distinctly.

He went to sleep with the light of the dial on the side of his face, smiling at the mellow music that he could hear all the way from Fort Wayne, Indiana, where the rain would be freezing to ice before morning. In April.

Mackey took a bus back from the cemetery to Bull and Broughton streets. She started to walk back to the Barnard Street house, but decided she didn't want to go back into it just yet. Not by herself. So she sat down on a bench in Percival Square, across from the post office.

Almost before she was settled on the bench, a young man came up to her and said hello. The way he did it, she knew she was supposed to remember him.

"I know you, don't I?" she said. There was something about his face that was vaguely familiar. But she couldn't connect it with a name.

"Oh, the beautiful times we had. Have you forgotten so soon?" He spoke in an exaggerated way, with his hands clasped over his heart. "An *interlude*," he said, putting emphasis on the word. "Ah, so sweet."

"How would I forget?" she said. "Come on." She stood up.

"Saaay . . ." The young man cocked his head to the side, giving her an arch look. "Same old Mackey," he said. "What a heart on that girl." He dropped his eyes to her bosom, with a look on his face that was very nearly a leer—but a friendly one.

She walked away without looking at him, and he fell in beside her. "Where's the fire?" he said. "Don't you want me to court you a little? Let's go get us a beer first."

He tried to keep up the patter, but since she didn't respond, he finally gave it up, and the two of them walked rather grimly, like couriers on their way to deliver dispatches.

She turned left off Oglethorpe onto Barnard, walking across Orleans Square in the fire lane without turning her head to look at the pile of charred bricks and rubble where the auditorium had stood on the west side of the square.

She marched him right up to the door of her apartment, then she turned and looked him in the eye. The walk had settled her face into a droopy grimness, like a small child on the verge of tears. "Not today," she said.

"What?"

"I've changed my mind."

"That's a hell of a thing."

"I know," she said. "I'm sorry."

"Sorry. Sorry," he said. "Fuck 'sorry.'"

"Listen. I lost a friend today."

He looked at her for a minute. "You mean dead?"

"Yes," she said. She didn't look at him when she said it. "A very good friend."

"Well," he said. "You might have mentioned it before. You could have saved the both of us some time."

"I just came from the funeral."

"Well," he said.

"Look. I'm really sorry. It's just that I'm upset. It was a very good friend."

"I know it can be tough. It's just that . . . you were the one suggested it."

"I know. I'm *sorry*." She shrugged her shoulders.

"John," he said. "John Wade. You didn't remember me, did you?"

"I'm sorry, John."

"I know how it is." He stood there a minute. "It's been a shitty day all around." He started to move away.

"Try me another time, John. We had a good time together, didn't we?"

"You're the light of my life, Mackey," he said. He gave her a little salute.

"Try me again, John Wade," she said.

"Well," said Ducker, "we put him away decent and respectful."

Horse Fosdick nodded without saying anything. Canty Greb didn't nod.

"I wouldn't say everything came off without a hitch," said Ducker. "But we gave him a decent burying."

For a while nobody said anything.

"Was he as good as they say he was, Ducker?" said Fosdick. "All we ever heard about was Curran and Rooney."

"He was good," said Ducker. He had lit up a cigar and was placing his Sir Walter Raleigh can so it would be handy. "No doubt about that. He took Rooney in the alumni game. Nearly killed him." He took a puff on the cigar. "You know how the season came out."

"Sometimes a story like that will grow, you know. I just wondered how good he really was."

"They do get away from you sometimes," said Ducker. "Ain't no shortage of bigmouths. There was ten other men on the field, of course."

"One man can't win a football game," said Fosdick.

"That's true," said Ducker. He took a pull on his cigar. "We were a *team*. You can't beat teamwork."

For a while they sat without saying anything. "You played fullback, Fosdick. Dimmy Camack was the fullback on the 'forty-seven team. I used to see a lot of old Dimmy. The last I heard he was running his own shrimp boat down at Thunderbolt." Ducker chuckled. "*Captain* Dimmy," he said.

"Horse Rooney was the only fullback anybody could talk about. Of course I heard about Camack, too. But Rooney was the one they were always talking about."

"I used to see old Dimmy now and then," said Ducker. "We had us some good times." He told them about stealing Oglethorpe's coffin, and breaking his leg. "It kept me out of college, but old Dimmy couldn't help it. I never could hold it against him."

"Camack was probably pretty good, but Curran was the only one they ever talked about from the 'forty-seven team. Some people they don't ever talk about."

"Listen," said Ducker. "Camack was a pretty fair ballplayer, but he wasn't no Doc Blanchard. Dimmy was kind of—you know—stupid. But we had us some good times."

"I just meant some people get the credit."

"Fosdick," said Ducker, looking at him. "Every man on the 'forty-seven team was on the 'forty-six team, too. Every man but one. You know how many games we won in 'forty-six?"

"I know it wasn't a good year."

[374]

"We won *one* game," said Ducker, holding up his finger. "Some people *deserve* the credit, Fosdick. Not that I ever felt like I ought to be kissing Curran's ass. He was an irritating bastard sometimes."

"That's what I mean," said Fosdick.

"He was an irritating bastard sometimes," said Ducker, not hearing Fosdick, "but the son of a bitch was a *football* player."

Fosdick didn't say anything for a while. "Yes," he said.

Ducker took a pull on his cigar. "I wonder what old Dimmy is doing these days? Maybe I ought to look him up." He put his cigar back into his mouth and looked at Fosdick. "Me and Dimmy and Whistler Whitfield. We used to have us some good old times." He thought a minute. "*Captain* Dimmy Camack. For Christ's sake." Then he laughed.

Dendron took Jack's name tag out of his wallet—the one Ducker had given him the night before. He wondered if maybe Feeb or Mackey might have a better claim to it than he did, but he never saw them anymore, and didn't know how to go about getting in touch with them. Anyway, it might be they had keepsakes of their own.

He couldn't remember just what Jack had looked like, particularly when he thought about it. He had no memory for faces, and didn't pay much attention to the things that were going on around him. He had no picture of Jack to go by.

But he remembered things *about* him vividly enough. Like the dreams. Even without the face, the dreams and the name tag would help him to keep his friend in mind. Especially the shark dream, which was the one that impressed him the most.

He still didn't have dreams of his own, but once in a while he would almost have the dream of the sharks. He could get as far as the green haziness of the water. But he always woke up before he could get any sharks to come into it for him. Which was something he was thankful for, to tell the truth. He didn't *want* that dream to happen to him when he was asleep, though he couldn't shake off his fascination with it, and knew it would be the one that would come for him if one ever did. He would have to go through it to get to the others.

Still, he had another knack, and if he couldn't have sleeping dreams the way that Jack did, he was able to bring things to life in his room very clearly, while he was lying awake with the lights out *before* he went to sleep. Somehow he didn't think that was the equal of having regular dreams like his friend had them. And though some of them were horrendous—like the sharks—they didn't bother him especially, as long as he knew he was awake. He always knew that he was in his own room, so that what was happening wasn't *there*—the way it would have been if he hadn't been awake. If he hadn't been awake, he would have been more *in* the dream.

Still, he hoped that he would have a dream of some kind before it was over—even if it would have to be the shark dream—as it probably would.

He never did make up his mind about the thing in the bathroom—the rat, or snake, or whatever it was. He had heard the noises and seen it—or thought he had—with the lights *on*, which was unusual. The other night thoughts only came to him after the lights had been turned off.

Also, the things that came to him in the dark weren't his own. He had always gotten his inspiration for them from Jack. Now that Jack was dead, with no one to tell him about the dreams they were having, he wouldn't have anything to go by. He felt that he might not even be able to make anything come into his head in the dark.

He put the name tag back into the secret compartment of his wallet and got ready for bed. After he turned out the light, he lay there in the dark, waiting for some kind of vision to come to him. There were times when he could wish them up when he wanted to—especially the sharks, which would glide silently back and forth in the air over his bed, passing noiselessly through the walls of the room. Huge silver shapes that were graceful and benign—as Jack had said they were.

He was sorry that his friend was dead, but also he was preoccupied with what it would mean to him.

"I'll never have any dreams," he said to himself sadly, looking up at the sharks gliding above him in the room. "Not any *real* ones."

Feeb could take off from his curb market only long enough to attend the funeral. By four o'clock he was back and waiting on the customers. Feeb liked church services of whatever kind. And the sadness of funerals appealed to him in an intrinsic way. But he had a wife and two sons, and the business which he had to see to, so two hours was the most he could give up to it.

At home that night he talked to his wife about it, after they had eaten supper and the boys had been put to bed.

"It was a sad life, Corinne. A waste."

"I know. He was just your age, wasn't he?"

"He was too much of a natural. He did the things he was good at. That's all he could ever do."

"He was a very young man."

"I don't just mean being dead," he said. "It's what went before that was so much a waste. He could have been anything."

"He didn't work out in the curb market too well."

"You know what I mean. Anything *big*, he could have done it. It was the little shitty things got him down."

"Well. It's always sad for a young man to die."

"Mary. You knew Mary Odell. That was the first mistake he made. I'll have to take it back. He wasn't good at all the things he tried to do."

"Mary was all right. You always wanted to blame the whole thing on her."

"She was too thin and bony."

Corinne didn't say anything.

"You don't know how he pulled us together—the 'forty-seven team. We thought he could do anything after he did that."

"You didn't even like football."

"That's what I mean. None of us could let him down. It was the same way when we used to live on Waldburg Street. I've known him all my life."

"Well," she said. "I never did know him that well."

For an hour they talked about it. Feeb had put on weight around the middle, but his face was sleek and almost handsome. Corinne was beginning to look matronly.

"I'd get out the Arak if tomorrow wasn't Saturday."

"No more sundaes," she said. "You've had it for the month."

"I've known him a long time, Corinne."

Saturday was the busiest day of the week for him. He had to open the store at seven o'clock.

[377]

"I need to get the corrective shoes for John tomorrow. And Robert has to start his allergy shots Monday."

Feeb looked at her. "Fuck-a-duck. Maybe I'd better open at six."

For nearly an hour he lay awake in the dark, thinking about the things Jack could have done—the aspirations Feeb had had for him—that they all had had for him. Mourning the loss of them, and thinking how it would be if the time had come for him to die himself. They had been good friends for twenty years, and how seldom they saw each other—that didn't make any difference. It was almost as if he had been disappointed in himself. Jack had been a person he had looked up to all his life.

He reached out and touched Corinne's warm meaty haunch. "Good, solid flesh," he said to himself—thinking how the bones stuck out on Mary Odell.

"You mean it's lit up again? They cut it off during the war."

Maybe the radioman caught the family resemblance, though Jack looked more like Kate than Johnny. Maybe it was just the size, and the fact that the time of day was the same, with the days between so short—Wednesday to Friday, from son to father.

"Two to five, mister. Two to five." He said it in his high-nosed voice, with the hard northern accent. The clock on the wall said five minutes to five.

Johnny looked at him. "I'm not going to argue with you, sonny," he said, opening the iron door to the stairway. He said it with determination but without any particular menace. "I don't want no trouble."

The radioman looked at him for a minute, thinking—a humming noise vibrating his sinuses. "Ummmmmmmmmm . . ." he said. "Don't sign the register."

Johnny went through the door, letting it slam behind him. Then up the stairs one at a time, slowly, but without stopping. At the top, in the dome, he sat down on the catwalk, his feet on the ladder, his knees drawn up under his chin. Sitting the way a small boy would sit—a cramped and uncomfortable position for a grown man.

The afternoon sun was bright, collecting inside the glass dome and dancing on the water outside, making it sparkle, the light erasing the dirty brown patch that the river made going out into the ocean.

He tried to think about Ireland, the green way he had always thought about Galway Bay, with the silver boat and the great white bird on gliding wings. Only—fatherly thoughts kept coming in, breaking the vision and bringing him back where he was. He and Jack hadn't really been close to each other, not in the sense of being pals and seeing eye to eye. The thing was—the one had always been *there* for the other. And now Jack wasn't. He had thought he wanted to go over the time that they had come up into the lighthouse when Jack had been little. It was on his mind at the funeral, and had brought him out from town and up the spiral staircase, putting him in the dome of the tower with his chin on his knees. Now he wondered why he had come exactly. He couldn't think of the reason. All he remembered was the urgency of it. What he would be remembering of Jack, that was the thing that was there for him now. The time in the lighthouse, and the few other times they had been together—too few to count them, and all Jack's doing except for the one time when Jack had been little and he had led the way, fatherly.

He thought about the time that he had cheated to keep him from winning the arm-wrestling. It wasn't a fair test, but he shouldn't have cheated on him just the same. Maybe he could have beaten him in his prime—with both of them in their prime. That would have been the real contest—the one he could have come to rest on. And he thought that he could have done it so that they would have been happy with it—the both of them. He was convinced that he could have.

The thing was—and he was beginning to resent it already—that shouldn't be his problem anyway. Which was what it had become, since the wall came down in the fire on Hull Street. *He* wasn't the one to add it all up and see where it might come out. That was an unnatural thing. Nor was it that he wanted to be dead in Jack's place, which would have been a crazy way for him to think, even if it had been possible for him. But there should be a kind of fitness in the way the world worked. One thing should follow the other in orderly progression. This wasn't a problem to lay on the father, the sins of the son. This was something for Jack to do, thinking back on the way things had been, after he was gone—adding it up to see how it all came out. Under the circumstances, he had done the right thing to cheat, because the absolute proof was something that no one should have—least of all the father.

Only he wished that he hadn't had to cheat at all.

Of course, *he* had been the one to suggest that they wrestle in the first place. Yes. Well, that was the way it had been for him— all of his life things had always been that way. And he had a ready sense of honor where games were concerned, and other activities of little consequence.

There was a ship moving on the horizon—a wisp of smoke that did not fill him with the longing and wishfulness that he wanted and could remember from the other time twenty years before. It didn't make him feel anything at all. Probably the ship was going down to Jacksonville or Brunswick. That was the only way he could think about it. He didn't know where it was going, of course, only that it wasn't going to Ireland. And no one was there to make it worth his while to tell lies about it.

When he looked back the other way—toward town—there was nothing that he could see except the blank green-brown of the marsh grass and the shrimp boats at Lazaretto Creek. Too much haze. Fort Pulaski was clear, and the pink spots in the walls where the federal batteries had pounded at it. But even the bridge at Bull River—less than half the distance to town—even that was lost in the grayness between the marsh and the sky.

He loosened his tie and unbuttoned the collar of his shirt. The afternoon sun seemed to be collecting inside the dome, making him hot and uncomfortable. Where it came through the lens of the light it cast small rainbows of color on the catwalk—pure bands of red and yellow and purple that fused only slightly at the edges of the bands where the colors came together. His shadow, too, was outlined in a thin rainbow nimbus where it fell on the floor of the catwalk. He looked at the spots of color, not knowing at first where they were coming from. Then he looked up at the lens, filmed pink and yellow in the lowering light of the afternoon. And there he saw himself, his reflection, blown fat and grotesque on the round surface. For a moment it reminded him of the way Jack had looked during the worst of his drinking, when his face had gone swollen and grotesque, with rolls of fat that bulged his face until his eyes nearly closed.

Then he was looking into the heart of the lens, seeing what he remembered of Wednesday night—the sheet of flame dancing red and yellow, with the stark black shadows cast in the foreground.

He had seen the movement before he saw Jack. With the wall out on the side of the auditorium, there was light for him to see by and shadows cast on the side away from the fire. There was not much of him to see. Only the head. Sticking out through the hard-edged squares of hot bricks. More like some creature up from the bottom of the sea than anything to be recognized as human. The head that was not a head. A balloon. A mushroom. Swollen red in the light from the fire. With growing eyes. Swelling and oozing out of their sockets in great, round, egglike balls. The whites showing all around. The pupils floating small and dark on the surface. Out of his open mouth a great bubble swelled, shiny purple and leathery. The fire-red skin of his face was split in a jagged line. Coming out of his hair. Going down the side of his nose. Breaking his upper lip where two teeth gleamed white in the tear.

The head.

He stood looking down at it, thinking of it as a separate creature. Not as part of the body that was buried under the bricks. While he looked at it, the jaws moved. Trembling. Chewing and working at the leathery bubble where the scream lay dark and ready.

Then the eye moved. Only one, rolling slowly up as a crab's eye would. Turning to look at him in stealth and profundity. It was the movement of the eye that terrified him. The thought that it might see him and know him. That out of the meeting some filial conundrum might be propounded, which he would have to answer.

He bent and grasped a great loose block of masonry—bricks and mortar. Taking the fire into his hands. Raising it high over his head and dashing it down where the eye lay turning at his feet. Burying the eye. Picking up other blocks of hot masonry and piling them on top of the first. Heaping and mounding them to obliterate the great white eye and stop its turning. Crushing and

burying it under the light of the flames. And the muffled sound of
the scream where the bubble broke.

Except for Ireland and the idea he had of Kate, there was nothing that Johnny had been able to hold on to and nourish. And he
didn't want to make death his own. The terrible head. Like a red
and growing mushroom with the scream inside.

He balled his hands into fists and began to pound on the lens
of the light. Smashing blows that should have shattered the smooth
and shiny surface. But the blows hurt his hands, and the lens of
the light was hard and smooth. So that finally he had to think of
the bones in his fists. His own bones and flesh.

For a minute he sat holding one hand in the other, feeling the
deep dull pain of the blows inside the fire-bitten skin of the
blisters. Then he reached out his arms, putting them around the
smooth globe of the lens. Laying his cheek on the hard curved surface where the waning light of the afternoon was collecting. His
black shadow, outlined in the colors of light, fell on the floor
among the small pieces of rainbow—purple and yellow and red.

"Busy, busy, busy. A rushing day, dearie. Daddy's a tired daddy
tonight, dearie."

Charlie Carne scuffed into the office in his slippers, the dog's feet
clicking on the floor behind him. He took the pins with the green
heads out of the map and stuck them into a cluster of pins in the
lower right-hand corner.

"A rushing day, dearie." He leaned down and picked up the
dog, carrying her back to the kitchen with him, holding her close
to his cheek and talking into her ear. "Did you miss your daddy
today?"

He got the steak out of the refrigerator and leaned down, holding it in both hands where she could see it. She stretched her neck
and sniffed it with her long ratlike nose.

"Steakie tonight. Lovely steakie tonight for dearie and daddy."

The dog sat looking up at him while he put the steak into a
cast-iron skillet on the stove. Her eyes were bright and black, protruding from her head like buttons. When the steak began to
sputter and sizzle, Charlie prodded it with his fork, sliding it

around in the pan. The rich smell of the cooking clouded the kitchen. Sub shifted the weight on her front legs, then opened her small pink mouth and licked her chops.

"A rushing day, dearie. Oh, so tired tonight."

He lifted the steak out of the pan with the fork and put it on a saucer, where he trimmed off the gristle and fat and sliced it into smaller and smaller pieces, mincing it fine. When he had finished, he poked the pieces with his fork, holding the saucer up close to his face to be able to see it better. Satisfied, he put the saucer back on the counter and poured gravy from the pan over it.

When he moved away from the counter, the dog did a nervous little dance, clicking her feet on the floor.

"Hot-hot, dearie. Too hot." He pursed his lips and made a face. "Burn dearie's little mouth." He touched the dog's nose with his finger. "Daddy's not forgetting dearie's steakie."

He put bread into the toaster, then went back to the counter and cut up his piece of steak. He said the blessing for them, then put her bowl on the floor and they ate together—Charlie standing at the counter, the dog at his feet gobbling the steak out of the yellow bowl.

"Slowly, slowly, dearie. Lovely steakie. Mustn't choke on lovely steakie."

After they had eaten, he went back into the office and took four of the green-headed pins out of the cluster in the corner of the map. He made flags for them, reading the new locations off a paper, then placed them carefully, pushing them in with his thumb.

"Oh my, dearie. Busy, busy, busy. Rushing day for daddy to-morrow."

While he was talking, the dog walked away.

"Rushing day tomorrow, dearie," he said.

But the dog didn't hear him. She was licking the yellow bowl in the kitchen.

Savannah:
July 4, 1956
and
January 16, 1957

July 4, 1956

The eye was big and yellow, divided by the vertical black slit of the pupil—shining gold and burnished like a jewel in the twelve o'clock sun. A lazy eye, but a cruel one, too, if you looked at it long enough in the right way.

George had his head shrugged over to the side, sighting through the prongs of the slingshot, the rubbers pulled back at full tension, his thumb pinching the shot in the sling—just barely touching his right cheek. While he looked, the nictitating membrane rolled up in a flickering movement, filming the bright yellow jewel of the eye.

George was aiming for the eye itself—the target within the target—as he had learned to do. There was no wind to allow for, only a pulsing wateriness in the air. When he released the sling, he could see the dull silver of the slug tumbling away from him, and he heard the sound it made when it hit, though there wasn't any mark to show the place. They were hardheaded animals, and even a lead slug wouldn't kill one outright. He would have to finish it off with his knife before he took the legs.

The frog lay slumped on a water-cut ledge, rolled a little to the side, so that part of its white underbelly showed. George started down the bank to get it, keeping a handhold on the honeysuckle vines that trailed over the edge and into the water of the canal. The bright, hot sun came up into his eyes off the water, filling his head with the brightness, opening it to the white glare and heat of the still air. Stretching to reach for the frog, he began to feel the numbness coming up behind his eyes, rising in the heat. He frowned, not believing it at first, because of the unfairness and surprise. He had all the vindication in the world on his side. And, in spite of everything, he still thought of the world as an orderly place where fairness counted in the long run.

It was no time to change the rules—at the very moment when he was sprung out into space, hanging by one hand to a tangle of honeysuckle vines with the brown water below. He had learned to follow the arrows of his life carefully, and had built his expectations on the accommodations that he had learned to make with that feeling of numbness when it rose behind his eyes. Thirty-eight years of it. Such an old and intimate relationship that there was no hostility in the way that he felt about it anymore. Just something that he had learned to bear. But the fact that he could tell ahead of time—the *fact*—that was something he counted on. The days when the time was coming, there was a lightness in his head—even early in the morning. That was the rule that he had learned to live by. The arrow that pointed the way.

But, today. Today. Nothing. His head had been clear as a bell.

When the glare of the sun had come up from the water, catching him unawares, he was as surprised and resentful as he would have been if he had gotten up in the morning to find three red noses where his ear ought to be.

For half a minute he swung on the vines with his eyes blank to the glare—picturing the close darkness of his room, with only the orange glow of the radio, and soft out-of-town music coming to him out of the dial. Then the vines gave way, and he pitched into the dark water of the canal. He was unconscious when he went in, but it wouldn't have made any difference. He didn't know how to swim.

And that was the end of law and logic. Wherever justice lay, the way was dark and winding.

The search party found what was left of him on Thursday. The body had snagged in a backwash that was scummed and clogged with garbage. And clicking blue-shell crabs that menaced them with their claws. The sun was going down when they took him out of the dark water and wrapped him in a rubber sheet—with the tender gentleness of finality.

There was a short notice in the paper on Friday, but the reporter didn't mention the blue-shell crabs, even though that was his most vivid remembrance of the event. There was almost not enough to say about him to make a proper obituary. It was seven days short of three months since the night Jack had walked into the fire on Hull Street. But no one knew that they had been friends, and the fact went unremarked. There was only his single death to make the story.

When they told Mrs. Bogger, all she could say was, "George?

[388]

My George? . . ." Then she sat down on the couch in her living room, and they had to watch her crying in her dry, old woman's way. Grieving weary for her flawed son as she might have grieved for a true and glorious hero, who never had attacks and didn't swallow his tongue.

"My George? . . ." she said. Biting her handkerchief, and making wet sucking noises through her dentures.

January 16, 1957

The doctor looked down at them in the bed. "What are you going to call him?" he said.

Mackey looked up at him. "It wasn't so bad, you know? You've got a pair of hands like a gorilla, but except for that it wasn't so bad."

"Why would it be bad for you? You're a healthy girl."

She looked down at the baby's head. "Would you say that was a good-looking head?"

The doctor looked at him. "Not especially," he said. "It's a big one."

"*You'd* say it was? Like a bowling ball."

"What are you going to call him, Mackey? You need a name."

"How about something Irish?" she said.

"Irish would be fine. I've got to put something down on the birth certificate."

"I want to think it over," she said. "How we start him out could make all the difference."

The doctor looked down at them wisely, pulling at his chin. "Yes," he said. "Beginnings are important."

She stroked the baby's head lightly with her fingers. "Yes," she said. "They certainly are."

In the clean light of the room, the doctor stood regarding the face-within-a-face of the baby beside the mother. Pulling at his chin and nodding. Deep and wise and debonair.

·